HIGH PRAISE FOR RAY GARTON!

"*Live Girls* is gripping, original, and sly. I finished it in one bite."

—Dean Koontz

"The most nightmarish vampire story I have ever read."

—Ramsey Campbell on *Live Girls*

"It's scary, it's involving, and it's also mature and thoughtful."

—Stephen King on *Dark Channel*

"Garton never fails to go for the throat!"

—Richard Laymon, author of *Into the Fire*

"Garton has a flair for taking veteran horror themes and twisting them to evocative or entertaining effect."

—*Publishers Weekly*

"Ray Garton has consistently created some of the best horror ever set to print."

—*Cemetery Dance*

"Ray Garton's *The Loveliest Dead* eases the reader into what is easily the most mature, heartfelt, and unflinchingly disturbing novel of his career. The unspeakable horror that lies at the center of *Dead*'s mosaic-like mystery is the darkest nightmare of every parent, only in Garton's hands, the revelation of this nightmare is only the beginning. A powerful, terrifying, unforgettable achievement. Ray Garton is back, and he will shake your soul's foundation with this one."

—Bram Stoker Award–winning author Gary A. Braunbeck

FEEDING

Afterwards, she stood slowly, her mouth dripping. She ran long fingers over her lips, then licked them clean. Reaching out a hand, she flicked off the lamp. She was more comfortable in the darkness. The darkness was cool and soothing.

She leaned against the wall a moment, feeling her strength return, warm behind her eyes, making her feel as if she glowed in the dark room. She felt whole, strong, satisfied.

She bent forward, threw a bolt lock on the floor, then another. She wrapped her fingers around the flat handle and lifted a trapdoor, stepping aside.

They clumsily began to pull themselves up with twisted hands and knobby fingers. Some of them had lost the flesh at the tips of their fingers and bone protruded from the ragged skin.

Others shot up from below, their vein-webbed wings flapping softly as they fluttered near the ceiling, their red eyes gleaming in the blackness.

All of them were disfigured in some way, bent, crippled. They swarmed over the still form on the floor, their teeth and claws tearing the flesh, their lapping tongues filling the room with quiet sounds, wet sounds, as they fed on what remained of the girl's blood....

Other *Leisure* books by Ray Garton:

THE LOVELIEST DEAD

LIVE GIRLS

RAY GARTON

LEISURE BOOKS   NEW YORK CITY

For Dawn.
The book that
brought us together.

A LEISURE BOOK®

August 2006

Published by

Dorchester Publishing Co., Inc.
200 Madison Avenue
New York, NY 10016

ISBN 0-8439-5674-7

Visit us on the web at www.dorchesterpub.com.

ACKNOWLEDGMENTS

While mine is the only name on the cover of this book, there are several others greatly responsible for its existence. I'd like to thank them here, in no particular order.

Scott Sandin and Derek Sandin for their helpful suggestions and priceless friendship; Susan Davis, Ellie Gallardo, Ruth James, Debbie Allen, Anita Mistal, and Paul Meredith for keeping me awake.

And an extra special thanks to Sarah Wood, Jessie Horsting, Nancy Lambert, Joan Myers, Francis Feighan, and my parents, Ray and Pat Garton, for late nights, lots of laughs, and the kind of understanding that's hard to come by.

LIVE GIRLS

After work, Vernon Macy had the cabdriver drop him off a few blocks from Times Square, just to be safe. Briefcase in hand, he walked the rest of the way, his gray eyes darting mouselike around him, making sure there was no one around who might recognize him, in which case he would hurry down to the subway, catch a train home, and forget the whole thing.

He wasn't a tall man. He had a big nose and his salt-and-pepper hair, now covered with a gray fedora, had begun to disappear on top nearly fifteen years ago. His skin was pasty and flabby from forty-seven years of avoiding sunshine and exercise. When he wasn't sitting at his desk in the office, he was in his study at home, reading, smoking a cigar, doing anything to avoid being in the same room with Doris, his wife, or Janice, his twenty-two-year-old-daughter, who spent far too much time nervously flitting about her parents' apartment and not nearly enough in her own, where she seemed to do nothing but snort coke with her unwashed boyfriend and postpone her college education.

1

To make the coming weekend at home more tolerable, Vernon Macy had decided to do something he'd never done before. Something he'd never *thought* of doing before.

A week ago, he had overheard two of the younger men in the office talking about the strip joints and peep shows in Times Square, and how some of the girls, if given generous tips, would give blow jobs through holes in the walls. At the time, Vernon Macy had given it little thought. But that night, lying in bed next to Doris, the perfume she applied several times a day filling the dark room with a sickening sweetness, he thought of what that young man had said, and Vernon Macy wondered. . . .

And in the early morning of that Friday, as he ate his breakfast and as Doris complained about the length of his toenails, he decided that he would give it a try.

The lights of Times Square flashed and glittered with lives of their own. The litter on the sidewalk became more unpleasant: a pile of shit that may or may not have been left by some stray animal, a moist yellowish puddle that had caught and held a newspaper blowing in the breeze. Some of it was human: lying beside the trash cans, against walls, at the openings of alleys—old women wearing tattered feather boas and torn paper party hats, carrying all their belongings in shopping bags; old men with three-day beards, their ratty clothes stained and crusty, lifting bottle-shaped paper bags to ragged lips.

Vernon Macy tried not to notice. He pressed on as night gave way to the neon awakening of Times Square. He slowed before each strip joint, each peep show, each movie theater and video shop, trying to keep his head down as much as possible.

2

Chapter One

By the time Davey Owen climbed the steps out of the subway station at Broadway and Fifty-second, the rain that half an hour ago had been pounding against the panes of his apartment window had given way to a thin but chilling drizzle. The sky was dark with clouds that seemed to hover just above the towering buildings of the noisy city. As he started down the sidewalk, Davey opened his umbrella and lifted it over his head, hitching his shoulders forward. The hem of his overcoat flapped around his knees as he walked.

Weariness seemed to stick to the soles of his shoes, making each step an effort. He wanted to turn around, get back on the subway, go home and get drunk, maybe sit in front of the TV and wait for Beth to come back. He knew that would be a mistake, though; if she did not return, it would only make him feel worse.

If she comes back? he thought. *How long will I kid myself?*

Then, after a few more steps:

As long as I need to.

He hurried through the doors of the building, collapsing the umbrella and tucking it under his arm as he stepped into the elevator.

"Good morning, Penn Publishing, may I help you?" Tammy answered the phone as Davey came out of the elevator. She sat behind a rectangular window across from the elevator, plump and rosy-cheeked. She smiled at Davey as he turned right and passed the window, walked to the big door at the end of the corridor. The lock buzzed and clicked loudly as Tammy pressed the release button at her desk.

Beyond the door, Davey took a left and began winding his way around the desks and cubicles, smiling dutifully at the others who were typing, talking on the phone, hunched over manuscripts. He went to his own cubicle in the far corner.

His stride was smooth and his smile looked genuine despite his dark mood. He was lean, of average height, with thick wavy brown hair, a few curls of which fell down on his forehead. At twenty-six, there were already wrinkles around his eyes. His features were not particularly strong—no sharp angles to his jaw, no pronounced cheekbones. It was a gentle face, the face of someone any father would be happy to see his daughter date.

Davey stared for a moment at the clutter on his desk, then removed his overcoat and hung it on the wall hook. He straightened the lapel of his suitcoat and adjusted his tie, glancing down at himself and looking forward, once again, to being able to afford a few new suits someday.

His cubicle was just that—a cubicle. It had three

walls, one of which held two shelves with books and manuscripts and copies of the magazines cranked out weekly and monthly by Penn Publishing. There was just enough room for his desk, his chair, himself, and a visitor—if the visitor stood nice and straight. In the cubicle, Davey did work for just about every department in the office: Subscriptions, Research, Copyediting for fiction and nonfiction. Well before he was finished with one job, there was always another on his desk.

As he wearily seated himself, he found a note on his typewriter. Red ink, delicate feminine handwriting:

> *Davey—*
> *Three more mss. for* Brute Force.
> *Need a gun check ASAP.*
>
> *Sheri*

He lifted one of the manuscripts. The title: "I Blew Away the Punks Who Tried to Rape My Sister." He scanned the first two pages and spotted several references to guns; he would have to verify their accuracy. He would call Morris at Target Guns in Jersey; Morris was an expert on guns and quite a fan of *Brute Force* magazine; he considered it an honor to contribute whatever he could.

Davey sighed, propped an elbow on the desktop, and put his chin in his palm, fighting the urge to put on his coat and go back home where he could read a good book, or the *Times*, maybe even this week's *People*, for Christ's sake. Anything would be better than the stuff Penn put out: vigilante rags, "true" crime and romance magazines, the kind of magazines that crowded grocery store racks with covers dulled by greasy fingerprints. But this was his job.

It was a job Beth had always held against him.

"Almost nine months I've been living in this dump with you," she'd said to him angrily that morning, emptying her dresser drawers into her suitcase. "Nine months and you're *still* working for that cheap-shit publishing company, waiting for a break so you can maybe have a little extra money to play around with. But nothing ever happens. *What*," she'd snapped, spinning around to face him, a strip of perspiration glowing on her upper lip, "you think somebody's just gonna walk in one day and *hand* you a goddamned promotion? 'Cause you smile nice, maybe? Uh-uh, my friend. It doesn't work that way."

A sigh dragged heavily from deep inside Davey's chest and he shook his head to empty it of the echoes of her voice.

He'd tried to tell her about the promotion he'd be getting any day now. Fritz, one of the assistant editors, had left and his position was open. Davey was certain he'd get it because he'd been there the longest. It was time for him to move up, dammit. It seemed he'd been sitting in that little cubicle reading trash forever. He'd tried to tell Beth all of that, but it didn't do any good.

"I don't want to hear it, Davey," she'd said. "Really. I mean, how long have you been working there? They *know* they can shit on you, so they're going to. They'll give the job to someone they can't push around." She'd paused to slam the suitcase shut and flick the latches. "I know you, Davey. You'll stay there in your shitty little cubicle getting shitty little wages forever. And if I stay with you, what then? What about *me*?" She faced him. "I mean, I'm a very social person, y'know? I like to go *out* once in a while, right? *You* sure as hell can't afford to take me, and with the pennies I make selling tickets at the Union, I can't either. So I find some guys who can. Like I did last night. And last month. And a couple weeks before that. And I would just *keep* doing it. And, of course, you would put up with it." She shook her head slowly. "No, Davey, I just don't want to hear it."

He belched hungrily. He'd missed breakfast that morning; Beth's departure had destroyed his appetite. He'd spent the morning, after his shower, sitting at the kitchen table with a cup of coffee and his sketch pad, drawing. Some people smoked, some people cracked their knuckles. Davey Owen drew. He never knew exactly what he was drawing, even as his pencil swirled over the paper. He just pulled out whatever was inside of him and let it spill onto the page. That morning, he'd become more and more uncomfortable with the images appearing on the page. At first, hair. Then a forehead, an eye, another eye. He began to recognize the face he'd looked into so many times.

Beth.

He'd flipped the page and begun drawing again. The lines and curves began to take shape. A mouth. *Her* mouth, with that odd little slant on the left side that gave her a permanent smirk.

He'd torn out both pages and tossed them into the trash, leaving early for work.

At his desk, he considered going to the lounge for a cup of coffee, but decided not to, knowing that Chad Wilkes was probably there. Chad Wilkes was *always* there. And the coffee in the lounge was simply not worth an encounter with Chad Wilkes so early in the day.

"Son of a bitch." He sighed, rubbing his eyes with the heels of his hands. He ached with frustration.

Adjusting his chair, he leaned over "I Blew Away the

Punks Who Tried to Rape My Sister" and turned to the first page, hoping he would see Casey sometime today. Seeing Casey always seemed to help.

Walter Benedek collapsed his umbrella and went into the lobby of his sister's apartment building.

"Hello, Norman," he said to the doorman with a friendly nod.

"Good morning, Mr. Benedek," the short round man replied with a smile, touching two fingers to the shiny black bill of his cap.

Benedek punched the UP button with his gloved thumb, then stood with hands folded in front, facing the silver mirrorlike doors of the elevator. He was a very tall man, with broad shoulders and a deep chest; he was hefty but not fat. His face was long and rubbery and had been compared, on occasion, by a few abhorrently honest people, to the face of a basset hound. His black hair was sprouting ever-growing patches of gray, and there were some wiry silver hairs mixed in with the bushy blackness of his eyebrows. He was forty-seven years old and looked no younger, no older.

"Want me to call ahead, Mr. Benedek?" Norman asked.

"No, thanks. She's expecting me for breakfast."

The elevator arrived with a quiet *ding* and the doors rolled open silently. Benedek stepped inside, hit seventeen, and waited. The doors closed and he heard the music he'd come to hate so much playing from the speaker overhead, barely distinguishable. This morning it was a choir singing an old Beatles tune. Lots of strings. A soprano solo. Benedek took his gloves off and stuffed them into the pockets of his overcoat.

Walter Benedek's sister Doris Macy lived on the seventeenth floor. Vernon would be gone by now, presumably at work, but, Benedek thought, probably not. Janice, who didn't actually live there but certainly seemed to, would probably be watching game shows with her mother. And Doris. Well, Doris would probably be curled up on the sofa staring at the TV, but not really seeing whoever was giving away the money this half hour. She would be sitting there chewing a thumbnail, nervously twitching her slippered foot, worrying about Vernon.

She had come to Benedek a little over two weeks ago. He'd opened his apartment door to find her standing in the corridor, eyes narrow with worry. She was concerned about Vernon. He was acting . . . different. He wasn't himself. He came home late from work, sometimes not until dawn, and then only to take a shower and go back to work. He didn't eat, lost his temper easily, and he was so very pale. At first, she told him, she'd thought he was having an affair. Then she'd become afraid for his health.

"He's always been so stoic," she'd said to Benedek as they sat at his kitchen table having coffee. "He would never tell me if he were ill. Even seriously ill. Please, Walter, you have a vacation coming up, don't you? Do you think you could . . . oh, just spend some time with him, maybe? I don't know what, really, but he needs something. Some*one*. And *I* don't seem able to get through to him. Could you help me, Walter? Please?"

Poor timid, dowdy, bighearted Doris who, when she was a young and single woman, could have done so much better for herself than that doughy, pudgy-fingered businessman with his clipped speech and his permanent frown. Benedek sighed and shook his head, remembering how lively his big sister had been when they were kids, and how different Vernon had made her.

Benedek had not talked to his brother-in-law. He hadn't even tried. He'd never been comfortable with Vernon Macy. They had always rubbed one another the wrong way. But he did have some time on his hands, a few weeks of long-awaited vacation from his job at the *Times*. So he'd followed Vernon one morning, staying out of sight. The man had not gone to work, but to Times Square, straight into a dark little place called Live Girls. Benedek's years as a reporter had sharpened his eye and he'd had no doubt that morning as he watched his brother-in-law walk through that black curtain with such purpose that Vernon Macy not only knew where he was going, but had been there before.

Benedek had followed him a few times after that, and each time Vernon had returned to Live Girls. That disturbed Benedek, although he wasn't sure why. Neither was Benedek·sure exactly what it was about that dark, inconspicuous little peep joint that unsettled him so. Maybe it was his reporter's intuition, a hunch. But Walter Benedek, in all his years of reporting, had never for a moment believed in intuition or hunches.

He had not spoken with Doris about her husband since she'd asked for his help a couple of weeks ago. He knew she would ask him about it over breakfast, and he didn't know what to tell her. He supposed that the news of Vernon's seedy pastime would be better than no news at all. It would at least assure her that he was not sick, was not seeing another woman. At least, not in the way she'd suspected.

But with the relief would come the hurt in her face.

Her top lip would curl under like an old leaf and tears would glitter like diamonds in the corners of her eyes.

Doris would be very hurt.

The elevator whispered to a halt and the doors slid open. Benedek turned left down the corridor. He stopped outside his sister's apartment and punched the button beside the door. He decided, as he heard the muffled buzz inside, that he would tell Doris that Vernon was simply going through the much-talked-about midlife crisis, a second adolescence of sorts. Benedek wasn't entirely satisfied with that story, but it would have to do. He didn't think he could bear those glittering tears.

He waited for the familiar sound of movement behind the door, the rattle of locks being unfastened. All he heard was the television.

". . . and Jerry Mathers as the Beaver," the announcer was saying happily over the perky theme music.

Benedek punched the button again.

The television continued to play loudly inside.

His bushy eyebrows drew together tightly above his nose as he raised a big hand and rapped his knuckles on the door several times.

"Follow your nose," the television sang, "it always knows . . . the flavor of fruit . . ."

This time, Benedek made a fist and pounded on the door, calling, "Doris? Janice? It's Walt." He turned an ear to the door.

"And *you'll* find the flavor of fruit in every bite . . ."

Benedek turned the doorknob. The door unlatched and opened a crack. A cold spot bloomed like a flower in Benedek's stomach. Doris seemed to have a new lock installed on the door every month and she *never* left them unlatched, even so early in the day.

After a moment of hesitation, Benedek pushed open the door and stepped inside. From the doorway, he could see half of the television set in the living room at the end of the short hall. Before the television he saw two feet in furry white slippers, two bare legs lying very still, and around them splashes of reddish brown on the creamy carpet.

"Oh God, Doris?" he called, nearly a shout, as he rushed down the hall, leaving the door open behind him. When he rounded the corner, he saw his sister lying face-up on the floor. Her blood was dark and crusty on the carpet around her.

Benedek's palm slapped over his mouth as he retched, then swallowed and gasped several times to keep from vomiting. He staggered forward and got down on one knee beside his sister's body. Then the other knee. Then one hand. He reached the other hand out to touch her, but couldn't.

"Oh, dear Jesus, sis? Sissy?" he croaked.

Her robe was open and her nightgown—silk, dark blue, very matronly—was torn nearly all the way down the front exposing her flesh, which was now marble white. Her mouse-brown hair was tangled and stringy with blood. Her eyes and mouth were open wide. So was her throat. The flesh had been torn open, clearly exposing blood, gristle, and her trachea. It looked like a garden hose that had been chewed in two by a dog. Her flesh had been torn open all the way down to her chest and pinkish-white bone showed through the drying blood. Her hands were the worst. The fingers of one hand were tangled in the tendons that ran along her neck and the fingers of the other were clutching her left clavicle, like a choking man trying to pull away the tight collar of his shirt.

"Oh, Christ, sis . . ." His tears fell freely onto her body and his big shoulders shuddered with quiet sobs. He sat up suddenly, scrambled to his feet, gasping, "Janice!" He said the name softly at first, then roared "*Jaaah-nice!*" as he bounded across the living room and into the kitchen.

There was a single streak of blood on the door of the white refrigerator. Through the kitchen, Benedek could see into the dining room where his niece was sitting up against the wall by an overturned chair. With a pained, rumbling groan, Benedek hurried to the girl's side.

"Please, God . . ." he hissed as he knelt beside her.

She was wearing blue jeans and her legs were sprawled on the floor before her, feet bare. The plaid shirt she'd been wearing had been ripped off and lay half in her lap, half on the floor. Her arms were limp at her sides, hands palm up. She was naked from the waist up and part of her left breast had been torn away and was dangling from her chest. Her head hung at a sharp angle to her right and her long silky blond hair—"the stuff angels' wings are made of," Benedek used to tell her when she was little—hid her face and tangled in the yawning hole that was once a smooth and graceful throat. Her blood was splashed in dark designs on the beige wall behind her.

Benedek pushed himself away from the dead girl, moving crablike over the floor. He bumped into one of the stools at the bar that separated the kitchen and the dining room and the stool fell. Benedek leaned against the bar, pressed his back against it hard as he clutched his face with his big hands and sobbed into his palms. He realized that he was breathing in small bursts and he tried to take deep breaths and think.

15

"Okay," he said soothingly to himself, "oooookay."

Without looking at the corpse against the wall, Benedek stood, crossed the dining room, and went to the doorway that opened onto the hall.

"Vernon?" he called, his voice cracking.

Silence.

All the rooms were shut except the master bedroom. Benedek started down the hall, looking at the tracks of blood on the floor. They led straight to the open doorway. Benedek's legs quivered as he neared the bedroom, trying not to look at the blood at his feet.

"Ver-Vernon?" he said again, softer, more cautiously than before.

He stopped a foot or so short of the bedroom, took a deep breath, then stepped through the doorway.

Vernon Macy's suit was lying in a heap on the floor; a shirt was tossed onto the bed. They were soaked with blood. The drawer of the bedside stand lay on its side on the floor, its contents scattered everywhere.

"Vernon!" Benedek shouted through tears. "Goddammit, Vernon, if you're here, come out! Come . . . out . . ." His voice broke. He stared at his brother-in-law's clothes for a long time, then crossed the bedroom to the bathroom on the other side.

A bloody bar of soap lay in the middle of the tile floor and a gray towel, blackened with blood, had been tossed over the toilet seat. Puddles of pink water had gathered just outside the shower. A bloody handprint was smeared on the opaque glass of the shower door.

Benedek gagged once, twice, bent over gasping for air as he spun around and stepped out of the bathroom. It wasn't that there was a great deal of blood, it was knowing from whom the blood had come.

He stood outside the bathroom for several minutes. Then, when he was finally sure of himself, he went to the phone and called the police.

"Yeah, Target Guns."

"Morris? This is Davey Owen at Penn Publishing."

"Hey, kid!" Davey could hear Morris's smile through the phone. "How's it hangin' over there, huh?"

"Just fine, Morris, and how are you?"

"Oh, I'm mean, kid, mean as usual, you know me."

Actually, Davey didn't know him. They'd never met. But they spoke on the phone so often, they talked as if they'd known one another for ten years, when they'd been speaking for less than two.

"What can I do you for?" Morris asked, his dentures clicking through his words.

"Well, I need a little help with a story. I got a mousy type of guy whose sister is being attacked by a bunch of punks. He takes a shotgun to them. Pump action."

"Why use pump action with all the automatics you've got to choose from? Pumps're obsolete."

"Really?"

"Yeah. Oh, you can still buy 'em at Sears, I think, but that tells you something right there, know what I mean, kid?"

"Yeah. What do you suggest?"

"Maybe a twelve-gauge."

"Of course."

"I don't wanna be steppin' on your toes, though, kid. I mean, maybe you *wanna* use a pump action, what do I know?"

"No, no, thanks for the tip, Morris."

"I gotta ask, though . . . how come the writer didn't

know that? I mean, these are supposed to be true stories, right?"

Davey chuckled. "Well, sometimes the truth needs a little help."

"Yeah, know what you mean. So, kid, when you gonna drop by the shop? Meet in person? I never met a real magazine type before. Lunch'll be on me."

"One of these days, Morris," Davey said with a smile. "When things calm down a bit."

"Problems?"

"No, just busy. That's all."

"Well, take a break some day. I'll show you around the joint. Maybe you'll buy yourself a gun. It's a jungle out there, y'know." He lowered his voice. "I'll give you the special discount. For friends of the management only, kid."

"Thanks, Morris. Well, I've got to go. Maybe I'll talk to you later in the week."

" 'Kay. You take care of yourself, you hear?"

After Davey hung up the phone, he thought maybe he *would* drop in on Morris one day. He might enjoy himself.

Davey pushed the manuscripts aside and rubbed his watery eyes. Casey had not come by yet. She usually came to see him when she arrived, to chat. Maybe she was late, or home sick.

He looked around at the three walls. They seemed to creep in just a bit when he wasn't looking.

Swearing under his breath (he'd been swearing all morning) Davey stood and grabbed his coat, putting it on as he hurried out of the cubicle and stepped across the aisle to Pam's desk.

"I'm taking an early lunch, if anybody asks," he said.

She looked up and nodded. "Yeah, sure. You okay?"

"Just really hungry. I missed breakfast." He hurried down the hall to the elevator, realizing how claustrophobic he'd actually begun to feel in there.

Outside, a sharp, icy wind shot around corners and straight down the sidewalks as Davey walked out through the glass doors of the building. He wasn't hungry, although he hadn't eaten, and he wasn't thirsty. So he decided to just walk for a while. He took a right and pushed into the cold with his hands in the pockets of his overcoat and his head bent forward slightly, winding through the stream of rushing pedestrians.

I should be tired, he thought. He'd gotten very little sleep the night before because he kept waking to see if Beth had come back yet.

Her disappearances were not rare, but they always worried him. And hurt him. This time, he'd planned to talk to her about it. He'd lain in bed half the night practicing his speech. He must have gone over it a dozen times, choosing just the right words, trying not to sound too possessive and yet making it clear that she was being inconsiderate to him.

She'd arrived at a little before five that morning. He'd been asleep, but had awakened to the sound of her packing.

"Are you all right?" he'd asked.

"Don't I look all right?"

"Well, you look . . . you look tired, that's all. Where've you been?"

"What difference does that make?"

Still shaking the cobwebs from his head, he'd realized what she was doing.

"C'mon, Beth," he'd said, "stop that for a minute and let's talk."

19

"We've tried that already. I doubt it would work any better now than it did then, so why waste the time?"

He'd gotten out of bed and tried to go to her, but she just kept packing. "Jesus, you act like *I've* done something."

"No, Davey, you haven't done anything. That's just it. You haven't . . . done . . . *anything!*" She stopped and faced him. "Not at work and not here. You just go around letting people walk on you, y'know? You don't even get pissed off! I'm beginning to wonder if you're human! And I'm beginning to feel like a fucking *jerk* every time I turn around, because you just won't . . . you don't—oh God, I just can't take it anymore, Davey."

He'd thought then that if he could convince her he was getting that promotion, she would stay. But a jarring thought shattered his certainty.

Then what's to keep her from finding another reason to see other men?

He'd pushed the thought from his mind and said, "Look, Beth, Fritz is gone. He's left Penn. That leaves an assistant editor position open and I'll—"

"It's not just the money and the rent and . . . it's you, Davey. I can't stand getting away with—with treating you the way I do."

He still wasn't sure if that was the truth or just a good way of getting out smoothly. In any case, he'd thought perhaps it was time to show a little anger. "Okay!" he'd snapped. "*Okay*, so I'm angry! This makes me *angry*, Beth, it really does. I've never been very good at getting angry, but I'm trying to handle it as well as I can! Would you rather I scream and shout? Maybe throw things around and rough you up a little? I know you've enjoyed that from your male friends in the past, maybe you *miss* it!"

20

That made *her* so angry she'd broken a bottle of perfume throwing it into her small overnight bag.

She'd packed the rest of her things in silence, then stalked out of the room with a bag at each side. He'd followed her to the door, where she'd stood a few moments. Turning, she'd said quietly, "Look, Davey, you're a good person. I love you a lot, you know that. But . . . well, you're just letting your life pass you right by, know what I mean? You're just *sitting* there! And I can't live with that anymore. Really, Davey. You're gonna have to start grabbing things by the short and curlies." And then she'd left.

Davey crossed an intersection, weaving through the cars and trucks. He had no destination in mind as he walked, scuffing his shoes on the concrete. His knees and elbows ached, a sure sign of not enough sleep, but he didn't actually feel tired.

He wondered where Beth would live now. Alone? With a girlfriend? A man? Maybe someone who would break things when the cable television went on the fritz? Someone who would knock her to the floor and then kick her because she didn't buy toothpaste that day? Someone like Vince, the man she was living with when she met Davey? He often wondered about her relationship with Vince. If he had never gotten in trouble with the police—Beth had told him it had something to do with selling drugs—would she have given Davey a second thought? Maybe, maybe not. Maybe she had really seen something she needed in Davey . . .

Like a way out.

A wadded newspaper skidded over the sidewalk with the breeze. Davey kicked it out of his way, so hard that he nearly tripped. He was startled by the sudden anger he felt, and stopping on a corner to wait for traffic to pass, he took in a few deep breaths, exhaled a ghostly white vapor that was swept away by the icy gusts.

Casey had disapproved of Beth from the beginning. She'd disapproved of Patty, too. After meeting Beth for the first time, Casey had said, "I hope you're not planning to get serious with her, Davey. You've got to break your pattern, and she isn't gonna help."

"What pattern?" he'd asked.

She'd looked a bit surprised. "You really don't see it, do you? Oh well, you will. Someday."

Davey wondered about that pattern a lot.

He remembered something his mother had once told him, not long after his father had left them. Up until that time, his mother had been a moderately religious woman, attending church every Sunday, helping out with church socials. After Donald Owen left, though, she leaned more and more on her religious beliefs, searching her Bible as if for a reason for her husband's desertion. One day, while Davey was doing his homework, his mother looked up from her Bible, her eyes sparkling with unspent tears, and said softly, "Remember, Davey, no matter who you fall in love with, no matter how right it seems, she'll hurt you. That's the way love is."

From then on, she repeated that statement frequently, and always at the most unexpected times. In fact, they were the last words she'd ever said to him; it was during a phone conversation his sophomore year in college. Davey had called to say he was coming home for the weekend.

When he got home that Friday, he'd found her dead.

She'd choked to death on a bite of steak and died beneath the small table in her dining room.

Davey hadn't thought of her remark for some time, but he thought, as he shuffled down the street, *Maybe she was right.*

Then: *Or maybe I've made her right.*

He passed a tall black man who paced back and forth on the sidewalk as he spoke into his handheld microphone.

"And you wanna know *why* you's unhappy, brothers and sisters?" the man bellowed. "You is unhappy 'cause you's livin' inna worlda *sin*, my friends! And *you* is a *sinner!*"

A wiry man wearing tattered denim strolled toward Davey. His hands were deep in the pockets of his dirty denim jacket, fumbling with something.

"Smokes? Toots? Smokes? Toots?" he muttered as he passed.

Davey turned away from him. The pusher passed and walked on down the sidewalk, his quiet voice quickly swallowed by the sounds of the street.

Davey stopped and the other pedestrians flowed around him like a stream around a fallen tree. He looked around.

He had not been paying attention to where he was going and realized now that he wasn't even on Broadway anymore.

There was a dingy taco stand with a window open to the street. Next to that was an adult bookstore, which boasted the largest selection of rubber goods in New York City. In front of that, two old men, both wearing darkly stained clothes, stood against the wall, one chewing on a stubby cigar, the other drinking from an unlabeled bottle, dribbling some of the liquid down his stubbly, deeply wrinkled cheeks.

Times Square.

Davey checked his watch; he still had plenty of time, he hadn't been through Times Square in a while and he'd always been fascinated by the facade of glamour that failed to disguise the squalor beneath. It held a sort of pathetic beauty, like an old, gritty, low-budget movie that tries hard to entertain. Davey continued walking.

He passed a junk shop called N.Y.C. Souvenirs, going slowly by the window to look at some of the cluttered merchandise. There were bongs, rubber gorilla masks, dirty little Cabbage Patch Kids rip-offs that looked well-used, boxes of Ping-Pong balls with I ♥ NY stamped on them in black and red. Cobwebs fluttered in the corners of the window and there was a fine coating of dust on the items behind the smudged glass, making them look even more worthless.

After the junk shop, he came to a long rectangular picture of a naked woman with only her nipples and pubis covered, one hand raised, beckoning to passers-by. The picture was surrounded by white lightbulbs that flashed in succession, giving the illusion that a burst of light was shooting around and around the frame of the picture. Written above it in big block letters was: LIVE SEX SHOW. Beyond were more flashing lights, more pictures of naked women, and a very skinny young man in a long leather coat smoking a cigarette and waving to the men walking by.

"C'mon in, guys!" he said, his voice happy. "Finest women in this city, lemme tell ya! Beautiful! They're waitin' for ya in there. Hey, how 'bout you?" He waved to Davey. "C'mon in, pal, they'll show ya a good time! First drink's on the house. How 'bout it?"

Davey slowed to a stop in front of the man and stared at one of the pictures. It was of a very tall woman who, in fact, looked a bit like Beth.

Who doesn't these days? he thought.

A gold chain hung around her waist, her hands were in front of her crotch, and her arms were pressing her bare breasts together, pushing them out, her lower lip tucked under her upper teeth, her eyes half closed.

Davey opened his mouth to ask, "Is she inside?" But he didn't. He closed his mouth, half smiled at the man, turned, and walked away.

"Aw, c'mon, Jack, you gotcherself a good time, here!" the skinny man called. "Jeee-zis!"

Davey continued slowly down the walk, reading the signs in front of each of the strip joints he passed: COUPLES ON STAGE! LESBIAN LOVE SHOWS! N.Y.'S ONLY GAY BURLESQUE! Something for everyone.

A silver-haired man in a beige overcoat stepped quickly out of the gay burlesque theater, briefcase in hand. He looked around him, glanced at Davey as they passed. His every move seemed to scream, "Wrong door! I just took the wrong door, that's all, I didn't really *mean* to go in there!" It almost made Davey laugh.

"Hey, m'friend," said a fat man with a toothpick in his mouth, "we got 'em all right here, best-lookin' women in town, models is what they are, right here, totally nude, dancing their tits off, waitin' to get to know ya. How 'bout it, friend, how 'bout you?"

Davey found himself slowing again, and stared beyond the fat man to the club's entrance.

"Whatta ya say, fella?" the man asked, smirking.

Davey had never gone into such a place. He thought of the man he'd seen coming out of the gay burlesque theater. The man probably had a wife, grown kids, who had no idea where he went on his lunch hour, and what dark fantasies he fulfilled there.

Davey realized, with a faint pang of disappointment, that he had no dark fantasies. Just a nibbling curiosity stirred, perhaps, by the picture of the girl who resembled Beth, or maybe by the cold, empty hole in his chest.

The drizzle returned and Davey decided it was time to go back. He headed for the end of the block, figuring he'd walk back on the opposite side of the street for a little variety. It was on his way back that he noticed it.

He stopped on the sidewalk and looked up at the sign. In the dim light of the overcast day, the flashing red letters glowed faintly. The black curtain in the doorway was fluttered gently by the wind. The curtains parted occasionally as they shifted and Davey tilted his head to see inside, but there was only darkness. The absence of garish lights and signs, obnoxious hawkers, made it somehow appealing.

He wondered how much it would cost, quickly thought about how much cash he had in his wallet, then glanced at his watch. He still had time. Curiosity may have killed the cat, but, Davey supposed, the cat probably died quite satisfied. He smirked at himself as he walked toward the entrance (the closest he'd come to a genuine smile all day) for feeling like a guilty teenager, looking around to see if there were any familiar faces nearby.

An old Sunday school teacher, maybe? he thought with a chuckle.

Davey stepped through the black curtain.

The I in GIRLS flickered and buzzed.

Inside, Davey had to take a moment to let his eyes adjust to the darkness. The air was damp and had a sort of locker-room smell to it: sweat and stale clothes with a strange sweetness just beneath it all. He blinked several times as the darkness slowly dissolved. A corridor, narrow and low-ceilinged, stretched before him. A few yards down it turned to the right and a very dim glow came from around the corner.

He turned to his right and faced a box office-like cage; there were bars over a square window with a space below. Beyond the bars, which seemed bumpy with rust, was only darkness. Deep, black darkness. Davey peered through the window, but saw no one. He turned to go down the corridor.

"Tokens?"

Davey started and looked through the bars again. He still saw no one.

"Excuse me?" he said uncertainly.

"Tokens?" the voice asked again. It was a woman's voice, soft, almost a whisper, but rich, full, a voice that would carry far if raised. It held within it a great deal of power.

"Uh, yes." Davey took his wallet from his coat. "Um, how much?"

"One dollar minimum."

He looked once again through the bars, trying to find her, but she was lost in the blackness. Davey had not expected to find a woman in there. Her presence, even though he could not see her face, made him uncomfortable. The what-the-hell attitude that had brought him inside gave way to an almost childish nervousness.

As he opened his wallet, Davey stared through the bars, hoping to get a look at her. He saw nothing. Except, for a moment, something seemed to catch a bit of stray light and reflect it for just an instant: a blinking glimmer of red. He pulled a bill from his wallet, held it up to his face to make sure it was a one, then held it under the bars.

A hand slid from the darkness, a beautiful hand that, despite its delicate appearance, moved with a swiftness, and a certain tenseness that suggested great strength. Long, thin, pale fingers plucked the dollar bill away from Davey and then its unhealthy whiteness was swallowed up by the wall of black behind the bars. An instant later, the hand reappeared. Davey opened his palm and the hand dropped four small coins into it, then pulled away. Davey stood there a moment, waiting for something, although what it was he did not know. Then he turned and started down the corridor.

The smell thickened as Davey neared the corner and the darkness began to give way to soft light. The farther down the corridor Davey went, the colder it got, almost as if he were going into a cave. As he neared the corner, he could hear the soft murmurs and sighs of the others.

He rounded the corner and came into a small room that had only one light in the center of the low ceiling. The bulb was covered well and shed only a minimum of light on the small square room. There were four men. They did not look up when Davey entered. They paced back and forth, hands in pockets, heads bent forward. One stopped pacing and quietly leaned against the wall, looking at nothing.

They all wore dark clothes. One wore a brown hat with fur flaps on the sides which he'd pulled down over his ears. Another wore a fedora pulled forward on his forehead so that it cast a dark shadow over his face. None of them seemed to notice Davey. In fact, they hardly seemed to notice one another.

They were all silent.

The other sounds seemed to come from all around them. Davey took another step into the room and listened. Soft sighs, moans, whispers. They were coming from behind the six doors in the room, a pair on each of the room's three walls.

Across from him on the wall between two of the doors was a sign. He stepped forward and squinted to read it in the poor light:

> *INSTRUCTIONS*
> *—ENTER BOOTH (ONE PERSON ONLY PER*
> *BOOTH)*
> *—INSERT TOKENS IN BOX*
> *—PANEL WILL RAISE*
> *—INSERT TIP THRU SLOT*
> *BELOW WINDOW FOR SEXY SHOW*

Davey held in a laugh. *Insert tip of* what *through slot?* he thought. He looked around at the men again. Each of them had chosen a door and was standing by it. Each seemed to think he was the only person in the room.

Davey turned away from them and faced the nearest door. Setting his jaw, he took a step forward. *I'm here, I'll do it and get it over with.* He wrapped a fist around the knob (it was cold and felt a little sticky) and turned it.

The door burst open and Davey jerked back. He was face-to-face with an old man who looked like a walking corpse: his mouth hanging open like a hole between two sunken cheeks, his eyes deep in their sockets, watery, unfocused, his teeth long and yellow, and his breath—dear God, his breath—hit Davey in a hot, moist wave. Davey had smelled a smell like that once before . . .

When he was a little boy. His dog, Brat, a scruffy little mutt, had disappeared. Davey had gone out hunting for the dog on a hot summer day.

He'd found Brat lying beside a narrow side street, his abdomen split open like a melon, small white worms crawling through the remains. The smell that came from Brat's corpse was exactly like the smell that came from the old man's mouth. . . .

The man brushed past Davey and disappeared down the corridor. Davey stepped into the hot black booth and closed the door behind him.

Something small scuttled around his feet on the floor and Davey stamped a foot around until the sound stopped with a crunch beneath his shoe.

The booth was saved from total darkness only by a tiny, blinking red light on the coin box attached to the wall at Davey's right, and by the soft light that shined through what he decided must be the SLOT BELOW WINDOW to which the sign outside had referred. It was in the wall just below a rectangular panel, waist high. It might have looked like a slot at one time, but not anymore. He bent forward and looked at it closely. It had apparently been sort of like a letter slot in a door, but now it was more a rounded hole in the wall, crudely widened by a knife, perhaps, or a jagged piece of metal. Looking at it a bit more closely, Davey had a silly thought, a thought that, at first, made him smile a slight, nervous little smile:

It looks like it's been chewed open.

He stood up straight and sighed, regretting ever walking through that black curtained doorway into this dirty little place and wanting to leave as soon as possible. He felt his back beginning to perspire in the stuffy booth and removed his overcoat, folding it neatly over his arm until he bumped his head on a hook mounted on the back of the door behind him. He turned around and reluctantly hung up his coat, then once again turned his back to the door and opened the fist that held those four corpse-gray tokens. One at a time, he dropped them into the slot next to the tiny red light. They made thick, heavy *per-clink* sounds as they fell into the coin box.

Davey squinted as a rectangular section of the wall before him began to slide up with a low hum, pouring gentle but sudden light into the dark booth.

He saw her calves and knees first, then her thighs: skin that looked as smooth as the finest silk, the color of rich cream, was stretched tautly over firm muscles and perfectly structured bones. Her left knee was bent ever so slightly and she seemed to be swaying from side to side. The graceful fingers of her right hand fluttered through a triangle of hair of blackest black, moving in gentle, small circles below the tiny navel that was centered in the middle of her flat, firm belly. Her left hand rested lightly on her tight hip, rising and falling as her pelvis moved around and around in slow, luxurious circles. Her small rib cage was lightly outlined against the skin below her firmly uplifted breasts, two scoops of vanilla flesh topped with generous dollops of rich chocolate that had hardened in the center. Above them, two sharp ridges of bone sloped slightly toward regal shoulders and a slender, tightly muscled neck curved into a finely chiseled jaw. Her lips were dark and full, glistening and wet, and her cheekbones were prominent beneath huge dark eyes that sparkled with pupils that seemed to descend into a comforting darkness into which one might fall forever without ever reaching bottom. Thin black brows arched over long, thick lashes and midnight fell in long shining waves over her head, resting gently on her shoulders and shifting with her gentle movements.

Everything seemed to stop as he stared up at the woman who stood behind the thick glass.

This was not what he'd expected. He'd pictured hardened, coarse runaways who had been picked up in bus stations upon arriving from Nebraska, used to their limit, then discarded like paper napkins after a birthday party, dirty and torn. This woman did not belong in this place with its shuffling, faceless men and its disinfectants and its artificial indoor twenty-four-hour-a-day night!

He gawked at her like a little boy seeing his first department-store Santa Claus, feeling a strange sense of . . . comfort.

After a few moments had passed, he realized what was expected of him. Without taking his eyes from her, he reached around for his coat, groped for his pocket, found his wallet, and took it out. Still without looking away, he removed a bill from his wallet, stuffed the wallet into his back pocket, and carefully reached down, pushing the bill through the slot below the window.

Her delicious lips curled into an emotionless, but

embracing, smile. She knelt down gracefully; her right hand wrapped around the bill, tugging it from Davey's hand while, at the same time, her left hand gently took Davey's wrist.

He started at her touch. It was smooth and cool.

Her right hand moved behind her, then returned smoothly, the bill gone, and without the slightest hint of effort, she pushed the sleeves of Davey's suitcoat and shirt up his arm, at the same time pulling his arm through the hole all the way up to his elbow.

The inside of Davey's mouth became moist and he slid his tongue back and forth over his lips as she began to lightly dance her fingers up and down his forearm.

She tilted her head back slightly, her eyelids lowered until they were almost completely covering her deep, dark eyes, and the smile grew to one of promise and anticipation, her lips almost, but not quite, parting. Then she moved forward, pulling his hand toward her and touching it to her left thigh.

Davey's heart skipped a beat; he did not move his hand, did not react, at first, to the touch of her velvety flesh. He just watched her as she moved his hand over her thigh, up and down, her smile never wavering. She brought his hand up as she straightened her back and moved her pelvis forward. His fingers brushed lightly over the black mound of hair.

She bent her upper body down, then toward him, sliding his hand up over her strong belly, over her ribs, to her breasts, pressing it to one, then the other. His fingers began to gently flick the erect nipples and squeeze the breasts delicately.

This is illegal! he thought frantically. *This must be illegal! But it's okay, it's okay, because she's letting me touch her.*

It seemed strange to him how very important touching her had suddenly become, but he took no time to question it.

She leaned forward even further and moved his hand to her throat, bent her head down and kissed his palm, then directed his hand back down over her breasts, her belly, and down between her legs. She pushed his fingers through the hair, leaned her head back, and closed her eyes as his fingers moved over her vulva, through the flowery folds and, finally, inside her.

He gasped softly and goose flesh rose on the back of his neck when he felt her moist center, moist but strangely cool and tingly. She pressed herself against his hand, and her long black hair swayed back and forth behind her.

Davey heard a sound in the distance and realized, after a moment, that it was the sound of his own pleasure. His eyelids fluttered and closed, but he snapped them back open immediately, as if not seeing her would mean his death.

She took his hand away from her, bent as far forward as she could, and brought his hand, fingers glistening, to her lips. She kissed his palm again and again, then the back of his hand, his fingers . . .

Davey's breathing became sporadic, his heart hammered in his chest, and a dull ache began to pound in his crotch.

Her hair brushed across Davey's arm, tickling him slightly.

Even her hair feels cool, he thought.

The tip of her tongue slipped between her lips and she looked up at him through strands of her hair as she slowly licked the length of his exposed arm, first up, then back down, wrapping her lips around his index finger, rolling her tongue over it lazily, then sliding her mouth up and down over the knuckles. She did the same with the next finger, and the next, until she came to his pinky.

When she backed away from Davey's hand, stood up straighter, he thought it was over, thought that perhaps she wanted more money. But her smile seemed to say, *There's more, my friend, much more. . . .*

Very carefully, she pulled his sleeves back down and gently pushed his arm out of the hole. Her eyes remained locked with his. She gave his hand a small squeeze as it slipped out of the hole.

When he felt her hand on his leg, Davey looked down and saw her arm snaking through the hole. He watched as her hand glided across his thigh to the bulge beneath his pants. Her arm twisted slowly until her palm was facing upward. She tucked her elegant fingers between his legs, just below his crotch, laid her thumb flush with the line of his zipper, and squeezed. Just a slight whisper of a squeeze, but enough to send white threads of electricity up the center of his body.

Davey looked through the glass again, saw the lids of her eyes grow heavy as she cupped his genitals in her palm. She pulled the zipper down with dreamlike slowness and wriggled her fingers through the opening. Through the thin material of his briefs, Davey felt her fingernail travel the length of his erection teasingly and he moaned, a long breathy moan. Her fingers pulled open the front of his briefs.

Her fingers were cool and velvety; they wrapped around his penis and pulled it carefully out of his pants.

Davey leaned forward and pressed a hand to the wall on each side of the window. His head drooped and he looked down at her hand, smooth and gentle, as it tugged him toward the hole. He took a small step forward. Another.

She nodded encouragingly to him, fondling a breast with her free hand. Her lips parted just enough for her tongue to ease out and slide across them, glistening lusciously.

"Oh, God," Davey breathed as he allowed her to pull him through the hole. Its hard, ungiving edges, so harsh compared to her glassy-smooth skin, made him wince. He leaned almost his entire body against the thick glass as her tongue lightly touched him, her black hair draping each side of her head like curtains on a window, private and concealing. She flicked her tongue over the darkened head of his penis first, then slipped it underneath, running it the length of the shaft slowly, lovingly.

Davey swallowed several times.

She pulled her mouth away for a moment and held him close to her face, her fingers caressing him as she moved his penis just a bit to one side, holding it as a jeweler might hold a precious stone.

Davey felt her lips wrap around the side of his shaft, felt her wet, pillowy tongue, her teeth, then a slight sting so sudden that, amid all the other overpowering sensations, he wasn't even sure it was real.

She took him all the way into her mouth so swiftly that Davey's knees began to buckle and it was only with effort that he kept them from collapsing completely. She began sucking on him hungrily and he grunted as if he'd been slugged in the stomach.

He cried out, softly at first, his breath clouding the glass.

Cooooool, he thought, *she feels sooo cooooool.*

His orgasm pounded inside him like an animal throwing itself against the bars of its cage, and when it was just a breath away from release, he clenched his teeth to hold back the cry. It came anyway, ripping from his chest as he slammed against the glass and shuddered uncontrollably, sweat rolling down his body, his heart drumming in his ears.

She finally slid her mouth from him but continued to stroke him with her hand.

His eyes were closed and he didn't seem to have enough energy left to open them. The panel began to hum down over the glass and he opened his eyes in time for one final glance, and saw her smiling, her mouth sparkling with his juices and . . . something else . . . smeared lipstick?

She was gone.

He pressed his cheek to the panel as she continued to stroke him on the other side. Then she let go and he pulled away, fell to the wall on his right, and slid down until he reached the floor. He remained there, curled up like a baby, trembling, trying to catch his breath, staring with wonder at the panel, at the hole through which soft light cast a glowing bar that landed in a distorted puddle on his hanging overcoat.

With effort, he stood, leaning on the wall. He zipped up, took his coat from the hook on the door, and clumsily slid his arms into the sleeves. He kept looking at the panel. Before he opened the door and left the booth, he reached out and touched his fingertips to the hard wood.

He burst from the booth and hurried through the shadows of Live Girls. He passed the cage by the entrance and looked through the bars as he went by. He saw nothing in the darkness, but he knew that someone was sitting there, someone with large, beautiful, pale hands. Someone watching him.

Chapter Two

Casey Thorne headed for the lounge as soon as she arrived at Penn Publishing, lighting a cigarette as she walked down the corridor. She was a small woman with a fast, lively walk that swept her into the lounge like a sudden gust of wind. She went straight to the coffeepot, ignoring Chad Wilkes.

"Hey, Casey," he said happily. "G'morning."

"Morning, Chad," she said with an intentional chill as she took a styrofoam cup from the stack on the counter and tipped the steaming coffeepot over it.

"Your hair looks wet. Forget your umbrella?"

Her short strawberry-blond hair was damp and stringy; strands of it were still sticking to the sides of her face. "My umbrella broke this morning," she replied slowly, trying to keep her voice from raising. All the way from the lobby up, people had been asking her, "Forget your umbrella?"

Not only had her umbrella broken, but her alarm clock had not gone off and she'd slept too late to fix breakfast or even have coffee. She'd gotten caught in the middle of a fight between her roommate Lisa and her boyfriend, Selig, then she'd missed her bus.

It was Monday.

Hunger was beginning to gurgle crankily in Casey's stomach as she tucked her cigarette between her lips. Chad was sitting at one of the two long rectangular tables in the lounge—the one closest to the tray—eating a Mars Bar, a cup of coffee on the table next to a manuscript he'd apparently been reading. He smiled at her as she stepped around the chairs that were scattered in disarray along the table, trying not to spill her coffee. She did not smile back.

Chad was smartly dressed, as usual. There wasn't a wrinkle in sight anywhere on his stylish gray suit, his narrow maroon tie lay straight as an arrow against his blue shirt, and his blond hair was perfectly in place. The only thing that kept Chad Wilkes from being attractive was his face, his mouth in particular. It was very small, the lips were thin, and it looked a bit like a little rectum that had formed beneath his nose. He wore little wire-rimmed spectacles over his squinty eyes. He had a personality to match those tight, pinched features: most everyone at Penn agreed that he was an asshole.

"You have a good weekend, babe?" he asked.

Casey turned her back to him as she puffed on her cigarette, pouring some cream into her coffee. "You know, Chad," she said casually, "I've told you before to stop calling me babe. If you do it again, I'm going to sneak into your apartment one night and poke holes in all your rubbers." She glanced over her shoulder and saw the shock that passed briefly over Chad's face, as if he thought she might actually be serious.

"Come on, now, Casey, honey," Chad said good-naturedly. "You're so mean to me. We have to work together, you know. We might as well be friendly, don't you think?"

She turned to the table where Chad was sitting, leaned forward, and tapped her cigarette over the ashtray in front of him. "I'm perfectly happy with our relationship the way it is, Chad," she said. "Filled with hostility and intense dislike." She tore open a blue packet of artificial sweetener and shook some of it into her cup. She could hear Chad chewing on the last of his candy bar, wadding the wrapper up, and pushing his chair away from the table.

"Well," he said with a smile in his voice, unfazed by her remark, "I've got to be off. Miss Schuman has asked to see me. I don't want to keep her waiting."

Casey turned and watched with relief as Chad walked briskly to the door.

"Have a good day, hon," Chad said with a little wave and a pursed smile. "See you later."

"The later the better," Casey muttered. She went to the row of cupboards above the sink and opened the one closest to the wall. There was a mirror on the inside of the cupboard door and Casey stood on tiptoes to see her reflection. "Oh God," she sighed, frustrated. She reached up with a hand, her cigarette between two fingers, and plucked at her hair hopelessly. It was a mess. In the mirror, she saw Davey come in behind her.

His curls were loose from the drizzle outside, his tan overcoat was spotted with water. His shoulders sagged and . . . was he limping? Just a little? He didn't notice her when he entered.

"Hi, Davey," Casey said, turning around and closing the cupboard.

Davey stopped suddenly, startled. "Hi," he said. His voice was tired.

Casey stepped forward and put a hand on his shoulder. "Hey, you don't look so good, mister."

"Mm?" He smiled, and his face, although very pale and drawn, seemed to regain a little life.

"You look kinda sick. You okay?"

"Yeah, I suppose."

"You suppose. Coffee?"

"Please." He went to the sink and washed his hands.

Casey put her cigarette out in an ashtray, set down her coffee, and poured a cup for Davey. "How was your weekend?" she asked.

"Oh, I've had better." Davey's hands smacked wetly as he rubbed them together under the stream of water, rinsing off the soap.

"You want sugar in this? Cream?"

"Black."

She went to his side and set the coffee on the counter as Davey dried his hands.

"Trouble with Beth again, or what?" Casey asked. She watched his eyes slide slowly to her, heavy-lidded. It was a look of inward weariness, a silent *What do you think?* She decided not to pursue it just yet. She knew he would get to it in his own time. He always did.

Davey reached for his coffee, but leaned forward heavily, his hands clamping the lip of the counter, a look of surprise on his face as his knees buckled.

"Davey!" Casey gasped, grabbing his arm. "Jesus, sit down!" She pulled a chair away from the table for Davey, who seemed barely able to stand. "Sit!"

Davey fell into the chair and leaned forward with his elbows on his thighs.

She squatted down beside him, her hands on his arm.

"Is there anything I can do?"

"No, no," he breathed, "I'm fine, really."

"Fine?" she said softly. "Fine is not falling in the sink, Davey. What's wrong?"

He looked at her. His eyes seemed sunken, the rich brown color that she loved so much dulled, and the flesh beneath dark and sagging. Even his cheeks seemed hollow. His skin was ashen, made even worse by the fluorescent lights in the lounge. One corner of his mouth trembled.

"I didn't sleep last night. I'm just tired."

Casey reached up and wiped away a drop of rain-water just below Davey's hairline. "Did she leave again?"

Davey leaned back in the chair and exhaled slowly, nodding. He reached up and massaged his neck.

Casey stood and folded her arms over her breasts, thinking, *God, how I hate that woman.*

"She took everything with her this time," Davey said. "She's not coming back." He started to stand, but Casey put a hand on his shoulder.

"Want your coffee?" she asked.

He nodded and she handed it to him.

"Stay there for a while."

He blew on the coffee a few times. "It was inevitable, I guess."

Casey knew *exactly* what was coming and closed her eyes a moment, hoping she would be wrong and he would surprise her. He didn't.

"I suppose it's my fault," he said quietly.

Casey pushed herself away from the counter and got her coffee. "That did it. I don't want to hear any more."

"What?"

"If it's your fault—and, of course, it always is—I don't want to hear any more." She faced him, one hand on her hip. "Somehow, Davey, you always manage to get involved with women who are such experts at relationships that it's impossible for them to make the smallest mistake. So you, a complete clod, come along and single-handedly ruin one relationship after another. Every time, without fail."

Davey avoided her gaze.

"I hope what I just said sounded stupid to you, because it was. But it's how you *think*," she said with frustration, "and I wish, for Christ's sake, you would *stop* it, because it takes two people to make it and two to break it!"

He stood carefully and paced slowly to the other side of the lounge. "Yeah," he said, "but I . . . I think I . . ." He stopped, staring with tight lips at the floor between his feet. "She said that I'm . . . well, what it boils down to is that she thinks I'm too *good!*" He looked across the room and she saw clearly the confusion and hurt in his eyes. "What the hell's that supposed to mean? I didn't beat up on her like her old boyfriends. I was faithful, which is more than I can say for *her!* And she says"—he started laughing through his words; cold, disbelieving laughter that sounded very unlike Davey—"she says she can't stand me because I make her feel like a jerk! I don't know—I mean, I just—" He shook his head in defeat.

Casey had heard this before; a few times, in fact. It hurt Casey to see that puppydog look he always got on his face. It made her want to hug him, hold him tight. Kiss him.

They had spent one night together about two years ago and Casey had thought, for a while, that Davey was finally exhibiting good judgment. But things, for some reason, had not clicked after that, despite how well the evening had gone. It had not happened again since.

But not for lack of trying, girl, she thought.

"So," Casey said softly, "what if she's right?"

"Hm?"

"It is possible, you know, to be just a bit too nice. So nice that you turn yourself into a victim. I've always said that Beth is a mercenary bitch, and you'd be a hell of a lot better off without her. But the woman is right on that point, I'll give her that." She sniffed, waiting for his reaction.

He simply stared into his coffee.

"But that's not what you want to hear, is it?"

Davey shrugged finally, shook his head. "I don't know. I guess I just want to hear that there's nothing wrong with me." He looked at her. "You know, my mother used to tell me that whoever I fell in love with, no matter how great it seemed, I would always get hurt. 'That's the way love is,' she'd say."

"Oh?" she replied. "So you feel some obligation to prove her right? Sounds like a self-fulfilling prophecy to me."

"Well," he said, frustrated, "maybe she *was* right."

"Prove her wrong."

"Any suggestions?"

"Yes. I would love more than anything to say there's nothing wrong with you, Davey, but I can't. There *is:* your taste in women and your lack of spine, Davey. You have no spine." When he didn't respond, Casey started to go on, but was interrupted by Chad.

"Hel-*lo* there!" he exclaimed, grinning as he took broad steps to the coffeepot. His fingers were snapping at his sides and his shoulders were bouncing, as if he were listening to music no one else could hear. "Glad you're here."

"We're having a talk here, Chad," Casey said. "Do you mind?"

"Not at all, go right ahead. Um, do we have any tea bags left? I really don't think I'm in the mood for coffee right now."

"No tea bags, Chad. Could you excuse us?"

"Sure. But before you go," he said, standing before them and holding up both palms, still grinning, "I'd like to give you both the opportunity to congratulate me. Christ, Davey, you look like hell."

Casey sighed and gestured with her hand toward Chad, an okay-get-on-with-it wave.

"Okay, okay," he said, snapping his fingers again, "I just got back from Stella's, um, Miss Schuman's office, and she's informed me that *I* am to fill the position left behind by Fritz." He spread his arms at his sides, gloating, self-satisfied. "How do you like *that?*"

Casey felt her stomach shudder as she realized how Davey must be feeling. She looked over at him, saw the sudden looseness in his jaw, the disbelief in his eyes.

"She . . ." Davey whispered, then cleared his throat. "She gave you that job?"

"Yes, isn't it great?"

Casey saw the glimmer in Chad's eyes. He knew exactly what he was doing to Davey. And, goddamn him, he was enjoying it.

"Chad," she said with distaste, "don't you have something else to do right now?"

"Yes," Chad said, frowning suddenly, "as a matter of fact, I have an appointment with my doctor. A general physical. They'll probably take blood. God, I hate that." He went back to the coffee tray and began searching the rectangular compartments for a stray tea bag. "I especially hate it when the nurse pops the cap off the needle and smiles and says, 'Just a little blood, Mr. Wilkes. This won't hurt a bit.' " He shuddered slightly. "I could've *sworn* there were some bags in here earlier."

"Chad, you are such a fucking creep, it brings tears to my eyes," Casey said softly.

"*What?* No congratulations? No slap on the back?" He grinned again and stepped closer to Casey. "In fact, I thought you and I might even go out for a little celebration tonight."

"I have plans," Casey said without the slightest pause.

"We could go to the Trench. They're gonna have a great live band there tonight, and we could—"

"I *said* I have plans, Chadwick."

His mouth snapped shut—she actually heard his teeth clack together. He hated being called by his full name.

"I'm . . . I'm going out with Davey," she improvised.

Chad's eyes got big and round and his mouth pulled into a tiny *O*. "Ooooh," he said, glancing at Davey, who was staring at his feet silently. "Do I have some competition here?"

"You were never in the contest, Chad. Now will you go away, *please?*"

"Mmm," Chad mumbled, turning again to the tray and poking through the packets of sweeteners, "I suppose I should go." He brushed his fingers together to rid them of the little white specks of Equal. He smiled. "Wouldn't want to keep the doctor waiting. Plus, I have to move into Fritz's office. You two enjoy yourselves tonight." He started out of the lounge but stopped and turned in the doorway. "Oh, Davey, I almost forgot. I have a message for you."

Davey's head rose slowly, and he looked at Chad.

"Miss Schuman said she would like to see you as soon as possible. In her office." He frowned. "You know, you really don't look well." He hurried down the corridor.

Davey turned back to Casey, massaging his neck. "Well, you can't say my life isn't consistent."

Casey clenched her teeth. Giving Fritz's job to Chad Wilkes instead of Davey was a low blow from Miss Schuman. Davey had been at Penn longer than Chad and he did much better work.

"Look, Davey," she said, going to him and kneading the tense muscle in his shoulder with one hand, "Chad is a talentless slug who just happens to be a consummate ass-kisser, and we all know how much ass good old Miss Schuman has to kiss, don't we?"

He nodded slightly.

"I've said it before, Davey, and I'll probably have to say it again and again: you should leave this dump. You're better than this, you're being wasted here. If you're going to stay, you're just going to have to be as much of an asshole as Chad to get anywhere."

"Oh, c'mon, Casey," he said, standing. "Who's gonna take me?" He dumped his coffee in the sink. "I've been working *this* long at Penn Publishing—which, as I'm sure you know, is not exactly a point in my favor as far as everybody else in this business is concerned—and I'm still only an editorial assistant, for Christ's sake! If I can't get anywhere *here*, what good will it do to go somewhere else?"

Casey was surprised at the anger in his voice; he so seldom showed any. She noticed that his hands were clenched into fists at his sides. When he turned to her again, standing just inside the door, his face was shining with perspiration.

"I suppose I should go see what she wants," he said, so quietly it was nearly a whisper.

"Wait, Davey. Why don't we get together tonight? There's a great old Karloff-Lugosi flick on TV. I can come over to your place with munchies and booze. We can get shit-faced. It'll be better than sitting home alone brooding, right?" He started to speak and she could tell by the look on his face that he was going to say no, but she didn't want him to. She went on quickly, before he could reply: "And if you're *really* good, maybe I'll even give you a hand job."

He laughed and shook his head. "Okay," he said finally. "How can I turn that down?"

"Great. We'll have fun."

His face was drawn again.

"Anything else wrong, Davey?" she asked. "Besides Beth?"

After a moment, he shook his head. Casey did not believe him.

"Gotta go," he said.

"Okay. Give that city block we work for a kick in the teeth for me, willya?" she said in a stage whisper.

Davey tried to hurry down the corridor without looking hurried. He couldn't go see Miss Schuman yet; he was a mess. He was sweaty and sticky; he could still feel the wetness trickling down the insides of his thighs. He was glad he was wearing dark pants.

He had to make an effort to avoid limping; something between his legs was stinging him, making it difficult to walk steadily.

He went out front, past Tammy's desk, around the

corner to the restroom. He stepped into the far stall and locked the door, experiencing a shiver of *déjà-vu* in the small rectangular compartment, thinking again of the woman behind the smudged glass. . . .

Davey opened his overcoat, dropped his pants, and fell back against the door of the stall, his head spinning as he stared down at himself.

His white briefs were soaked with a sticky reddish brown. Spots of it glistened in the darkness of his pubic hair and were smeared on the right side of his penis.

"Dear Jesus," Davey breathed, "I'm bleeding."

When he returned to his cubicle, Davey had to sit quietly for a moment at his desk to calm down. He stared at his hands, watched them tremble like leaves in a breeze.

He'd cleaned himself up, washed thoroughly and clumsily in the stall with soap and water from the restroom sink. Beneath the blood, he'd found two scratches on the side of his penis. They had barely broken the skin above the vein that was visible along the side of the shaft. He'd cut himself. Pulling his pants back up, he'd hissed curses at himself for being so stupid earlier, for sliding his cock through that rough-edged hole in the wall of the booth.

Davey had had to sit on the toilet seat for some time. He'd buried his face in his hands and prayed that he hadn't picked up some god-awful disease.

Standing in front of the mirror before he left the restroom, he'd realized that Chad Wilkes was right; he did not look well. He'd rubbed his pasty cheeks, trying to work up a little color in them. He'd washed his face with cold water, run his fingers through his hair. Staring into the mirror, he could see her, almost as if she were superimposed over his reflection, smiling up at him with her deep welcoming eyes that seemed to pull him slowly, powerfully, toward her, toward those dark, candy lips that had felt so good on him, sooo cooool and smooth and comforting. . . .

He'd started suddenly, and thought impatiently, *I've got to get some sleep.*

Now he stood, steeled himself for his talk with Miss Schuman, and started down the hall.

He tried to think confidently, tried to tell himself that he was going to be very firm about her unfairness in giving Fritz's job to Chad.

Jasmine Barny, Miss Schuman's secretary, sat behind her desk in the outer office, talking on the phone. She was a small young black woman with a very large smile that never quite went away. Standing before her desk, Davey suddenly felt very dizzy. He grabbed the edge of Jasmine's desk to keep from hitting the floor.

Jasmine hung up the phone and looked at him with concern. "Are you okay, Davey?" she asked, standing.

"Yeah, yeah, I think so," he said quietly, straightening up as the sensation began to fade. "Sit down, I'm fine."

"You sure? You don't look so good."

He took a deep breath and smiled. "Yeah, I'm fine. I just haven't eaten today. Is she in?"

"Yes," Jasmine said uncertainly, watching him carefully as he moved around her desk. "She's expecting you. Go on in."

As usual, Miss Schuman sat behind her desk, seeming to be in competition with its size, smoking a cigarillo, scanning a paper she held before her in one thick-fingered hand.

"Miss Schuman?" Davey said.

"Ah." She put the paper down and took a drag on the

cigarillo, motioning for him to come toward her. "Come."

Davey stepped inside, closing the door behind him.

"Sit," she said, waving her hand toward a rusty-red vinyl-covered chair that faced her. She wore a bracelet with several silver seashell-shaped charms that dangled and clinked loudly when she moved.

Davey sat and crossed one leg over the other.

Miss Schuman reached over to an ugly wooden box filled with cigarillos on the corner of her desk and offered it to Davey. "Smoke?"

"No, thank you."

"That's right," she said, "you don't smoke." She leaned back in her chair and it squeaked painfully under her considerable weight. She was wearing one of her tentlike dresses that fell in folds around her huge upper arms and mountainous breasts. This one swirled with black and red and had a small red bow at the collar where her breasts just began to press together into deep cleavage. Large red beads were strung around her neck and little black cubes dangled from her ears beneath her curly, stiff, salt-and-pepper hair. Her glistening red lips smiled at Davey, pushing her fleshy cheeks up until they almost obliterated her eyes.

"You wanted to see me?" Davey asked.

"Yes," she said abruptly, her smile disappearing. She took another drag on her cigarillo and exhaled smoke as she continued. "I think it's about time we had a talk. *Another* talk, I should say, since this isn't a new issue." She leaned forward, not without effort, and tapped her finger on a notepad before her. "I want to talk to you about these stories you've been recommending to our editors. Like the one about . . ." She lifted the notepad and looked over it briefly. ". . . about the family who loses their son to a, uh . . ." Another peek at the pad. ". . . to a 'gun-cleaning accident.'" She looked at Davey silently, waiting for him to respond.

"Well," he said, wondering whether he should be honest or tell her something she wanted to hear. He decided to be honest. "I really thought it was an important story. And well written."

"Come *on* now, Owen," she said quietly. "That is a pro-gun control story you gave to Max. How many times do I have to tell you that is *not* what our readers want to read. We leave all that stuff to Phil Donahue. We publish action-adventure magazines, vigilante magazines, war magazines. In our business, Owen, *guns* are more important than *people*. We are read by people who have seen *Rambo* fifty-seven times and who tap-dance on the throats of those who support gun laws. If we were to print that story you recommended, they would storm this building and beat us all within an inch of our lives. If we were lucky."

"Well, maybe so," Davey said quickly, sitting forward in his chair, "but the truth is—"

"The truth is, Owen, that you are not doing your job. You're doing *a* job, but I'm afraid it's not the one you're supposed to be doing." She took a long drag on the cigarillo, sat back in her chair, and closed her eyes a moment. When she spoke, she gestured with her hand, leaving a swirl of smoke behind the cigarillo. "Your job, Owen, is to toss this stuff out, do you understand me? You may be a pacifist, and your tastes may lean toward literature of a more intellectually stimulating nature. America is, however, a country of armchair warriors, and those are the people to whom Penn sells magazines. We want gunfire, explosions, war, violence, mayhem. For our female readers, we want stories about handsome men and beautiful women with fascinating careers who meet, fall in love, and have no cares or worries except whether to spend the weekend in Paris or Rome and what they should wear." She looked again at the pad before her and continued, her tone exasperated, "Two weeks ago you turned in a story about an aging magician who falls in love with a young blind girl. For Christ's *sake*, Owen, this is *not* what we *want*, don't you *know* that by now?"

Davey uncrossed his legs and shifted his position in the chair, trying not to sound off the way he wanted to.

Your lack of spine, Davey. You have no spine.

"Yes," he said quietly. "I understand. And I'll, um, I'll try to keep that in mind."

"Good. Now, like I said, we had this talk last year. I would be very pleased if, next year, or a few months from now, we don't have to have it again. Because if we do, Owen, we aren't going to, do you understand me?"

You have no spine.

He exhaled his reply: "Yes."

She smiled again, pooching up her cheeks. "Good. Now. Unless you have any questions, that's all I wanted to say."

Davey stood. "No. No questions."

"All right." Puff. "Thank you for coming in."

"Sure." He tried to smile as he stood, but failed. He turned and started toward the door.

"Owen?"

He stopped. "Hm?"

Miss Schuman frowned as she stamped her cigarillo out in a big brass ashtray to her right. "You feel all right? You look pretty pale."

"I feel . . . yeah, I feel fine."

She removed another cigarillo from the box and

stuck it between her lips. "Are you eating right?" she asked, producing a butane lighter from somewhere in the folds of her billowy dress. "You know, your body might be trying to tell you something. You should pay attention to your body, Owen." She flicked the lighter and held the flame to the tip of her cigarillo. "It's not a bad one," she added with a sly smile, "you should take good care of it." She exhaled and waved smoke at Davey. "I've got a diet at home you might like to try. Maybe I'll bring it in tomorrow. Or maybe you'd like to come over to my apartment some time and I can show it to you."

Davey said nothing as he reached for the doorknob. Chad Wilkes's smug smile flashed behind his eyes.

"I do have one question, Miss Schuman."

"What's that, Owen?"

"Well . . . Fritz's old job? I understand you gave it to Chad Wilkes."

She sniffed. "That's right."

"Well, you know, Miss Schuman, I've been here for quite a while now. I hope to stay in this business. Make advances. I thought that, by now, I would've moved up a little here at Penn. I thought that I would be considered for that job."

"You were considered, Owen. You were. But Chad has a good eye. He knows what we're looking for, he's picked some winners. He . . . well, he knows"—she cocked one thinly penciled brow, speaking deliberately—"what I like." She leaned toward Davey, making no attempt to hide the scrutiny in her eyes as she looked him up and down slowly. "You know, Owen," she said slowly, choosing her words carefully, "we hardly know one another. Maybe if we spent more time together . . . *you* would know what I like, too."

I can't believe what she's saying, he thought.

"And next time," she continued, "maybe you'll get the assistant-editor position."

They know *they can shit on you, so they're going to!*

"Maybe some weekend soon," she went on, "we can have dinner. Spend some time outside of work, you know, getting acquainted."

They know *they can shit on you. . . .*

"What do you say, Owen?"

. . . so they're going to.

He thought of Beth's last words to him: *You're gonna have to start grabbing things by the short and curlies.*

And of Casey's gentle scolding: *You have no spine.*

Of Chad Wilkes's smug smile, and of the girl in the booth, of her breasts and her jet-black hair, and something seemed to uncurl inside Davey. He wasn't sure if it was confidence or anger, or both, but it was sudden and strong and it pushed the words up through his mouth.

"Not on a bet."

Miss Schuman blinked slowly. "I'm sorry?"

"I said: Not. On. A *bet*." Quietly, but firmly.

The corners of her mouth twitched. She clearly did not know how to react.

"Miss Schuman," Davey said, "I think it's time that I—"

What? his mind demanded. *Time that I what?*

"Yes?" she prompted.

"Moved on. I think it's time that I moved on."

She chuckled. "To what, Owen?"

"To a new publisher, I suppose. There doesn't seem to be anything for me here."

"And what makes you think there is elsewhere?"

Pause. "I'll turn in my two-week notice before I leave today." He opened the door.

"That won't be necessary."

Davey half turned to her.

"I don't like your attitude, Mr. Owen. If you want to be rewarded for your work, you must do something to deserve it. So far you haven't." Puff. Smile. "Chad has. If you're going to go around with your nose in the air making rude remarks to your superiors, then I'll let you go now so you won't waste two weeks of your time. Or mine. How does that sound?" She grinned. "You can take your things with you when you leave tonight. Good-bye, Mr. Owen." She went back to the paper she was reading as if he weren't there.

Davey left the office and closed the door quietly.

Davey got his things together in no time at all, and he did it with a smile. He felt better than he had in months, satisfied with himself. A little scared, too, of course. He had no idea what he would do next, but it would at least be something that would allow him a little self-respect, even if it were nothing more than bussing tables.

Having gathered together the few belongings he had in the cubicle—a few pens and pencils, a tin of aspirin, some newspaper articles he'd cut out for one reason or another, all of which fit nicely into his briefcase—he said a silent good-bye to the tiny space he'd occupied for so long, turned his back on it, and walked away.

"Where are you going?" Casey asked him on his way out.

"I quit."

"You *what?*" she hissed with a smile.

"Well, actually, I quit and then I was fired. I'll tell you all about it tonight if you're still coming over."

"Are you high? I wouldn't miss it for the world!"

He tossed a few good-byes to his coworkers as he left, smiling even at those whose names he could not remember. In fact, he was still smiling when he got into the empty elevator and as he crossed the lobby to the doors, opening his umbrella as he stepped outside.

He joined a small group of people waiting at the bus stop: two old ladies, a black woman juggling a baby on one arm and a bag in the other, and a few foul-mouthed teenagers. He collapsed his umbrella and tucked it under his arm; the rain had stopped, leaving only a chilly mist.

He looked around him at the others, catching snatches of their conversations. Then, for no reason, she came to mind again.

Smiling and cool.

Soft and smooth.

And oh so promising.

She was *that* way. Just a few blocks, around a few corners, and he could see her again.

He remembered the uncomfortable stickiness in his pants earlier. The shame and anger he'd felt.

The *pleasure* he'd felt at the touch of her soft, moist lips.

There was a hiss and wrenching sound as the bus came to a stop at the curb. The others filed in; Davey stepped toward the bus, looking from its door to his right, toward her . . .

He stepped up on the first step and reached into his coat pocket for a token. He felt its round flatness, so much like those four tokens he'd held in his hand earlier, the ones that had lifted the panel from the glass . . .

"Well," the driver grunted impatiently at Davey, "you comin' or goin', fella? I ain't got all fuckin' day."

"Uh, I-yuh . . ." Davey looked up at him, fingered the token a moment, then let it drop again. He smiled at the driver and shook his head. "Never mind. Never . . . mind." Davey stepped away from the bus, the doors rattled shut, and it drove away in a belch of stinging exhaust.

Her booth was empty and she was still there, as if she had been waiting for him to return. When the panel rose, she was smiling.

As he walked out of Live Girls afterward, his hair was mussed, his breathing uneven, and his gait a bit unsteady. He could feel the biting sting again. He could feel the moist warmth soaking into his briefs against his skin.

He was bleeding.

Chapter Three

Walter Benedek belched fire into his napkin at the same instant that Davey Owen walked out of Live Girls for the second time that day. He pushed aside the paper plate with leftover egg foo yong on it and leaned toward the window to watch the young man across the street. He seemed to be limping, trying hard to stay on his feet as he walked into the crowd and quickly disappeared from Benedek's view.

He leaned back in the small plastic chair and belched again, wishing he hadn't eaten the day's special in Lim's Chinese Kitchen, New York's Fastest Oriental Eatery. The acidic sizzling in his stomach showed on his face as he stared across the street at Live Girls.

Such a plain little place, and yet something about it held Benedek's gaze, something that he couldn't actually see but something he *felt*, maybe.

He'd waited for the police in the apartment next to Doris's. Mrs. Shaunessy, an old widow, had heard him shouting and came over to see what was wrong. When she saw the bloody mess in the apartment, she'd taken

Benedek's arm, ushered him to her apartment muttering comfort and assurances, then put him on the sofa and poured him a glass of scotch.

Riley had come, Detective Kenneth Riley. They'd met on a number of occasions, never pleasantly. Riley did not like Benedek because he was a reporter and reporters got in the way. Benedek, as a rule, did not judge people by their occupations; he did not like Riley because Riley was simply not a nice man.

After seeing the bodies in the apartment, however, Riley had shown Benedek a rare moment of compassion.

"I'm . . . very sorry, Walter," he'd said, coming into Mrs. Shaunessy's apartment.

"Yeah, thanks," Benedek had said hoarsely.

Riley had seated himself on the sofa beside Benedek. "You know, Walter, I'll have to question you," he'd said softly.

"Right now?"

"Well, I'd like to get as much information from you as possible now."

Had Vernon Macy been acting strange lately? Were there some domestic problems between Mr. and Mrs. Macy? Where might Mr. Macy be found?

Benedek had told Riley everything he could, especially about Vernon's strange behavior of late and his visits to Live Girls.

"That was out of character for your brother-in-law?" Riley had asked.

"You kidding? *Way* out."

After a pause, Riley had asked carefully, "You think he might have done it?"

Benedek had looked up at him with disbelief. "*Might* have? Isn't it as obvious as the fucking *weather*, Riley?"

"Well, we'll see. We've gotta find him first. We're going to start with his place of work."

"Go to Live Girls. Times Square."

"Yeah, we'll go there, too, eventually."

"Go there first, Riley."

Riley had frowned at him, apparently puzzled at Benedek's insistence. "What're you thinking, Walter?" he'd asked firmly. "If you know something, you'd better tell me now."

Benedek had started to speak, but his voice never came and he'd finally swallowed the unspoken words with another shot of scotch. He was sure of nothing. He just *felt* something, but that didn't count.

When Benedek didn't answer, Riley stood and said, "We're looking to contact his dentist, too. You wouldn't know his name, would you?"

Benedek shook his head. "Why?"

Riley hesitated. "They were, um, bitten. Extensively. M.E. thinks they might've . . . bled to death if . . . if they didn't go right away."

"There wasn't that much blood," Benedek had said.

"Yeah, that's what's got the M.E. scratching his head. You go home now, Walter. I'll have to talk to you some more, but it can wait till tomorrow. You can work out all the arrangements and . . . Just go home now. Get some rest."

He'd gone to Times Square. He'd walked for a while up and down the sidewalk across from Live Girls, watching. Waiting to see a familiar dumpy figure hurrying through the crowd. But it never appeared.

Not long after he'd arrived, around ten-thirty, maybe eleven, he'd noticed the young man. He'd stood out of the crowd, totally unlike most of the customers going in and out of Live Girls. All the others looked like typi-

cal peep-joint clientele, maybe a little on the unhealthy side, gaunt and worn. This guy, however, was
young and in apparently good shape; he was well
groomed and wearing a suit. When he came back out,
Benedek had noticed that he was limping, almost
staggering. Then he'd seemed to make an effort to
hold his balance as he fell into step with the others on
the sidewalk.

Now why, Benedek had wondered, *would a
respectable-looking young man like that visit a place
like Live Girls?*

A few minutes later, though, the young man was almost completely forgotten. Benedek was just watching
for Vernon, smoking, drinking coffee, letting his mind
wander.

He'd stepped into the Chinese place because the
view was good from the window. He was not hungry
but he ate anyway. Now he regretted it.

The irritation of his upset stomach was forgotten
when the young man returned. He'd gone in and, after
a while, come out again, walking unsteadily, just as
before.

Okay, Benedek thought after the guy was gone, *once
is fine. Maybe he was just curious. But twice within a
few hours? Uh-uh. And why the limp?*

Something was not right.

Benedek stood and left the humid little restaurant.
He went to the corner and stepped off the curb to
cross the street, go inside Live Girls, see for himself. But
he didn't. He wasn't sure why but it didn't feel right.
Not yet.

He watched Live Girls for a long time. Even as night
began to fall, Benedek watched the black-curtained
doorway and tried to see in whenever someone

walked in or out. But all he saw was darkness. And that darkness made him strangely uneasy.

He finally gave up and took a cab home.

The moment he slipped his key into the lock, he heard Jackie hurrying through the apartment to get to the door. She stood in the doorway in her red and white bathrobe, worry creasing her smooth, gentle face. She opened her arms and took him in, held him for a moment. She smelled of lavender bath soap, clean and fresh.

"I heard," she whispered, her head on his big shoulder. "God, I was so worried when you didn't show up all day. Riley called"—she moved back and looked into his eyes—"to see if you got home okay. Are you all right?"

He nodded, closing the door. "Riley called?"

"Mm-hm."

Benedek chuckled. "He better be careful. Somebody might get the idea he's a nice guy, or something."

"Come sit down. Would you like a brandy?" she asked, slipping his coat off.

"Please." He watched her leave the living room, her robe fluttering around her feet as she moved; her prematurely silver hair shimmered in the apartment's soft light. Chopin played quietly on the stereo.

He'd met Jackie Laslo at a dinner party he hadn't wanted to attend. She made reporter jokes when she found out he was a reporter; he made gynecologist jokes when he found out she was a gynecologist. He'd asked her to move into his apartment eleven years ago and they'd been living together ever since. They'd never seemed to find the time to get married, but they referred to one another as husband and wife most of the time for convenience.

"Here," she said, bringing him the brandy. "Anything else?"

"No." He sipped. "Just stay with me."

She held his hand, sitting on the armrest of the chair.

"I'm sorry you had to find them," she said.

"So am I, hon. Did Riley say if they'd found Vernon yet?"

"No, they haven't."

"Mmm." He leaned back his head, closed his eyes, and sighed as she began to gently stroke his hair.

"You think he did it, huh?"

He nodded.

"Jesus Christ, what could've . . ." She didn't finish. "You want to go to bed, Walter?"

"In a little while." He was enjoying the attention she was showing him. She was usually busy with one thing or another. If she wasn't, he was. Feeling her close was nice.

Benedek thought of that young man stumbling out of Live Girls and wondered if he would return there tomorrow. Probably. Benedek decided he would return, too, and wait for him. And follow him.

"You're frowning," Jackie said.

"Yeah. Thinking."

"About?"

"Well . . . you know how I've always said I don't believe in hunches?"

"Mm-hm."

"It's the damnedest thing. I think I've got one."

That night in bed, long after Jackie's breathing had taken on the rhythm of sleep, Benedek lay awake, staring into the darkness. He thought of Doris and Janice, how thrilled Doris had been when she got pregnant, how inquisitive Janice was as a little girl.

Before he slept, Benedek cried. . . .

Chapter Four

It was a cold night and the air was brittle.

Sondra lit a cigarette, cupping a hand over the lighter's flame to protect it from the wind. Its warmth felt good on her palm. She leaned against the wall on the corner of Eighth and Forty-third just outside Donut Heaven. Tall and striking in black fishnet stockings, black leather mini, and a gray fur jacket, Sondra turned heads with no effort. Men smiled at her and she smiled back with a toss of her blond hair. She nodded at men who slowed down as they drove by the corner.

A short man with a big nose eyed her and slowed his pace as he walked by. In a moment, he turned around and came back, leaning against the wall just a few feet from her.

"Cold night, ain't it?" he asked.

"Yeah, well . . ." Sondra shrugged. "You just gotta find yourself a way to keep warm, know what I mean?" She smiled and drew on her cigarette.

"Yeah." He wore a long, pea green coat, his hands

deep in the pockets. The wind blew his stringy hair off his creased forehead. He shifted his weight from one foot to the other rapidly, never meeting her eyes. "Yeah, so, how much'll it cost me to keep warm, huh?"

Sondra smiled. "Depends on what you want warmed up. And for how long."

"Yeah? Well . . . how about a blow job?"

"Twenty-five."

"Shuh . . ." He paused, stepped away from the wall and fidgeted. "Showers?"

Sondra immediately turned away from him. "Nope. Wrong corner."

The man pushed his hands deeper into his pockets and hurried away as if he'd been slapped.

"Got 'em," Hildy said, coming out of Donut Heaven. "Cruller, right?" She was a petite Asian girl with a streak of magenta running through her long black hair on the left side.

"Yeah."

"They only had the vanilla frosted kind." She handed over a cruller wrapped in a napkin.

Sondra tossed her cigarette away and bit into the donut. For nearly an hour, she'd had a craving for something sweet, one of those cravings that buzzed like an abscessed tooth. As she chewed the donut she regretted getting it; the taste reminded her of the last time she saw her daughter.

"Any sign of Chase?" Hildy asked, reaching into the bag again.

"Uh-uh."

Holding a chocolate-covered custard bar in her hand, Hildy wadded up the bag and threw it down on the sidewalk.

"So what's his fuckin' problem?" she asked, annoyed. "He was supposed to be here forty-five minutes ago."

"*If* he got the blow," Sondra reminded her. "Maybe he didn't."

"Yeah." Hildy took a bite of the custard bar and purred.

Sondra looked down at the cruller, remembering the smile on Maggie's face when she'd bitten into her donut two months before. Sondra had visited her in Connecticut; they'd spent the afternoon together.

"My daughter loves these," Sondra said quietly, smiling.

"I didn't know you had a daughter," Hildy muttered.

"Yeah. Maggie. She's six."

"God, this is good. So what's your daughter like?"

Sondra took another bite of the cruller, dabbed her lips with the napkin. "Curly blond hair, big blue eyes. And smart! She was talking long before I ever did. 'Course, I wasn't around when she started; I was working for that prick Cedric. Till somebody comes along and does the whole fuckin' world a favor by sticking a knife in that asshole's neck." Her voice became bitter. "He was found in a trash bin behind some Italian joint on Broadway."

"Yeah. Heard about it."

"Best thing to happen since the invention of penicillin." She turned the half-eaten cruller around in her hand. "She's staying with my sister in Connecticut. Maggie, I mean. I hate my sister and she hates me. But she's really good with kids, so I figured that'd be best for Maggie." She started to bite into the donut again, but didn't. "I try to see her as often as I can." She wadded the crescent-shaped remains of the cruller into the napkin and threw it away.

Two young Hispanic men, one holding a portable stereo that throbbed with a heavy beat, hurried by. They both smiled at Sondra and Hildy.

"You threw away your cruller," Hildy said, wrapping her lips around the end of her custard bar. When she pulled it away, a bit of custard clung to her lower lip; the tip of her tongue slid out and licked it up.

"Not hungry anymore."

"Hey," a voice called. "I like the way you eat that."

They turned as a man in a rainslicker approached, his eyes and smile on Hildy. He had frizzy hair that was disappearing on top and very thick eyebrows that tangled with his lashes.

"You do, huh?" Hildy said with a smirk.

"Yeah." He stood before her. "Think I could get you to eat *my* custard bar like that?"

"If you're nice enough, I'll eat your whole fuckin' bakery, friend."

"Yeah?" His head bobbed up and down. "Yeah, sure, I think I can handle that. Whatta you say we take a little walk and talk about it?"

Hildy turned to Sondra and held out the custard bar.

"You want the rest of this?"

Before Sondra could reply, the man grinned and said, "No, no, bring that along," his head bobbing like a beachball on the surf.

"See ya," Sondra said as Hildy walked away with the man.

Sondra lit another cigarette and paced on the sidewalk. The wind was icy and her stockinged legs ached with cold. She was twenty-three years old but the lines around her eyes and mouth, though not unflattering, made her look over thirty.

"Heya, babe," a slurred voice said.

A fat, disheveled man, probably in his late fifties, approached her. When he was still several feet away, she could already smell the gin on his breath and on the front of his coat.

" 'Cha doin' with yerself out here inna cold, huh?"

"Waitin' for my limo, thanks." She walked back to the wall.

"Aw, c'mon, honey. How much? Twenny bucks? I got twenny bucks."

"Sorry."

"C'mon, babe."

"Walk."

"You ain't gonna turn away bidness now, are ya?"

"Go to bed and fuck yourself, friend," she snapped.

He staggered toward her, sneering. "Can't handle it all m'self." He cackled. "Need some help. You wanna gimme a hand?" He stepped forward and reached for her arm.

"Hey, *hey!* Back off!"

He laughed a strained, wheezy laugh. "Whatta you gonna do, sweetie, call a *cop?*" His laugh turned into a cough and he doubled over a moment, holding his stomach. He spat, then stood and took another step toward her. "C'mon, babe, let's have some—"

"Excuse me."

The deep, clear voice made Sondra turn. A startlingly tall figure stood at the corner of the building, blanketed in shadow, his hands in the pockets of a long black coat.

"What do you say you go somewhere else for com-

71

pany, hm?" he said to the drunk, his voice barely raised above a whisper.

The drunk waved a hand in dismissal. "Aw, fuck off, I was just lookin' for a little fun's all. Who the hell you think you—"

"Go. Away."

The drunk straightened his posture, jutted his jaw. "It's a free country, buddy. I'll do whatever the fuck—"

The man stepped forward and closed a fist over a clump of the dirty coat and shirt, and lifted him off the ground, backed him against the building. The drunk's feet dangled heavily several inches from the sidewalk.

"I said go. Now." The man let go and the drunk fell in a heap onto the sidewalk. He scrambled to his feet and staggered down the walk away from them, mumbling curses into his collar.

The man turned to Sondra and stepped into the light.

"Well," Sondra said, uncertain at first. "Thanks. I guess."

"No problem."

Sondra put a hand on her hip and looked up at the man, half smiling.

"So, is there anything I can do to show my appreciation?" she asked.

"Maybe," the man said, nodding slowly. "Why don't you walk with me?" He stepped closer, held out a hand.

Sondra squinted slightly as she looked him over. Very tall, thin reddish brown hair that fell almost to his shoulders, pale skin.

"Where to?" she asked.

"Just a few blocks."

"You haven't answered my question yet."

"Well, actually, it's for a friend."

"A friend, huh? Sorry. He'll have to come see me himself."

"She doesn't get out."

"Oh, she? Well, that's interesting. So what is she, a crippled dyke? I don't do amputees, none of that shit."

"She's in perfect physical condition, I promise you."

"Yeah?"

Roger smiled with strangely dark lips. His hand was still held out before him, waiting for her to take it.

"Well," Sondra said, looking around, "I gotta friend, too, see. She'll be back pretty quick and she's gonna wonder where I am."

Roger lowered his hand and slipped it into a pocket. "I can pay very well." He held up a handful of bills.

"Well, *Christ*, buddy, why don't you just throw the money up in the air and see how much attention we can attract?"

He put the money back in his pocket. "Sorry," he said quietly.

Sondra put a hand on her hip, brushed her hair back with the other, and said, "You sure this ain't for you? You're, um . . ." She smiled. "You're pretty interesting, you know? I like you."

He shook his head slightly. "For my friend."

She sighed and looked around for Hildy again. "Well, shit." She narrowed her eyes. "Okay, money in advance, right?"

"Of course." He reached over and pressed some money into her hand. "Two hundred dollars?"

She blinked. "Jesus, you gotta horny friend." She

stuffed the money in her purse at her side. "Okay, where to?"

"This way."

She walked with him across the street, along the sidewalk, their feet splatting softly against the wet cement.

"So what's your friend into?" she asked. "I don't do just anything, you know."

"Sucking."

"Into sucking, huh? Two hundred bucks just for me to come suck her?"

He turned his head to her only slightly, one cheek raising with a gentle smile. "No. *She* does it."

After a few blocks of silent walking, Roger slowed in front of a small black storefront with a flashing sign that read LIVE GIRLS.

"Hey, hey, wait a sec," Sondra snapped. "This is a peep joint."

"This is where my friend is," he replied, leading her to the curtained doorway.

"Nope." She stopped. "Uh-uh. I'll have a world of shit, I go into a place like that to turn a trick. What, she wants me to go into one of them dirty little booths with her, or somethin'? The management'll shit a brick sideways, I go in there."

He smiled again. "She *is* the management."

Sondra stood outside the black building and thought of the two hundred dollars in her purse. "First sign of trouble," she said, "I'm haulin' my ass outta there."

"Fair enough," Roger said. He took her arm and led her through the curtain.

"Jesus," Sondra breathed, "it's pitch black in here."

"Just come with me."

She reached out a hand and felt cold, rusty bars, then a wall. Just beyond that, Roger opened a door and led her through. She heard it close, then heard a lock click. Sondra detected the presence of a third person in the dark with them. She sniffed; something smelled sweet. She heard Roger speak to someone in a whisper, but she could not understand what he said. There was an unintelligible reply. Sondra closed her eyes for a moment, then opened them. The darkness was thinning slowly. She looked through the barred window at the curtained doorway through which she had come; light from outside shone through the narrow part in the curtains.

"Come this way," Roger said, never letting go of her arm. He led her through another door; its hinges sounded like the laugh of an old woman. It shut behind them. There was definitely someone with them now, someone standing just behind Sondra to her right.

Roger let go of her arm and stepped away from her. With a click, soft light came from a small lamp on an end table against the wall, landing in a round pool on the dirty floor. Sondra looked around the tiny room; Roger stood by the lamp looking at someone over her shoulder. She turned and could see a figure in the dark. No face. A shadow cast by nothing. Roger smiled at her, then spoke to the figure behind Sondra.

"Shall I go?"

"Yes," a voice said from the darkness at Sondra's back. "I'll let them up when I'm finished." It was a woman's voice, deep and touched, perhaps, by the accent of a language unfamiliar to Sondra.

She heard scratching, like a kitten pawing at a door. At first, she thought it was coming from outside the door behind her. Then she realized it was in the room with them. Not exactly *in* the room, but . . . coming from beneath the floor.

With a nod to the shadowy figure, Roger turned and went back out the door, smiling in at Sondra before closing it behind him.

The faint scratching became a heavy scraping against wood.

Sondra turned to the woman hidden in the darkness. For the first time in a long while, Sondra was scared, and when she spoke, her voice trembled. "Look," she said, "I don't like the feel of this, know what I mean? No offense, or anything, but, tell you what. I'll give you your two hundred dollars back and just take off. How 'bout it?"

The woman stood there, a part of the darkness around her, motionless and unnervingly silent.

"Okay?" Sondra asked, smiling uncertainly.

The scraping became a thumping.

The woman stepped into the circle of light cast by the lamp and all Sondra could see were her eyes. Deep, red eyes that gripped her and held. For several moments, she saw no other part of the woman's face except those two enormous, embracing *eyes*.

"You're very pretty," the woman said, her voice as quiet as a lustful thought. "Very healthy and *soft* looking. Desirable."

Sondra could not speak. She could not move. She wasn't even sure she was breathing.

"I'm glad Roger found you," she continued, taking another step forward. Sondra realized the woman was holding open her arms to Sondra. She moved toward the woman, unable to resist. Sondra saw her face as the woman's hands touched her shoulders.

She saw the white white flesh, the silver hair framing the long face, narrow, upturned ears, the flat nose, the lips, and when the woman smiled hungrily, Sondra saw her teeth, long and narrow and sharp, dripping with saliva.

The pounding beneath the floor became frantic. Sondra's last thought was a memory of her daughter; her last sensation was the woman's mouth pressing to her throat. . . .

Afterwards, she stood slowly, her mouth dripping. She ran long fingers over her lips, then licked them clean. Reaching out a hand, she flicked off the lamp. She was more comfortable in the darkness. The darkness was cool and soothing.

She leaned against the wall a moment, feeling her strength return, warm behind her eyes, making her feel as if she glowed in the dark room. She felt whole, strong, satisfied.

She bent forward, threw a bolt lock on the floor, then another. She wrapped her fingers around the flat handle and lifted a trapdoor, stepping aside.

They clumsily began to pull themselves up with twisted hands and knobby fingers. Some of them had lost the flesh at the tips of their fingers and bone protruded from the ragged skin.

Others shot up from below, their vein-webbed wings flapping softly as they fluttered near the ceiling, their red eyes gleaming in the blackness.

All of them were disfigured in some way, bent, crippled. They swarmed over the still form on the floor, their teeth and claws tearing the flesh, their lapping tongues filling the room with quiet sounds, wet sounds, as they fed on what remained of the girl's blood.

She passed quietly through the room, through the door, closing it softly behind her. She sat once again in the cage, blending into the darkness behind the bars, sated and waiting.

Chapter Five

"My God!" Casey shrieked, rocking with laughter. "I can't believe she actually said that to you! Are you, are you . . ." She stopped, recovering from her laughter. "Are you sure that's what she had in mind?"

"Sure sounded that way to me," Davey replied, his voice a little hoarse. He was lying on the sofa in an old gray jogging suit. Casey was sitting Indian-style on the floor turned toward him, a white carton of take-out Chinese food in her lap. The television was on, the volume low. The gray images of *The Black Cat* cast a flickering glow on Casey and Davey in the otherwise dark room. "Now we know the *real* reason Chad got that job."

"Well," Casey said, a little bitterness in her voice, "I knew it wasn't because he deserved it. I don't think he even knows what he's doing half the time, he's so preoccupied with that damned singles bar he hangs out in every night."

"The Trench?"

"Yeah. Slime. Wonder if Miss Schuman knows that her little pet is going out and getting it on with bouncing bimbos a few times a week. Anyway, Chad is just what Penn is looking for. He wouldn't read more than two pages of a truly good manuscript if you made him. You know, I read the manuscript about the magician and the crippled girl? Good story. You just wait, it'll sell somewhere." She scooped some noodles into her mouth and chewed, smiling up at Davey. "You made the right move," she said.

"Yeah," Davey agreed. "I think I did. I feel good about it. I just don't know what I'm gonna do now."

"Don't worry too much about it."

"Well, now that Beth's gone . . . She was helping out with the rent and stuff. Not much, but let's face it; selling tickets at that slimy theater doesn't exactly keep caviar on the crackers, you know? But it was something. I'm gonna have to move fast so I can put some groceries in the fridge. Maybe if I'd done this sooner . . . maybe she wouldn't have left."

"Hey, bucko," she snapped, "don't start that with me. If *that's* why she left, you're better off without her. Of course, I don't give a damn *why* she left, you're better off without her *anyway*." She held up the carton. "Are you sure you don't want any of this? It's good."

Davey looked down at the carton with its mash of noodles and vegetables and sauce and his stomach did a little flip. He hadn't been feeling too well since he'd gotten home; his appetite had been gone since morning and he hadn't eaten all day. The thought of food in his mouth only made him feel worse.

"Positive," he said. "My stomach's a little upset."

Casey leaned forward and squinted at him. "You do look a little pale. Maybe you should just eat some soup. Get a little food in your stomach."

He shook his head. "No, thanks."

"Get lots of Vitamin C," she suggested, taking another bite of food.

"Thanks, Mom."

"And don't be a smartass. You've got to stay well if you're going job hunting. Nobody in their right mind'll hire you if you look anemic."

He chuckled, staring at the television. "You know, I'm gonna kind of miss the trash at Penn."

"Gimme a break."

"No, really. Some of that stuff was fun. *Some* of it. I learned a lot of weird stuff from those stories. How to break into very secure buildings, how to defend yourself with a pocket comb. How to blow up cars with Ping-Pong balls and—"

"Whoa, wait a minute. Ping-Pong balls?"

"And Drano."

"You're shitting me."

"Uh-uh."

She took another bite, then set the carton aside, leaning toward Davey with interest. "Okay. I'll bite. How do you blow up a car with Ping-Pong balls and Drano?"

"You take a Ping-Pong ball, inject some Drano into it, then drop it into the gas tank of your favorite Godless communist, and . . . boom!" He spread his fingers wide.

"C'mon, now. Drano explodes?"

He shrugged and turned on his side toward her. "Some sort of chemical reaction. The gasoline dissolves the Ping-Pong ball after a while—that way the good guy has enough time to haul ass—then when the Drano and the gas mix, it explodes. Any petroleum distillate is supposed to work. I"—he covered his mouth with his palm as he yawned—"don't know. I just read it in one of those 'true' adventure stories."

"Well, it's certainly good to know if you ever go into the terrorist business."

They both chuckled.

Boris Karloff and Bela Lugosi were playing chess for the lives of a young couple who had wandered into Karloff's huge art-deco mansion.

After several moments of silently watching the movie, Casey turned toward Davey and watched him as his eyes grew heavy, as the gray light flickered over his pleasant face. When he finally noticed she was staring, Davey said, "What?"

"Nothing. Just thinking."

He waited, but she just continued looking at him, smiling softly.

"Well?" he pressed.

"I was just thinking that . . . I'm kind of glad that Beth took off."

Davey blinked a few times. He was used to her joking about his choice of women friends, but her tone now was serious. Sincere.

"I'm sorry," she said, shaking her head apologetically. "That probably wasn't a very nice thing to say. However I may have felt about her, I know she meant something to you. But, well, I *am*, dammit! My reasons are kind of selfish, I guess, but that's the way I feel."

"Okay, so what are your reasons?"

"Well, she was bringing you a lot of heartache, for

one thing. But I also think that maybe you and I will have a little more . . . time together."

Davey sat up a bit straighter. "There's more, I can tell. Go on."

She squirmed, took another bite of her food, then set the carton aside and scooted closer to Davey.

"What happened between us, Davey?" she asked suddenly, her voice so quiet he almost had to strain to hear it. "I mean, that day we spent together, walking around the park, making up stories about all the bums and bag ladies, harassing the pigeons, then, when we came back here, spent the night together . . . that was wonderful, Davey. I mean, it. Really. Was. *Wonderful.* Then afterward, we never talked about it, never did anything about it, it was almost like it never happened. So, what'd we do wrong?"

Davey watched her for a moment, hoping she would continue. "I really don't know," he finally said.

"Neither do I, which makes the whole thing even more stupid and frustrating! You didn't need to go off and shack up with Beth, and I didn't need to quietly sit on the sidelines and watch, wondering if you'd ever come to your senses again!"

He sighed but didn't say anything.

"Anyway, now she's gone and you're available, and all that shit, and . . . if you're interested . . . I'd kind of like to, well, I think we'd be . . . oh, I'm fucking this up. I didn't even plan on talking about this, you know." She got a tight-lipped look of determination on her face, and she said, "Davey, are you interested? Yes or no."

He almost laughed at the cards-on-the-table tone of voice. "Casey," he said, "I'm sorry. Sorry if I made you feel—"

"Don't apologize!" she snapped, bringing her face so close to his that he could smell her not unpleasant Chinese-food breath. "That's all over now and we've got another shot at things. Life's too short to spend apologizing. So what do you say?"

Davey finally laughed. Softly. "You're a tough cookie," he said.

"Mama Thorne didn't raise no airheads."

He sat up on the sofa and she scooted over, waiting for a reaction.

"I've got to admit, Casey, I'm a little puzzled. I mean . . . I'm not really your type, am I?"

Casey slid away from him. "And just *what* is my *type?*" She didn't let him reply. "If anybody has a *type*, it's *you*. And I can't fit into it!" She stood and paced with her hands on her hips.

"Oh?" Davey said. "And what's *my* type?"

"You still don't know, do you?" She turned to him. "Remember Patty?"

Davey had met Patty in the elevator on his way to work one morning. She'd said she was going to apply for a job at Penn but was sure she would never get it. When he asked why, she'd replied, "I can't do anything, and I sure can't keep a job. Well, except for one. But I don't like it."

Sure enough, she hadn't gotten the job, but he'd taken her to dinner that night. She had talked him into giving her a place to stay until she could get a job. She'd claimed to be looking for work, but she never found any, though she'd somehow managed to always have spending money.

One day, six months later, Davey came home from work early with the flu to find her in the bathroom with a grossly overweight black man. She was giving him an enema in the bathtub.

"It's nothing personal, just a job!" she'd shouted just before leaving a short time later. "But *everything's* personal to you, isn't it?"

Davey looked up at Casey, wondering what she was getting at.

"She needed help, didn't she?" Casey asked. "Needed, oh, I don't know, *caring* for. Right?"

"Well, yeah, she—"

"She needed a good shot of self-respect and confidence, right? You thought you had something to offer her. And Beth. You found her in the lobby of the Union being knocked around by her boyfriend. You took her home, gave her a place to stay, took good care of her, let her cry on your shoulder . . . really, Davey, don't act confused when I say you have a *type.*"

Casey stopped pacing and stood before him.

"You let them use you, Davey, and then when they're finished, you fall into a big pout. Why don't you take a *look* at your problem and *do* something about it. Stop thinking that no woman will have you unless you can *do* something for her."

She sat down and stretched an arm out on the back of the sofa.

"I don't want you to do anything for me, Davey," she said softly. "I don't want to change you, I don't want to help or pamper you. I just think you're a pretty terrific guy with whom I want to . . ." She thought a moment, and giggled. ". . . get naked."

Davey laughed, but briefly. He felt tired. Not just physically tired, but exhausted from the juggling he'd been doing during his relationship with Beth, and before that with Patty, trying so hard to . . . what?

To make them happy.

She's right, he thought with disgust.

"Casey," he began slowly. "I'm not so sure it's a good idea."

"And Beth was?"

"Touché." He sighed. "Look, I'm not saying . . . I'm not telling you that . . ."

"Yes or no, Davey."

He put a hand on the side of her face and gently moved his thumb over her soft skin. He honestly did not know what had happened between them. If Patty hadn't come along, perhaps something would've developed with Casey, something more than their strong but (with the exception of one night) platonic friendship. He would probably have never become involved with Beth.

Davey touched Casey's hair.

"Not right now, Case. But that's not a no!" he added quickly. "I just need a rest, okay? An intermission. Maybe if we just sort of . . . worked up to it?" He waited. "Well?"

She smiled. "I think that's the smartest thing you've done since you left Penn. You're beginning to display some good judgment, my friend. I'm proud of you." She bent down and kissed him. It began as a simple peck, but lingered. She pulled away and got up on the sofa with him. "Scoot over," she said. "The best part's coming up, where Lugosi skins Karloff alive." She cuddled up next to him. As Casey stroked his hair and Karloff screamed in pain, Davey fell asleep.

* * *

He awoke from a dream of the girl in the booth. He was on the sofa, a blanket twisted around his legs, sweat trickling over his temples. The television was off, the room was dark, and he was alone.

"Casey?" he said. The name came from his dry throat as a rasp. He swallowed a few times, coughed, sat up. "Casey?" He looked around the room and found a note taped to the television set.

Dear Mr. Van Winkle,
Sorry you're not feeling well. I hope you're better in the morning. Rest up tomorrow, I'll call you after work, and we can plan your job-hunting strategy.
Kisses,
Casey

He lay down on the sofa; he felt terribly weak.

He'd dreamed of her, her creamy skin . . . her long black hair . . . The panel had hummed up, but there had been no dirty glass between them. Only her.

Davey went into the kitchen and splashed a little vodka into a glass of orange juice. He got out the sketch pad he kept in a kitchen drawer, found a pencil, and began scribbling.

Shadows within shadows on the paper, shapes forming, shifting. Eyes, lips, a breast, a triangular patch of darkness . . .

He tore out the page, wadded it up, and tossed it toward the trash can. It missed and rolled on the floor.

Davey was still sweating. It was not hot, but he opened a window, and let in the cold air and the noise of the city.

He wondered if she was still working in the booth

behind the window, or if she'd gone home to bed, perhaps with a lover. He imagined her hair spread about her face, an ebony pool over the pillow . . . her breasts rising and falling in her sleep.

Davey went to his bedroom, dressed, and grabbed his umbrella.

Downstairs, he caught a bus to Times Square.

Chapter Six

Tuesday

Times Square was alive.

It throbbed with light: red, orange, yellow, blue, green, white, all flashing at a staggered pace, creating a silent harmony of color, softened through the mist left behind by the rain.

Davey looked at his watch—it was just past midnight—then through the rain-speckled window of the bus. The next stop was his. The bus lurched to a halt, the doors opened, and Davey stepped down onto the sidewalk.

He faced the bus, hands in his pockets, as it slowly rolled away, billowing fumes. On the other side of the street, its sign glowing a deep red above the blackened doorway, was Live Girls. The red letters were reflected on the wet pavement below, the reflection passing in and out of sight as cars hissed over it. Davey stepped off the curb, waiting for a break in the traffic when he spotted movement in the darkness of the alleyway to the right of Live Girls.

Someone stepped from the alley onto the sidewalk. Someone tall and slender in a long coat, black leather with a gray fur collar. A woman.

She held her hands before her face and flicked a butane lighter; the flame glowed a soft orange on her delicate face, creating small shadows above her high cheekbones. Dark hair fell to the side of her face. The flame disappeared; she put the lighter in her coat pocket and brushed the hair aside.

It was very long hair.

Davey felt something clutch in his chest as he watched her walk to the corner. She waved at a cab, but it drove on; she scanned the street for another.

It was the girl from the booth.

Davey took long hurried steps over the street, his only thought that he get to her before she got into a cab.

A horn blared and Davey gasped as a car jerked to a stop less than two feet from him. The driver stuck his head out the window and pushed back the bill of his cap.

"What the fuck 'er you, re-*taahhh*-ded?"

Davey ignored the man and rushed to the other side of the street. For an instant she disappeared behind a cloud of steam rising from the pavement, then he saw her again, hailing another cab; this one slowed to a stop at the curb.

Davey broke into a run, dodging pedestrians as he rushed toward the corner.

The girl grabbed the door handle and had the door halfway open when Davey waved and shouted, "Wait!" His voice was lost in the sounds of traffic and he began to run faster. She was sliding a leg into the cab when Davey reached her. "Wait wait wait!"

Startled, she pulled her head back and raised her thin brows. "Are you talking to me?" she said firmly, her face tightening. She pulled her leg from the cab and stood behind the open door as if it were a shield.

"I . . . I . . ." Davey's voice left him and he stared at her awkwardly, his mouth open. A white light flashed rapidly above them, having a strobelike effect on her face. The cold breeze tossed her hair against her cheek and she brushed it away.

"Well?" she said, impatience in her voice. "What do you want?"

"I . . . I was coming to see you just now. I mean"—he gestured over his shoulder—"back there. I saw you earlier today. Er, yesterday." He tried to smile. "Twice, in fact."

"Come back tomorrow. I'm off for the night." She started to get in the cab again.

Davey put a hand on the door and said, "Wait."

She stopped, and turned to him again, cocked a brow. "Yes?" She sounded vaguely annoyed. Her leather coat crinkled softly when she moved. She took a quick drag on her cigarette.

"Are you in a hurry?" Davey asked uncertainly.

"As a matter of fact, I am. I'm on my way to work."

"I thought you worked here."

"Sometimes," she said patronizingly. "I'm also a dancer."

"A dancer!" Davey said through a pleased smile. "Where? I'd like to see you."

"Hey, lady," the cabdriver said, "you coming or going?"

She bent down and looked into the cab. "As long as your meter's running, what does it matter?" She stepped forward and put an elbow on the door. Smoke rose between them from her cigarette, dancing in the breeze. "A club. The Midnight Club."

"Oh. I'm . . . not familiar with it." Her hand was inches from him, the same hand that had touched him.

"Well, then, you should come in sometime. I'm there five nights a week." She smiled tightly, her lips glistening. "Good-bye."

"Can I come with you?" Davey asked quickly.

She pursed her lips, as if concealing a smile.

When she said nothing, Davey added, "I'd really like to see you. Dance, I mean. Tonight."

She remained silent, watching him.

"I'd be glad to pay for the cab. My name is"—he cleared his throat—"Davey Owen."

She drew on the cigarette and exhaled smoke through a gentle smile. "All right. You can come. But you don't need to pay the fare. I would've taken the cab anyway." She slid into the cab smoothly.

Davey moved slowly around the door, his heart pounding anxiously. He stood by the door for a moment, then got inside, pulling it closed.

She leaned forward and said to the driver, "Hudson and Watts, please."

As the cab jerked away from the curb, she turned toward Davey and leaned back against the door, one elbow propped on the back of the seat, her cigarette held up beside her head. Her dark eyes remained fixed on Davey, studying his face as she drew on her cigarette. She blew the smoke in a thin, slow stream at the ceiling of the cab, watching him.

Davey began to feel hot and claustrophobic. He wanted to speak to her, but did not know what to say; the look in her eye did not encourage conversation. It was a look of analysis that made Davey feel like a germ under a microscope.

"I'm not a prostitute," she said.

Davey blanched and shook his head.

"I never thought you were!" he replied quickly.

Her mouth curled into a half smile of disbelief. "Surely the thought crossed your mind. Just for a moment?"

"Well, yeah . . . maybe. But that's not why I approached you."

"Then why did you?"

"Like I said, I'd come to see you. You're the only reason I wanted to go back into that place."

She nodded, but did not seem convinced. "Do you go into Live Girls often?"

"First time today. I was . . . curious, I guess."

"You came in twice."

Davey looked away from her, embarrassed. The cab-driver braked suddenly.

"Get offadah road, moron!" he growled.

Davey tried to smile. "I just . . . wanted to see you again."

"Mmm." Her eyes moved over his face slowly. "You don't seem the type."

Davey simply shrugged.

In the silence that followed, she turned from him and stared out the front window. Her fine profile was outlined against the passing lights outside the cab.

"How often, uh, do you work back there?" Davey asked.

She turned to him, almost as if she'd forgotten he was in the car. "Off and on," she answered.

"Do you have a . . . oh, a specific schedule?"

She arched a brow.

"I'd like to come see you again."

From deep in her throat came a low, honey-thick laugh, a laugh of pleasure, but with, perhaps, a touch of mockery. "A fan," she said, cocking a brow.

"Yeah." Davey chuckled. "I guess you could say that."

"The atmosphere in the Midnight Club is much more pleasant," she said, looking out the window again. "If you want to see me perform in the future, I suggest you go there."

With a twinge of disappointment, Davey realized she was not going to tell him when she would be at Live Girls.

A club would be much better than that booth, he told himself. But in a club, he would not be able to touch her; she would not be able to slide his hand over her smooth, cool thighs, her breasts . . .

Davey flinched and shifted in the seat, ashamed that the mere thought of being in that dark, close booth was making him erect.

When he looked at her again, her lips were wrapped around the end of her cigarette; she looked as if she could sense his shame and was amused by it.

She glanced through the front window and said, "We're almost there. I'll have to get you a table," she added. "It's nearly impossible if you don't have reservations."

"Thank you."

"It's nothing," she said, taking a small billfold from her coat pocket. She gave him a sidelong look, her lashes low over her deep eyes, and smiled. "I'm rather glad you came, Davey."

The cab stopped, and Davey got out as she paid the driver. He looked around for some sign of the club, but saw nothing; the dark Tribeca neighborhood was deserted. The sidewalks were lit only by pools of light from the streetlamps. The entrance to a nearby parking lot was chained off and the lot was strewn with litter and broken chunks of cement. Davey saw only one lighted window on the top floor of an old cast-iron building; it flickered a soft grayish blue.

"This way," she said. Her heels clacked on the wet street. "I usually go in the back," she told him, "but I can't take guests that way." She led him to the end of the block and stopped at a door set in the corner of the building. She pushed the door open and Davey followed her inside.

They walked into a vacuumlike silence. The deep purple carpet and black walls of the foyer seemed to soak up sound like a sponge. Davey heard music playing faintly, as if from a great distance, its melody no more distinct than the buzzing of a housefly.

She turned to a man standing at the right of the entrance. There was a book open before him atop a solid black pedestal.

"Hello, Malcolm," she said. "This is Davey, my guest this evening. Do we have a table for him?"

He checked the book, running a long finger down the page. The top of his skull was large and dome-shaped with thinning gray hair slicked straight back; he had sunken temples, sharp cheekbones with deep shadows beneath, and a razorlike jaw. His fair skin was smooth and clear as a child's. He wore a black tuxedo; a diamond stud sparkled just above his left nostril. Malcolm looked up and smiled.

"Table twelve," he said. His voice was sibilant, feminine. "Tell Cedric when you go in."

"Your coat, sir?" A young blond girl stood behind a

counter across from Malcolm. She held a tiny hand
out to Davey.

Davey slipped his coat off and gave it to her. She
handed him a ticket in exchange; he stuffed it in his
pocket.

Davey turned to his companion; she was taking long
strides toward a huge black door framed with red across
from the entrance. With a slight wave, she said, "Later,
Malcolm." Then to Davey: "Come, Davey, I'm late."

Davey saw Malcolm push a button on the pedestal
and the black door swung open heavily; the music that
had sounded so distant a second before suddenly
pounded from beyond the doorway.

Following her out of the foyer and into the club,
Davey glanced back to see the door shut smoothly behind them.

The club was dark inside; smoke, diffused with dim
light, writhed above bobbing heads. She led him
around a crowded, U-shaped bar and through the
crowd.

Overhead lights with purple shades gave everything
in the room a bruised look, relieved only by small
white lamps on the center of each of the round tables.
The walls were black and covered with a white grating
on which were mounted geometrically shaped neon
tube lights; the lights flashed red and purple, blue and
white.

A Hispanic man with close-cropped hair and a mus-
tache approached them. Like Malcolm he wore a
tuxedo, but filled it with a much more impressive
physique. He had a hard street face, knowing and sly.

"Cedric," she said loudly. She lightly touched Davey's
arm as she spoke. "Could you show my guest to table
twelve?"

Cedric turned to Davey.

"This way, sir," he said with a heavy accent.

"Wait!" Davey called to her as she began to walk away.

She stopped and turned.

"Your name!" Davey said. "I don't even know your name."

That half smile again: "Anya." She was swallowed by the crowd.

"Sir?" Cedric said. "This way, please."

Reluctantly, Davey followed him through the crowd toward the source of the music.

Davey saw middle-aged couples, some in formal attire and jewels, others casually dressed, mixing with younger people wearing the most current fashions and sporting extravagant hairstyles. Ice clinked and smoke swirled.

Cedric led him around the crowded dance floor just below the stage to one of the front tables. "Here you are, sir," he said. His hard-edged voice and steely eyes clashed with his formal manner.

Davey seated himself and looked up at Cedric, who was watching him carefully. His eyes moved from Davey's face, down his chest and stomach to his lap, then back up again.

"A cocktail waitress will be with you in a moment," he said.

As the man walked away, Davey noticed a scar just below his left ear; it was perhaps two inches long and had apparently been a very deep cut. Cedric wound his way through the crowd until he was out of sight.

Davey looked up at the perfectly dark stage and blinked several times in disbelief. White disembodied hands were playing white instruments: drums, guitars, a saxophone, a keyboard. The instruments shone like polished ivory in the darkness of the stage. They moved and bobbed and swayed; the white hands glided over the keyboard gracefully. The effect was hypnotic.

The beat of the music was heavy but not unpleasant. It seemed to move the bodies on the dance floor as strings move a puppet.

"Something to drink, sir?" a waitress asked. She had short red hair; gold eyeshadow sparkled beneath her brows. She wore the top half of a tuxedo with tails and, from the waist down, only black panties and black stockings.

"Uh, vodka gimlet, please," Davey said. "No ice."

As she walked away, Davey watched the tails flap against her legs.

Davey spotted a table of three women, all in their forties, each immaculately dressed. They were laughing raucously. One of them, a plump black woman, gracefully lifted a hand above her head and waggled her fingers, not unlike a schoolgirl asking a question in class. Light glinted on her handsome diamond wedding ring; the spot of light was filtered through the hovering smoke and shined, for an instant, like a star. Cedric went to her side, joined his hands behind his back, and leaned toward her, smiling. She lightly placed her fingers on his elbow and said something in his ear. Cedric nodded and stepped behind her, pulled her chair back as she stood. He took her arm and led her through the crowd.

Davey watched them as they stepped around tables and shouldered their way between the other patrons. Cedric led the woman to a door, rumbled with the knob as if unlocking it, then pushed it open. They stepped inside.

Davey turned back to the table from which the woman had come. Her two friends were hunched forward over the table, their lips moving frantically in turn, their expressions mischievous and conspiratorial.

Davey sat back in his chair, puzzled.

The ladies' room, maybe? he wondered. *But why did he have to unlock it? And why did he go in with her?*

The song ended and applause rose from the dance floor. The dancers laughed and chattered as they returned to their seats.

The hands and instruments on the stage faded and disappeared.

The waitress returned with Davey's drink. He winced at the price, but paid her. He sipped the gimlet slowly; at that price, it would have to last.

Davey watched the door through which Cedric had led the black woman. No one else went in, and no one came out.

He was startled by a sudden silent movement before him. The cleared dance floor began to rise until it was on a level flush with the stage; it was no longer a dance floor but a runway.

The lights dimmed and the crowd hushed.

Music began to play, soft and slow, mournful and somehow reverent. The tune was unsettlingly familiar. A spotlight came on as something began to descend from the darkness above the stage, something white and rectangular. As it was slowly lowered, the music became louder and richer. Only when Davey realized what the object was did he recognize the song.

It was a white cross floating down to the stage, and the song was an old church hymn Davey remembered from his days in Sunday school. He found himself remembering the words:

*"On a hill far away . . . stood an old rugged cross . . .
the emblem of suffering and shame . . ."*

The cross came lower . . . and lower . . .

*". . . and I love that old cross . . . where the dearest
and best . . . for a world of lost sinners was slain . . ."*

The base of the cross gently came to rest on the floor of the stage and the soft, sorrowful music exploded with wailing guitars and thunderous drums. Red light bled over the cross and two dancers, a man and a woman, leaped from the darkness behind it.

The man wore only bulging bikini briefs and a clerical collar. He had bushy dark hair that swept around his head as he danced; shadows rippled over his sleek, muscular body.

The woman wore a black and red teddy and a nun's cowl over her long black hair. It was Anya.

They writhed around the cross, their movements sensual and flowing, then they closed in on it like sleek, predatory animals. They put their hands on it, caressed it, pressed their bodies to its sides, rubbed themselves against it. Anya wrapped one leg around the bottom of the cross and slid her crotch up and down its edge; her head fell back limply, mouth open and eyes closed, and her long hair swayed from beneath the cowl. The man locked his hands around the top of the cross and squatted until his jutting knees flanked the base; he thrust his hips forward several times before standing.

As the man stepped away from the cross, Anya held it to her, lifted it, and began dancing with it as if it were a partner.

The music throbbed like the pulse of an aroused giant.

The light changed from red to white to red again.

The man danced around Anya as she twirled and dipped the cross. She tilted it, straddled it, and began riding it like a lover.

Davey sipped his drink as he watched her. He noticed, as he lifted the glass to his lips, that his hand was trembling. Something deep inside him squirmed. A small remainder, perhaps, of his childhood, when his mother would dress him up on Sunday morning, lead him by the hand to the small church a few blocks away where he would squirm through Sunday School and the endless services. Hymns like "The Old Rugged Cross," which was now thundering through the walls around him, an entirely different song now with its erotic beat, propelling the two hard, glistening bodies over the stage.

The song's words echoed in his head and his mind's ear heard them sung by his mother, her voice high and breathy and slightly off-key.

"And I'll cherish the old rugged cross . . . till my trophies at last I lay down . . . I will cling to the old rugged cross . . . and exchange it someday for a crown."

For a moment, the voice was so vivid in his mind that he was afraid if he turned to his right, he would see her beside him, hymnal in her hands.

He blinked his eyes several times, dissolving the memory but not the guilt. Childish guilt. And he knew why it was there.

Because he enjoyed the feeling of the music rattling his bones. And he *especially* enjoyed Anya humping the cross with abandon, her tongue sweeping around her sparkling lips.

She slowed her movements, swinging her head to the beat of the music. Setting the cross upright, she stepped back and the man grabbed it, danced with it, then set it on its side. He lifted the base of it off the floor until it was sticking from between his legs like an enormous erection. He began sliding his hands up and down the shaft, rolling his head slowly as Anya danced around him. She dropped to her knees before him and wrapped her arms around it, opened her mouth wide, and began sliding her head along its length. The music became louder and more frenetic; the man bucked and writhed orgasmically.

They both stood, righted the cross, and flanked it, still moving with the beat, and backed away from the cross, slowly disappearing into the darkness. The music became deafening as it neared its finish. On the final roaring chord, the cross burst into flames; the flames instantly disappeared in a *whump* of purple smoke.

A spotlight shone on the pillar of smoke as it shifted and snaked through the air, gradually clearing to reveal a tall figure.

The music stopped.

Applause shattered the brief silence. Hoots and whistles rose above the sound of clapping hands.

Davey stared slack-jawed through the remaining wisps of smoke. After a moment, Davey began to applaud with the others.

The woman standing in the circle of light wore a black mask with glittering silver fringe and fine screens over the eyeholes. Only her mouth and chin were visible. She smiled at the crowd and raised her arms in greeting. Her sleeves bunched around her elbows, revealing shapely arms with unblemished, fair skin.

"Thank you!" she said loudly. She had no microphone, yet her voice carried quite clearly above the applause. She lowered her arms. "Thank you very much. Anya and Marcus—our dancers!"

Anya and her partner came out and took a bow. The applause swelled; there were more cheers. When the dancers slipped back into the darkness, the audience quieted down.

"Welcome to the Midnight Club," the woman continued. "For those new to this establishment, I'm Shideh, your host."

There was more applause, but she raised a quieting hand.

"Thank you, but that's not necessary. We have a full evening of entertainment ahead and we've hardly begun."

Davey was certain he had never seen her before. But there was something oddly familiar about her. The folds of her purple and black costume moved gracefully over her curves. A diamond-shaped opening over her chest revealed pale, smooth flesh and deep cleavage. Her hands were large and elegant and somehow powerful.

". . . want you all to relax now and enjoy yourselves," she went on. "For some, it's late. But here it's early, and the evening has just begun."

There was a flash of light, smoke billowed up from the floor and swallowed Shideh. The disembodied band appeared once again, and when the smoke began to clear, Shideh was gone.

When the music ended, the comedian came onto the stage and introduced himself. He was stylishly thin, stylishly dressed.

Davey looked around, hoping to see Anya again; he could not spot her in the crowd. He wondered if she would come back out at all. As his eyes scanned the smoky room, he noticed the side door opening. The black woman came out first; Cedric followed close behind. He escorted her back to her table.

She moved differently, slower, with less bounce in her step. A languid smile rested on her lips. Cedric seated her, touched her shoulder, and walked away. The other women leaned toward her and began chattering. She simply closed her eyes, smiled, and gently nodded.

". . . but *everybody* seems to be afraid of death, am I right?" the comedian said. "Now me, I look at it this way. Dead people don't have to deal with public parking, you know what I mean?"

There was scattered laughter.

". . . had a girlfriend die on me once," the comedian went on. "Right in the middle of sex. She was giving me head and then she was dead."

A few quiet laughs.

"Only good thing was she didn't gag when I came in her mouth."

A roar of laughter and applause.

A hand came to rest on Davey's shoulder and he looked up with a jerk.

Anya smiled down at him.

Davey started to stand but her hand pressed on his shoulder and she laughed. "No, no, don't get up," she said, seating herself. She wore a simple black and white dress with spaghetti straps. A necklace of tiny, glittering white beads hung from her slender neck.

Davey smiled and leaned toward her. "I . . . I'm very impressed. You're an incredible dancer. Really, I've never seen anything"—he cleared his throat—"like that."

"Thank you, Davey."

"In fact," he continued, "this whole *place* is like nothing I've ever seen before. I'm overwhelmed."

She raised her hands beneath her chin, her elbows propped on the table. "We take great pride in that."

Davey cocked a brow. "We?"

"Something to drink?" the waitress said, standing beside Anya.

"Yes," Anya said. "House special for me and another of those for my friend."

"Oh, no," Davey said. "I don't . . ."

Anya put her cool hand on his and Davey's whole arm tingled. She leaned toward him. "It's on me," she said.

The waitress left.

Anya's hand remained on his.

"It's not every day," she said, "a devoted fan waves me down on the street, you know." She slid her hand away slowly.

"That dance . . ." Davey said.

"Irreverent, wasn't it?" She smiled mischievously.

"I recognized the song."

"Yes? Are you a churchgoer, Davey?" She gave him a sidelong look and smirked.

"Well, not anymore. I used to be. When I was a boy. But I've long since"—he chuckled—"veered from the straight and narrow path."

"Haven't we all." Anya looked around the club. "Yes, the entertainment here is a bit out of the ordinary. Like him." She nodded toward the comedian. "His humor is too . . . oh, too dark, I suppose, for most tastes. But he fits in here."

"The woman with the white hair," Davey said. "Does she always wear a mask?"

"Whenever she has an audience. Shideh is very

theatrical. She prefers to surround herself with mystery. You met her earlier. She runs the token cage at Live Girls most of the time."

"That was her?" Davey asked, his brows rising with surprise. "It was so dark I couldn't see her."

"See what I mean?" She narrowed her eyes dramatically and said in a loud stage whisper, *"Mystery!"*

The waitress returned and set down their drinks. Anya's was in a tall clear glass; it was brownish red and looked thick.

"What is that?" Davey asked.

"House special. It's for employees and members only."

"This is a members-only club?"

"Not exclusively, no. Nonmembers have to pay more and make reservations well in advance."

"How do you become a member?"

She smiled. "There's a long waiting list. And it's expensive. *Very* expensive."

Davey's attention was torn. He was fascinated by his surroundings, but he could not take his eyes from Anya. She sipped her drink, produced a cigarette, and lit it. Every angle of her face, her body, was pleasing to the eye; every move she made was beautiful.

One side of her mouth rose in a half smile. "You're staring," she said quietly.

He blinked and turned away. "I'm sorry." Looking again at the closed door across the room, he asked, "What's in there?"

"Why do you ask?"

"Just curious." He shrugged.

Her fingers curled around her glass and her nostrils flared delicately. "Restrooms," she said simply. Her expression made no attempt to hide the untruth of her reply. She seemed entertained by his curiosity, but a brief coldness in her eyes suggested he not pursue it.

Davey sipped his fresh drink. It was stronger than the first and went down heavily.

"Will you be dancing again tonight?" he asked.

"Once more, then I'm done."

"Do you have any plans after work?"

"I was going to go home. Why?"

"Well, I thought maybe we could go have a drink, or something."

What am I doing? he thought. *Beth just walked out on me, Casey wants to start something, and I'm pursuing this total stranger who* . . . His eyes moved slowly over her perfect face. . . . *who is absolutely gorgeous.*

"We're having a drink here," she said.

"I mean someplace a little quieter. I'd . . ." He ignored his apprehension and folded his arms on the table as he leaned toward her.

Anya tilted her head back a bit and cocked a brow, prompting him.

"I'd like to get to know you," he said.

She smiled with satisfaction. "*Would* you, Davey?"

"Yes."

"Are you sure that would be a good idea?"

"Why wouldn't it?"

She smoked her cigarette and sipped her drink, closing her eyes as the rim of the glass touched her lips.

"Surely you have a wife? A girlfriend?" she asked. "You seem to be a nice, respectable fellow. I would think you'd have *someone*."

"You say that as if you aren't nice and respectable."

"Well." She shrugged. "Some wouldn't think so."

"I'm not some. You seem very nice to me. And I'm . . . I'm very attracted to you."

She chuckled behind closed lips, watched him closely, then stood, putting out her cigarette.

"Well?" Davey said. "What about later?"

She lifted her drink as if to sip it, considered it a moment, then placed it back on the table.

"Meet me in the front lobby after my next performance," she said, her hand resting on the glass. "We'll go to my place."

Davey nodded, vaguely uncomfortable under her unwavering gaze.

"You're not going to finish your drink?" he asked.

She shook her head. "I won't be needing it."

Chapter Seven

The moment Davey stepped into Anya's dark, chilly apartment, she embraced him, opened her mouth, then closed it over his, running her tongue across his lips.

Davey stiffened—partially because the kiss was such a contrast from the cool behavior she'd exhibited all night and partially because her tongue was so startlingly cool—then slowly relaxed and put his arms around her.

Anya pulled her head away.

"You're not getting boyish on me, are you, Davey Owen?" she asked. "It was *your* idea to get together."

"Yeah, I know. I just . . ."

She laughed. It was filled with genuine pleasure.

"You didn't expect this all at once?"

"Not really," Davey said. "No."

"But it's what you wanted, isn't it?"

He nodded.

Her eyes examined his face carefully. "You're a very weak person, Davey," she said quietly.

He flinched. Davey remembered what Casey had told him the day before.

You have no spine.

"Why do you say that?" he asked with an edge to his voice.

She smiled. "Because you're here."

Taking his hand, Anya led him through the living room. The windows were open and white curtains fluttered in the cold wind like ghosts. Down a hall, she took him into a bedroom.

She turned and kissed him again, and slipped a hand between the buttons of his coat.

Davey sucked in a breath at the chill of her palms through his shirt. She drew his tongue deeply into her mouth. When Davey put his hands on her back, he felt bare skin, soft as a baby's and cool from the night air. She lifted one leg and pressed it between his, against the hard lump in his pants. When Davey stepped back to take his coat off, he saw that her dress lay crumpled around her feet. She slipped her shoes off as his coat fell to the floor, then led him by the hand to her bed, pulled the covers back, and began unbuttoning his pants. Davey put his hands on her breasts, and caressed the round undersides with his fingers.

Davey undressed slowly with trembling hands as she kissed his face. He remembered the look in her eyes when he first saw her behind that smeared glass in the booth, that look that promised so much. This is what that promise had been, the fresh, clean smell of her, the way his skin tingled when she touched him. She pulled his undershorts down and kissed his erection, then licked her way back up over his stomach and chest to his throat. He touched her thick black hair and kissed her temples, her eyes.

There was nothing in the darkness but her skin and her smell and her hands, nothing in his life but her breasts and lips, her tongue and her teeth tugging gently at his flesh. He hadn't lost his job, Beth hadn't left him, he didn't live in a huge, dirty city that sat on an island like a dark, hunkering beast waiting to gulp down anything that wandered by. His whole body quivered as he fought the urge to furiously devour her beneath him.

He wanted it to last, to linger, so he forced his movements to come slowly.

"You like this, Davey Owen?" she asked him. He could not see her lips in the darkness but he could feel them moving against his shoulder. "You like all this?"

Davey tried to speak, but couldn't.

She rolled over and knelt by him; her hair swung lightly over his face and shoulders.

"You like surrendering yourself like this, don't you, Davey?"

Surrender? he thought, but the word dissolved in his mind and fluttered away like a breath of vapor on a cold night. He ran his hands down her slender body as she leaned forward and kissed his neck and ears, his throat, his chest.

Davey tried to reciprocate, to kiss her and touch her in return, but his energy seemed to be flowing from his body, leaving him through every spot of flesh touched by her tongue, her lips, her fingers.

Anya wrapped her fingers around his moistening penis and slid her hand up and down slowly.

Davey moaned and lifted his pelvis toward her.

She gently rubbed her thumb over the head of his cock and touched his testicles lightly with her fingertips.

"You want to be in my mouth again, don't you?" she whispered.

He wanted to reply, but his lips would not come together. He nodded, eyes closed, chin jutting, and she put her lips on him, teasing him with her mouth, running the tip of her tongue along the bottom of his shaft, and then, as she had in the booth, she plunged her mouth down on him, all the way to his groin, and began lifting her head up and down, up and down, while Davey's whole body squirmed and shifted over the mattress. He gulped air and moaned, touching her head with his hand; his arm was so weak he couldn't hold it up and it slid heavily back down to the bed.

Anya moved around with her mouth still full of him until her legs straddled Davey's face. The skin of her thighs was like satin against his cheeks and his face was gently smothered in her pubic hair, and in her fleshy lips. He slipped his tongue inside her, wanting to give her pleasure but able to concentrate very little because of the waves of sensation flowing through him.

Anya began sucking vigorously. Davey could hear her gulps and feel her fingers clutch his thighs hard. He felt a sudden draining sensation, a feeling of being emptied, not unlike that of relieving a full bladder but without the feeling of relief. With each of her deep, throaty gulps, a tremor passed through him, and with each tremor came a euphoric weakness. He let his head fall to the pillow, unable to keep his mouth on her. Anya moved herself luxuriously over his face as she sucked him. Davey's body became helplessly limp beneath her. He could not move or participate, only feel.

Only when she finally stopped and lifted her head did it occur to Davey that he had not yet come.

Anya pulled herself away from his face, turned

around, and mounted him. There was a controlled frenzy in her movements as she rode him, bending forward until her breasts were swaying just above his face.

Davey wanted to bury himself between them but he couldn't lift his head. His body felt heavy as iron.

Slipping an arm beneath his neck, Anya lifted his head to her breasts. Davey opened his mouth and licked her, inhaled the musky smell of her skin. Perspiration trickled down his sides, over his ribs, but she remained dry and smooth and cool.

Anya leaned back and, with surprising strength, lifted him with her, one hand between his shoulders and the other behind his head. She pressed his face to her neck.

"Bite me," she hissed, never losing the rhythm of her movements. "Bite me, Davey."

He tried to kiss her, but she wouldn't let him; she kept pushing his head back to her neck.

"*Bite* me!"

Bite her? He couldn't . . . do . . . that . . .

"I *said bite me*, Davey Owen!"

"I . . . I can't . . ."

She held his head down, pressing his open mouth to her neck just below her ear. She pressed harder and harder; Davey teetered on the edge of orgasm and his body tensed, his eyes clenched, and he closed his mouth over her, vaguely feeling his teeth break through her skin.

She bucked on him, moaning in his ear.

Davey's cry was muffled as he came inside her. His lips were wet with sticky, warm fluid and he ran his tongue over her skin, sucked on it.

"Suck it!" she gasped. "Suck it, Davey, suck it in . . ."

Davey felt himself slipping away; the darkness around him deepened.

Everything went away. . . .

When Davey awoke—he wasn't sure how much later—Anya was kneeling between his legs. She was silhouetted in the soft glow from the bathroom as she gently dabbed a warm, wet cloth between his legs.

Davey opened his mouth to speak and his lips peeled apart, sticky and dry. There was a sharp, harsh taste in his mouth. Anya reached up and patted his lips with a corner of the white cloth.

"How long have I slept?" he asked.

"Not long. But it's late." She got off the bed and walked to the bathroom. "You'll have to go."

Davey sat up and put his legs over the edge of the bed. His limbs were weak and a dull ache throbbed between his legs.

When Anya came from the bathroom, she wore a heavy black robe that reached to the floor.

"You can use the bathroom before you go if you like," she said.

Davey stood, picked up his scattered clothes, and went into the bathroom. He washed his face with cold water, rinsed his mouth, then stood over the toilet to urinate. Touching his penis made him wince; it was tender and, in one spot, sore.

The cut. It was pink and streaked with red. He carefully rubbed a finger over it and held his hand up. Blood.

He took in a deep breath, exhaled slowly, and leaned on the edge of the sink. The room seemed to tilt a bit; his head felt light.

After he relieved himself and began to dress, Davey

spotted the cloth draped over the edge of the tub. It was stained with deep red.

It's not a cut, he thought suddenly. He realized he'd known since he'd first discovered it in the restroom at Penn. He looked closely at the two small lacerations; they were puncture wounds. *It's a bite.*

Davey peered through the slightly open door and saw Anya moving about in the dark room. Although he'd rinsed, his mouth still tasted . . . metallic. Coppery.

Bite me, Davey . . .

Suck it . . . suck it in . . .

He hurriedly finished dressing and went into the bedroom. Anya stepped before him and smiled.

"Do you have cab fare?" she asked.

He nodded and said, "I want to know what—"

Anya took his hand and his mouth snapped shut as she looked into his eyes. His throat felt tight as she led him through the apartment to the door.

"Good night, Davey Owen," she said as he stood in the doorway.

He opened his mouth.

What did you do to me? he wanted to ask. *What's wrong with you?*

But those eyes calmed him, reassured him, and made more silent promises.

"Will I . . . see you again?" he asked, his voice forced.

She said, "Of course. And soon." Then, very softly, as she closed the door: "You'll *have* to."

The lock clicked on the other side.

Chapter Eight

It began to rain again as Beth started down Avenue C toward Vince's apartment building. She took her retractable umbrella from her bag and opened it. The rain sounded like machine-gun fire above her head.

After leaving Davey's early the previous morning, she'd gone straight to Vince's apartment and let herself in with her key; Vince had never asked for it back when she left nine months ago. She'd put her things in the bedroom and showered. Vince still hadn't returned when she left for work later in the day.

Beth wondered if he was back now. She wondered how he would react when she showed up.

Up ahead, four very large men were mounting motorcycles parked at the curb. One of them tossed a bottle over his shoulder as he settled his bulk on the seat. The bottle shattered on the sidewalk.

Beth stepped around the chunks of glass and wrinkled her nose at the powerful smell of whiskey.

"Hey, sweetcheeks!" one of the men shouted.

She ignored them and hurried on.

Beth thought about Davey; surely he wouldn't be too crushed. She hadn't been good for him; Davey had a lot of love to give, but he would have to give it to someone who knew how to take it.

She climbed the steps of Vince's building as someone opened the door on the way out. Beth collapsed the umbrella and looked up at the smiling face of the man holding the door open for her. He had slicked-back hair, plucked eyebrows, crooked teeth, and a spike through his right cheek.

"Hi," he rasped as she went in. When she didn't reply, he spat, "Cunt," and stomped out.

Upstairs, she slipped the key in the lock and opened the door. She heard his voice even before she was inside.

"Well, fuck *me!*" he said loudly. "Look who groveled in!"

She closed the door and turned to him.

The apartment was dark and stuffy. All the windows were closed and the only light came from the fluorescent light above the stove in the small kitchenette. Candlelight flickered in the bedroom. He'd been doing business.

Vince wore an open white robe that came to his knees, and his gaunt body was bare except for blue briefs. He was nearly bald on top and his dark brown hair was mussed and thinning on the sides. His face shimmered with perspiration and his eyes were wide.

"I'm not groveling, Vince," she said calmly. "I just came back, is all. If you don't want me here, give me a day or so to get my—"

He dashed across the room toward her so suddenly, she flinched, expecting him to hit her.

"Why wouldn't I, babe?" he breathed. He put his arms

around her and pulled her to him until their noses touched. "Missed you, babe. Things are great now. Heat is off with the cops. Business is good. Got me a little customer in the bedroom right now. Things are fuckin' great."

"I'm glad, Vince," she said, trying to smile.

"So what broughtcha back, babe? Your little boyfriend broke? Can't get it up? Doesn't wanna go down on ya? What?"

Beth recognized the look in his eye, the fire in his movements; Vince was flying. Probably dexies. In this condition he was a time bomb; his mood could change in a heartbeat.

"It just didn't work out, Vince. That's all."

He buried his fingers in her hair, closed his fist, and pulled her head back. Not hard, but firmly. "Knew you'd be back. Knew you'd miss me. But you shouldn't just pop in, you know? Liable to get your little throat cut, babe. My work makes me a little edgy, like. Know?"

"Sorry, Vince. I didn't think you'd mind."

"Still thinkin', are ya?" He grinned unpleasantly.

"Viiiince!" a girl whined from the bedroom.

He let go of her hair and stepped back. "Got some business goin' down here, babe." He started toward the bedroom. "Yeah, business as usual. Didn't think I was gonna be mopin' around waitin' for you, didja? Didja?"

"Course not, Vince." She put down her bag and took off her coat.

Vince went into the bedroom and shouted, "Okay, get the fuck outta here!"

"But Vince, I wanna—"

"I said *out!*"

Beth heard rustling and whispering.

"No," Vince said.

"Please . . . please, Vince."

A sharp slap made Beth close her eyes. Business as usual.

"Put your clothes on and get out," Vince growled.

In a moment, a painfully thin young girl—seventeen at best—staggered out in dirty clothes. She stumbled across the room and shut the door quietly on her way out. Beth heard her stumble and cry out in the hall.

Beth went into the bedroom where Vince was clearing a stack of clothes and soiled underwear off the bed. On the nightstand, Beth saw the burning candle, a belt draped sloppily over the stand, a syringe, and a couple wet spoons.

Vince shrugged off the robe and flopped on the bed, grinning wildly. His erection was sticking out from the briefs.

"C'mon, babe," he said, patting the mattress with a jittery hand. "Wanna welcome you home."

"I'm pretty tired, Vince. I didn't sleep last night, I've been working at the—"

The grin turned cold. "The fuck you think this is, a hotel?" He lifted his ass and pulled off the briefs. "Little Penny couldn't do shit," he said. "Too fucked up. Good customer, always finds money, but gives head like a dead fish and I got me some ashes to haul, babe, so . . ." He cackled. "You just get your little ass over here."

Beth rubbed her eyes a moment. When she pulled her hands away, Vince was tugging on his penis; his eyes were half closed and the tip of his tongue sparkled in the corner of his mouth. "Cmon, babe, get it over here, now," he panted. His hand slowed down and his eyes opened. "You gonna suck me or am I gonna kick ya?"

She began to undress.

"And how many times I gotta tell ya," he said, "open the fuckin' window, it's like a tomb in here!"

She opened the window and finished undressing, knowing that in the morning, he would be better. Usually, for the first couple hours of the day, Vince was almost a sweet guy.

Walter Benedek was at his sister's wedding once again.

Doris stood at the altar facing Vernon. Benedek sat in a pew near the front, sweating in his stiff, prickly suit.

The reverend spoke, but very quietly. It sounded like he'd said, "You may kill the bride."

Benedek leaned forward and clutched the back of the pew before him.

Vernon lifted Doris's veil and smiled as his lips twitched back over his teeth.

"No!" Benedek shouted, shooting to his feet. "No, *kiss* the bride!"

Doris's eyes were closed and her head was tilted back; she was smiling gently in anticipation of the kiss. Vernon plunged his head forward and buried his teeth into the soft skin of her throat, pulling his head back sharply as blood gushed from the opening and darkened her snowy gown. A ragged patch of skin dangled from his mouth.

"*Kiss* the bride, goddamn you!" Benedek roared. "*Kiss* her!"

Vernon turned his head toward Benedek and smiled around the meat clenched in his teeth, then spat hard. The bloodied flesh slapped onto Benedek's cheek and clung there. Vernon pressed his face into the hole in

Doris's throat as she gasped and jerked, clutching desperately at her collar. Vernon began to bite and suck.

"No, *kiss* her, goddamn you!" Benedek screamed, sobbing now, stumbling into the aisle. Something was holding his feet, snagging them. He looked down.

The floor was covered with hair. Blond hair—Janice's hair—matted with blood. It tangled around his ankles like wet weeds.

"No!" he bellowed. "No, no, *kiss* the bride, that's my sis and you're supposed to *kiss* her!"

He awoke in Jackie's arms.

"Dreaming, Walter, that's all, you're okay," she whispered.

He felt her lips on his ear, her fingers in his hair. His face was moist with tears.

"I'm sorry," he croaked.

"Don't be." Her voice was soft, her breath cloudy with sleep.

"I'm . . . I can't . . ." He took in a deep breath and released it with a groan. "I want to find him, Jackie. I want to find that fucker and kill him."

Casey woke from a fitful sleep at the sound of Lisa's sobs in the next room. She'd been on the phone crying and arguing with Selig since Casey had gotten home. Words occasionally became clear when Lisa raised her voice.

". . . expect from *me* after that . . . want the same from *you* then . . ."

Rain pattered against the small window in Casey's room.

Her period was about to begin and she felt achy and irritable. She was annoyed by the ongoing argument between Lisa and Selig; she was annoyed by the people she had to work with, even more so now that Davey was no longer there to make the job a bit more tolerable. The only thing she felt at all good about was Davey.

Casey was very pleased to see him showing a little maturity, a little self-respect, by not jumping from one relationship right into another. He was giving himself a little time to regroup.

Maybe when he got his act together, they could really enjoy one another. Casey thought they deserved that.

She took a cigarette from her nightstand and lit it as a sharp cry came from Lisa's room. She heard the phone slam down hard. A few moments later, it rang and was picked up on the first ring.

Davey hadn't looked at all well when Casey left him earlier. She hoped that he would get a good night's sleep and feel better in the morning. She wanted him to get things rolling, find a new job.

Casey smiled at her impatience as she reached over and stubbed her cigarette out in the ashtray.

Davey lay exhausted in bed, but he could not sleep. He'd considered getting up and drawing for a while, but he was too weak. He'd turned on the radio beside his bed, but the jazz it played seemed off-key. The volume was low, but the music stabbed needles into his scalp, so he'd turned it off.

The normally soft sheets on his bed scraped against his skin like sandpaper, so he threw the top sheet and covers off.

His bedroom seemed hot and stuffy, but when he

tried to get up to open a window, he nearly fell over with dizziness.

He wouldn't see her again. He would stay away from that filthy booth in Times Square and that flashy club with its perverse entertainment. And he would stay away from that sick woman. That sick . . . beautiful . . . soft . . . woman . . .

"This is a very sick world we live in, Davey," his mother had once told him on the way home from church. They passed a woman sleeping in a doorway; his mother looked away and sniffed. "Very sick," she had continued. "And the only medicine is Jesus. I'll be dead and gone someday, but you can always turn to Jesus. Remember that."

Davey suddenly felt ice cold, as if he'd been stripped of his skin and his bare bones were chilling. He pulled the grainy covers over his body and curled up, shivering, beneath them.

When sleep finally came, he dreamed.

He fucked Anya violently, biting her skin, as his mother stood over them screaming hymns at the top of her lungs and crying, after each verse, "Jesus is the only medicine! The *only* medicine!"

And somewhere deep in his muddy sleep, Davey bathed in blood.

Chapter Nine

Casey's ashtray was full. Ashes were scattered around it on the desk and a stray butt had toppled over the ceramic rim.

Halfway through proofreading a story for *Loves Lost and Found* magazine, she struck a match and lit another cigarette, blowing the smoke hard from her lungs.

Her mind was not on the story. She'd called Davey three times that morning and had gotten no answer. He might have awakened after she'd gone last night and unplugged the phone before going to bed, but surely he would have plugged it in this morning. She'd told him she would call.

Casey was startled by a hand on her shoulder. Chad put his head next to hers and spoke in her ear.

"Hey, hon, how about lunch?"

She shrugged him off. "What *about* lunch, Chad?"

"Are you eating alone today?"

"Yes."

"No sense in that."

"I'm not up to it today, Chad. All right?"

"Okay. How about tomorrow?"

She spun her chair around, standing so suddenly that Chad had to step out of the way.

"I didn't mean I'm not up to *lunch*," she snapped. "I meant I'm not up to *you*. Not today, not tomorrow, and not a *week* from Saturday. Okay?"

"Fine," he chirped with an optimism that made Casey's veins chill.

She grabbed her coat and stepped outside the cubicle. Chad stood in the doorway with arms folded.

"I just thought that, since Owen's gone now, you'd be—"

"Don't even bring him up, Chadwick!" She tried to whisper but she was so angry her words came out in a harsh rasp. "Quitting this dump was the best thing he ever did, but he *would've* gotten that promotion if you weren't fuh—"

She was going to say, *If you weren't fucking that noxious slab of fat!* But she knew word would get back to Miss Schuman and Casey wanted to keep *her* job for a while longer.

"I'm sorry?" he said.

She plucked the cigarette from her mouth and blew smoke in his direction as she said, "Nothing." She left the room.

Chad followed her.

"You know," he said, "the way I heard it, he didn't leave. He was *ousted*, if you know what I mean." He chuckled.

"The way *I* heard it, he *left*, and I heard it from *him*." She stormed through the big door and into the lobby.

Chad was just a step behind her.

"Well," he said, "of course *he* would tell you that."

Casey hit the elevator button so hard the tip of her finger was numbed. The doors slid open instantly and she stepped inside.

"Can't you take the stairs?" she snapped when Chad followed her. She hit the *L* button with her thumb.

"I want to have a word with you."

She turned away from him and blew smoke at the NO SMOKING sign on the wall. The elevator doors closed, and the car began to descend.

"Casey," he began, his voice suddenly lowering. "I understand."

"Understand what?" she asked.

"Why you treat me the way you do. You're nice to Davey because . . . well . . ." He shrugged then coolly stretched an arm out and propped himself against the wall. "Because he's not a threat. But you try to keep your distance from me because . . . because you're afraid of your attraction to me."

Casey's jaw dropped and she started to tell him he was so full of shit that his ears reeked, but Chad stepped forward and put a hand on her neck, slipped his fingers into her hair, and pulled her face toward him, his tiny mouth puckering.

Casey gasped and pulled back, at the same time slipping her cigarette into the breast pocket of his suit coat.

Chad stepped away from her and began slapping the smoking pocket.

"What . . . Jesus Chrrr . . . this . . . this is a brand-new suit!" he sputtered, his voice rising to a high pitch.

Casey took in a steadying breath. "Next time," she said through clenched teeth, "it goes in your eye."

The elevator stopped and the doors opened.

"That shit may work with *her*," Casey hissed as she stalked out, "but not with *me*."

Chad's hand froze an inch above his pocket, holding the butt gingerly between thumb and forefinger. His face hardened. "With *who?*" he asked.

Casey turned and pressed her hand to the edge of the elevator door. She couldn't resist. "I'm curious. Chadwick, does she ever get on top?"

Chad's mouth snapped shut and his little nostrils flared.

Casey pulled her hand away and the doors rolled shut.

"Bastard!" she whispered to herself, wiping her mouth with the back of her hand as if he had actually kissed her. The very thought made her feel dirty.

She went to the bank of payphones in the building's lobby, dropped a quarter into the slot, and punched Davey's number.

It rang eight times; he didn't answer.

She sighed as she replaced the receiver. Leaving the building to go to lunch, Casey thought, *Please, Davey, be all right.*

Benedek wearily paced the sidewalk across from Live Girls, hands in his coat pockets, his hat pulled low over his forehead, until his knees seemed unable to hold his weight any longer. There was a bench facing the opposite side of the street, but it was filthy and he was cold. The only other possibility was Lim's Chinese Kitchen, New York's Fastest Oriental Ulcer. He went inside and ordered tea and a few fortune cookies and took a seat by the window.

He'd gotten little sleep the night before. Jackie had insisted he spend the day inside.

"I'll cancel my appointments," she'd said. "I don't have anything important today, nothing that can't wait. I'll stay with you and—"

"I can't just sit here, Jackie," Benedek had interrupted quietly. "I've got to arrange the cremation and I just can't stay around here. You go to work. I'll be all right."

He'd eaten a light breakfast, called a few mortuaries until he'd found one that sounded reasonable, then he'd gone down and arranged to have his sister and niece burned down to two small piles of ashes.

He'd sat there in that plush, deadly silent office listening to portly, toupeed Mr. Birnbaum talk about "our various plans, all of which are designed with your convenience in mind," all the while thinking, *I'm having them slipped into a giant oven and burned to gray little ashes I could blow away with a single breath.*

Afterward, he'd taken a cab to Times Square.

He bit into a fortune cookie. Crumbs of it clung to his lips as he chewed.

The day was dark with clouds; tires splashed through puddles outside.

A man shuffled by with his head low, talking loudly to the sidewalk—something about pressing charges and pressing flowers.

Benedek wondered if Vernon would ever show up at Live Girls again. He was raising another cookie to his mouth when he spotted the young man he'd seen the day before. A meat truck passed slowly, blocking Benedek's view, and he nearly knocked the table over standing up. Tea sloshed from the cup and the cookies wobbled over the tabletop. Benedek hurried to the door, pushed through, and stood on the curb, watching.

The truck passed and Benedek got a glimpse of him

just before he stepped through the black curtains. It was the same guy, no doubt about it. Same coat, same walk. Except . . .

Yesterday, the guy had seemed dizzy and off balance when he came out of Live Girls. Today he seemed that way *going in.*

Benedek held up a hand to the oncoming traffic and stepped into the street. A car horn honked and the driver's mouth worked angrily as he shook his fist at Benedek.

"Yeah," Benedek snarled, waving an annoyed hand at the man, "your mother sucks warts, buddy."

On the other side, he faced the doorway of Live Girls. He took out a cigarette, lit it, and paced. Going in after him probably wouldn't be a good idea. Probably best to wait for him to come out.

Yeah, he thought, *I'll wait.*

Davey slipped a dollar bill beneath the bars and said, "Tokens, please."

The woman in the darkness—Shideh—silently dropped the tokens in his hand. He went down the dingy corridor.

He'd slept late and awakened screaming. A vague nausea had prevented him from eating; he couldn't even drink coffee. The face in the bathroom mirror had been drawn, cheeks gaunt and eyes sunken with dark patches beneath them. There had been a harsh taste in his mouth, metallic and sticky. He'd stared at himself in the mirror for a long time, wondering what was wrong.

The phone had rung; on the third ring, he'd unplugged it, unable to tolerate the shrill sound another moment. He'd paced, then collapsed wearily on the sofa before the television. He'd watched it, unseeing.

He'd bitten her. She'd *made* him bite her. He remembered the powerful hold of her hand on the back of his skull as she'd pushed his mouth down on her neck.

Bite me.

Going back to the sofa, he'd begun biting his nails until one pulled to the quick and a spot of blood oozed from the small tear. When he'd put it in his mouth and tasted the blood, a rush of dizziness made him lie down.

When he recovered, he'd put on his coat and gone out to see her, to ask her what she'd done to him.

In the booth, he dropped his tokens into the box. As the panel lifted, he folded his arms tightly across his chest.

I shouldn't be here, he thought. *I should be home in bed, I'm sick, I shouldn't be here, why am I here?*

When he saw her, he knew. He began to grow hard instantly and looked away, angry and ashamed.

When the panel stopped humming, he looked up. "Your neck," he breathed.

There was no bite mark.

Her sultry look disappeared when she saw him and her face became blank.

"Not here," she said flatly, her voice muffled, and reached out of his view. The panel began to close.

"I just want to talk to you," Davey said quickly. "I want to—"

"Not here."

The panel thumped shut.

There was movement behind the slot. When Davey looked down, he saw her mouth framed by the rough wooden edges. She spoke quietly.

"I have a break at three. For two hours. Meet me in front of my apartment building."

"But I just want to *talk* to—"

"Later."

She went away.

The booth suddenly seemed smaller, darker. It smelled of sweat and sex. Davey pushed the door open and hurried out, thinking of the smooth, unbroken flesh of her neck.

A few moments after Davey had fallen into step with the foot traffic outside, a deep, lazy-sounding voice beside him said, "Excuse me?"

He ignored it.

"Sir? Excuse me."

Davey turned, expecting one of the street people to ask him for a quarter. It was a tall man with a long, droopy face. He smiled at Davey, satisfied to have his attention.

"My name's Walter Benedek," he said, walking beside Davey. "I'd like to ask you a couple questions if you don't mind."

Davey felt a quick flash of fear. "About what?" he asked.

"Well"—Benedek puffed on his cigarette and tossed it away—"I'm a reporter for the *Times*. Right now I'm doing a feature on the, um, sex industry."

Davey stopped and looked at the man suspiciously.

"Here." Benedek pulled out his wallet and showed Davey an ID card. "See? *New York Times*. Been there almost twenty-seven years." He put the wallet away. "Now, I'm doing this piece on the business, okay? It seemed like a good idea." He spread his arms. "It's booming, right? But it's not so easy. Nobody wants to talk about it."

Davey started walking again.

"Oh, a few people, sure, but most of those who talk

are a little"—he waggled his fingers around his head—"a little loopy, know what I mean? So I saw you coming out of that place, that Live Girls place. You seem intelligent. *Coherent.*" He laughed. "I'd like to talk to someone—you'll remain anonymous, of course—about what it's like to patronize places like that."

Davey frowned. "Sounds like you'd be patronizing *me.*"

"No, no, not at all. See, if I don't write this, there's this guy in the office—a Moral Majority type? *He's* on a mission from God to clean up the city, if you know what I mean. I think the piece should be unbiased. I just want to hear your thoughts. If you're not pressed for time . . ."

"I am," Davey said quickly, hurrying his pace.

Benedek kept up with him.

"I'll buy you a drink? Lunch? Just a half hour is all I need, really. How about a drink? Perfect weather for a nice hot buttered rum, huh?"

Without looking at the man, Davey thought about it. Despite his clothes and heavy coat, he felt cold, light, as if he'd lost a great deal of weight. A hot rum *would* be good—if he could keep it down. The sound of another voice—even a stranger's voice, *especially* a stranger's voice—might be welcome.

"My name won't be mentioned?" he asked

"You won't have a name at all," Benedek replied.

"Okay. A half hour."

"Great. C'mon, I know a place."

Benedek watched the young man slide into the booth in the quiet, shadowy bar. Davey had inconspicuously held on to rails, benches, walls, and doorjambs all the way over to the bar, as if to keep from falling. His eyelids were so heavy, the mere sight of them made Benedek feel a bit sleepy himself.

"So, Davey, what kinda work you in?"

"Publishing. At least, I *was*. I worked at Penn Publishing. But I, well, I quit. I got fed up."

"If you don't mind my asking," Benedek said, getting comfortable at the table, "are you feeling okay?"

Davey scratched his chin and nodded. "I'm fighting the flu."

When the waitress came, Benedek ordered two hot buttered rums, then lit a cigarette. He took out his pad and pen and cleared his throat loudly.

"What was it," he asked, "about that place, Live Girls, that attracted you?"

Davey shrugged. "First time I went in was yesterday. I was, I don't know, curious. My girlfriend had just left me that morning and I just wanted a diversion."

"Mm-hm." Benedek made notes as if it were a legitimate interview. "Had you ever been in a place like that before?"

"No."

"What was your initial reaction?"

"A little sorry I'd gone in at first. It was dirty and dark and . . ."

The waitress brought their drinks and Benedek paid her.

"Look," Davey said, "are you sure you don't want to talk to someone else? I mean, I don't exactly frequent those places."

"How many times you been in there?"

Davey sniffed and looked down at his drink.

"Three times."

"In two days? That's pretty frequent. Why'd you go back?" Benedek sipped his rum.

Davey lifted his drink and stared at it. He sipped the drink like a child taking cough medicine, and put it down. His face tensed, his lips pressed together hard. He smiled apologetically at Benedek.

"Sorry. My stomach's been a little upset."

Benedek nodded at Davey's drink. "That'll do you good. So, why'd you go back? Nothing better to do? They selling more than peep shows in there?"

"Why don't you go in and see for yourself?"

Good question, Benedek thought.

"Because," he said, "my opinion doesn't matter. I want this piece to focus on *your* feelings and the feelings of others who go in that place and places like it. I want the point of view of those who work there and the—"

Davey's brow creased. "Have you talked to the employees? From Live Girls, I mean?"

Benedek was intrigued. It seemed he'd almost snagged something here. "Should I?" he asked.

Davey took another drink without meeting Benedek's eyes. "I just . . . wondered."

"Okay, back to my question. What made you want to go back in there?"

"I guess I was intrigued."

"That's all? Look, Davey, if they're doing something illegal in there, you can tell me. Like I said, your name and the name of the establishment will not be mentioned." He slapped together a little fiction in his mind. Benedek had learned long ago that nothing loosened the tongue like a common experience. "When I was a young man living in Jersey, working my ass off to get into the newspaper business, there was this bar. The chicks'd get up on the bar and dance around and strip. Never all the way, not back then, but enough, you know? And this guy who'd been going there a lot longer than me told me a secret. The girls had this code. They'd look you in the eye, and if you wanted something, you were supposed to reach up and kinda pinch your nose, like you were scratching it. Then, while she was dancing, she'd put her finger in her mouth, meaning, 'You wanna blow job?' Or she'd make a fist—hand job. Or put her hand over her crotch—'You wanna fuck?' When she hit on the one you wanted, you pinched your nose again. Then she'd meet you in the employees' bathroom, you'd pay her, and she'd do you. I used to go there all the time until the joint was busted one night—while I was there! I wasn't in the back, thank God. I wrote it all up and the story nailed me a job on some little rag." He laughed, pleased with himself, thinking, *Walter, you are one consummate bullshit artist.*

"So," he went on, "I didn't fall off the melon truck yesterday, Davey."

Davey stared at his rum. "Well," he began slowly, "there's this girl . . ."

Benedek frowned. Davey seemed very nervous suddenly. No, afraid.

"Yeah, go on."

Benedek listened closely and made notes as Davey talked about his experiences inside Live Girls, about Anya, then, haltingly, like a shy young boy talking about his first kiss, about the blow job Anya had given him through the opening in the wall.

"Okay," Benedek said with a grin. "Some gorgeous girl gives you a blow job, of course you go back, right?"

Looking at Benedek for the first time in several minutes, Davey opened his mouth to speak, then looked away.

"What is it, Davey?" Benedek asked quietly.

Davey shook his head.

"Come on, kid, is there more?"

"I think . . ." Davey whispered. His head was low and his fingers twitched around the glass. "I think she . . . did something to me."

This is it, Benedek thought excitedly. *Whatever it is, this is it*.

"What?" he asked. "What do you think she did to you?"

Davey took a big gulp of his drink and grabbed his coat. "I think I should go," he said tremulously. "I'm not feeling so well and I should be in bed."

"Wait a sec, kid," Benedek said as Davey slid out of the booth. "Don't go."

Davey stood, started to put on his coat, and fell down.

"Jesus," Benedek muttered, kneeling beside him. "You okay?"

"I'm fine . . . fine," Davey breathed, sitting up. "Just drinking on an empty stomach, I guess."

Benedek looked at him closely. There were dark circles under his eyes and his face was pale.

Maybe he's always pale, he thought, *what do I know?* But he doubted it. When Benedek saw him yesterday, he'd seemed, even at a distance, quite healthy.

The waitress dashed to their table, plump and breathless and bleached blond. "What is it?" she asked. "What's wrong?"

Benedek scowled up at her and said, "Can't you see the man hasn't had enough liquor? Bring another hot rum." He helped Davey to his feet and seated him at the table, then sat across from him. "Davey," he said quietly, "tell me about this girl."

"Well, she's . . . beautiful. Absolutely, unbelievably beautiful." His eyes brightened. "I went back later that afternoon. Then last night. I met her outside the place. She was on her way to this club where she dances. The Midnight Club."

Benedek wrote it down. "Think I've heard of it. That's the one over on . . . let's see, the corner of . . ."

"It's in Tribeca."

"*That's* right." Benedek made a quick note of it.

"As far as I can tell," Davey continued, "the club is run by the same people who run Live Girls."

Benedek looked up from his pad. "Really?"

"Anyway, I went there with her and watched her dance, then I went—" He sighed. "I can't believe I'm telling you this. I don't even know you." His words came slowly and slurred a bit from the rum.

"All the better, Davey, believe me. Strangers are the best confidants. They don't know any of your friends, so they can't gossip. So what did you do, take her home?"

"I went to her place."

"And?"

"I went to bed with her . . ." His face clouded. "And she sent me away."

"You see her today?"

"I'm going to. Later today. We're meeting."

Benedek reached up and rubbed his forehead hard. Something about this was all so wrong it smelled. "You said earlier, Davey, that she'd done something to you. What was it?"

"I'm not sure, but I think she . . . bit me . . . and now I'm . . . sick."

Benedek chilled. "She *bit* you? Where?"

Davey simply shook his head as the waitress brought another rum.

"Between . . . between my . . . legs." The words seemed to stick in his throat like fishbones.

Benedek had to fight the urge to grab Davey's arms and shake answers out of him. He scrubbed his face with his big hand, lit a cigarette, and took a good swallow of his drink.

"Look, Davey, I want to talk to you more about this, okay? Something's not right here. Tell you what, my wife's a doctor. You come home with me and she can—"

"No." He took his coat again and stood, slowly and carefully this time.

Benedek could see by the look on his face that Davey regretted having talked with him. He could also see that Davey hadn't told him everything.

"Davey, wait. I wanna help you."

"I'm fine. It's nothing. Thanks for the drink." Davey started out of the bar, walking quickly, but careful to keep his balance.

Benedek grabbed his pad and followed him outside. He watched Davey stagger until he fell to the sidewalk.

"Here, Davey," Benedek said, squatting beside him.

"Really, I'm okay."

"You're *not* okay, goddammit."

Benedek got him on his feet and supported him with a big arm. "C'mon, we'll get you home," he said, leading Davey to the curb and waving for a cab. Two ignored him; the third pulled over. Benedek opened the door, helped Davey inside, and slid in beside him. He turned to Davey. "What's the address?"

Benedek repeated the address to the driver and they drove into the halting traffic.

"I wish you'd just leave me alone," Davey said quietly.

"Look, Davey, I want you to listen to me, okay? I'm not writing a feature article on the sex business. I'm not writing *anything*. I'm a reporter for the *Times*, but I'm on vacation right now. The reason I asked you all those questions is that I think there is something very wrong about Live Girls, something dangerous."

"Like what?"

"I don't know yet, that's why I talked to you. I saw you go in there twice yesterday. I was—"

"You were following me?"

"No, no, not you. I was looking for my brother-in-law."

"I don't understand."

Benedek explained to Davey the change in Vernon's behavior after he started frequenting Live Girls; he told him about the murder of his sister and niece. "For a while," Benedek said, "Doris thought he was sick. He became pale, lost some weight. She also thought he was seeing another woman." He watched Davey, waiting for a reaction, hoping he would make the connection. Davey's face remained weary and unaffected. "Like I said, Davey, my wife's a doctor. If you'd just—"

"No! I don't want to see a doctor." He looked away from Benedek. "I'm going to be fine." He shrugged. "Well, maybe I picked up something in that place. If it doesn't go away, I'll see someone."

"Okay, fine. But will you at least do one thing?"

The cab stopped at Davey's building.

Benedek asked, "Will you stay away from Live Girls? From Anya?"

Davey turned to him again, his brow creased as he shook his head slowly. "I don't know if I can."

Benedek paid the driver then led Davey into the building and escorted him onto the elevator.

"You don't have to come up with me," Davey said as the elevator started up. The doors opened on the ninth floor. "Really, I'm—"

"Davey!"

Benedek saw a young woman with mussed strawberry-blond hair and a cigarette in her mouth approaching them.

"Where've you been?" she asked. "I've been calling and calling and then I went out to lunch and couldn't eat so I came here, and now I'm late." She put a hand on Davey's arm and turned to Benedek. "Who're you?"

"This is . . ." Davey began.

"Walter Benedek. Friend of Davey's." He turned to Davey and gave him a cautioning look.

"Davey, Jesus, you shouldn't be out of *bed,* let alone your apartment." To Benedek: "I'm Casey Thorne, by the way. Nice to meet you. C'mon, Davey."

She led the way to Davey's apartment, where Davey unlocked the door and let them in.

"You sure you don't want to . . ." Benedek began.

"Positive," Davey said, nodding. "But thanks."

Benedek took out his pad and scribbled on a page. "This is my number. Call if, well, if you need anything."

"C'mon, Davey, you look really awful."

As if neither of them were in the room, Davey disappeared into his bedroom.

"Miss Thorne?" Benedek said quietly.

"Hm?" She seemed anxious for him to leave.

"Do you know anything about a place called Live Girls?"

She frowned. "No. Should I?"

Benedek pursed his lips. He knew nothing of her relationship with Davey; telling her about his visits to

Live Girls might cause some problems between them. He shrugged. "I guess not."

Giving her a small so-long wave, he left the apartment.

Davey sprawled on his bed fully clothed; he didn't even bother to remove his coat, which was still damp from the air outside. He heard the door close in the next room as Benedek left. Eyes closed, he heard Casey enter the room, felt the small jolt of her weight on the mattress. She spoke, but her voice was no more than white noise to him because his attention had been captured by an odor.

It was just a whiff, a vaguely familiar smell, dark and musky. His stomach gurgled and churned.

". . . really have to get back to work, okay?"

Davey jerked his head toward Casey.

"What?" he asked.

She shook her head and sighed, exasperated. Touching his face, she said, "You don't seem to have a fever. In fact, you're pretty cool. I want you to stay in bed, Davey, please. Get some rest. I have to go back to work, but you can call me if you need anything, okay? Promise me?"

He nodded.

"I'll come back this evening. If you're not better, you're going to see a doctor."

"You don't need to come back."

"But I'm going to." She stood. "Will you get undressed and into bed?"

"Yes, Mom."

She winced and touched his hand. "I'm just worried, Davey. Have you looked in the mirror? You look *awful*."

That smell again. For an instant, Davey's head felt

light and he became aware of an emptiness in his stomach, at once a hunger and a nausea. He almost asked Casey if she smelled anything.

"Just take care of yourself, Davey. I'll be back this evening." She squeezed his hand then started to let go, but Davey held on. She frowned. "What?"

He looked up at her small, roundish face and felt a rush of warmth. Remembering the steady gaze of her eyes when she'd asked him if he wanted to start a relationship, Davey smiled, although he suddenly and inexplicably felt like crying. Casey had always allowed him to lean on her whenever he'd needed it, and he'd taken advantage of her generosity. He'd gone to her with every problem, from disastrous to trivial, but he'd taken his joys, his happiness, to Patty and to Beth. And when those relationships had become rocky and, eventually, failed, she'd given him her shoulder once again along with a gentle chiding and a lot of pampering.

Davey suddenly wanted to get out of bed and kick himself. Kick *anything*. But he had only enough strength to lie there and look up at her face. He knew that if he asked her to stay, she would call in sick for the rest of the day. She would do anything. And he would probably let her, and give nothing in return.

What does she see in me? he wondered.

You have no spine, Davey.

She was right. He suddenly saw that with a clarity that had, until then, somehow escaped him. If he had any spine, he wouldn't meet with Anya that afternoon. Or any afternoon.

She'd been so confident when he asked her if he would see her again.

Yes, she'd said with that smug smile, *soon. You'll have to.*

142

You have no spine, Davey.

"What's the matter?" Casey asked, squeezing his hand again.

Afraid his voice would crack, he spoke quietly. "Nothing. Just . . . come back tonight. I'd like that."

She smiled. "I will. I've got a great story to tell you about Chad." She laughed and shook her head. "He's such an asshole. Okay, gotta go. Stay in bed." She backed out of the room, smiling. " 'Bye."

The door closed.

The thought of Benedek's brother-in-law came to him, unsummoned. An image of slashed throats flashed before him and he curled into a ball on the bed. He began to shake; his arms and legs no longer seemed to be his own.

Surely the murders had had nothing to do with that man's visits to Live Girls.

For a while, Doris thought he was sick. He became pale . . .

A coincidence, that's all . . .

. . . lost some weight. She also thought he was seeing another woman . . .

It had nothing to do with him . . .

You like surrendering yourself like this, don't you, Davey? Anya had asked.

Surrendering . . .

Davey sat up on the bed and looked at the time. Still a couple hours before he was supposed to meet her. He had to ask her what she'd done to him, what she was *doing*. He wanted to see the bite mark on her neck. It *had* to be there! He'd just missed it in the poor light of the booth. He would go talk to her, but he wouldn't go into her apartment. Not again.

You have no spine, Davey.

He lay back on the bed, scared, confused, and trembling.

The seconds ticked by on the nightstand clock and three o'clock drew steadily closer.

Davey arrived at Anya's building at twelve minutes after three. Less than five minutes later, Anya slinked out of a cab at curbside. She said nothing as she approached him.

"I just want to ask you a couple of questions," Davey said. "I don't want to go up."

She took his hand and led him to the entrance.

"I said I don't—"

Her eyes locked onto his as she turned.

"We can talk upstairs," she said quietly, and led him inside.

Anya greeted the doorman pleasantly before stepping into the elevator. As the car rose, she said nothing, eyes front, holding Davey's hand.

There was a fluttering in his chest as the crotch of his pants grew tight. It angered him, but his anger and shame were lost in the touch of her cool hand, in the beautiful way she held her head, and in the smooth curves of her breasts and shoulders, her clean and unblemished throat. . . .

They entered her apartment and she locked the door. Davey realized he felt better. The windows were still open and winter gusted through the apartment, but he felt warm and at ease, although he trembled slightly with anticipation.

Ask her, he thought. *Ask her what's happening!*

"I came to . . . to talk to you," he said as she turned to him.

Her coat fell at her feet, she stepped out of her shoes, and put her hands on his chest.

"I wan-wanted to ask you a, a question."

She began to unbutton his coat.

"What, what have you—"

"Shhh," she hushed him, touching his lips with hers.

"But your . . . your throat is—"

"Shh-shh."

Davey had the feeling of being caught in a vortex and sucked down a small, narrow tunnel as she began to touch him all over. His questions remained unasked.

When Benedek got home, he went to his desk, took his phone book from a drawer, and looked up the number of Ethan Collier.

Benedek had known Ethan for seventeen years. He wrote an entertainment column for the *New York Post* in which he reviewed films, plays, nightclubs, and restaurants. He also hosted a local late-night cable talk show on which he interviewed celebrities and socialites.

Collier was six years older than Benedek, a very flamboyant homosexual who took pride in his position at the *Post* despite its reputation for printing less than the truth and leaning heavily on sensationalism.

"Hello," Collier's voice said, "this is Ethan Collier. I am otherwise occupied at the moment and am unable to come to the phone. If I'm here, and if you're lucky, I will pick up before you cut the connection. If not, I'm either gone, or I don't like you. Thank you for calling."

"Pick up the phone, you aging faggot." Benedek chuckled.

"Walter! My friend! How are you?"

"I'm getting by. How about you?"

Benedek pictured the fashionably thin, silver-haired man curled on his peach-colored sofa reading the latest Jackie Collins novel.

"I'm leading a *very* productive life, Walter," he said, his voice soft and effeminate, "don't worry. I'm so sorry, it's been *months* since we've been in touch. I was going to call you and extend my condolences. I'm so sorry about your sister, Walter."

"Thanks, Ethan. I appreciate it."

"Are you holding up, my friend?"

Benedek winced, knowing that the man meant well. "I'm holding up, Ethan. I have a favor to ask."

"*Anything, love.*"

"Ever heard of a place called the Midnight Club?"

"Of course. Who hasn't?"

"What can you tell me about it?"

"Well. It's definitely not for everyone. It's for those who prefer their entertainment a bit more . . . oh, I suppose a bit darker than usual. It's expensive. Reservations aren't easy to get. To be quite honest, Walter, it's not exactly your style. Why do you ask?"

"I need to get in there tonight."

"Oh, dear, Walter. You're broadening your horizons?"

"You could say that."

"What would you like of me?"

"I need to get in. Tonight. Can you help me?"

"Well, I'm not sure. When do you want to go?"

"Early in the evening."

Benedek heard the man sucking on his teeth thoughtfully.

"Let me see what I can do. May I call you in a couple hours?"

"Sure. I'd appreciate it, Ethan."

"Nothing at all." Collier paused. "Are you sure you're okay, Walter?"

"I'm fine."

"Good. Talk to you in a while."

"Thanks."

When Benedek hung up the phone, he was smiling. It was his first genuine smile all afternoon.

Davey felt suspended in a reddish mist; he lost all sense of time and, for a while, place. He became vaguely aware of his own voice: ". . . bleeding again . . . what have you done to me?" but he couldn't tell if he was shouting or whispering.

When the mist began to clear, he felt as if he were waking from a heavy, dream-filled sleep. A smiling face with heavy-lidded eyes hovered inches above his own.

"I have to go back to work, Davey," Anya said softly. "You can rest. I got tonight off at the club, so I'll be home by nine. You can stay here until then if you like, or you can come back. But be here."

Davey lifted his head and watched her cross the room. She was fully clothed and buttoning her coat. He tried to speak, but his voice would not come; he could do no more than exhale.

"Remember," she said, turning to him at the door, "it's very important that we be together tonight. We'll have the whole night, Davey," she added with a slow smile. She turned and left.

The sheet was sticky beneath him. He sat up on the edge of the bed and looked down at himself. There was no blood, but he could feel the familiar sting. She'd probably cleaned it all off, like a mother washing her child. In fact, she seemed oddly motherly in other ways, too. Her kiss before leaving had been just a light touch of her lips with her hand resting gently on his chest, almost as if she were tucking him into bed.

The bedroom window was open and hazy daylight shone through the narrow space between the shifting curtains. The room's dimness was strangely comforting.

Davey's stomach suddenly cramped and he hugged himself and retched violently. Nothing came up.

He couldn't remember the last time he'd eaten, but the thought of food repulsed him. He put a hand atop the nightstand to brace himself as he stood. Before taking a step, he noticed a thick book with a black padded cover, like a photo album. Curious, he switched on the bedside lamp and opened the book at random.

A newspaper clipping was pressed beneath plastic. The headline read, DANCER WORTH THE PRICE OF ADMISSION. It was a review of a nightclub in New Orleans where Anya had apparently been a dancer. The critic praised her performance at length. But the paper was slightly yellowed.

Davey looked at the top of the page and saw the date: December 2, 1962. On the adjoining page was a photograph of Anya on stage in a dark bodysuit. She looked not a day younger in the picture than she did now.

Frowning, Davey flipped a couple of the stiff pages over. Another article and another picture, these from a Chicago paper dated June 8, 1956.

Davey exhaled slowly as he lowered himself to the bed again. This could not be the same Anya . . .

He turned another page, making his way to the front of the book. There was another article. San Francisco, May 12, 1949. The years had tinted the page a spoiled-fruit yellow.

He turned another. Los Angeles, January 24, 1946.

"What the hell is going on?" he breathed.

He turned the pages in the opposite direction, thumbing to the back of the book. The final clipping in the book was fresh, the paper was white and clean. It was from the *Times* and dated eight months before. A review of the Midnight Club, praise for Anya's dancing, and a picture . . .

Davey began paging through the book frantically, something that would give reason for what could not be. All he found were more articles, more pictures.

The oldest of all was on the first page. The edges of the clipping were tattered and creases cut through the type. It was dated August 9, 1920. In the grainy, blurred picture was the same Anya—just as beautiful, just as young—who had left the room minutes earlier.

Chapter Ten

Casey stood on a crowded bus with her fingers wrapped securely around the sticky handrail. Standing beside her was a fat wheezing man with a cane. He smelled like a dog kennel; the odor made her wince.

One annoying person after another, she thought. She'd spent the whole afternoon dodging Chad Wilkes after the incident in the elevator. Now she had to stand next to a walking sewer.

Casey had decided to go straight to Davey's rather than to her apartment first. If he wasn't any better, she was going to insist he see a doctor. Sick people made her very nervous. Her father had died of cancer when she was twelve. After he'd died, she'd learned everyone had known he was dying but her. Now whenever someone close to her got sick, she feared there was something she wasn't being told, and it made her anxious. She couldn't imagine Davey keeping anything that serious from her and tried to tell herself that it was, indeed, just the flu. But she'd never seen the flu have such a drastic effect on someone's appearance.

A hand came to rest on her ass and she stiffened. Turning to the fat, smelly man beside her, she saw him smirk. The fingers touching her squeezed ever so slightly.

Casey's teeth clenched, and she said, "If you don't take your hand from my ass, I'm going to rip it off and stuff the fingers down your throat one at a time."

The man's eyebrow, speckled with snowy bits of dried skin, rose slowly, and the hand relaxed but did not pull away.

Casey swung her hand down and grabbed his crotch, squeezing hard. "How do *you* like it?"

He pulled his hand away and moved as far from her as he could.

"You shouldn't live in New York," her mother often told her. "Your mouth is going to get you killed. You're the kind of person who would slap an armed mugger in the face and tell him he was out of his mind because you don't seem to realize that when you have a gun, it's *okay* to be out of your mind, it's okay to be anything you damn well *please*."

When the bus came to her stop, Casey got off and hurried down the sidewalk with her umbrella at her side. The darkening sky was still filled with clouds, but at least the rain had stopped.

Upstairs in Davey's building, she knocked on the door of his apartment; it swung gently open. She frowned; it was very unlike Davey to leave the door open.

When she stepped inside, she heard the voice of Mister Rogers on the television.

". . . and Mr. Cogswell is an electrician. Can you say 'electrician'? I knew you could."

"Davey"—she laughed—"what the hell are you watching?"

He was sitting on the sofa, his back to her, facing the television. His hair was mussed; spikes of it sat upright.

"Davey?"

He turned to her slowly. The white of his face stood out against his brown hair.

"Case?" he said softly.

She closed the door and stepped toward him. Davey stood, pulled the front of his robe together tightly, and took a step back.

"Maybe you shouldn't come in," he said. "This might be catching."

She stared openmouthed at him. He actually looked like he'd lost more weight in the last day or so than she could lose with a week of serious dieting and he was so pale his skin seemed almost creamy.

"How are you feeling, Davey?" There was something odd about the way he was standing.

"Not bad. Really." He rounded the sofa, but kept a distance from her. His movements were jerky; he seemed tense and nervous. "I'm going to see a doctor tomorrow."

"Who?"

"Remember the guy I was with today? Walter Benedek?"

She nodded.

"His wife's a doctor. I'm calling tomorrow."

Davey didn't seem to be telling the truth. His tongue poked out between his tightly pressed lips and moved back and forth like a small, quick animal.

"He left his home number," Casey said. "You should call tonight."

". . . time to go to the Land of Make Believe," Mister Rogers was saying.

Davey always kept loose phone numbers by the phone on his nightstand.

Casey hurried into the bedroom, found the slip of paper, and began to dial the number. Davey came in behind her. He put a hand on her arm and pulled the receiver from her ear, using the other hand to push down the button on the cradle.

"Please, Casey, I'm going to call her in the morning. Early. I'll call her at home before she leaves. Would that make you feel better?"

She turned to see him smile. It was forced and stiff.

His nostrils flared and he leaned toward her. Hanging up the phone, he asked softly, "What's that smell?"

"What smell?"

"I don't know. I smelled it when you were here earlier. Kind of, I don't know, maybe musky?"

"Well, it's not my perfume."

He put a hand on her shoulder and said, "It's you. It's on you." His grip tightened and he moved closer to her, sniffing. "Take off your coat," he said, unbuttoning it for her.

"Davey, what's—"

"It's on you. I know it is."

He pulled her coat down over her shoulders; it slipped to the floor. His smile slowly grew, wide and genuine.

"It smells good," he breathed. He leaned forward and kissed her, long and deep.

"Davey," she murmured, pulling her mouth away, but he kissed her again. He slid his hands over her breasts and began to unbutton her top. His touch left a brief tingle just beneath her skin, but it scared her, too. Something was wrong. She pushed him away hard.

"What's the *matter* with you?" she said with an unintentional laugh.

"You smell so good," he whispered.

"Well, you've certainly had a change of heart, haven't you?" She started to rebutton her top.

He stopped her. "Please don't." He leaned forward and kissed her neck, clumsily got her top open and reached beneath it, passed his hand over her skin.

"Davey . . ."

He moved her to the bed and began to undo her skirt, but then gave up. He pushed her back on the bed and slipped a hand beneath her skirt, moving it over her thigh.

"Davey, I can't," she said.

He didn't seem to hear her. His hand moved above her thigh, above the top of her stockings, to her panties.

"Davey, I said I *can't*. I'm on my period."

He exhaled suddenly; there was a moan behind his breath as he pressed his mouth hard onto hers. He slipped his fingers beneath her panties and pulled them down. She trembled at the feel of him touching her there.

"Davey," she gasped weakly, "please . . ."

He kissed her neck and her chest, her belly, her thighs. He lifted her skirt, pressed her legs apart, and nuzzled her. His fingers explored for a moment, found the string, and pulled it out smoothly. His tongue moved over her folds, her body stiffened with pleasure, and she moaned.

Casey heard the sounds of his mouth on her, smacking sounds, slow and wet, and she felt the movements of his lips and tongue, nicking, sucking. Heat rose from between her legs and spread throughout her body.

Mister Rogers's voice droned placatingly in the next room.

". . . can't always be happy, can we, boys and girls? We must remember that it's okay to be sad sometimes. It's natural. Can you say natural? I knew you could."

As Davey lapped at her like a dog, she heard him mumble between her thighs.

". . . what I needed . . . so good . . ."

He reached up and covered her breast with his hand, pushed aside the material of her bra. The combination of his fingers on her nipple and his lips and teeth and tongue flicking over her clitoris made her cry out.

Why is he doing this? There's something wrong . . . something wrong . . .

". . . tastes so good . . ."

"Davey . . ."

She felt his mouth pull away from her as he lifted himself up. Casey raised her head and looked at him. She sucked in a breath to scream, but the sound lodged in her throat.

Davey was propped up on stiff arms. Clotted, viscous blood was smeared around his mouth, on his nose and cheeks, even in his hair. His eyes were sparkling in the dim light and his smile was broad and rigid.

It was that smile, that smile she'd never seen before, and the look in his eyes, a lusty, exhilarated look that was so unlike Davey it made his whole face seem unfamiliar.

In a low, guttural voice, he said: "Can you say menstru-ation? I *knew* you could . . ."

His mouth opened to its limit and his lips pulled

back over his teeth, until they were all exposed, shining white and red, and he leaned his head far back and she *knew* without a doubt that Davey was going to plunge that soft, kind, gentle face downward and sink his teeth into the lips of her vagina until they broke through the tender skin. Casey screamed and began frantically pulling herself away from him.

"Davey Davey my God Davey what're you *doing?*" she shrieked.

Davey's face suddenly relaxed; he blinked several times as if waking from a deep sleep. "I'm . . ." he began. He ran his tongue around his bloody lips twice. "I'm . . . sorry." He moved from the bed quickly and stepped away from her, turning his back. "I'm sorry, Casey, you should, you should get out of here and stay away from me, there's"—he sobbed—"there's something wrong with me. Something very wrong." His shoulders hitched and he gasped for breath through his tears.

Casey stood, and pulled herself together. When she moved toward Davey, he dashed into the bathroom. She heard him retching into the toilet. Casey took a tissue from the box by the bed, wrapped the tampon in it, and tossed it in the trash can in the corner.

"Davey, let me call her now," she said, approaching the doorway.

Davey was kneeling at the toilet, his robe crumpled around his legs. He stood slowly and leaned on the sink. Washing his face, he said, "I'll be okay. Why don't you go now?"

As Davey was drying his face, Casey stepped into the bathroom and stood at his side. Davey pulled away as if struck.

"Just go, Casey, okay?"

She saw that his hands were trembling and his fingers were worrying the edges of the towel.

"Davey, you're keeping something from me," she said firmly. "If you'll tell me what's *really* wrong, I'll try to help you, but I don't want to be lied to!"

Casey immediately regretted her angry tone when she saw Davey's face screw up. Tears sparkled in his eyes and he stumbled backward, sitting heavily on the edge of the tub. Through his tears, he began to tell her about Anya. . . .

Benedek was led to a table by a man named Cedric. Something about the man—was it the scar on his neck?—made Benedek think he should know him. The man's dark, angular face was very familiar, but Benedek couldn't pin it down.

The gaunt, balding man at the door had grudgingly let him in, giving Benedek the once-over with his beady eyes. Benedek was certain that, had Ethan Collier not called ahead the thin, hollow-cheeked man behind the pedestal would have smilingly turned Benedek away.

Once Benedek was seated at his table, Cedric told him a waitress would be with him in a moment, and walked away. Benedek took in his surroundings carefully but casually.

It was dark and sleek with a sparse crowd, which was not surprising at that hour—it was just past seven. A smiling blond waitress took Benedek's order: a rum and Coke on the rocks. When she left, he lit a cigarette and looked around at the other patrons.

Two women huddled close over their table talking. One of them, perhaps in her early fifties and strikingly attractive with high cheekbones and thick, sandy-colored hair, waved at Cedric after Benedek settled himself at his table. Cedric escorted her to a door on the other side of the room and let her through.

Restrooms, Benedek thought absently, until he noticed that there were no signs.

"Are you going out?" Jackie had asked when she'd come home to find Benedek getting dressed.

"Just for a while."

"That's too bad. I was looking forward to an evening in bed with the television. *Ninotchka*'s on tonight."

"Not this evening, sweetie."

"Where are you going?"

Benedek had considered lying to her so she wouldn't worry, but as good a liar as he was, she always seemed to see through it. "I'm going to a place called the Midnight Club."

"A nightclub this early?"

"Business, not pleasure." He'd finished tying his tie and given her a hug and kiss. Still holding her, he'd said, "There's some connection between the club and Live Girls."

She'd pulled back gently. "Walter, don't you think you should leave this alone? They'll find him."

"They'll find *him,* maybe. But I don't think they'll find what I'm looking for."

"And what's that?"

After a pause: "I'm not sure yet."

"Walter." She placed her hand on his neck and squeezed. "Your sister and niece have been killed. They're dead. You're suffering a loss. Shouldn't you be . . ."

"Mourning?"

She nodded hesitantly.

158

"Sweetheart, I am. In my way, I *am*. And part of it is *doing* something about it."

"And what are you doing, Walter? What aren't you telling me?"

He pulled his eyes from hers for a moment. "You're right. There's something I'm not telling you. When I know more . . ."

She touched his face. "All right," she whispered, nodding. "I trust you. Do what you have to. But be careful."

"Don't worry, honey, I just want to have a look around."

"Christ." She chuckled, stepping into his arms again. "What you call looking around *most* people call breaking and entering. You and your lock-picking . . ."

"Don't lose any sleep over it," he said, smiling. "Go to bed. Let the machine answer the phone. Relax. I'll be back in a while."

"Famous last words."

A few tables away, two couples—yuppies, Benedek decided immediately—laughed over glasses of white wine.

Only one person other than Benedek sat alone: a jowly Asian man in a blue business suit. He fidgeted and shifted in his seat, looking over both shoulders every few seconds, as if expecting someone. After watching him a few moments, Benedek realized the man was waiting for a waitress. Each time one passed, even if not nearby, the man timidly waved a pudgy hand toward her. He wasn't obvious enough. He became more and more agitated, tugged at his collar and wiped his brow, glanced at the door and . . .

That's why he kept looking over his shoulder. He was watching the door.

The waitress came with Benedek's drink and he paid her. As she walked away from his table, the Asian man waved at her; she didn't notice.

What the hell's he need, permission? Benedek thought.

Finally, the man stood and walked to the door alone. He tried the knob, apparently found it locked. He knocked hard with one knuckle, then took a few nervous steps this way and that before the door.

It opened.

Someone peered out.

A round, fleshy face. Salt-and-pepper hair. Thin lips and a wrinkled brow. There and gone.

The Asian man stepped through and the door closed.

Benedek's cigarette dropped from his fingers to the floor. Without even thinking, he stamped it out with his foot, burning a black spot into the carpet. He had a simultaneous feeling of triumph and fear.

The face in the doorway had been that of Vernon Macy.

"For Christ's *sake,* Davey!" Casey snapped. "What the hell possessed you to go into a place like that?" She lit a cigarette as she paced before him in the little bathroom. Her voice was sarcastic and accusatory, even though she knew he needed a friend. Well, she *was* being a friend by not giving in and showing him undeserved pity. What he needed more than anything, she decided, was a good kick in the ass. "If all you wanted was a blow job, you could've come to *me.* You know *I'm* clean. Jesus, who knows *what* you picked up in there. And you went *back* to her! *Jeee-zus!*"

"She bit me," Davey whispered, staring at his lap.

160

"*Bit!* She *bit* you? Holy God." She stopped pacing and faced him. "Have you talked to her? I mean, did you at least ask her what she *has?*"

"I tried to, but—"

"You *tried,*" she spat. "Davey, I am so fucking *sick* of your attitude. You keep digging these holes and jumping in, then asking me to pull you out. Or at least *expecting* me to. And I keep doing it. Well, *you* handle this one. I can only be so understanding and so helpful, then I have to draw the line. You apparently *like* being miserable or else you'd start *thinking* for a change. You'd grow up and take charge of your own life and stop acting like a fucking whiny *child!* You'd—oh, fuck it." She started to walk out. "Christ, I hope you didn't give *me* anything."

"Casey, wait. It's not what you think. There's something wrong . . ." He pressed a hand to his forehead and closed his eyes. "*Inside* me. I'm having . . . nightmares and . . . thinking awful things. I can't . . . stay . . . *away* from her. Maybe if I'd stayed away the first time. But she's doing something to me that . . . I *need* now. I don't know what or why, but there's something I *need;* it's a craving. That smell . . . your smell . . ." He met her eyes for the first time in several minutes. "It's driving me crazy," he said huskily.

Casey took an involuntary step away from him. She realized then what was different about Davey. It was the hungry stare, the stare of a child peering into a pastry display case.

A *sick* child.

His whole body quaked as he stood, licking his lips. "I'm hungry, Casey," he whispered. "But I can't eat."

She backed into the bedroom and he followed her.

"Davey, you *have* to *see* a *doctor,*" she said.

His voice quavered as he whispered, "I'm afraid he'd have me put away. I just have to wait for it to pass."

She reached the bedroom doorway and stopped. "What if it doesn't?" she asked. Tears were stinging her eyes; she was suddenly terrified of her best friend.

"Then it doesn't. Like you said, it's my problem. I'll . . ." He turned away from her and went to the bed, sat down, and began rocking back and forth. He spoke rapidly, running his words together. "I'll handle it, now will you just go away please."

He rocked and rocked, like a retarded child, his arms folded tightly across his stomach, acting as if she weren't there.

"All right, Davey," she said, trying to speak levelly and confidently. "I'll go. But will you do one thing for me? I have some Librium in my purse. Lisa gave them to me months ago. Will you take a couple? They'll calm you down, help you sleep."

At first, she thought he hadn't heard her. Then he nodded rigidly.

Casey got her purse in the living room, took out her pillbox, and went into the kitchen. As she held a glass under the faucet, she realized her hands were trembling.

She was afraid. Davey was dangerous. Maybe the pills would keep him from doing anything harmful for a while. Casey was aware of no disease, social or otherwise, that exhibited itself so suddenly and with such symptoms. But what did she know about diseases? What if that woman, Anya, *were* spreading something around? Surely she was aware of what she had, knew she was exposing her customers to it. Could she *really* not care?

She felt a rush of anger at the woman's irresponsibility. And at Davey's.

What kind of woman could knowingly do that? she wondered, tightening her grip on the drinking glass. *How could she—*

The glass shattered and a jagged edge sliced into the pad of flesh between her thumb and forefinger. She held the cut between her lips for a moment, then got another glass and filled it, ignoring the broken pieces in the sink.

In the bedroom, Davey was still rocking himself on the edge of the bed.

"Here," Casey said softly, holding out the pills in her palm.

Davey opened his eyes and stared at the blood on her hand. His lips parted and his chest heaved as he began breathing rapidly, shallowly. He crawled backward on the bed and turned his face from her.

"Put them down and go!" he shouted hoarsely. "Just get the hell away from me!" He curled up on the bed in a fetal position.

Casey's heart was hammering as she put the pills and water on the counter. The slip of paper with Benedek's number on it lay beside the phone. She picked it up, grabbed her coat, and, with weak legs, hurried out of the apartment.

Outside, she hurried to a payphone. She deposited a quarter and dialed the number.

"We're not in right now," the man's recorded voice droned, "but if you'll leave a message, we'll get back to you. Thanks."

After the beep, Casey said, "This is Casey Thorne. Davey's friend. Davey Owen. You left your number. He said your wife is a doctor and I think . . . Davey's very sick and I think he's in trouble. Big trouble. He needs help. I left him just a few minutes ago. Um, right now it's . . ." She looked at her watch and started to say "seven twenty-two," but the machine cut itself off and a dial tone hummed coldly in her ear. She slammed the receiver down and pushed out of the booth. She had to do *something*, but she was not certain *what*.

After several seconds of thought, Casey hurried to a corner to catch a bus to Time Square.

Chapter Eleven

With his mouth dry as a desert rock, Benedek stared at the closed door for a long time. The blond waitress walked before him on her way to another table.

"Miss," he said.

She spun around and approached him, smiling.

Taking a quick sip of his drink, Benedek stood and said, "Where's the restroom?"

She pointed a finger and said, "Right back there, sir."

To the left of the entrance, Benedek saw a door with a small sign above that read, in blue neon letters, RESTROOMS.

Resisting the urge to break into a run, Benedek walked across the room and went through the door. On the other side was a softly lit corridor; the ladies' room was to the left, the men's to the right. At the end of the corridor was a door. There was no sign, not even a NO ADMITTANCE or EMPLOYEES ONLY.

Moving quickly, Benedek fished a small leather pouch from his breast pocket. He took out two thin, flexible pieces of metal—lock picks—and replaced the pouch. The picks had been given to him twelve years before by his friend Grover Dumont on the occasion of Dumont's retirement from the police force.

"I've used these puppies plenty of times in the pursuit of justice," Dumont had told him with the twinkle of experience in his eye. "Maybe you can use 'em in the pursuit of truth, huh?"

Taking a cautious look over his shoulder, Benedek tried the knob. Finding it locked, as he'd expected, he slipped the picks smoothly into the lock and jiggled them delicately, precisely.

The door at the other end of the corridor opened with a whisper and the music from the main room thundered in. Benedek jerked the picks from the lock, clutched them in his fist, spun around, and started back up the corridor at a casual pace.

A short, dowdy woman in a long blue dress and a cream shawl came through the door, turned to the ladies' room, and stopped to look at Benedek. She raised a brow, sniffed, and pushed through the door, ignoring his pleasant smile.

"Jesus," he breathed, returning immediately to the lock, working it until he heard the familiar click. The knob turned, the door opened, and he stepped through. Hoping there was no one on the other side to discover him, he closed the door silently.

Widely spaced lights glowed a soft purple overhead. The corridor, lined with closed doors on each side, went left and right with thick carpet that would silence the footsteps of anyone coming around a corner.

Benedek could feel his pulse throbbing in his throat; he turned to the left and began walking, hoping the

GET UP TO 4 FREE BOOKS!

You can have the best fiction delivered to your door for less than what you'd pay in a bookstore or online—only $4.25 a book! Sign up for our book clubs today, and we'll send you **FREE* BOOKS** just for trying it out...**with no obligation to buy, ever!**

LEISURE HORROR BOOK CLUB

With more award-winning horror authors than any other publisher, it's easy to see why CNN.com says "Leisure Books has been leading the way in paperback horror novels." Your shipments will include authors such as RICHARD LAYMON, DOUGLAS CLEGG, JACK KETCHUM, MARY ANN MITCHELL, and many more.

LEISURE THRILLER BOOK CLUB

If you love fast-paced page-turners, you won't want to miss any of the books in Leisure's thriller line. Filled with gripping tension and edge-of-your-seat excitement, these titles feature everything from psychological suspense to legal thrillers to police procedurals and more!

As a book club member you also receive the following special benefits:

- **30% OFF all orders through our website & telecenter!**
- **Exclusive access to special discounts!**
- **Convenient home delivery and 10 days to return any books you don't want to keep.**

There is no minimum number of books to buy, and you may cancel membership at any time. See back to sign up!

*Please include $2.00 for shipping and handling.

YES! ☐

Sign me up for the Leisure Horror Book Club and send my TWO FREE BOOKS! If I choose to stay in the club, I will pay only $8.50* each month, a savings of $5.48!

YES! ☐

Sign me up for the Leisure Thriller Book Club and send my TWO FREE BOOKS! If I choose to stay in the club, I will pay only $8.50* each month, a savings of $5.48!

NAME: _____

ADDRESS: _____

_____

TELEPHONE: _____

E-MAIL: _____

☐ **I WANT TO PAY BY CREDIT CARD.**

☐ VISA   ☐ MasterCard   ☐ DISCOVER

ACCOUNT #: _____

EXPIRATION DATE: _____

SIGNATURE: _____

Send this card along with $2.00 shipping & handling for each club you wish to join, to:

Horror/Thriller Book Clubs
20 Academy Street
Norwalk, CT 06850-4032

Or fax (must include credit card information!) to: 610.995.9274. You can also sign up online at www.dorchesterpub.com.

*Plus $2.00 for shipping. Offer open to residents of the U.S. and Canada only. Canadian residents please call 1.800.481.9191 for pricing information.

If under 18, a parent or guardian must sign. Terms, prices and conditions subject to change. Subscription subject to acceptance. Dorchester Publishing reserves the right to reject any order or cancel any subscription.

JOIN NOW!

corridor would lead him to the door through which he'd seen Vernon.

A sound up ahead made him stop and listen.

A giggle.

From behind him, a sigh.

A long and lusty moan.

Benedek looked behind him. Pools of gentle light spilled on the carpet before door after door after door.

Pressing a hand to the wall, he leaned toward the closest door and cocked his head.

"Yes, yes, *suck* me . . ." He couldn't tell if the muffled voice was male or female. But he had no doubt what was going on behind the door.

Prostitutes? Probably. That might explain the Asian man's nervousness. But what about the woman he'd seen escorted through the door earlier? Male prostitutes were not uncommon, but they were, more often than not, gay.

In any case, there was more than just drinks being sold at the Midnight Club. That made sense considering its connection with Live Girls. But how many people knew? Surely not *all* of the patrons. Maybe just the members.

Too many questions, Benedek thought as the voice behind the door began to cry out.

"I'm coming! Don't stop, I'm coming!" It was still muffled to the level of a whisper, like a disembodied voice in a half-remembered dream. Something about it made Benedek uneasy.

He moved ahead to an intersecting corridor. To the left was a door—the door leading into the main room, he was sure—and at his right, a wall of darkness. Ahead, the corridor led around a corner.

Benedek heard a door open behind him and ducked into the blackness, hoping it would conceal him.

Hushed voices from around the corner came closer; a door closed quietly.

". . . incredible as usual," a woman purred. "Oh God, I'm weak-kneed." She giggled.

"The pleasure was all mine," a deep male voice said.

"Here, here, let me . . ." the woman breathed, rustling something.

"But you already . . ."

"No, no, this is for you, Cedric. And there's more where that came from. I've reserved a table for a week from next Friday. Will you be here?"

"I'm *always* here." Benedek could hear Cedric's smile.

"My friend Pamela doesn't know what she's missing," the woman went on. "She seems to prefer that black fellow."

They were coming closer and Benedek pressed his back hard against the wall, willing the darkness to swallow him. His stomach was tight with fear as he held his breath.

Turning left at the intersection, they approached the door with their backs to Benedek. He recognized the tall, sandy-haired woman from the main room.

"Well," Cedric said, reaching for the doorknob, "to each his own."

Cedric opened the door, and the woman's laughter was drowned out by the music.

Benedek let out a long breath once the door was closed again. He slid his hands over the wall behind him. The corridor ended just a couple feet to his right. Facing the back wall, Benedek lifted his hands and passed them over the smooth surface before him, looking for . . .

A door. It swung open just a crack beneath his big hands. Finding the knob, he turned it; the door had been locked. Apparently, it had not been completely shut.

A soft, fluorescent glow came through the narrow opening. Benedek could hear no movement, but there was a low, almost inaudible hum beyond the door. With a gentle push, the door swung open further.

There was a small, square room on the other side. On a table against the far wall were two metal trays holding rows of glass tubes. The tubes had red stoppers and were empty except for a filmy gloss along the sides, as if they'd recently been emptied of a dark fluid.

Light poured through an open doorway to the left.

Benedek stepped into the room, his eyes darting around him cautiously. Except for the table, the room was absolutely bare. Walking on the balls of his feet, he went to the open door. The hum became louder and he could hear a soft clicking. No, it was a steady, rapid drip.

Through the doorway, Benedek saw a refrigerator. As he drew nearer, he saw another.

A *kitchen?* he wondered. The white linoleum floor and white walls shone beneath fluorescent lights.

Across from the doorway was a row of cupboards above a white tile counter and sink. The faucet was dripping. There were more trays on the counter holding more glass tubes, but these were filled with a very dark red liquid. Benedek put a hand on the doorjamb and started to step inside when he heard footsteps. He pulled back from the doorway. There was someone in the room.

He heard clattering; the faucet was turned on.

Peering around the doorjamb, Benedek saw a man standing at the sink, head bowed, arms moving vigorously before him as he washed his hands. After turning off the water, the man spun around and smiled.

"Walter," Vernon Macy said, drying his hands on his white, red-stained smock, "I've been expecting you."

Casey stood before a brightly lit hot-dog stand a few yards from Live Girls smoking a cigarette. A plastic clown's head with fat red smiling lips hung above the service window; a light flashed on and off behind the face, silhouetting the tiny insects that crawled and jumped behind the round cheeks.

Her hand trembled as she raised her cigarette to her lips. Now that she'd arrived in Times Square, she wasn't quite sure why she'd come. She certainly had no right to be angry at the people in Live Girls because Davey had caught something from one of their girls, did she? What had Davey expected? It was his problem.

No, she thought, *no, it's their problem, too. One of their girls is spreading something around, and they should do something about it!*

Thinking that she was probably being very naive, Casey tossed her cigarette to the sidewalk and hurried into the cold wind toward Live Girls.

She pushed aside the black curtain and stepped into darkness. The damp air and dirty, musky odor made her wince.

The darkness began to thin as her eyes adjusted and she saw the bars to her right.

"Hello?" she said, leaning toward the cage. "Is anybody—"

"Tokens?"

The deep female voice startled her and she pulled back.

"Uh, I'm sorry?"

"Would you like some tokens?" The voice sounded mildly impatient.

"Tokens?" Casey asked, confused. She squinted, but could still see no one. "Uh, no, no, I'm here to—"

"Then please go away."

"No, wait a second. I have to talk to someone about one of the girls working here."

"I'm asking you to—"

"Believe me, I don't *want* to be here. Just give me a second. A friend of mine came in here a couple days ago. He claims that one of your girls . . ." She paused; it sounded so ludicrous. "He says she bit him. Since then, he's gotten sick. I mean, he's *very* sick. I'm worried for him. I think maybe your girl has—"

"If you don't leave, I'm going to have someone take you out," the woman said firmly.

Feeling a jolt of anger, Casey stepped forward and snapped, "I'm not leaving until I'm *finished!* You've got a very sick girl in here and she's probably spreading some—"

Casey stopped midsentence when she heard a sudden movement in the darkness before her. Her inability to see the woman made her feel very vulnerable, like swimming in dark, still waters, unable to feel bottom. She reached into her coat pocket, pulled out her butane lighter, and flicked it.

There was a flash of white and red and, with a throaty hiss, a hand shot between the bars and clutched Casey's wrist in an iron grip. The light of the quivering flame flickered briefly over a long white face

171

with blood-red eyes centered with pinpricks of black, an upturned, flattened nose—*a snout*, Casey thought wildly, *dear Jesus, it looks like a snout!*—above ruby lips and long white teeth that glistened wetly and narrowed to fine points; white hair fell around her face in long shiny waves through which two long tapered ears protruded and her eyes—large and almond-shaped, of a pure, deep red marred only by the tiny black pupils—seemed to pull on Casey's eyes like magnets, sparkling as if with a light of their own.

The cigarette lighter slipped from Casey's fingers and clattered to the floor. The woman leaned forward so that her face became visible through the bars even in the heavy darkness. With shocking ease, she pulled Casey's arm through the bars so hard that her face almost slammed against them.

"Let go of, of—" Casey made a gagging sound as the fingers tightened on her wrist like steel cables; she clenched her eyes in anticipation of the dull crack of her wrist.

It never came. But the fingers tightened more and the pain shot up Casey's arm and caught in her throat like a lump of tough, dry meat. When she opened her eyes, she saw the woman's other hand sliding between the bars, felt the fingers wrap around her coat collar. She pulled Casey's face against the damp, rusty bars.

With sweet, meaty breath, the woman hissed, "I told you to *go!*" She opened her mouth and her teeth sparkled like deadly needles.

Casey began screaming and thrashing, scratching the skin of her face against the lumps of rust on the bars, throwing herself back and forth, back and forth, until suddenly—so suddenly she was startled—she was free! She fell back against the wall behind her and slid down to the floor. When she looked up, the woman was gone.

Casey struggled to her feet and tripped. Leaning against the wall, she turned toward the doorway. But not before one last glance . . .

Something was crawling beneath the bars, something long and sleek, glistening white, with little red eyes. Its mouth opened around razor-sharp teeth as it slithered under the bars in a fluidlike motion.

A snake.

And it was looking straight into Casey's eyes.

She threw herself toward the doorway and hit the black curtain, slapping at it, trying to find the opening. It wrapped around her arms, blanketed her head, twisted around her neck like strangling hands; each desperate movement only tangled her up in the heavy material a bit more.

Something wrapped smoothly around her ankle and began to spiral up her leg beneath her coat and dress and Casey began screaming, her voice lost in the folds of the curtain.

The snake was just below her thigh when Casey felt it swell and grow heavy on her leg until it was pushing up her dress and coat, reaching up her back and around her waist with strong, restricting arms.

Casey struggled, but the arms were powerful and held her still, moving only enough to pull her from her black cocoon.

A vile, soft voice spoke into her ear:

"It's too late now . . ."

Vernon Macy wadded up the smock and, still smiling, tossed it onto the counter. He wore dark blue slacks, immaculately pressed, as always, and a salmon-pink shirt with the sleeves rolled up to his elbows.

"I heard you were coming," he said. "Malcolm mentioned your name earlier. He said Ethan Collier had called ahead for you. Malcolm was annoyed, but then"—he chuckled—"he always is, it seems."

Benedek had almost forgotten how unnervingly soft his brother-in-law's voice was; his sibilant *S*'s had always set Benedek's teeth on edge. Macy's speech, however, was not as discomforting as the smile Benedek saw on his face then. It was content and at ease, a genuinely happy smile.

"Doris used to tell me you're a very clever, sneaky man, Walter," Macy went on. "So when I heard you were coming, I knew you were looking for me. I don't know what led you here, but that doesn't matter. I knew you'd find me." He lifted one of the trays from the counter and carried it to a refrigerator. The vacutaner tubes clinked together gently as he moved across the room. Opening the refrigerator and sliding the tray onto a shelf, he said, "Doris spoke of you often, you know. If you weren't her brother"—he smiled at Benedek over his shoulder—"I think I would've been very jealous." He turned from the refrigerator for another tray.

Benedek's throat burned with anger. The ease with which Macy spoke of Doris made Benedek want to throw up.

"He's a good man," Doris had told him upon announcing she'd decided to marry Vernon Macy. "He'll make a good life for me, Walter. And I love him."

Arranging the trays on the refrigerator shelves, Macy said, "You were very dear to your sister, Walter. She was

174

always terribly sorry that you and I didn't get on better. I remember saying to her once that we—"

Before he fully realized what he was doing, Benedek dove toward the man from behind; a strangled sound squeezed from his throat as he joined his hands together and raised them to begin beating on the back of Macy's neck.

The soft little man spun around with surprising speed and grabbed Benedek's arms, holding them up firmly. Macy snapped his mouth open wide and hissed like a cat.

Two long, sharp teeth gleamed.

Benedek tried to pull back, but Macy's pudgy hands were stronger than he anticipated.

"Relax, Walter," Macy whispered. "Let's talk."

Benedek stared with disbelief at the now unfamiliar face. "What the fuck's happened to you, Vernon?" Benedek breathed. "What's *wrong* with you?"

He smiled, slowly lowering Benedek's arms. "Nothing is wrong, Walter."

"You killed your wife and daughter," Benedek snapped, pulling his arms away and stepping back, "*something's* sure as hell wrong!"

Macy's smile faltered as he moved away from the refrigerator, letting the door slowly swing closed. He went to the counter, to rows of empty, clean tubes laid out on a cloth. He began putting them, one by one, on an empty tray. "I had to do that. She kept hounding me and . . . prying. I wanted to just walk out. Quietly. But she got hysterical and I was . . . hungry."

Benedek swallowed a lump in his throat. "You were . . ."

Macy turned to him again and smiled. It was such a warm, friendly smile, incongruent with the cold eyes. "There are a lot of things you don't know about, Walter. Now that you're here, you'll have plenty of time to learn."

"Others know I'm here. If I don't go home, they'll start asking questions."

"And we'll tell them you never arrived."

"There are witnesses. Customers. It'll draw attention to the place. And if *I* can find you, the *police* will, too."

Macy leaned back on the lip of the counter with a sigh. "First of all, Walter, you were *allowed* to come back here. All the employees know who you are. You're going nowhere. Secondly, do you know how many important people come here? How many *wives* of important people? Very lonely wives. They come here to meet their friends, have a few drinks, and go in the back rooms for a little much-needed companionship. I suppose you noticed that, didn't you? These are the wives of city officials, politicians. And you know how much influence wives have over their husbands." In a whiny, feminine voice, he said, " 'Oh, dear, the Midnight Club is a *delightful* place, a *charming* place, the girls and I meet there all the *time*, surely there's nothing untoward going on there, all the people are above reproach.' " He leaned forward and whispered, " 'And they eat pussy like you never could, husband dear.' " Then he threw back his head and laughed. "You're no threat, Walter."

Benedek wanted to step forward and squeeze the man's throat with his hands, but decided to pursue the conversation. "And what's all this?" he asked, gesturing to the refrigerators and the trays of tubes.

"This is their payment for our favors. Oh, they think their money is what's important to us. You know, it's amazing how much more people appreciate and value things if they have to pay good money for them. I learned that long ago. But . . ." He walked to the refrigerator and opened it, showing Benedek the shelves of trays, the rows of dark red tubes. "*This* is what we really want. They just don't know they're giving it."

"And who are *'we'?* Who are the people who run this place?"

"They aren't people at all. They're gods. And they've made me one of their own. My life was a small sacrifice to get here. Killing Doris? Killing Janice? Very, very small prices to pay, Walter." There was a sparkle of challenge in his eyes.

Benedek could take no more; he threw himself on Macy, grabbed his fleshy throat and squeezed. Macy smiled as he flung his hands up and snapped Benedek's arms away from him effortlessly. Before Benedek realized he'd lost his edge, he was pressed against the open refrigerator door and Macy's hands were on his neck, squeezing just enough to make his breath gurgle in his throat.

"Walter, Walter," Macy whispered, shaking his head slowly, smiling like a disturbed child taking pleasure in breaking a toy, "I'm not the same man who married your sister, Walter." He tilted his head back slowly, opening his mouth, exposing the two deadly sharp teeth. "Not the same man at all." He pressed his thumbs harder into Benedek's throat as he slowly leaned forward.

Benedek swung a fist into Macy's soft stomach with

no effect. His right arm hit one of the refrigerator shelves and the vacutaners clattered together noisily. His hand brushed cold glass, his fingers wrapped around one of the tubes, pulled it from the tray, and hit it against the inside wall of the refrigerator. A splash of red dribbled down the shiny white surface and speckled the lightbulb, and shards of glass snickered against the metal shelves. Benedek pulled his arm from the chilled air clutching the remaining half of the broken tube. His face felt swollen so he could not take aim; he stabbed blindly and felt the vacutaner's jagged edge sink through doughy flesh, cut through cartilage and muscle.

Macy's hands fell from Benedek's throat and the man staggered backward with a dreadful hawking sound. Benedek held on to the glass tube; it slid from Macy's throat as he moved away. A dark gout of blood cascaded down the front of the pink shirt and spattered onto the white floor. Macy backed against the counter and leaned forward, clutching his throat and gagging. Blood dribbled out of his mouth and continued to flow from the hole in his throat.

Gulping air like water, Benedek looked at his right hand. A small piece of flesh had caught on one of the sharp points; the hand was striped with red. Bile stung the back of his throat, but he held it back and sidestepped Macy, nearing the door.

Macy suddenly stood straight and grinned at Benedek, still holding his throat. Blood glistened on his mouth and chin, but the flow from the wound had stopped. He sucked at the air, pulling his hand away.

"Jesus Christ," Benedek rasped.

Macy's throat was healing before his eyes.

Benedek felt light-headed and realized he was hyperventilating. He took a deep breath and let it out slowly, steadily. He closed the door and turned to his brother-in-law.

Macy was still coughing and wheezing, but his breath was coming easier. His throat was closing quickly.

Clenching his teeth, not wanting to but knowing he *had* to—*for Doris*, his mind screamed, *I'm doing it for Doris and Janice, I have to!*—he stepped forward and swung his arm in an arc, plunging the bloody tube into Macy's throat again, then pulled it out just as quickly.

There was another rush of blood as Macy curled his fingers into claws and fell forward, grabbing at Benedek, who stepped aside, letting the man thud heavily to the floor. Macy rolled over, reached up, and babbled. There were no words, only blood and a ragged hissing as he snapped at the air, flailing his arms helplessly.

Benedek stood at a safe distance, watching him writhe. Macy's eyes rolled toward him and he reached his hand out to Benedek, wheezing . . . wheezing.

Benedek knew he would never rid himself of the memory of that awful, nightmarish wheeze.

The wheeze thickened and became a gasp, and the gasp began to sound like a voice.

Walking around Macy, Benedek stood at his head and watched the wound begin to heal once again.

"Oh God," he grunted through clenched teeth, "oh Jesus, oh *God!*"

He got down on one knee and tried to hold down his gorge as he stabbed the tube into Macy's throat again. Then again. And again . . .

A black, ragged-edged hole opened beneath Macy's chin and he began thrashing like a fish on land. His hands slapped on the linoleum and his legs kicked as his blood pooled around him. When he tried to cover the hole, his fingers slipped through and disappeared in the black-red gash.

The convulsions stopped. His arms and legs became still.

A smell like rancid meat rose from Vernon Macy as his skin began to darken. His eyes bulged and his stomach bloated, straining the buttons of his bloodied shirt.

His skin became purple, then slowly blackened as tiny splits appeared in the puffy flesh of his face.

A sound like an enormous belch came from the body and the smell of excrement mixed with the rotting odor, making Benedek wince.

A thick, viscous mixture of pus and blood oozed from Macy's nostrils and rolled slowly down the sides of his face.

The broken tube slipped from Benedek's hand and shattered on the floor. He pressed the sleeve of his suitcoat to his mouth and nose trying, unsuccessfully, to block out the smell as he stepped to the counter and grabbed the crumpled smock. He wiped as much of the blood from himself as he could and hurried to the door. Turning slowly, he looked once again at the bloated body.

Macy's eye sockets were empty and his fingernails were blackened.

It made no sense; he'd died less than a minute before, but looked like he'd been dead for weeks.

Benedek spun around, knowing he would vomit if he didn't get away from the smell.

He knew he couldn't go out the way he'd come in;

they would be waiting for him. In fact, they'd probably be sending someone into the room any moment.

Benedek looked around the room frantically. At the other end was another door; when he looked through it, he found a small storeroom. Boxes were stacked neatly against the walk and there was a high window across from him. He stepped inside, closed and locked the door, then hefted a few of the boxes, one at a time, until he found one that was packed solid. He put it beneath the window, stepped up, and struggled with the latch. It loosened, and he pushed the window open.

He fell to the pavement in an alley outside. Wincing and panting from exertion, he got up, ran down the alley, and hurried around the corner of the building.

Three women were climbing out of a cab, laughing and chattering. He wanted to tell them to stay as far away from the Midnight Club as they could, but he knew they would think he was crazy. Running a hand through his thick hair, he waited for them to leave the cab, wishing the cold night air would take the clinging, putrid smell of death from his nostrils.

When the women were gone, Benedek got into the cab and snapped the address of his apartment loudly through the transparent partition.

Once the cab was moving, Benedek tried to calm himself, knowing Jackie would be upset if he came home in such a state. He leaned his head back and rubbed his eyes, breathing deeply. Then it hit him. His head jerked up and he stared openmouthed out the windshield of the cab, not seeing what was ahead but, instead, the face of Cedric, the tall waiter in the club.

Those deep eyes, that cocky smile, and, most importantly, the scar on his neck, all fell together in Benedek's head.

"Shit on a stick," he muttered, leaning forward and banging on the partition. "Driver! Take me to the *New York Times*. Hurry!"

Chapter Twelve

By the time the Librium had settled fully into Davey's bones, he was lying naked in bed drifting in and out of a murky, restless sleep. Occasionally, he opened his heavy-lidded eyes and looked at the clock radio only to find that minutes had passed when it had felt like hours.

He rolled away from the clock with a deep sigh and closed his eyes again. His mother came to him in his sleep. She wore her Sunday best and smelled of cocoa butter hand lotion. Clutching her old ragged-edged Bible to her breasts, she leaned forward to speak to him but could only make a strangled gagging sound. She spit up a half-chewed lump of blood-flecked meat. It landed beside Davey on the bed where it began to pulsate quietly.

"Remember, Davey," she said hoarsely, "no matter who you fall in love with, no matter how right it seems, she'll hurt you. That's the way love is."

He wanted to scream at her, to curse her, but he couldn't speak up.

She leaned closer to him and he saw that her lips were blue and puffy. "Jesus is the *only* medicine," she said. Turning from the bed, she sang off-key at the top of her lungs as she left the room. "There's power in the blood, power in the blood . . ."

When she was gone, he looked down at the piece of meat to find his old dog Brat lying beside him. White, fat worms moved sluggishly in the animal's split-open stomach.

Davey grimaced, sickened. He was confused. The smell that came from the scruffy corpse was the same as it had been on that hot summer day so many years ago, but something about it seemed pleasant. Inviting . . .

As his stomach gurgled hungrily, Davey lowered his hand, trembling, until his fingertips touched the sticky edge of the gash. Then his hand slid into the squirming mass of maggots. His hand was swallowed by the moist warmth; the movement of the worms tingled against his skin. He wriggled his fingers a bit, then pulled his hand out. Flecks of dark, bloody meat clung to his fingers and he raised his hand to his open mouth.

Davey awoke suddenly and found himself chewing on his pillow. His tongue felt like a thick strip of leather. The sheets were damp with his sweat. Looking at the clock again, he saw it was a quarter of ten. He was supposed to be at Anya's.

Even if he were physically able to go, he told himself he wouldn't. He *couldn't*. Whatever she was doing to him had to stop. And whatever she *was* . . .

Those pictures had been yellowed and blurred with age, and yet Anya had been as beautiful as ever, her skin just as unblemished, her breasts just as firm today at the age of . . .

How old was she? Surely she wasn't old enough to have been in those pictures. The reviews must have been referring to her mother . . .

The window shade was up and the glow of a street-lamp rose from the sidewalk below. It was raining again. Raindrops pattered against the pane, and as Davey drifted off again, the sound incorporated itself into his dream in the form of white empty shoes that tap-danced on darkness . . .

Voices spoke to him softly over the tapping.

You have no spine . . .

. . . by the short and curlies . . .

She'll hurt you. That's the way love is . . .

Scratching . . . scratching . . . Mice in the walls?

Davey turned his head toward the window and gasped.

Anya smiled at him through the wet glass. As if she were underwater, her long black hair floated around her head. She smiled as she pressed her palms to the window.

Can't be, Davey thought. *Nine floors up . . .*

She ran her nails down the glass with a harsh grating sound, leaving behind long scratches as she silently mouthed his name:

Daaaaveeeeyyy . . .

Her smile broadened and she opened her mouth wide. Snakelike fangs caught the light like small knives.

"Oh, Jesus, Jesus," Davey gasped, closing his eyes, but instead of comforting darkness, the backs of his eyelids flickered with grainy yellow images of Anya, images from decades ago, images that couldn't possibly be.

When he opened his eyes again, he could see that

she was naked. Her breasts rose above the bottom edge of the window.

Daaaveeey, she mouthed, her perfect lips sliding over the deadly teeth, *let meee iiinnn.* Her nails scratched against the pane, cutting trails in the glass.

She'll cut right through, he thought, *Jesus Christ, she'll cut right through it!*

"Leave me alone!" he croaked, trying to sit up in the bed. "Stay away from me!"

Her lips moved again: *It's toooo late . . .*

Floating gracefully in the mist, she rose until he could see her belly, her thighs, her knees. She slowly spread her legs and touched the patch of black hair and ran two fingertips along her pink, glistening lips . . .

As if he were in the booth again, watching her through the smudged glass, Davey slowly became erect. A deep warmth spread through his body as he sat up on the edge of the mattress.

Anya smiled at him as she touched herself.

It's just a dream, he thought as he stood on weak legs. *It's impossible so it has to be a dream, I'm sick and I have a fever and I'm dreaming . . .*

He pressed the heels of his palms to the sash and opened the window. In a rush of rain and icy air, Anya's arms were around him and her lips were brushing his cheeks, his ears, his throat as she whispered, "You didn't come to me, Davey, so I came to *you.*"

Their bodies tangled together on the bed and Davey lost himself inside her.

Benedek raced around the desks in the city room on the way to his small office in the back.

"Hey, Walter!" someone called. "Thought you were on vacation."

Sal Burkett fell into step beside Benedek. He was small and wiry with long blond hair. He was a staff photographer, but in the three years Burkett had been at the *Times*, Benedek had never seen him carrying a camera. Nor had Benedek ever seen him without a wad of bubble gum in his mouth.

"I am on vacation," Benedek said, a bit winded, "but I missed the place so much, I had to come in and look around."

"You okay?" Burkett asked, following Benedek into the small office. "You look like you just caught the pope beating off."

Benedek sat down at his desk and faced his computer terminal, lighting a cigarette.

"You know I don't bother with that small-time stuff anymore, Sal. Carlysle in?"

"Left a couple hours ago. What's up?" Burkett blew a large pink bubble; it popped and left behind it a sugary smell.

"Need some info, that's all." Benedek typed in STAB-BING/PIMP and started to add a month, but paused, fingers hovering over the keyboard.

"Maybe I can help you," Burkett said, stepping behind Benedek and peering over his shoulder.

Benedek's chair squeaked as he leaned back and puffed on his cigarette.

Looking at the screen, Burkett said, "Looking for a dead pimp, huh?"

"I'm not sure he's a pimp, but I'm pretty sure he's dead."

"Well, it's not like it's a rare thing in this city, you know. Dead pimps, I mean." He chuckled. "Those're the best kind. When did it happen?"

"Not sure of that, either. Maybe, uh, April? May? I

187

remember seeing a picture of the guy. Hispanic. Cocky looking. I think he was found in a trash bin just off of, um . . ."

"Broadway?"

Benedek blinked up at the younger man. "Yeah."

"Stabbed in the neck?"

"That's the one. You gotta good memory, Burkett."

"Not really," he said, standing beside Benedek and leaning toward the computer. His thin fingers clattered over the keys as he said, "The reason I remember this one is that it was kinda weird."

"How so?"

Burkett backed away from the computer and a brief article flashed on the screen in amber print.

"Holy shit," Benedek breathed.

The body of Cedric Palacios, a convicted pimp found stabbed to death Thursday, was stolen from the Bellevue morgue this morning. The thief's motive and method of entering remain a mystery. With no sign of a break-in and . . .

Perching himself on the corner of the desk, Burkett studied Benedek's face with interest.

"Hey, Walter, you on to something?"

Benedek shook his head slowly without taking his eyes from the screen. "They ever catch the killer?" he asked.

Burkett popped another bubble. "Nope. Doubt anybody cares. I mean, the guy was a *pimp*, you know?"

"You remember anything unusual about his death?"

"Well, let's see." He got off the desk and turned to the computer again. In a moment, the piece reporting

Cedric Palacios's murder appeared. Benedek read it quickly.

The knife wound had not been fatal. It had missed the jugular and Palacios might have lived.

If he hadn't bled to death.

The authorities assumed Palacios had been killed elsewhere, then moved to the trash bin because there had been so little blood around the body.

"Walter, you don't look so good," Burkett said quietly. "You okay?"

"Just out of curiosity, Sal . . . have you heard of anyone else dying like this? Bleeding to death, I mean?"

Burkett's face brightened. "You *are* on to something, Walter. You gonna need pictures?"

A long ash dropped from the end of Benedek's cigarette as he continued staring at the screen.

"Close the door on your way out, Sal."

"Oh. Okay." He went to the door, turned, and said, "By the way, Walter, I'm really sorry about your—"

"See you in about ten days, Sal."

"Yeah. See you." He closed the door quietly as he left.

Benedek pressed his dying cigarette into the bottom of the ashtray and lit another.

He didn't like what he was thinking. It was the kind of thinking that could land him in Central Park picking up old milk cartons and used rubbers with a pointy stick for a living.

As weird as his thoughts were, however, they made a frightening kind of sense.

Doris and Janice had bled to death, but there had been little blood in the apartment.

Cedric Palacios had bled to death, but little blood had been found around the body.

But he's alive and waiting tables, for Christ's sake! Benedek thought. *He's fucking lonely middle-aged women in dark little rooms!* Then, an unwelcome thought occurred to him: *Unless he's not really alive at all . . .*

Within seconds, Vernon's corpse had reached an advanced state of decay, as if he'd died weeks ago.

Maybe he did . . .

And Davey Owen . . .

I think she bit me, he'd said, *and now I'm sick.*

Benedek snatched the telephone receiver from its cradle and called Jackie.

" 'Lo?" she answered groggily.

"Hi, hon. Sorry to wake you, but it's kind of important. Do me a favor?"

"Where are you?"

"My office. Check the answering machine and see if there are any messages for me."

"Just a second."

He waited while she listened to the recordings.

"Riley called," she said finally. "He wants to talk to you tomorrow. And someone named Casey Thorne called. Says she's a friend of Davey's and that he's really sick. She sounded worried and said something about seeing your wife the doctor. Walter, have you been generously offering my services without—"

"Did she leave a number?" he asked urgently.

"No, the tape—"

"*Shit!* Look, Jackie, I gotta go. I may call you later. This guy might need to see you."

"What's wrong with—"

"I don't know yet. Thanks. Love you." He hung up as he stood and dashed from the office.

Downstairs he caught a cab to Davey's and offered

the driver twenty bucks if he would erase his memory of all traffic laws for the duration of the ride.

Benedek was trembling and very afraid.

Only after they had finished did Davey realize it had not been a dream. His lips were sticky and his mouth tasted of blood. The cold air from the open window helped clear his head, although he felt very dizzy, and by the time Anya rose from the bed, he was quite alert.

She went into the bathroom and returned with a wet rag.

"Get away from me," Davey said.

"I just want to clean the—"

"Get away and *stay* away!" He sat up against the headboard. "You've given me something, you've . . . you're sick, you have . . ." He wiped his mouth and looked away from her.

Standing at the foot of the bed, Anya laughed as she pushed a long strand of black hair from her face. She dropped the rag onto the bed.

"You think I have a *venereal disease?*" she asked cheerfully. "Come, Davey, you're no fool. What do you think I've been doing these last few days? How do you think I got to your ninth-floor window? And Davey." She moved to the side of the bed. "Why do you think I left that scrapbook beside the bed today? Do you think that was an accident?"

"What have you done to me?"

She smiled. "I've given you a new life, Davey. A life of endless potential and power you've never—"

"Go *away!*"

"No. You shouldn't be alone tonight. The transfusion is complete and you'll—"

"Trans*fusion?*"

She sat on the bed, reached over, and wiped a bit of blood from the corner of his mouth with her finger. Sliding the finger into her mouth, she licked off the blood and smiled.

"The blood in your veins," she whispered, "is no longer your own. It's the blood of gods, Davey, and it's changing you. Right this instant. Tonight, you will die. And when you wake, you will have—"

"Get the hell away from me!" he screamed, turning his back to her. He pulled the covers over himself and curled up beneath them. He felt her get off the bed.

"I'd rather not leave you alone, Davey," she said softly. "Some things will come instinctively, but others . . . But then, if you insist. You know, Davey, *I* didn't do this to you. You *allowed* it. As I said before, you're a very weak man."

He wanted to shut out her voice, but it was so low and smooth, so very soothing.

"I'll see you again soon, Davey Owen."

He opened his mouth to tell her to stay away, that he never wanted to see her again, she was fucking crazy and sick, and he just wanted to get better, goddammit, but before he could speak there was a strange shift in the air, an odd swirling.

Davey rolled over to see something flutter away outside the window and finally it hit him, a cold, almost tangible fear that swallowed him whole, the feeling of plummeting down a bottomless pit with nothing to hold on to and no hope of breaking the fall if the bottom came, and all the wind gushed from his lungs as he tried to sit up, his vision blurred and his head felt disconnected from his body, and all control left him so he wet himself as he stood and staggered away from the bed, groping for support, but falling on his face with the sound of thunder in his skull, and he tried to scream but he couldn't because there wasn't enough air, he couldn't get his breath, and when he pushed against the floor to lift himself, the room spun and fell and he cried out softly but his voice caught in his throat and he retched and spit bile onto the floor.

Tonight, you will die.

Through the pounding in his ears, Davey heard a knock at the door. He turned himself painfully toward the bedroom doorway. The knock came again.

"Davey?" It was a man.

He opened his mouth and tried to speak but could only gasp fragments of words.

"He . . . hel . . . help . . . plea . . . *pleeeaa* . . ."

His insides seemed to be collapsing, his body felt as if it were turning in on itself. His blurred vision darkened until he could see no more than shards of soft light.

"Davey, it's Walter Benedek! Let me in!"

He wanted to slam a fist to the floor, hoping he would be heard, but his hands would not clench. When he tried to inhale, he retched again and felt as if his stomach were ripping open.

Walter Benedek continued pounding on the door and the sound bored through Davey's skull like a drill.

Tonight, you will die.

Breath would not come, it was cut off completely, and when he closed his eyes, he saw blinding flashes of red as he began to disappear, like a morning fog slowly clearing away, and his guts began to dissolve in a bubbling mass inside him. The voice and the pounding fell farther and farther away . . .

"Davey? It's Wal . . . nedek . . . me in, Da . . ."

And even the red began to dim until there was nothing and Davey Owen was no more.

* * *

Benedek cursed through his teeth as he fumbled the picks into the lock, hoping that, despite the fact that this was not a secure building, Davey had no bolts on the door because the picks would do no good in that case and he *had* to get in, something was very wrong.

The lock clicked, Benedek turned the knob and pushed the door open. Inside, the dark apartment was freezing cold and the air was damp.

"Davey? It's Walter."

Benedek's joints felt stiff. He was afraid to look around, afraid of what he might find. He couldn't bear the sight of any more blood.

"Davey?"

He stepped hesitantly into the kitchen.

Nothing.

The bathroom was empty.

He's in the bedroom, Benedek told himself, *you know he is, that's why you're avoiding it.*

Davey Owen was lying on the floor, his naked body twisted as if he'd been struggling against something. His eyes and mouth were open but Benedek knew immediately that he was dead.

Cold air blew rain through the open window and the curtains flapped against the wall as Benedek knelt beside Davey and touched his throat for a pulse.

There was none. His skin was cold, as if he'd been dead for some time.

Unable to stand the cold any longer, Benedek went to the window, closed it, and did a double take at the pane. Something had cut the glass in long streaks, something *outside* the window. The cuts were grouped together by fours, almost as if a human hand had clawed and run down the glass.

He turned away from the window and crossed the room, muttering "Son of a *bitch*" as he turned to Davey's body again. He leaned against the wall, thinking about the piece he'd read on his computer.

The body of Cedric Palocios . . . stolen from the Bellevue morgue this morning . . . no sign of a break-in.

What had Vernon said about a sacrifice?

My life was a small sacrifice to get here. Killing Doris? Killing Janice? A very, very small price, Walter.

Benedek fingered his lower lip as he stared at Davey. He went to him and checked his pulse again. Nothing. He put a hand over Davey's mouth. No breath. He was definitely dead.

Apparently, someone had thought Cedric Palacios was definitely dead, too. Dead enough to put in a morgue drawer. But he wasn't dead anymore.

He wasn't stolen from the morgue, Benedek thought. *He got up and walked out.*

That was a possibility too insane to consider. But it was beginning to make perfect sense to Benedek.

I'm not the same man who married your sister, Walter, Vernon had said. *Not the same man at all.*

Benedek paced around the body as he thought.

How dead was Davey Owen? Dead enough to have no pulse, no breath, but was he dead enough to stay that way?

Benedek stopped his pacing and looked frantically around the room until he spotted the curtain cords. He went to the window, grasped one of the cords, and pulled down hard. The rod fell to the floor, the curtains bunched in a heap. He freed the cords and went back to the still body on the floor.

He tied the hands and feet tightly, then sat on the bed, lit a cigarette, and watched Davey, waiting.

* * *

Casey awoke in darkness. The air was stale and sweet smelling. She felt a hand on her thigh and realized she was naked.

A man spoke: "Do you want me to go down and get—"

"No," a woman interrupted. Her voice was deep, rich. "I want this one to stay with us."

Footsteps. A door closed quietly.

"Are you hurt?" the woman asked, gently passing her hand up and down Casey's thigh.

"No, I'm . . ." She tried to sit up and found that she had been tied. She jerked her shoulders up hard, tried to kick her legs. "Let me *go!*"

"You'll only hurt yourself if you struggle. I'm not going to harm you. Just relax; lie back and relax." She continued stroking Casey's thigh, moving her hand higher and higher. "My name is Shideh. Who are you?"

"Get your fucking hand off me!" Casey spat. She could see nothing more than a vague shape over her in the darkness and an occasional glimmer of red. "What . . ." Her voice broke and she took in a breath. "What do you want?"

Casey felt more than saw the figure lean close to her. She felt hot breath on her ear as Shideh spoke.

"Your friendship."

"My . . ." Casey was incredulous. Her head burned with anger and she pulled uselessly against her bindings again. "What the fu—"

With a startling *scratch*, a match flame hissed to life in the darkness. Its halo of soft light was passed to the wick of a candle so black the flame seemed to be burning on the end of a shadow. The yellow glow flickered over Shideh's face, making shadows dance beneath her sharp cheekbones and sparkling in her blood-red eyes.

The woman's gaze grabbed Casey and held.

"What's your name?"

Casey opened her mouth, intending to curse her, but all that came out was, "Ca . . . Casey. Thorne."

"Thorne," she said, hissing the name. "Pretty as a rose, but your name is Thorne." She placed a cool hand on the side of Casey's face.

Shideh's pale, animal-like face seemed to fade away until all Casey could see were her red eyes and her tiny black pupils that seemed to open to her like waiting arms.

"I was going to kill you, Casey Thorne. You made me very angry. But you have such a pretty face. Such lively eyes. You must have a beautiful smile, Casey. Will you smile for me?"

Casey felt the hand slide down her face, over her throat, to her breast. The thumb lightly brushed her nipple and it hardened instantly. Unable to resist, Casey smiled at the eyes, at the same time repulsed at herself for giving in. If she could only look away from those eyes . . .

"A beautiful smile," Shideh whispered; her voice was like the caress of a skinless hand. "I won't harm that smile. Would you like to stay with me awhile, Casey?" she asked, pressing her fingers between Casey's legs.

No! Casey heard her own voice scream inside her head, but the eyes held like a silk-covered vise.

Shideh leaned forward and kissed Casey's throat.

Casey closed her eyes, but the image of those two red orbs, deep and unblinking, remained.

"I can teach you things," Shideh whispered, flicking

her tongue over Casey's ear. "I can do things to you that you never thought were possible." She nibbled Casey's earlobe, sucked on it. "I can make you into something you never dreamed you could be." She touched her tongue to the corner of Casey's mouth.

"Immortal . . ." and kissed her gently.

". . . undying . . ." then slid her tongue into Casey's mouth, around and around.

". . . and *sooo* powerful . . ."

Casey's mind reeled at Shideh's touch, at her deep and lingering kiss, at the odd sensation of her sharp teeth against her upper lip. She was vaguely aware of the sickening disgust inside her, the urge to bite and scream and pull away, but it was weak as a distant memory.

"It's been so long," Shideh hissed, moving her mouth down Casey's throat, over her breast, to her nipple, "since I've taken a lover."

Shideh's cool tongue swirled over Casey's nipple, pulled it into her mouth, and sucked on it with vigor.

Casey couldn't speak. Tears welled in her eyes and she sobbed once quietly as the woman's mouth moved over her stomach and settled between her legs. The tongue slipped out again and wedged itself inside her, where it lapped slowly, dipping in and out of her opening. She could hear the slurping and sucking sounds the woman made, the moan of pleasure that came from her as she continued to lick and gulp.

In spite of herself, ripples of pleasure passed up through Casey's body, but she remained unaffected by them, tried to suppress them, ignore them.

Shideh's teeth flicked over Casey's clitoris and the rush of feeling that came was warm and thick.

The woman spoke and her words were muffled:

". . . none like a woman's . . ."

Casey shuddered and involuntarily lifted her pelvis, pressing it to Shideh's mouth.

Her lips writhed over Casey's pubis, the tongue was relentless, and she sucked, and sucked . . .

Casey's orgasm made her cry out with pleasure and anger, frustration, helplessness.

Shideh moved over her, slid her tongue back up Casey's belly and over her breasts, stopping now and then to kiss her skin gently, until her face was above Casey's, her breasts pressing to Casey's breasts. Her white hair draped down around Casey's face.

In the candle's shifting light, Casey watched Shideh lift a hand to her own throat and press her thumbnail against her flesh until it cut through. She pulled her thumb downward, cutting a slit that immediately began to bleed. Locking her hands together beneath Casey's head, Shideh lifted it to her throat.

Casey's lips slid over the warm, sticky wound and her tongue slipped into the gash. Instinctively, she tried to pull back.

"No!" Shideh breathed, holding Casey's mouth to her throat. "Suck it! Suck it *now*, before it closes!"

She tasted blood and gagged once, but then found herself doing as she was told.

Like whiskey, the blood was pleasantly hot going down. A relaxed warmth spread through her body and she whimpered at the luxurious feeling that clouded her head like a drug, pounding thunderously through her veins, eating its way into her bones.

"Isn't it *gooood,* Casey Thorne? You'll have more, as much as you want."

Casey sucked and gulped furiously.

"Yes, keep sucking . . . don't stop."

Unable to hold it in, Casey pulled her mouth away and laughed a girlish, gargling laugh, feeling drunk and strong and *new*.

Before opening his eyes, Davey felt a burning emptiness inside. The sickness was gone, the cold certainty that he was dying had passed, but the hunger was strong and pressed hard up into his throat.

He opened his eyes and rolled over, staring up at the ceiling.

"Davey?"

Davey turned his head and saw Walter Benedek sitting on the bed smoking a cigarette.

"How do you feel, Davey?"

Davey blinked and tried to move his arms but found his hands and feet had been tied.

"How long . . ." His voice was a rasp, like rusty pipes rattling in the walls. He coughed a few times. "How long have I been like this?"

"I got here about an hour and a half ago. It's almost midnight."

"You found me . . . did you come in and . . ."

Benedek put his cigarette out in a drinking glass and walked over to Davey, looked down at him. "When I found you, you were . . . unconscious."

"Un . . . un . . ."

Benedek squatted beside him. "Davey, you weren't breathing."

"I wasn't . . ." Davey closed his eyes and gently tried to shake out the fog behind them.

"You had no pulse. Your heart wasn't beating."

Opening his eyes, Davey looked up at Benedek. He was serious. "I don't know what . . ."

"Davey, you were dead. When I came up here, I found you *dead*."

What was it Anya had said? She'd said that tonight . . . tonight he would . . . would . . .

Davey nodded his head slightly. "She said I would die tonight."

"Who?"

"Anya."

"You went to her?"

"No. She came here. Through the bedroom window."

Benedek glanced over his shoulder at the window, then looked back down at Davey. "Did she make the scratches?"

Davey nodded.

"You're nine fucking stories up!"

Pulling against the ropes, Davey said, "Why am I tied up?"

Benedek put his hand on Davey's shoulder and squeezed. "Davey, did you *hear* me? You're nine floors up, how could she come to your goddamned *window?*"

"I don't . . . I'm . . ." Davey wanted to be left alone. He didn't want to think about *anything*, but the image of Anya hovering outside the window would not go away. "She was just . . . she was just *there*."

"And you let her in."

Davey nodded.

Benedek stood suddenly and walked away from Davey, lighting another cigarette. "Jesus Christ," he bellowed, "if you wanted to get laid, couldn't you have found a woman who doesn't *float?*"

After a long pause, silent but for Benedek's pacing footsteps, Davey croaked, "Walter, why am I tied up?"

His question was ignored.

"Davey, there's a man at the Midnight Club by the

name of Cedric. Tall, Hispanic, scar on his neck. Know the one?"

Davey nodded, flinching at a cramp in his stomach.

"About six months ago, Cedric was found dead in a trash bin off Broadway. He'd bled to death, but there was no blood around the body. Later, his corpse disappeared from the morgue. Because the idea of a corpse walking out of a morgue is too fucking ludicrous for *anyone* to swallow, it was assumed to have been stolen." He stood over Davey again. "Now he's working in a nightclub where he fucks middle-aged women—and *men* for all I know—and, as far as I can make out, takes blood from them, which is stored in refrigerators in the back by my brother-in-law who, I suspect, has been dead for the last three weeks. Does any of that make sense to you?"

The cramp would not go away and Davey curled up on his side.

"Just leave me alone," he grunted. "Untie me and go. I'm sick."

"Davey," Benedek said softly, kneeling, the anger in his voice replaced by concern, "you should be *dead*, do you understand? I want to *help* you. If you can explain any of—"

"I'm *hungryyyy!*" Davey wailed, tilting his head back and opening his mouth wide.

Benedek suddenly jumped to his feet and backed away, gasping, "Holy Christ, your teeth!"

Davey blinked at him.

"Open your mouth again," Benedek whispered tremulously.

Davey gingerly ran his tongue over them. They were long and very sharp. Davey groaned and turned away from Benedek.

"Just like Vernon," Benedek muttered.

The emptiness inside Davey seemed to bloat his stomach until it felt as if it might split open. A pounding ring sounded in his ears and he had to close his eyes because the room had begun to spin. He couldn't think about what was happening to him, he couldn't give any thought to the teeth in his mouth that had not been there an hour and a half ago, because the hunger in him was eating him up.

"Walter," he rasped, "in the refrigerator, second shelf, there's some hamburger. Will you bring it to me . . . please?"

Meat, he craved meat.

"Do you want me to cook it?" Benedek asked uncertainly.

The thought of the hamburger being warm and brown made Davey want to retch.

"Just *bring* it!"

He heard Benedek's hurried footsteps, the refrigerator open and close, the sound of cellophane crinkling as it was torn away.

"Here," Benedek said, returning to his side.

Davey turned onto his back and looked up at the man. He seemed as tall as a building.

"Will you untie me, Walter?"

Benedek slowly shook his head. "Afraid not, Davey. Not yet."

"Then put it in my mouth."

Bending down, Benedek tore away a chunk of the moist burger and touched it cautiously to Davey's lips.

Davey sucked the raw meat into his mouth ravenously, pressing it to his palate with his tongue. The cold, coppery taste of blood was faint and only fed his hunger like dry wood on a fire. He writhed, spitting the meat from his mouth and crying, "It's not enough!" He looked up at Benedek and saw fear in the man's eyes, fear and helplessness. And he saw something else . . .

Even in the dark, Davey saw the pulse beneath the skin of Benedek's neck. A steady pulse that made the flesh bulge slightly with each beat.

"Leave, Walter," Davey said imploringly, unable to take his eyes from the vein. If he could just get close enough to brush his teeth over the skin, open it up, the blood would push itself out, onto his tongue and down his throat. His penis began to harden. "Get the hell out of here *now!*"

"Davey, I'm gonna call my wife and have her come—"

"Walter, I'm hungry," Davey hissed. "I'm not sure what's happening to me but I'm hungry and I'm going to hurt you if—"

"That's why you're tied up," Benedek said confidently.

Davey moved his hands and without any effort at all the cord snapped and fell away from his wrists. He sat up, his eyes on Benedek's neck.

"Walter," Davey said, his voice guttural and harsh, "I'm hungry and you have what I need."

Benedek reached the doorway in an instant.

"Davey, I want to help you."

"Then go, Walter. I don't want to hurt you." Tears stung his eyes and disgust clogged in his throat, making it hard to speak. "But I will. I can't help it."

"Okay, Davey, listen. You have my number. When you're . . . better, call me. I'll try to help you if I can."

"Thank you, Walter. Now go."

Benedek's footsteps were silenced by the closing of the door in the living room.

Not trusting his legs, Davey crawled to the bed and

lifted himself to his feet. The room tilted and he sat on the edge of the mattress for a moment, then carefully walked to the window. With a heave, Davey lifted the sash and let the cold night air wash over him.

The transfusion is complete, Anya had said.

He'd become like her. He'd *allowed* her to change him, and now that it was done . . .

Davey couldn't think about it now. He imagined the entire city stretched before him, alive with millions of people, millions of hearts pumping warm blood through veins and arteries . . .

He knelt at the window and laid his head on his arms.

He knew he needed blood. Each second that passed without his hunger being satisfied seemed to drain his body of energy. The very thought, however, of drinking the life out of another human being was . . . was . . .

He shuddered. Although he tried hard to imagine the act to be repulsive, he couldn't.

Lifting his head, he looked up at the murky night sky. His tongue felt like sandpaper and his dry eyes burned.

A life of endless potential and power.

He imagined gliding over the city, swift and silent, his senses raw, acutely aware of everything around him, every sight and sound, even the faintest scents on the breeze.

Some things will come instinctively.

With his eyes on the sky, the fantasy became so vivid that he was unaware of the changes taking place in his body, the shrinking of his bones, the shifting of his skin . . .

The window seemed to grow, become enormous,

and the view beyond became wider and wider until there was no floor beneath him, no walls around him. The city was a passing blur below, its lights filtered through what seemed to be a mist in his eyes, and as if the plan had been tucked away in his mind all along, Davey knew upon whom he would feed.

Chad Wilkes watched the girl's back as she walked away from the bar stool next to him and burrowed into the crowd on the dance floor. She was petite and blond and had a tiny mole just above her mouth. Oh well. She was probably a ballbuster anyway. She certainly didn't have a sense of humor.

Chad had used one of his favorite icebreakers on her, the one he used when he was in an up kind of mood, which he was that night because he'd canceled a dinner date with Stella Schuman (something he'd been trying to muster the guts to do for quite a while) but the girl had not been at all amused.

"So, what's your sign?" he'd said, and after her abrupt reply: "Oh, Aries? I'm a Sagittarius. I'm a little rusty on my astrology, but if I'm not mistaken, tonight's the night my Milky Way is supposed to slide into Uranus."

She'd tossed back the rest of her drink and walked away.

And she'd been his fourth try! It was just short of midnight and he was having no luck. Oh well, having nothing was better than having dinner with *her*. It hadn't been so bad at first because he'd known that it would get him somewhere. But now that he'd received his promotion, and especially now that talk of their relationship was spreading—Casey Thorne's little remark in the elevator had *really* pissed him off—he didn't know if he'd get near her again.

Leaning against the bar, Chad surveyed the crowd, his wine cooler in hand, waiting to find someone interesting—and interest*ed*.

He finished his drink and decided a good piss might make him feel better. He walked casually away from the bar, smiling and nodding at each woman with whom he happened to make eye contact.

The restroom was cramped and dirty and not very well lit, the smell of urine and feces thinly covered by the stinging odor of pine-scented cleaner. A small rectangular window was open in the back of the room, just above the last stall, but what little fresh air got in didn't get far.

There were two urinals: one was piled with wet toilet paper, the other had an OUT OF ORDER sign taped to it.

Clicking his tongue, Chad walked to the first stall and pushed the door open. It squeaked as it turned heavily on its hinges and something in the restroom fluttered.

Chad looked back over his shoulder at the restroom's entrance.

Nothing.

The stall door began to slowly swing shut again and he stopped it with his hand. It seemed pretty heavy for such a thin, rickety door. He stepped inside, shouldering around the door so it could swing closed.

Spreading his feet before the yellowed toilet. Chad opened his fly, but before he could relieve himself he heard the fluttering sound directly behind him, so close that it ruffled his hair. He spun around, zipper gaping, to look into two small red eyes and a snout lined with razorlike teeth hanging upside down from the hook on the door. Two wings mapped with thin delicate veins spread wide and then sprang on him and wrapped around his face, making him fall back on the toilet.

Pain shot down his legs as his hips landed hard on the dirty porcelain bowl. Chad screamed but the sound was muffled by the thing smothering his face. He raised his hands and tried to slap it away, but it held on tight and seemed to be . . . it was getting *heavier* and holy Jesus it was getting *bigger* and *stronger*, spreading over his whole body until . . .

The thing pulled away and Chad scrambled to get to his feet but couldn't because a strong hand was holding him down. It was a *man*, a *naked* man—*oh Jesus Christ a homo a fag sweet Jesus I'm gonna be raped!*—not a *bat*, which was what it sure as hell *looked* like a few seconds ago, and Chad lifted his eyes to the man's face and sucked in his breath so hard that he nearly gagged.

"Hello, Chadwick," Davey Owen said through a grin, letting the name dribble from his mouth like spittle.

"Davey, what the hell're you *doing* here? You're naked, Davey, Jesus, what's . . ."

"I came to find you, Chad."

"Did you have to scare the *bejeezus* outta me like that?"

"Sorry," Davey said, smiling.

Adrenaline was still racing through Chad's body but his fear had passed now that he knew it was only Davey Owen. Probably Davey was pissed off about the promotion and about losing his job, none of which, of course, was *Chad's* fault. He angrily tried to knock Davey's hand away from his shoulder. It wouldn't budge.

"Okay," Chad barked, "so you've found me, now what the *hell* do you *want?*"

"Just a little blood, Mr. Wilkes," Davey whispered.

"Huh, *what?* Davey, will you . . ."

Chad felt himself being lifted and slammed against the wall. His head banged the Sani-Sheet dispenser above the toilet. His eyes widened. Maybe Davey was on drugs, PCP, that made people really strong, didn't it? It *had* to be that because Davey Owen simply was *not* that strong.

"Look, Davey, I know you're upset about . . ."

Davey opened his mouth and the fangs sparkling with saliva made Chad want to scream.

"This won't hurt a *bit*, Mr. Wilkes," Davey said softly as he leaned forward.

Chapter Thirteen

Wednesday

When Stella Schuman opened her office door at twelve minutes past eight in the morning, she was met by a gust of chilled air. Two sheets of paper blew from her desk and fluttered to the floor.

Behind her desk, there was a jagged hole in the window from which several delicate cracks spread like webbing across the rest of the pane.

"Jasmine," she said stiffly.

Her secretary came to her side. "Yes?"

"Do you know anything about this?"

Jasmine Barny lightly touched her fingertips to her lips when she saw the hole.

"No!" she said breathily.

"Damn," Miss Schuman barked as she went into the office and put her briefcase on the desk. "Get maintenance up here right away and tell them to handle this, will you please?"

Jasmine was gone before her boss was finished speaking.

With a hearty exhalation, Miss Schuman lowered herself onto one round knee and retrieved the papers, then replaced them on their stack, using her cigarette box as a paperweight.

Below the window, a large water spot from the rain of the night before had spread over the carpet.

They were endless, these little annoyances, *endless*. Last night, her television had started acting up and made Pat Sajak look like a deformed Asian throughout *Wheel of Fortune*. Then Chad had canceled their evening together with an abrupt phone call.

"Don't have time to explain," he'd said, "but something's come up. I'll see you tomorrow at work."

Fine. You help someone climb the ladder and they start getting too big for the rungs. If she found out he'd gone to that repulsive meat-market bar he frequented, well, she'd give him a good scare. Maybe tell him they were going to be forced to lay off a few assistant editors because of a drop in circulation. Let the little bugger shake in his boots for a week or so.

The corners of the weighted-down papers snickered in the wind.

What could have done it? A bird? Certainly not vandals; the window was eighteen floors up.

"Damn," she said again, taking her briefcase from the desk and leaving her office. "I can't work in here." She stepped through the doorway and started to tell Jasmine she was going to the lounge but stopped when she saw a bald man leaning over Jasmine's desk.

"May I help you?" Miss Schuman asked.

The man looked up and smiled briefly. "Stella Schuman?"

"Yes."

"Detective Kenneth Riley, New York Police." He showed her his badge and ID, then slipped them into his coat pocket. "Do you have a few minutes?"

"What can I do for you?"

"I need to ask you a . . . could we go somewhere?"

"I'm on my way to the lounge right now." To Jasmine: "Tell Chad I want to see him."

"He hasn't come in yet."

"Well, when he does."

When they started down the corridor, the detective asked, "Was that Chad Wilkes you were asking for?"

"Yes. Why?"

"He's the reason I need to talk with you."

"Good God," she snapped, "what's he done?" Paper cup in hand, she approached the coffeepot.

"He's been murdered."

She turned to him with a start. "Are you sure?"

"Quite sure, Miss Schuman."

"In his apartment? On the street? Where?"

"In the restroom of a club called the Trench."

"Oh, Christ." She filled her cup, suddenly angry. Chad had been unaware that she knew he was going to the Trench, but she'd been planning to strongly suggest he avoid the place. She'd often worried about what he might pick up from the little tarts he met there.

"When was the last time you talked to him?"

"Last night. In the early evening, really. We were supposed to get together and he called to back out."

"Get together?"

She eyed the detective as she sipped her coffee. "For dinner. We were going to discuss the possibility of introducing a new magazine. Does that matter?"

"No. Did he say why he was changing his plans?"

"No." She sat at one of the tables.

"Miss Schuman, do you have any idea if Mr. Wilkes had any enemies that disliked him enough to kill him?"

"God, no. Chad worked during the day and went out at night. He wasn't particularly popular here because he was a climber, but nobody hated him *that* much."

"Just the same, I'd like to talk to some of his associates."

"Wait a second." Miss Schuman scratched a fingernail up and down the side of her cup. "A couple days ago a man named Davey Owen quit his job because he was *very* upset. Chad had gotten a promotion that Davey thought *he* deserved."

"Do you know where I can contact him?"

"My secretary will have his address and phone number."

They started back down the corridor toward Jasmine's desk.

"Mr. Riley, this might be a, oh, a crass thing to ask, but how was Chad murdered?"

"His throat was torn open," Riley answered in a whisper. "He bled to death. The man who found him claims he saw a large bird, maybe a bat, flying around the bathroom. The guy thought this bird or whatever had killed him had something that looked like blood all over it. That's impossible, though, because the teeth marks on Wilkes's throat are human."

"*Teeth* marks?"

213

"Yes."

"Jesus." At Jasmine's desk, Miss Schuman said, "Davey Owen's address for the detective, Jasmine."

Riley thanked Miss Schuman for her time and said he would be back later in the day to talk to some of her other employees.

"Did you call maintenance, Jasmine?" Miss Schuman asked.

"They're coming," she said as she flipped through the Rolodex.

Miss Schuman went into her office and got a cigarillo from the box. The detective had seemed almost disappointed that she did not burst into tears.

When he was gone, she stepped outside the cold room again.

"Miss Schuman?"

"Hm?"

"Come here, look at this."

She looked over Jasmine's shoulder at the Rolodex. One of the cards had been torn out; only the bottom half remained, still clinging to the rings. The cards before and after had black-red smears on them.

"This was your card," Jasmine said. "Did you take it?" She touched one of the smears. It seemed to be dry; none stuck to her fingers.

"What's this?" she asked.

Miss Schuman silently shrugged.

Endless, she thought, *the annoyances are endless*. For some reason, however, this felt like more than just an annoyance. Touching Jasmine's shoulder, she said, "Just a second."

Miss Schuman went to the corner and looked down the corridor. Detective Kenneth Riley was gone. She decided she'd mention it to him when he got back, maybe have him check with security to see if anything odd had happened the night before.

"Fix it," she said to Jasmine, waving her fingers at the Rolodex as she passed the desk. She went back to the office door to close it and cut off the icy draft. Her eyes locked onto the hole in the window.

A large bird, maybe a bat . . . blood all over it . . .

Miss Schuman stared at the broken pane for a long time, her cigarillo between two fingers, unable to understand the sudden discomfort she felt.

Endless, she thought again, closing the door.

"Jesus H. Christ in sneakers," Benedek grunted as he poured himself a glass of orange juice.

"Sorry to wake you," Riley said flatly, coming into the kitchen.

"No, no, I shoulda been up a couple hours ago." Benedek shuffled to the table and dropped into a chair, gesturing for Riley to have a seat.

The creases on Riley's forehead were so deep they looked like cuts. He cradled his sharp chin in his right palm, stroking his cheek with his thumb.

"How are you, Walter?" he asked quietly.

"I'm okay, I guess." Benedek polished off the orange juice in a couple of gulps. "You want coffee?"

"Sure."

Benedek got up and took a filter from a drawer and spooned in some grounds. "So what's up?"

"There was a murder last night, Walter."

"This is New York. There were probably a couple dozen."

"Yeah, but this one was just like your sister's."

Benedek's thumb stopped half an inch from the BREW switch. He flipped it and turned slowly to Riley.

"What do you mean?"

"A man's throat was torn open. *Chewed* open. He bled to death, but there wasn't much blood around the body."

"And you think Vernon did it?"

"Well, not exactly. The teeth marks weren't his. But there were . . . similarities."

"Like what?"

"I'll get to that. Since the murder was identical to that of your sister and niece, we naturally thought there might be some connection to Vernon Macy."

Benedek leaned against the counter and heaved a sigh. He would have to be careful; Riley was sharp and would quickly pick up on the fact that he knew something. It sure as hell wasn't Vernon who'd committed the murder last night, but Benedek would have to play dumb.

"So what do you want from me?" he asked.

"The victim was Chadwick Morgan Wilkes. He was an assistant editor at Penn Publishing. Ring any bells?"

"No," he lied. "Should it?"

"I thought maybe you'd know of some connection between your brother-in-law and Penn or this Wilkes guy."

"Maybe"—he cleared his throat—"Vernon had nothing to do with it."

"It's a possibility. I went to Penn today and learned a former employee was pissed off at Wilkes, so I'm going to check that out. But the details of both murders were so similar . . ."

The coffeemaker began to gurgle and Benedek turned his back to Riley to get mugs from the cupboard. He was willing to bet his next paycheck that Riley was talking about Davey Owen.

"Walter," Riley said as Benedek poured coffee, "this is all off the record, isn't it? I mean, you're not going to run to your word processor when I'm gone and put all this in print, are you?"

"No." Benedek took the mugs to the table and returned to his chair. "No. I'm working on something else anyway." He sipped his strong black coffee, desperate to change the subject.

"You wouldn't keep anything from me, would you, Walter?"

"Why would I do that?"

Riley shrugged. "Maybe you're hoping to find your brother-in-law before I do?"

"Nope. That's your job."

"Yeah." Riley chuckled humorlessly. "My job." He curled his fingers around the coffee mug handle but didn't lift it. "Sometimes I wish I was a plumber."

"Riley. Do I hear a little discontent in your voice?"

"Something like that." He wrapped both hands around the mug and looked at Benedek. "Walter, we haven't been the best of friends over the last few years."

"No, we have not."

"But even though you've been a pain in the ass at times, I've always thought you were a good reporter. I mean, you're not one of those jerks who goes around juicing things up just for a story."

Walter couldn't hold back his laughter. "Why *thank* you, Riley. You're mellowing with age. Either that or you're getting at something."

Riley stared at the table for a moment. "Yeah, sort of. Walter, how superstitious are you?"

Benedek's smile twitched away. Maybe Riley was even sharper than he'd thought.

"Well," Benedek said slowly, "if you're talking about walking under ladders or stepping on—"

"Not exactly. I mean, well, are you very religious?"

"Not at all."

"Do you believe in evil?"

Benedek leaned closer to the detective. "Look, Riley, before you start asking for my opinion, why don't you tell me what you're talking about?"

Riley fidgeted in his seat like a child in church. Benedek had never seen him so nervous and uncertain.

"The fact that your sister and niece bled to death and there was so little blood in the apartment is strange. *Too* strange. About six, seven months ago, we found some pimp dead in an alley. Stabbed. He bled to death. But there was very little blood around the body. It was decided he was killed somewhere else and moved, but between the coroner's estimated time of death and the time that the body was found was maybe ten minutes at the most."

It was Benedek's turn to fidget.

"I saw the body, Walter. That puppy was *drained*, white as a *sheet*." Riley chewed on his thumbnail, his eyes staring thoughtfully over Benedek's shoulder.

"The pimp's body disappeared from the morgue the next day. No locks busted. Just *gone*. Like he walked out."

Benedek got up from the table and got the sugar bowl from the counter. He never put sugar in his coffee, but he wanted to get away from Riley, feeling as if his secrets had suddenly become visible and he had to act busy to keep them hidden.

"The pimp," Riley went on, "your sister and niece, and now this Wilkes guy. And there've been more. I checked. Now and then, somebody gets torn open—

sometimes carefully *cut* open—and bleeds to death, but, like magic"—he spread his arms—*"no blood!"* Riley stood and walked slowly around the table holding his mug.

"I ran across something kind of odd, Walter," he continued. "In January, a woman called us to report that someone was turning her eight-year-old boy into a zombie. Said he was acting very strange, losing weight. Looked really pale, she said, like he was anemic. And she said there was a cut on his throat that wouldn't go away. She was told to take him to a doctor but said she couldn't until her next welfare check came."

Riley walked to the counter and leaned against it, facing Benedek's back.

"Two days later, Walter, she called to say she'd found him dead in his bed. She was hysterical, of course, and someone was sent out immediately." He touched the mug to his lips. "The mother was in the living room crying and carrying on. The boy was gone. A few drops of blood were found on his sheets. Never found the body." He seated himself again.

Benedek was idly turning a spoon around and around in his coffee. He cleared his throat and rubbed the back of his neck and sighed, "Okay, Riley. What are you saying?"

"Something very *un*-right is going on, Walter, something very *bad*, and nobody seems to be paying any attention. Do you know that there are people living beneath this city? Naked, crazy people who've become like animals, eating shit from the sewers, sleeping on piles of maggoty garbage? Do you know that there are rats in this city big enough to carry off a two-year-old child?"

"Well, I've heard—"

Nodding, Riley interrupted: "Yeah, you've *heard*, but you haven't given it much thought, have you? Nobody does. When something is too off-center, too awful, it gets ignored or excused. That's what I think is happening here. Something *very* off-center is going on, and it's being explained away."

"Maybe it's just not strange *enough* for anyone to think—"

"Look, Walter, I'm telling you this because we've known each other a long time and, despite everything, I trust you to keep it to yourself. And because it was, well, you're directly involved. I mean, it was your sister . . ." He hesitated. "The teeth marks on your sister and niece were definitely Vernon Macy's. But they were different from the dentist's X rays. There were two, um . . ."

Fangs. Benedek finished the sentence in his mind.

"Well, they were long and thin, like . . . like fangs." Riley looked away, seemingly embarrassed. "There's evidence that Chadwick Wilkes's killer also had them. I said there were similarities between the teeth marks? Well, the teeth are different, but they both seem to have fangs."

"Maybe they, you know, used something," Benedek said.

"Yeah," Riley replied with a curt nod, "that's what the M.E. says. 'Well, it looks like he's got fangs,' he says, 'but we all know *that* couldn't be, so he must've used some kind of needles, or something.' He's ignoring the obvious."

"The obvious?"

"Walter," Riley said, then paused. When he spoke again, the words came quickly. "Walter, if you were covering this story and I said it was my opinion that there were vampires—or at least people who *thought* they were vampires—roaming around New York sucking blood, would you make me out to be a nutcase in the paper?"

Benedek tugged on his chin. He could tell Riley the whole story right now, tell him where to find the dead pimp and all about the Midnight Club and Live Girls, and Riley would believe him, he'd believe every word because he was ripe for it. But something made Benedek hold back, something told him the time wasn't right.

"No, Riley," he said. "I wouldn't. I would quote you objectively and nothing more."

Riley nodded and smiled. "I appreciate that." He pushed his chair back and stood. "Gotta lot of work to do today. I should go. Thanks for the coffee."

Benedek stood, too. "You'd be laughed out of your job," he said simply.

Riley didn't speak again until he was standing in the corridor outside the apartment.

"Not if I can prove it."

Benedek was surprised by the man's confidence.

"You've never met my wife, Walter. She's a social worker, God bless her. She spends her days working in parts of the city I don't even want to *know* about. And I've got a sixteen-year-old daughter, too. Every day I worry about them, and that's just from knowing they're out there with all those crazy *human beings* in New York City. I'm not at all nuts about the idea of them being at the mercy of something *inhuman*. I can take a few laughs if I have to." He patted Benedek's shoulder once and said, "Have a good day, Walter."

Benedek closed the door and immediately went to the phone. He had to get to Davey before Riley did.

When he realized he didn't have Davey's number, he got it from directory assistance.

He stopped counting the rings at fifteen, and it was sometime after that Davey finally answered.

"Yeah?" His voice was thick with sleep.

"Davey? It's Walter Benedek."

"Walter?" He sounded as if he'd never heard the name before.

"Davey, remember me? Walter Benedek?"

"Just a second, I'm . . . just let me . . ." He coughed and sighed, trying to wake up. "Okay, yeah," he said.

"Listen to me, Davey, you might be in trouble. A police detective will be coming to your apartment today. Don't answer the door to anyone but me. And don't answer your phone. Just stay out of sight, okay? I'm coming over in a while. Do you understand?"

"Y-yes, but why is—"

"We'll talk about it later. Just wait for me."

He hung up the phone and hurried into the bathroom to shower and dress. He had a lot to do.

After Benedek's phone call, Davey sat up in bed and rubbed his eyes. Sleep seemed to cling to the inside of his skull like drying mud.

When he opened his eyes, he saw his reflection in the mirror across the room. Something dark was smeared around his mouth. Touching it, he found it was dry and caked.

Davey turned to the nightstand, hoping to find a washcloth or tissue to wipe away the smear, but instead he spotted a torn, red-stained index card. He read the name and address and the previous night began to come back to him in pieces.

He went into the bathroom and washed his face

with cold water, then stared at himself in the mirror for a moment, remembering the fear in Chad's eyes.

Chad Wilkes had been an asshole, a real *prick*, but Davey had *killed* him.

And it felt so good, he thought, *like a fix for a junkie, like sex, for God's sake.*

That was why a detective was coming to see him.

He turned on the shower and stepped under the stream. The hot water washed away his sleep and made what he'd done even clearer.

A mountain lion doesn't worry about whether a doe deserves to die, he thought. *The lion needs to eat, so it kills.*

But his conscience would not let him off the hook so easily.

You're not an animal! he argued with himself. *You're a human being and so was Chad!*

He leaned against the shower wall and turned his face to the water, closing his eyes.

Davey knew why he'd gotten that card from Jasmine Barny's Rolodex the night before. He wanted to know where Miss Schuman lived so when his hunger returned . . .

There had to be another way of feeding, a way that would hurt no one.

He remembered the thick reddish-brown drink Anya had ordered at the club.

House special . . . for employees and members only.

What had Walter said about blood being stored at the Midnight Club?

Stored in refrigerators in the back . . .

He would go there for what he needed.

When Davey turned off the shower, he heard knocking at the door.

He began toweling off, surprised, after the last few miserable days and nights, at how very good he felt, how strong and clear.

In his bedroom, he quietly dressed, waiting for the knocking to go away.

Benedek arrived with a brown paper bag cradled in his arm and caution in his eyes.

"Are you okay?" Benedek asked in the doorway. "I mean, you're not going to . . ."

Davey felt a pang of guilt; the man was afraid of him. "I'm okay, Walter. For now."

They sat in the living room, facing one another.

"Walter, why are you protecting me from the police? I mean, after your sister was . . ."

"You killed a man last night, am I right?"

Davey nodded hesitantly.

"Okay. I don't condone that, Davey, even though I know you had to do it, but I—"

"You *don't* know, I don't think you under—"

"I *do* understand, Davey, things are beginning to make sense. Not *good* sense, not *sane* sense, but a *kind* of sense. You died last night, you came back, and now you need blood, am I right? Like, say, a diabetic needs insulin. Now, if the police catch you, they won't be able to hold you, and if they try to kill you, they're in for the surprise of their lives."

"What do you mean?"

"How much do you know about your condition?"

"Not much."

Benedek took in a deep breath and told Davey about his experience with Vernon Macy in the back room of the club.

"The wound just kept healing up," he said with disbelief, "right in *front* of me. Jesus, I don't know how many times I had to . . ." He coughed and shook his head.

"I want to help you, Davey," he went on. "If I can keep you from slaughtering people—like *they* do—I'll be satisfied. And I'd like *you* to help *me*."

"How?"

"I'd like to walk away from this, Davey, I really would, but I can't. I know they're out there and I know what they're doing. I can't just run to the cops or whoever and say, 'You've gotta do something about these vampires, they're ruining the neighborhood,' I've got to have a place to start. I can't even take this story to my *paper*. They'd *never* print it. Even if I could *prove* it. But I have to do *something*."

He put the paper bag on his lap, reached in, and removed a wooden crucifix with a silver Christ on it. "Does this have any effect on you?" he asked.

Davey stared at the cross for a moment, then shook his head.

Benedek dropped the cross into the bag muttering, "Fuck you, Bram Stoker." To Davey: "You looked in a mirror lately?"

Davey nodded, smiling slightly. "Yes, and I have a reflection."

"Quit smirking. You think *I* like this? This could land me a quick job on the *National* fucking *Enquirer*." He took out a Ziploc bag, opened it, and reached inside. "Hold out your hand."

Davey opened his palm and Benedek gave him three cloves of garlic.

It seemed so ludicrous, Davey almost laughed. A vampire test! *Send in the form below and we will assess your potential for a rewarding career in vampirism!*

Davey caught a whiff of the garlic and started to share the joke with Benedek but when he opened his mouth to speak he found that his throat had closed and his eyes began to water and swell and his lungs burned as if on fire. He threw the smelly lumps to the floor and clutched his throat, sputtering. When he tried to stand he tumbled to the floor, retching and clawing.

It passed slowly, until his throat was open again and his vision had cleared.

Benedek had sealed the garlic back in the bag immediately; the smell was gone.

"Sorry about that," he said, helping Davey to his feet and back into his chair. "You okay?"

Davey nodded stiffly.

"Well, that's a start." Benedek wadded up the opening of the paper bag. "Listen, Davey, if I were you, I'd get the hell outta the city. Go to the country, suck on cattle, and stay out of trouble. I'm gonna do my best to bring all this out in the open in a way everyone can swallow, and don't ask me what *that* is, because I don't know yet. But when I do, it's gonna be open season on your kind. I don't think you're a bad person, and I wouldn't want anything to happen to you. Make the best of your situation now that you're in it. But do it outside of New York."

Davey was still trembling. Why had that happened? It was only *garlic*, for Christ's sake. And how could he leave the city? Where would he go? How would he live? And what would he tell Casey?

"I have to talk to Casey," he said.

"Your friend? She called my place last night. She was very worried about you."

Benedek went to the door and turned to Davey.

"You have my number," he said. "Call and let me know what you decide to do. Take care of yourself, Davey."

Davey called Casey but got no answer, then realized she would still be at work. He decided to wait until that evening.

Standing at his window, Davey closed his eyes against the daylight. Even though the sky was filled with clouds, the day seemed bright.

There was so much he didn't know about what he'd become, about what he was capable and *in*capable of doing. Maybe that was why Anya had not wanted to leave him alone.

Make the best of your situation now that you're in it.

Davey turned on the television and stretched out on the sofa to wait for the dark. As he relaxed, he felt the tingling beginnings of emptiness inside him.

When Benedek got home, he found Jackie had left work early. She was curled in her favorite chair reading a paperback. In blue jeans and a brown plaid shirt, she looked deliciously comfortable.

Benedek held two bags in his arms: the paper bag he'd taken to Davey's and a white plastic bag filled with garlic. The strange look he'd gotten from the Asian clerk at the produce market would be nothing compared to the reaction he was sure he'd get from Jackie; she'd probably think he'd gone around the bend.

Benedek had planned to set the garlic up—around all the doors and windows in the apartment—before Jackie got home. Now he wouldn't have that edge.

"You're home," he said on his way into the kitchen.

"So're you," she replied, and he could hear the smile in her voice. "We should get to know each other, we have so much in common."

He put the bags down on the counter, took his coat to the bedroom, and went to Jackie's side. He slid his fingers into her smooth white hair, bent down, and kissed her.

"Where've you been?" she asked.

"All over town." He put his arm around her and sat on the arm of the chair. "How come you're home so early?"

"My last two patients canceled and I'm exhausted, so I came home to do absolutely nothing."

"Good."

"Walter . . ." She pulled her head back and looked up at him. "Are you okay?"

"Tired."

"You look exhausted." She reached up and stroked his cheek, wincing at the scratch of his whiskers.

"Need a shave, I guess," he said.

"You sure everything's okay, babe?"

Through the worry in her face, Benedek could see love in her eyes and a gentle warmth passed through him. "Nothing to worry about," he said softly, kissing her again.

"Walter, why do you smell like garlic?"

"I bought some."

"Did you *roll* in it, or something?"

"No." He chuckled. "I, uh, bought quite a bit."

"Are you cooking tonight?"

No, not yet, he thought. *Work up to it.*

"If you want me to," he said, smiling.

She tossed her book onto the sofa and wrapped her arms around his chest with a sigh. "I've needed a hug all day. I don't care *what* you smell like."

"Me too." He held her close. "Bad day?"

"Mrs. Bennet lost her baby." Her voice was muffled

against him. "This is their third try. I was hoping . . . I don't think she's going to be able to try again."

"Sorry."

"Hazards of the trade." She looked up at him again. "The mortuary called. They left a message on the machine."

"And?"

"They wanted to know if . . . if you were sure you didn't want some kind of, you know, ceremony before the cremation."

"They're doing it today?"

She nodded.

Benedek's mouth became dry suddenly. He swallowed hard and said, "I'll call them in a while." He looked at his watch; it was a little before three. "Would you like a drink?"

She reached over to the lamp table and produced an empty glass. "Another brandy, Jeeves."

Benedek took the glass and went into the kitchen. He poured her drink, picked up the bag of garlic, and returned to the living room.

"Thanks. Aren't you going to have one?"

"Not just yet," he said, going into the bedroom. He hoped she wouldn't follow him. He took a couple cloves from the bag and went to the bedroom window. It was a long rectangular window that opened on each end. He pressed the two cloves to the windowsill and scrubbed them back and forth, grinding them in. He wrinkled his nose at the smell. He rubbed the garlic up and down the sides and above the window, then left the cloves on the sill. He was taking a couple more from the bag when Jackie stepped into the room.

She held the wooden crucifix before her, turning it around a few times in her hand.

"Walter?" she said quietly. She needed to say no more. They had long since reached the level of familiarity at which questions could be asked with a word, an inflection of the voice, sometimes a single facial expression.

"I bought that today," he said, "for a friend."

"What are you . . ." She sniffed. "Walter, what are you *doing?*" She placed the crucifix on the dresser and stepped toward Benedek as he went to the other window in the room. "Walter, what's going on?"

"I'll explain in a minute. Just let me—"

"I'd like to know *now.*"

He turned to her and saw that she was not only serious, she was worried. Benedek put the cloves on the sill. "I would've told you sooner," he said, "if I'd had something to tell you. Until last night, I didn't."

"Tell me what?" she asked, fear softening her voice.

They sat on the bed together, and slowly and carefully, Benedek told her everything.

Chapter Fourteen

Casey had no idea where she was or how long she'd been passing in and out of sleep. Sometimes she wasn't even sure if she was dreaming, or if the sounds she kept hearing in the dark little room were real. They came and went like a breeze: cries, laughter, scratching, voices: ". . . smell it . . . so hungry . . ."

She didn't know if it was daytime or night, if a week had passed or an hour.

After Shideh had doused the candle and left the room, Casey had wanted only to sleep. She'd felt at ease and content and groggy. As she slept, she dreamed of Shideh's touch, of her angelic white hair and her red eyes, of the way her tongue felt inside Casey. Once—Casey was sure it had not been a dream—Shideh stepped out of the darkness smiling, her white skin bare.

"It's time again, love," she'd whispered, lowering herself over Casey's face. She'd smelled Shideh's sex as it gently came to rest on her mouth.

Their lovemaking had seemed to last forever, ending, as before, with the sucking that filled her up so.

Afterward, Shideh had untied her and given her a cushion to lie on. Once she was alone again, Casey fought to stay awake. If she could muster the strength to get up now that she was no longer tied, perhaps she could find a way out, or at least find out where she *was*. Her arms and legs, however, felt like lead; she could not lift them from the cushion. She was too weary even to be angry. So she slept.

The dreams continued: murky red dreams that swirled and waved. And the sounds . . .

Frantic, purposeful scratching and thumping.

Garbled voices:

". . . can *smell* it . . ."

". . . it's *mine* . . ."

". . . she'll let us . . ."

Casey twisted and tossed on the cushion.

When she was finally awake—when she was *certain* she was awake and the dreams had stopped—she realized someone had lit the candle again. And she could still hear the sounds. They had *not* been a dream.

She tried to sit up. "Who's there?" The room seemed to be shifting around her, but it was only the candlelight wavering over the walls and floor.

Someone was hunching in the corner.

The stillness and silence of the figure made Casey's chest tighten with fear. Trying to lift herself up on her elbows, she rolled off the cushion and thudded onto the hard floor. She turned her head toward the corner.

A moment later, she laughed—a brief, hissing laugh through her nose.

It was a table with a small lamp on it.

But what was that incessant thumping? Casey was certain it was in the room with her. Then she saw the floor move. Her eyes were level with the flat surface, and with the next heavy *thunk*, she saw a section of the floor just a few feet before her rise only for an instant.

Casey squeezed her eyes shut, then opened them, trying to focus. With two more thumps, the section of the floor jerked up twice. A trapdoor.

"Who's there?" Casey asked again. Her throat was so dry, it hurt to speak.

There was a harsh, urgent whisper, but the words were garbled.

Someone beneath the floor was trying to *speak* to her.

"*What?*" she snapped, crawling toward the voice.

". . . to *help* you! We want to *help* you!"

Was it another dream? Was she still asleep?

"Davey?" she asked hopefully. She wanted to cry with relief. "Who are you?"

"Friends. We've come to get you out."

"Yes," she breathed. "Please get me out of here!"

"Open the trapdoor." The voice sounded thick, as if it were coming through a throat clogged with phlegm.

"How?" Casey propped herself up on her hands and knees. "How do I open it?" The room swayed a bit each time she moved.

"Pull the bolts on the—"

There was a sharp whisper of protest from another voice, but it was quickly silenced.

"Pull the bolts and open the door," the first voice continued. "We'll get you out."

Casey swept her hand back and forth over the floor. She felt the edges of the trapdoor, the hinges, a bolt.

She fumbled with it, slid it back.

"The other one, too!" the voice hissed anxiously. "On the other side!"

Casey could not move fast enough. She didn't know who they were or how they had found her, but that didn't matter. She wanted *out!*

Her arms collapsed beneath her and she slammed to the floor, but reached out, groped with her fingers until she found the other bolt. Her hand tried to get a grip, but she couldn't.

"*Open* it!" the voice growled.

"I'm *trying*, I'm *trying!*"

With another thump, the unbolted side of the door rose a couple of inches, then slammed shut. Stale air gushed from beneath the floor and Casey nearly gagged at the smell of rotting meat.

Her hand recoiled from the bolt as if scalded.

"Open the fucking door, cunt!" the gurgling voice demanded. "*Open* it!"

Casey backed away from the trapdoor.

The free corner rose again, but did not snap shut. Casey saw two eyes, large and rheumy, peering at her from the darkness; the smell became almost unbearable.

"Pull the fucking bolt or I'll *break* it!" The eyes widened and Casey felt her breath being pulled from her lungs and the eyes reaching behind her own, sliding into her skull like a mist and tugging on her nerves, her muscles, until her arm was lifting with a jerky motion, reaching for the bolt again.

"Open the door and I'll *help* you."

Her fingers trembled with resistance, but the creature's eyes were too powerful. Their hypnotic gaze pulled her arm closer to the bolt.

I can't let this happen again, she thought desperately,

I won't, but the thought was snatched from her mind like a cookie from a jar.

"You can come down here with *us*," the voice went on. The anger was gone; the creature spoke soothingly with the faintest hint of a childlike singsong rhythm bobbing beneath its words. "There's a *win* . . . dow . . ."

Her mouth formed the word *no*, but her voice was not there.

"We'll keep you safe from *her, safe*. You *know* what she's *doing* to you, *don't* you?"

Another voice hissed accusingly, there was a struggle beneath the floor, and the door slammed shut.

The eyes were gone.

Casey gasped, as if suddenly released from a stranglehold, and jerked her hand away, collapsing onto her back.

"No!" the voice spat. "I want her *now*, I don't *want* to *wait*, the *smell* . . . I want her *now!*"

The other voice whispered reproachfully.

Casey stared at the door, realizing that whatever was down there was far worse than what had been happening in the room. She had to relock the trapdoor, had to pull the bolt back so the corner of the door could not be lifted. She dragged herself over the floor, stretched out a watery-weak arm, and splayed her fingers toward the bolt when the corner of the door lifted with a sharp creaking of wood and a hand—a dreadful hand with puffy, purplish skin and pink, infected lumps that glistened with draining fluids and sharp gray bone sticking from the fingers where flesh had been torn away—clutched Casey's wrist firmly and pulled her arm into the stinking darkness beneath the floor, pulled it in up to the elbow until she could feel hot sticky breath on her palm and a rough tongue sliding up her middle finger.

Casey closed her eyes tightly, knowing what would happen if she looked through the opening, knowing that one glance of those two powerful eyes would take from her what little strength remained. She turned her head away and pleaded, "Let *go* of me let *go* oh Jesus Christ *please* let *go!*" She jerked hard on her arm, but the hand would not let go. The skin was rough and clammy and the naked bones that stuck through the tips of two of the fingers threatened to break through Casey's flesh.

There was a rush of movement in the darkness below, the sound of sighing voices.

There were more of them.

She felt another hand on her arm and opened her eyes, screaming because there were three more arms pulling on her, hands with fingers missing or no fingers at all, and pulling its way up from the darkness, squeezing between the arms, was something not at all human: a knotted, twisted claw.

She screamed until she could scream no longer, then sucked in a deep breath and screamed again.

"Stop!" The voice came from behind Casey and was so loud it seemed to fill the room. "Let her *go!*"

Casey turned her head to see Shideh towering over her, flat round nostrils flaring with rage.

All but one of the hands dropped away and slid back into the darkness.

"Let *go!*" Shideh ordered again.

"I won't wait *anymore!*" the voice beneath the door gurgled. "I'm *hungry!*"

Shideh bent down, took Casey's arm, and pulled it out until the bloated, diseased hand was visible. She wrapped her graceful fingers around the creature's wrist and flicked her arm upward. The wrist broke with the sound of a crisp celery stick being pulled from its stalk. An animal-like wail rose from below and the door clapped shut. Something fell heavily beneath the door and the wailing continued for several seconds before dissolving into a pitiful whimper and dying away.

"Are you hurt?" Shideh asked softly, throwing the bolt with her foot.

Casey could not reply; her sobs had gained such a momentum that, even though the hands and that god-awful claw—*Jesus*, she kept thinking, *what was that, what the fuck was it?*—were gone, she couldn't stop.

Shideh bent down and, with no effort, bundled Casey up in her arms, carried her to the cushion, and gently lowered her, then sat beside her.

Casey's sobs began to subside as Shideh stroked her cheek. When her tears stopped flowing, Casey realized that she was not out of danger. This woman was a monster, not even human, no matter how soft her skin, how gentle her voice, how beautiful her *eyes* . . .

Casey closed her eyes again and pressed her head back hard into the cushion.

"Stay away from that door," Shideh said. "Don't even go near it."

"What are they?" Casey asked.

Shideh did not answer for a moment, as if carefully examining her reply. "My children," she said finally. "Like you. But they were too quick to leave my care, too quick to feed on their own. They fed on bad blood. Blood filled with chemicals, dangerous chemicals. Drugs. Others ingested blood that carried the few diseases to which we are not immune. They're sick, crippled. But I care for them. There's a window down there and they could leave if they wanted, but they know better. They can't fend for themselves. They need me."

As she listened to Shideh talk, Casey's eyes filled with tears and her stomach lurched sickeningly at the woman's words.

"Like *me?*" Casey hissed, still not opening her eyes. "What do you *mean*, like *me?*"

Shideh touched Casey's hair. "I thought I'd explained that to you already. I'm changing you, giving you something you never thought you could have. After tonight, you will no longer be the woman you are now. You will be able to change your shape, your appearance, with a thought. You'll be stronger than you thought possible. If you cut yourself, your flesh will heal within minutes. So will your muscles, your organs. If you look out for yourself, Casey, you can live . . . forever."

"No," Casey whispered, shaking her head, trying to push Shideh's hand from her hair, "no, that's not true, it can't be true, you're lying to me."

Shideh stretched out beside Casey and put her lips to Casey's ear. "I have slept with kings, Casey. With emperors, pharaohs, queens, and princesses. I have lived in castles that are now ruins, in cities that no longer exist. I've watched battles from the sky and fed on the dying and wounded, men you've read about in history books. It's not a lie, Casey. After tonight, you will be virtually immortal. You'll laugh at the ones you leave behind, at their beliefs about you. Crosses and daylight. Holy water. None of it's real, Casey, they're just fantasies, things they've dreamed up to make them feel they have some power. They don't. You'll be a god, Casey, invincible, *if* you allow me to teach you what you need to know."

Casey kept shaking her head, eyes tightly closed, murmuring, "No, no."

"You must let me teach you about your weaknesses. There are only a few, but they can be fatal. A nasty allergic reaction to garlic, a minor sensitivity to bright light, bloods that must be avoided. Otherwise, you'll be like *them*, the ones down there in the furnace room."

"No . . ."

"You don't want that, do you?"

"Please, let me go."

"Think of yourself as my daughter until you're able to break away and live on your own. Until you understand your power."

"No, just let me go, *please!*" Her voice rose to a cry on the last word.

Shideh placed her thumbs gently over Casey's eyes and lifted her lids. "You can't leave," she said. "It's too late for that now."

Casey jerked her head from left to right.

"I don't *want* to be like you!" she shouted.

Shideh straddled her and held Casey's head still in her large white hands. "It doesn't matter what you want, Casey," Shideh said softly, smiling. "I want *you*."

She leaned forward and placed her mouth over Casey's.

Although she couldn't really afford it, Beth decided as she walked into the dirty dusk on Avenue C to take a cab instead of the bus. She had to be at work by seven, and it was almost six-thirty. When a cab finally pulled over, she got in and gave the driver Davey's address; she'd get to the Union a bit late, but she didn't care.

Stupid idea, she thought as she sat back in the seat and tried to get comfortable. That wasn't easy; Vince had thrown her a couple good ones before she left.

Her left shoulder ached and she had an ugly bruise on her right upper arm. Her lower lip was cut.

Beth knew she should wait until tomorrow afternoon when Davey would be at work. She still had the key—Beth always tried to hang on to keys, knowing that, sooner or later, they'd come in handy—so she could slip in while he wasn't there, get what she'd left behind, and get out. He'd never know the difference.

But she wanted to see him. She knew that for her to show up would probably hurt him. Okay, so she was selfish, she admitted it. It was no surprise, she'd known it for a long time, and unless he was totally blind, Davey had known it, too. How could he *not* think so, the way she'd bitched about never having enough money, the way she'd gone out with other guys who *did* have money.

Of course, money wasn't the only thing. If it were, she sure as hell wouldn't be with Vince. He had money, sure, but there were other guys with more of it, guys who would treat her better. No, that wasn't all.

Vince's apartment was a virtual highway of drugs. Pills, heroin, coke, *everything*. Not that she needed them, but once in a while, maybe an upper or two now and then, maybe a snort. She wasn't like Vince, or the women Vince hung out with; she *wasn't* a *junkie*.

Not yet, a nasty little voice sneered in the back of her mind. A voice she ignored.

Davey didn't know about the drugs. Sure, they'd smoked some grass once in a while, but nothing more. Davey wasn't *like* that. Maybe that had been part of his attraction, that innocence and naiveté.

That was part of the reason she was going to his apartment this evening instead of tomorrow while he was out—she wanted to see those little-boy eyes again, those eyes that she knew would look at her with affection, despite everything. She wasn't going to take advantage of that affection anymore. She just wanted to *see* it. Then she would get her things and go.

When the cab stopped, she paid the driver. She couldn't afford to leave a tip and ignored the angry remark he tossed over his shoulder as she got out.

Upstairs, she stood at Davey's door clenching her fists nervously at her sides. Maybe he wouldn't let her in. Maybe those little-boy eyes were gone.

Her first knock wasn't loud enough, she knew that, and she had to take in a deep, steadying breath before she could knock again.

No answer.

"Davey?"

Maybe he wasn't home after all.

She knocked again, waited, then fished through her purse for the key.

The television was playing; the news was on. There was movement in the bedroom.

"Davey?" she called again, a bit louder.

He came to the bedroom doorway, startled.

Beth timidly lifted a hand in greeting and smiled. "Hi," she said softly.

Davey said nothing, he just stood there in jeans and a gray shirt with the sleeves rolled up, his hands resting on the doorjamb. His eyes were wide, as if she'd caught him at something. He looked . . . different.

"I still had the key, so I let myself in," she explained. "I left some things here. I think. I mean, I can't find them, so I figured they were still here. Three pairs of shoes and my hand mirror. Remember the hand mirror my grandma gave me? I can't find it. So I thought I'd . . ."

He still hadn't moved a muscle.

"Davey, are you okay?"

He slowly nodded his head. "Yeah."

"I hope you don't mind that I just, you know, came in like this."

He shrugged.

Yes, he definitely looked different. There was something about his eyes. They were so round and strangely alert, like maybe he had a buzz on. Not Davey . . .

"So," she said, "how are you?"

"Okay." He finally moved, stepping out of the doorway. "You?"

"Fine." She moved toward him to go into the bedroom for her shoes.

"Your lip is . . ." He swallowed and looked away from her, almost as if he were ashamed. "It's cut."

She said nothing, went to the closet, and poked around until she found them. "You got a bag, or something?"

She heard him go into the kitchen. He came in with a brown paper bag and she stuffed the shoes into it.

"Have you seen my mirror?" she asked.

He turned away again; he looked nervous, maybe even a little afraid.

"No, I haven't. Check the bathroom."

Beth shouldered by him and heard his sharp intake of breath. "Davey, *what is wrong?*" she asked, more harshly than she intended.

His back was to her, his head bowed for a moment. Then he straightened up and lifted a hand to his mouth.

"You smell nice," he said.

Beth smiled. He wasn't *that* different.

"Thanks." She went into the bathroom and, after a

few moments of looking, found the mirror in the back of a drawer to the left of the sink. It was really pretty ugly; it had a gold handle and frilly frame with four sparkly rhinestones around the glass. But she didn't want it for its looks. She put it in the bag and went back to the living room.

"You're living with Vince again, aren't you?" Davey asked, still not looking at her.

"Yes. For a while, anyway," she lied. "The apartment's kind of roomy, so, you know, I don't have to be with him all the time. Not a great area. It's on Avenue C near Fourteenth, but it's kinda cute. The building, I mean. A red brick place, kinda rundown, but, oh, I don't know."

"He hit you."

Beth touched her slightly swollen lip. "I ran into a door."

"He hit you."

She started for the door. "Okay, so he hit me, so what? Maybe I *need* a good whack once in a while, you know? Maybe if *you'd* given me one now and then I'd still be *here!*" She immediately regretted the words and turned to him. "Davey, I'm sorry, I shouldn't have said that. I don't want you to think—"

Davey spun around and the look on his face cut off Beth's words. His lips were pulled back tightly, his teeth clenched. His nostrils flared and his head was craned forward slightly, as if he were sniffing the air.

"You should go," he said quietly in a tone she'd never heard before. Not angry, not hurt, but threatening.

"Okay," she said, "I will, but I just want you to know that—"

"Go," he whispered.

"Jesus, Davey, what's wrong, you look like you're gonna pass out." She stepped toward him, expecting him to collapse at any moment, but Davey took a quick step back.

"*Please*, Beth," he said, and for an instant the old Davey was back, the little-boy eyes looked at her softly.

But only for an instant.

The softness left his face, and his mouth opened wide as he turned away from her. For a half second, she thought she saw something different about his teeth, but his back was to her now and he was walking stiffly toward the bedroom.

"Please, just go away *now*, Beth!" he snapped. He slammed the bedroom door and she thought she heard him sob on the other side.

Beth rolled up the opening of the bag and left the apartment. In the corridor, she fought to hold back her own tears, to ignore the nasty bite of guilt in her stomach.

"I'm sorry, Davey," she breathed as she headed for the stairs.

Walter Benedek was not anxious to leave the comfort of his dreamless sleep, so when the mattress beneath him stirred slightly, he rolled over and drifted off again.

It had not been easy convincing Jackie of his story, but he'd kept at it. Having nothing she could see, or perhaps touch, had not made it any easier; Jackie was stubborn and reluctant to be convinced of anything without solid proof. She was finally swayed by the fact that Benedek possessed the very same skepticism she did. Then her disbelief turned slowly to fear. They'd sat on the bed as Benedek told her of the past three days' events. As he went on, they moved closer and closer together, until they were leaning against the headboard in one another's arms.

"You're shaking, Walter," she'd said.

"That's because I'm terrified. I'm sure they've found Vernon by now. They'll know I did it to him, and they'll come after me. And you."

She'd looked at him then with the stern expression she took on whenever there was too much of anything for her to handle: too much pain, work, information.

"Then let's keep them out of here," she said to him. "I'll help you."

Together, they'd spread the garlic around all the windows and even around the outside of the apartment door.

Afterward, sick of the smell of garlic, Jackie had taken a bubble bath. Benedek had joined her. They'd sat in the warm water for nearly an hour, their legs intertwined, Benedek smoking leisurely, Jackie drinking a bit more brandy than usual. When they got out, they'd gently dried one another off then gone to bed, where they'd made long slow love for the first time in far too long.

Lying close, they'd drifted into a deep, solid sleep.

Until the mattress had moved and Benedek had stirred, trying to fall back to sleep.

Until the whispers . . .

Benedek grunted, swimming gradually to the surface of his sleep.

It was Jackie's voice.

Something was making a heavy sliding sound.

Benedek opened his eyes and squinted.

Jackie was sliding the window open.

"What, hon," he mumbled thickly. "Whasamatter?"

There were two hands pressing against the windowpane as Jackie lifted it, but something was wrong, because they were on the *outside* of the window, and that simply could not be because their apartment was on the eighteenth floor.

Jackie stood stiffly at the window wearing her short, thin nightgown.

"Jackie?" Benedek snapped, his sleepiness leaving him quickly as he sat up on the bed.

Then he saw the face outside the window, a smiling face that seemed to bob up and down slightly in the mist, its eyes lost in deep shadows:

Cedric Palacios.

Perhaps it was a nightmare, because he suddenly found it nearly impossible to move, as if he were wading waist-deep in honey.

"Jackie, get away from the window!" he shouted, but she seemed not to hear him.

Jackie pushed the window up all the way and Cedric Palacios's arms moved forward as if to embrace her . . .

"Christ, Jackie, *mooove!*" His legs were thick and stiff and numb, two tree trunks attached to the bottom of his body.

But then they pulled back suddenly and Palacios made a painful groaning sound and retched as he backed away from the window but did not take his gaze from Jackie.

The garlic, Benedek thought, *it's working thank God it's working!*

She did not move from the window, no matter how loud Benedek shouted, "Jackie, get *away*, get *away!*" and Benedek knew that she *couldn't* hear him, she was hearing something else, something Cedric Palacios was telling her, *sending* to her without words, because Benedek knew she would not be standing at that window if she knew what she was doing.

He tried to lunge toward her, to throw her away from those long powerful arms that were reaching through the window, that slid under Jackie's arms and began to pull her out of the room until her feet dangled from the window, and the thing that bothered Benedek the most, the thing he knew he would remember most vividly about that moment for the rest of his life, was that her legs did not kick, they just hung from the sill limply, slipping away like ropes over the side of a boat being pulled downward by the anchor as it dropped to the deep dark bottom, and Benedek threw himself forward hard with his arms outstretched and his fingers clawed to grab her ankles, but the legs kept moving and his knuckles only grazed Jackie's calves, they just touched for a moment her skin, feeling the slight hint of bristle that had not been shaved, such a good feeling, a safe, familiar feeling he knew he would never know again except in his memory, the *last* feeling he would ever have of Jackie Laslo because she was gone, she was in the arms of Cedric Palacios eighteen stories in the air and Palacios was smiling as he held her tightly to his chest, and as her arms wrapped around him, he said in a voice as smooth as the movement of a snake, "Garlic. You *are* a very clever man."

Still on the floor, Benedek wanted to scream Jackie's name, to make her snap out of whatever stupor she was in, but he couldn't, his throat had closed with rage and horror at the knowledge that Cedric Palacios would probably be the last person—the last creature—ever to hold Jackie in her life, and he could only watch as they were swallowed by the night.

"Maybe *too* clever, huh?" Palacios sneered.

And they were gone.

There was a sound in the otherwise silent room and

it took Benedek a moment to realize it was coming from him. It was a pitiful babbling sound, childlike and helpless. He clambered to his feet and went to the window. Clutching the sill, he leaned out.

Crisp air hit his face and speckled it with tiny beads of chilly moisture.

"Jackie," he wheezed, "Jackie, sweet Jesus, Jackie." Tears rolled unnoticed down his cheeks.

Where would Palacios take her? The club? Probably. How long would they let her live?

He hoped it would be long enough for him to help her.

It was time to tell Riley. The detective was the only one prepared to believe the story.

Benedek knew he had Riley's home number around the house somewhere but hadn't the patience to look for it. He went to the phone and punched out the number of the police department, trying to forget the image of her acquiescent form being pulled away from him.

He shifted from his right foot to his left, rubbing his eyes and forehead with a big hand as he waited for an answer on the other end of the line.

"Yes," he said when he finally heard a voice, "I'm, uh, my name is Walter, uh, Benedek, I'm a friend of Kenneth Riley, and I need to speak to him right now, it's an emergency."

The woman on the line hesitated for a long moment. "Who did you say you are?"

"Walter Benedek. I'm a reporter for the *Times*." He made an effort to speak coherently, steadily. "Is he in?"

"No, no, he isn't in. How well do you know Detective Riley?"

"What do you mean, how well do I . . ." Benedek

suddenly had to lean against the wall so he wouldn't collapse, because he knew she was holding something back. "What's happened?" he asked, his voice gravelly.

"Detective Riley is dead."

Benedek slid down the wall until he was sitting on the floor.

"He and"—the officious-sounding woman cleared her throat—"his family were found murdered a little over an hour ago."

The receiver clattered to the floor. Benedek felt as if everything were ready to shut down: his body, his mind, his control. He could almost hear the seams splitting in the fabric of his life.

"Hello?" the woman said. "Hello? Are you all right? Are you there?"

Benedek didn't hear her. He heard nothing but the slowly building rumble of fear in his skull.

He should have told Riley what he knew when he had the chance. Too late now: *they'd* gotten to him first. And Benedek was certain they wouldn't rest until *he* was dead, too.

That left Davey Owen as his only remaining source of help, and if Davey was unwilling to work with him, he would have to go public with the story sooner than he'd planned.

Benedek lifted the receiver to his ear.

"I'm . . . I'm sorry to hear that," he said tremulously. "Is there anything I can do for you?"

"No. Thank you. I just wanted to talk to . . . him." Benedek slowly lifted himself to his feet and hung up the phone.

He would call Davey. But not yet. He needed just a little time to pull himself together. Just a little time.

* * *

Davey sat on the bus staring out the window, trying to focus his attention on the passing lights outside. His mind kept returning, however, to Beth.

Why did she have to come over that night? Why couldn't she have just *left* the goddamned shoes and mirror at his place?

He kept thinking about the cut on her lip.

He closed his eyes at the memory of how desperately he'd wanted to kiss her, to put his mouth over that cut.

Two young girls sat in the seat ahead of him, laughing and whispering to one another. The girl directly before him had platinum hair and exquisitely smooth flesh.

Davey couldn't stop thinking about what was beneath that flesh. He couldn't ignore the burning emptiness in his gut, the trembling of his hands. The bus was not moving fast enough; he wondered if he would get to the club in time.

The bus stopped and several more people boarded. There were no more seats, so they stood, swaying with the bus's movement, hanging on to the rails.

At the next stop, a few more got on.

The girl ahead of him lit a cigarette and turned toward the window to exhale the smoke, laughing at something her friend had said. Davey looked at her throat. The cords in her neck tightened when she turned, and he could see the pulsing of her jugular vein just beneath her skin.

Davey jerked his head away, looked out the window.

But he could *smell* them all, crowded into the bus, their hearts pounding . . .

When the bus stopped again, Davey stood quickly, pushed down the aisle, and went through the rear exit.

The cold air made him feel better. He began walking fast, head bowed, trying to ignore the few people he passed on the sidewalk. He wasn't far from the Midnight Club, only a few blocks.

When he pushed through the door of the club, Malcolm smiled broadly at him.

"Mr. Owen," he said quietly, "how are you this evening?"

He nodded distractedly. "Fine, thanks. I'm here to see Shideh."

Malcolm cocked a brow. "I don't know if she's here, Mr. Owen. Why don't you go in and ask for her." He pushed the button on the pedestal and the double doors swung silently open. A flood of sound poured through: loud music, laughter, glasses clinking together in toasts.

Davey stepped through the doors and was greeted by a tall blond woman. She smiled. She had round, doelike blue eyes and a slightly crooked smile that looked warm and trusting.

"He*ll*o, Mr. Owen," she said in a low, smoky voice. "We were hoping you'd come in tonight. My name's Robbie. Can I get you a table?"

She had olive skin, straight white teeth, so friendly and warm. She spoke as if she knew him, had *expected* him.

Of course, he thought. *I'm a member now.*

Davey wondered what she'd given up for this life. A man who loved her? A family? How long had she been dead?

"Mr. Owen?"

Davey looked into her warm, heartbreaking eyes and suddenly conjured a vision of Robbie biting out a man's tongue in the middle of a long, deep kiss.

"Would you like a table?" she asked again.

"No. No, I'm looking for Shideh."

"Oh, she's not here yet. She won't be in until eleven-thirty."

"Is she at Live Girls?"

"Yes, I think so."

Davey nodded and started to turn, but felt Robbie's hand fall gently on his shoulder.

"Are you sure you wouldn't like a drink, Mr. Owen?" she asked.

The concern in her voice made Davey angry, made him want to jerk away from her hand and hurry out.

But his stomach was gurgling, his head ached, there was a burning beneath his skin that he knew would only get worse if he did not . . .

Robbie leaned toward him and looked at him with a sly smile, as if she knew a secret he had not told her. "You look like you could use a house special," she said.

Davey's fists clenched at his sides. He didn't want to stay, he didn't want to be with *them*. But if he didn't have the drink, he would get what he needed elsewhere. From *someone*. He nodded with resignation.

"Yeah. I'll have a drink."

"Let me take your coat."

She stood behind him and slipped his coat off, folding it over her arm. "This way," she said with a toss of her head.

He followed her into the swirling smoke and laughing crowd.

Robbie seated him at a table near the front, said she would be back in a moment, and went to get his drink.

Davey looked around him. The club looked different than it had the first time he'd come. The *people* looked different. He somehow knew which of them were members and which were not. Something about the way they moved, the way they smiled. Something in their eyes.

"Here you are," Robbie said, returning with a tall glass of reddish-brown liquid. "I'll be back in a bit to check up on you." She smiled again, gave him a wink, and walked away.

Davey touched the glass. It was chilled. He lifted it, touched it to his lips, and began to drink.

Casey opened her eyes and watched the dark room spin around her. She didn't know how long she'd been sleeping.

Something beneath her moved and she started to get up.

"No, no, it's okay," Shideh whispered. "Lie back."

She was lying in Shideh's arms. Her head rested against the woman's breast.

Shideh stroked Casey's hair, leaned forward, and looked into her eyes. She smiled.

"How do you feel, love?" she asked softly.

Casey wasn't quite sure *how* she felt. The last thing she remembered was having her mouth on Shideh's throat, feeling Shideh's fingers inside her, getting horribly ill and being unable to breathe then fading away until . . . nothing.

"Casey?" Shideh prompted gently. "It's all finished now. How do you *feel?*"

Casey gave it a few moments of careful thought, then looked up into those red eyes.

"I'm hungry," she said.

* * *

Davey felt heavy as he stepped off the bus in Times Square. The drink had left a sour taste in his mouth. His hunger had calmed, but it had not gone away.

He swept the black curtain aside with his hand and stepped into Live Girls.

"Tokens," he said at the cage, shoving his bill under the bars.

The hand reached out of the darkness. The fingers uncurled like a spider's legs and the coins dropped into Davey's palm.

Without hesitation, he went down the corridor, around the corner, and straight to the booth in which he always met Anya. He pulled the door open, stepped inside and locked it, then dropped all four tokens into the coin box.

The panel began to creep upward over the glass.

He saw her legs.

But they *weren't* her legs. They were different, shorter, the hips were rounder . . .

Davey began to feel sick.

He staggered backward a step and bumped the door. Reaching out his arms, he touched the glass as the panel rose further.

"Casey!" The name twisted itself out of his throat.

She was naked and touching herself; she looked stiff and uncomfortable. She lowered her eyes to Davey and her lips silently mouthed his name, as if she weren't sure it was he.

Davey's mind raced with questions: How long had she been here? What had they done to her?

Casey leaned toward him slowly and put her hands over his on the other side of the glass. She looked frightened and confused. Something about her eyes—

a subtle, familiar coldness—told him exactly what had been done to her. And he knew it was his fault. He wanted to hold her, ask her to forgive him.

"I'm sorry," he rasped, pressing his hands to the glass, "I'm so sorry."

"Davey, I'm scared," she said, her voice muffled. "Take me out of here, Davey, *please.*"

He began nodding his head quickly. "I will, Casey, I promise."

She leaned even closer.

"I'm so *hungry,* Davey."

"Oh God," he breathed, closing his eyes and leaning his forehead against the dirty glass. He'd done it again, he'd gotten her involved in *his* problem. But *this* time was going to be different, *this* time he was going to act. He was going to make the best of his situation, just as Walter Benedek had said.

This time, he was going to grab the short and curlies.

Davey lifted his head. It seemed there were two people looking at him through Casey's eyes: someone who was willing to kill to satisfy her hunger, and someone else who was desperately afraid.

"Casey, I'm going to get you out of here," he said. "I don't know how, but I'm *going* to, I swear."

She nodded, sucking in her lower lip.

"Is there an exit in the back?" he asked. "Another way in or out?"

She frowned and shook her head. "I don't know. There's a window . . ."

"Where?"

"It's beneath the building, I think. A basement."

"*Where?*"

"I'm not sure, I don't know."

The panel started to close again.

"But Davey, you have to be careful because there are—"

"Which side of the building is it on?"

"I don't know, I don't *know!*"

The panel closed.

Casey peered through the opening below. "She's going to come back soon, Davey, to see if I've fed."

"I'll go. But I'm going to get you out," he said slowly, emphasizing each word, as if to convince himself as much as Casey. "I promise."

"Be careful."

Davey reached through the opening and touched her face for just a moment. Her skin was cool.

Davey burst from the booth and rounded the corner on his way out.

"Davey!"

Anya was hurrying toward him in a gray robe. "Davey," she said quietly, "I heard you were here. I'm supposed to be working but I—"

He backed her against the wall and whispered, "*Listen* to me. There's a friend of mine back there working a booth. A *good friend* of mine. I want to know who the fuck—"

She smiled. "What does it matter?"

"What do you *mean,* what does it matter?"

"Davey, we have to talk. There are things you need to know before you start feeding."

"You mean before I start *killing* people?" he snapped, leaning closer to her. "I've already done that *once.*"

"But you have to be careful. This city is full of very sick people. Their blood can hurt you. There are things you have to look for."

"Like?"

"Junkies—there are chemicals that can be very damaging. People who are frail, sick; it takes *time* to know the signs, that's why you need my help."

"I don't *want* your help."

Davey pivoted away from her to leave, but she took his arm and pulled him back.

"I know what you're thinking, Davey. You think you can avoid hurting anyone by going to the club and drinking the specials." She smiled. "Right?"

He said nothing.

"It won't work," she whispered. "It will hold you for a while, but not long. You need the blood while it's still warm, Davey. You *need* to feel it pumping into your mouth."

His lips twitched and he took his eyes from hers.

"You don't have to kill, Davey. I know it's hard not to, at first. The hunger is always strongest when it's new. But you don't *have* to kill. You can take what you need without even being noticed. But it takes time to become disciplined. Time and help, help that I can give you. If you like, you could work at the club. Like Cedric. You can feed and make money and no one will be the wiser. That's why we have the club. And Live Girls. And if you work at the club"—she smiled and affectionately squeezed his arm—"we can be together more."

He jerked his arm from her and took a step back. "I may be *like* you," he whispered, "but I'm not *one* of you." He backed a few steps down the corridor, then spun around and went through the black curtain.

As he hurried out, he heard her say quietly, "You *still* have to feed, Davey."

Outside he became dizzy and weak. He ducked into

the alley that ran along the side of Live Girls, leaned against the wall, and tried to steady himself. His stomach was beginning to clench; it felt as if it had been scraped clean. Tiny pincered insects seemed to skitter just beneath his skin.

He pressed his head back against the wall and groaned, realizing that Anya was right.

"Hey, buddy, you okay?"

Davey turned to his left and looked down at a raggedly dressed old man with a pencil-thin neck and pointy chin. He was squatting in the alley facing the wall, his hands hovering over a cracked-open window just above the ground. He wore a floppy-billed cap that looked like it had been dipped in mud. He smiled at Davey; the few teeth he had left were blackened with rot.

"You don't look tho good," he said.

Davey stared at him, puzzled. The man rubbed his hands together as if over a fire.

"Oh." The man laughed. He nodded his head toward the rectangular window and said, "There'th a furnathe down there. Keepth me warm."

Davey stared at the window. His hands were trembling and it was getting harder and harder to focus his thoughts, but the window was important. It was directly below Live Girls.

There's a window . . .

"You ever go down there?" Davey said.

He shook his head slowly. "There'th *thingth* down there."

Davey tried hard to think. If he could get in unnoticed . . . then what? He didn't just want to get Casey out, although that was most important. He wanted to hurt them. *Stop* them, if possible. But how?

His face twisted as he slid down the wall to the ground, weakening under the ache that passed through his body in waves.

You need the blood while it's still warm, Davey . . .

He had to feed.

You need to *feel it pumping into your mouth . . .*

Soon.

"Hey, what'tha matter, bud?"

The old man was standing over Davey, holding out a knobby hand.

"Get away," Davey said.

"Should I get thome help?"

"Just get *away!*" Davey rolled away from him and stumbled to his feet. He staggered down the sidewalk, dodging pedestrians. The rhythmic sound of feet landing on cement became louder and began to sound like a chorus of heartbeats. The lights around him seemed too bright, and the *smells* . . . he could smell them as they passed by, as they walked beside him . . .

He leaned beside a window lined with tiny flashing Christmas lights and saw his reflection in the pane. His face had filled out some; he looked stronger. He was still pale; his skin flashed red as the lights went on and off. Then something in the window, something beneath his own reflected face, caught his eye.

Two Ping-Pong balls with I ♥ NY on them in black and red.

Ping-Pong balls.

A furnace.

There was something significant about the two objects, something that hovered just out of his reach, a blurred thought that would not come into focus.

His eyes burned.
His mouth was paper dry.
Fire licked the underside of his flesh.
It wouldn't wait any longer.

Chapter Fifteen

Beth slowly climbed the stairs to Vince's apartment. Her feet were lead and the bag in her arms seemed to get heavier with each step.

Her eyes were still puffy and red from the tears she'd shed on the bus. She wiped a thumb across each one, hoping to clear them up so Vince wouldn't know she'd been crying, then tucked her hand under the bag, deciding not to bother. It was only a quarter of ten; Vince would know something was wrong because she was off work so early.

About an hour and a half after she'd started work at the Union Theater that evening, her boss, Stevie, had opened the box-office door and poked his round head inside. Stevie was a little guy, maybe five-two, with a potbelly and a black hairpiece. He always wore fat, cheap-looking rings on his sausage fingers. He'd told her with a smile that he was having to let some of his employees go and double up the work for those remaining.

"Sorry, sweetie," he'd said, "but you ain't been here as long as summa the others."

Beth had stood in the box office, stiff and expressionless, for a long time before the tears started. She was almost thirty and, possessing a minimum of education and skills, had been able to do no better than get a job selling tickets for bad horror movies and martial-arts flicks.

Now, she'd thought, wishing her tears would stop, *I don't even have* that!

She'd spent too many years depending upon others to support her, too many years hoping the Right Man would come along. Beth realized that Davey was the closest she had ever come to the Right Man, probably the closest she would ever come. That thought had only made her feel worse, and she had grabbed her purse and gone inside the theater for her coat.

"Hey!" Stevie had called as she slipped the coat on, heading for the door. "Where ya goin'?"

"Home."

"But it's only—*hey, hey!*—I didn't mean ya hadda quit *tonight!*"

Without a reply, she'd gone outside.

"Hey!" Stevie had called, following her. "We gotta have *somebody* runnin' the box tonight!"

"Run it yourself."

Beth stood outside Vince's door steeling herself to go inside. With a tentative knock—Vince insisted that she always knock before entering—Beth slipped her key in the lock, turned it, and went inside.

The air in the apartment was stale; she'd forgotten to open a window before she left. She tried to be quiet, hoping Vince was asleep or, better yet, gone. When she heard the muffled gurgle of the toilet being flushed, she thought, *No such luck*.

Beth went into the bedroom and put the bag on the bed as she took off her coat.

She froze.

A gun lay on the sheet of the unmade bed. Vince's .357 magnum. The only time the gun came out of its drawer was when Vince was in trouble, or when he was *making* trouble.

"The fuck're you doing home so early?" Vince asked as he came into the bedroom. He swept the gun off the bed and stuffed it into the bottom drawer of the nightstand on his side of the bed. He spun around and looked at her with wide eyes, his lips pulled into a rictus grin.

Beth recognized his birdlike motions, the expression on his face, and knew immediately why the gun had been out.

Over nine months ago, Vince had held up a pharmacy with that gun. *Two* pharmacies, actually; the first time he'd been unable to find what he'd wanted. Cocaine hydrochloride.

Judging from his behavior now, he'd gotten some more of the pharmaceutical cocaine. And Beth was willing to bet good money that he'd used his gun to get it.

"Whassis?" he barked, grabbing the paper bag from the bed. He stuck his hand in and pulled out the mirror. "What the hell is *this?* You *buy* this?"

"No, Vince," she said, hanging her coat in the closet. She went to the window and opened it. "I've had it since I was a little girl. I left it at Davey's, so I went to get it today."

"You went to *his* place?"

She turned to him and tried to smile. "Just to get that and some shoes I left. My grandma gave me that mirror. It's ugly, but"—she shrugged—"I want to keep it."

His grin remained, but one brow rose over his eye. "So you went over to his place to get it. Look, babe, you wanna come back here, *fine*. Just don't go fuckin' around with old friends if you're gonna be stayin' under *my* roof, you unnerstan' me?"

"Yeah, Vince," she whispered, nodding, turning her eyes from him. "I won't anymore."

"You're fuckin' *right* you won't!" he bellowed, throwing the mirror against the bedroom wall. The glass shattered and fell to the floor in pieces around the gold-colored frame.

Beth bit the inside of her lower lip. *I won't cry*, she thought firmly, *I* will not *cry!*

"You bring anything to eat?" he asked, tossing the bag with the shoes in it back on the bed.

She picked up the bag and took the shoes to the closet. "Uh-uh."

"Jesus *Christ,* there's no food in this place, it smells like a garbage can, all the windows're always shut, and what the *fuck*'re you doing off work so early?"

She knew what was coming. She couldn't even leave at this point. He would stop her.

She found it difficult to speak; her throat burned with tears even though nothing had happened yet.

"I lost my job," she whispered.

Vince was silent. Sometimes she thought his silence was the worst part. It always came just before his outbursts. And it was always a deafeningly loud silence.

Vince cackled. It sounded like half a dozen dry twigs being snapped in rapid succession.

"Y'got fired?" he asked.

She nodded.

He came closer to her.

"That's too bad, babe. I'm sorry." His voice was soft.

He crooked a finger beneath her chin and gently lifted her head, looking into her eyes. "Hope you don't think I'm gonna take care of you," he whispered with a smile.

She started to speak, to tell him of *course* she didn't think that, she'd get *another* job, that's all, but she didn't have the chance.

"'Cause if you think that, you are *wrong!*" His palm connected with her face hard.

Beth's head jerked with the impact and she stumbled backward. The cut on her lip burned and began to bleed again.

"I'm *not* your fuckin' *papa!*" he shouted, swinging the back of his hand across her face.

Beth fell against the wall.

"Okay!" she said, trying not to raise her voice too much, hoping she could hold her tears until he was through.

"You can't keep a job, that's *your* problem!" Another slap, even harder. He reached around her neck, grabbed a handful of hair, and pulled her head back. "You unnerstan' me?"

Her mouth had fallen open and she made a long, quiet creaking sound in her throat. It felt like her hair was going to rip from her scalp if he didn't let go.

"Y-yeah, V-Vince, I under-understand."

"You gotta place to *sleep*, you get the best shit in town for *free*, but I *ain't* gonna be your fuckin' *meal ticket!*"

"I-I n-never th-thought—"

"And how many times I gotta tell ya not to *think!*" He plunged a fist into her stomach.

Beth's knees buckled and she collapsed with a pained grunt; Vince bent down over her, not letting go of her hair.

"So what happened?" he hissed, moving his face close to hers. His moist breath smelled of stale nicotine and beer. "You takin' long breaks? Blowin' the restroom attendant in the back stall?" He cackled again.

She couldn't speak because she could not take in a breath. Her insides felt as if they had been shattered by Vince's fist.

"I. Asked you. A *question!*" Vince stood upright and pulled her with him, throwing her onto the bed. "You lose your fuckin' *hearing* along with your *job?*"

She landed on her back, bouncing on the mattress. Vince got on the bed and straddled her, buried his fingers deeper in her hair, and clenched his fist.

"I asked y'why y'lost y'job," he breathed.

"B-because th-they n-needed t-to . . ." She couldn't finish the sentence. Her face burned, her lip was bleeding into her mouth, and her stomach felt as if it had been split open. She turned her face away from him and her eyes fell on the open window.

Something was on the sill.

Something dark.

With teeth.

"V-V-V . . ." She couldn't even say his name. It was moving, crawling over the sill, pulling itself along with tiny hooked claws that grew from the top of its wings just like a bat, dear God, it was a *bat*, but it was so big, its dark red eyes were so goddamned *big!* "V-V—"

Vince roared, "*Look* at me—"

He curled his free hand into a fist—

"—when I'm—"

—and raised it above his head.

"—*talking* to you!"

Vince started to bring his fist down like a hammer and the thing in the window screamed and dove from the sill, wings spread, fanged mouth open. Its wings embraced Vince's forearm and its teeth cut into the underside of his wrist.

Vince wailed like a child and pulled himself off her, rolling over the bed and off the edge to the floor.

Beth heard his fist pounding the floor, trying to knock the animal off his arm. With a crisp flapping sound, the thing flew toward the ceiling and circled above the bed. It moved so fast, it was hardly more than a blur.

On his feet, Vince staggered around the bed holding his bloodied arm, keeping his eyes on the creature flying around above him.

"*Goddammit*," he screamed, "you left the fuckin' window open for Christ's sake, get me the broom, something, *Jesus*, where's my *gun?*"

The thing shot downward and, with a loud *slap*, latched on to Vince's chest and tore its teeth into his throat. Vince fell against the dresser; he slapped at the creature as he fell to his knees. Vince said something, but it was lost in a horrible gurgle and blood sprayed from his mouth as he fell to the floor at the foot of the bed.

Beth made a quiet whimpering sound as she rolled over and got to her hands and knees on the bed. She could no longer see Vince, but she heard his struggle, heard the wet rattling sound of his breath being sucked through blood. She crawled over the bed to the nightstand, grabbed the handle of the bottom drawer, and pulled it out so far it clumped to the floor. Her hands were numb with fear and she clumsily wrapped her fingers around the butt of the gun, lifting it from the drawer.

There was a new sound coming from the floor at the foot of the bed, a horrible sound.

Sucking.

The gun was so *heavy*, she couldn't believe how *heavy* it was, she'd never used one before, never even *held* one, and it felt alien as she hefted it between both hands, sat up, and waddled to the foot of the bed on her knees.

Vince's arms were splayed outward limply; his eyes were wide and glassy; his throat was a ragged, bloody hole. The creature was hunched on his chest, its wings spread over his shoulders, its head bowed in the wound.

Beth's chest began to hitch with uncontrollable sobs and she tried to raise the gun but couldn't because her arms were so weak and she was going to throw up, she felt her gorge rising into her throat and her arms collapsed, the gun dropped to the floor, and she screamed because she *needed that gun* and now it was down there and if she reached for it, her hand would be only inches from that thing.

It suddenly lifted its head from Vince's throat, pushed itself up from his body, and made an odd spitting sound. Its ears twitched and it jerked its head from side to side as it crawled backward down Vince's body. At his feet, it flopped onto its side and screeched, its mouth yawning open to its limit, its red eyes squeezing shut. One wing swung upward then slapped onto the floor as the creature cried out again. Falling flat on its belly, it flapped both its wings.

Jesus God it's trying to fly, she thought, moving backward on the bed, wanting to be as far from the creature as possible. *It's trying to fly and it can't something's wrong with it it can't fly.*

Its bloody mouth opened again and it spit, gasped for breath, then rose from the floor, its wings flapping, heading for the window, but it veered to the left and fell to the bed thrashing. Beth began screaming, pressing herself against the headboard.

The creature's body began to tremble and its head jerked back and forth until its features seemed to be melting together until it had no face, no discernible head, just a mouth and two glistening eyes and its wings pulled together and . . .

No no no can't be it just can't no Jesus please no!

. . . it actually began to swell, like a balloon filling with air and a wing pulled away from the shifting mass of leathery flesh and bristling fur, except it *wasn't* a wing, it was an elongating stump that suddenly sprouted five trembling fingers . . .

Jesus Christ make it stop make it go away make me wake up Christ oh Jesus please!

. . . and the fingers bunched into a wet, shifting fist and the mouth widened and screamed a frighteningly human scream . . .

Make it stop stop stop!

. . . familiar somehow familiar but that couldn't be it just couldn't be and the fist swung down and thumped onto the mattress as the scream dissolved into a long deep retch that sprayed blood from the yawning mouth all over the bed and on Beth's shoes and ankles and she instinctively pulled her feet in and curled her legs beneath her as she screamed and as the thing before her continued to vomit blood onto the bed.

Then it stopped.

It lay motionless for several moments, the vaguely human arm still outstretched before it, the mouth open and wheezing for air, the eyes tightly closed.

They opened.

And looked at her.

Beth's scream crumbled to breathy sobs as she looked into the eyes.

They were no longer red. They were brown. Big and brown and hurting. Sad eyes. Davey's eyes.

"D-D-Davey?" Her voice was thick with tears.

The eyes blinked.

"Jesus Christ, *Davey?*"

The mouth closed and the mass began to shift again. The arm pulled in, the creature rolled itself off the side of the bed and fell heavily to the floor.

She couldn't bring herself to look over the edge, didn't want to see whatever was there.

It wasn't Davey couldn't be couldn't possibly be dear God I'm losing my mind I'm fucking losing my miiiind!

She curled into an even tighter ball and huddled against the headboard, her arms crossed protectively over her breasts. She trembled uncontrollably.

Beth heard shuffling on the floor beside the bed and a moment later saw the creature pulling itself across the floor with its wings toward the window. With a quick flutter, it hopped onto the sill and slowly turned its head toward her.

The eyes were red once again, but they were pulled into a sad, scared expression, a lonely look, a look she'd seen earlier that evening. They were puppy-dog eyes. Davey's eyes. They blinked once, and the creature pushed itself out the window with a long, lonesome screech that diminished quickly with the flapping of its wings.

Her sobs began again, but they were filled with relief now. Her head fell back and her eyes closed and she knew that when she opened them again, it would all be gone, the blood, the mess, Vince would be in the next room shouting at her and everything would be as it had been.

But when she opened her eyes, the bed was splashed with blood. Flecks of red speckled the wall by the dresser. The room reeked of sweat and excrement.

Murmuring softly, comfortingly, to herself, Beth slowly lowered her feet over the edge of the bed. She went to the closet and got her coat. Below the clothes on the floor of the closet was a small overnight case in which Vince kept what he called his "desperate dollars," spending money that he used only when absolutely necessary. She pulled the case out, lifted it, and put it on the edge of the bed. Opening it, she found some tens and twenties bound together with rubber bands. She didn't care how much there was; she simply stuffed the money into her coat pocket, then went to the closet and grabbed a few of her clothes and put them in the case. She closed it, latched it, and went into the bathroom. She put her toothbrush, some toothpaste, and a hairbrush into her pockets, gently placed the case on the back of the toilet, leaned forward, and vomited until her eyes stung.

Beth slowly moved to the sink and rinsed out her mouth, trying not to think, trying to ignore the trembling of her hands. She took the case from the back of the toilet, left the bathroom, walked slowly and steadily through the living room and out the door. She didn't bother to lock it.

On her way down the stairs, she was overwhelmed with dizziness. She sat on a step and held her head in her hands. When she saw the blood that had spattered onto her shoes, she closed her eyes and cried softly.

She had no idea where she was going. She had no idea what had just happened.

Nothing, she thought. A sudden calm fell over her like a chilly breeze. *Nothing happened. I'm just leaving. Away. I'm going away.*

Beth stood carefully, went down the stairs, out onto the sidewalk. She began walking, still trying not to think about anything except getting a bus or a cab and taking it . . .

Away. That was all. Away. Maybe to a motel. Maybe an airport. It didn't matter.

Just away.

Casey was huddled behind the window, exhausted, enjoying the fulfilling warmth that was passing through her body.

The panel was closed, the man in the booth had pulled himself from the hole, and she could hear his breathing on the other side, the rattling of his belt buckle as he fastened his pants, the hiss of his fly as he zipped up. The sounds came to her through the soft buzzing in her ears.

Casey's eyes were closed and she was running her tongue back and forth slowly over her lips, savoring the coppery aftertaste.

She'd done exactly as Shideh had told her. She'd moved slowly at the glass for a while, maintaining eye contact with the man in the booth. She couldn't re-member what he'd looked like; all she remembered were his eyes. He'd given her some money and she'd begun touching him. When he eased his erection through the hole, Casey had taken it in her hand and, for a moment, had thought she would be unable to go through with it. Her mind changed, however, when she found the vein, felt the pulsing flow of blood be-neath the skin.

She'd fed to the sound of the man's grunts and moans.

A hand touched Casey's face and she opened her eyes to see Shideh bending toward her.

"Feel better?" the woman asked.

Casey nodded her head, even smiled a little.

Shideh took her hand and helped her to her feet, then gave her a thin gray robe. Casey put it on.

"Come lie down," Shideh said softly. "You can do it again later when you need to."

Casey felt strong and sturdy, light on her feet as she went back to the room with Shideh and lowered herself smoothly onto the cushion.

She lay silent for a long time, enjoying the darkness.

Davey was slumped against the trunk of a tree in the park, retching, naked, and sweating. His arms were pulled together tightly over his stomach and he hugged himself protectively, his muscles tensing against the searing burn that swept through him again and again.

There are things you have to look for . . .

After several minutes of rocking forward and back against the tree trunk, the shaking began to subside. Davey began to relax.

There are chemicals that can be very damaging . . .

Something had gone wrong. He'd eaten something bad, something dangerous.

His hands dropped in his lap limply for a moment, then he raised his left hand toward his face, frowning.

His fingers were curled under, clawed, the joints were knotted. He could not straighten them out. Clenching his teeth, Davey used his right hand to try and pry the fingers back. They wouldn't budge.

Their blood can hurt you . . .

He let the hand drop again and leaned his head back, taking in a deep breath of the cold night air.

There are things you have to look for . . .

On top of the pain he'd gone through, the hunger was gnawing at his insides. He had to feed, he had to try again.

He remembered the Rolodex card smeared with blood. In his mind's eye, he saw the address in bold type, the name in caps: SCHUMAN, STELLA.

Davey slid himself away from the tree and lay down on the damp grass, wanting to rest, if only for a little while.

But he felt that if he did not feed soon, he would wither up like a leaf in autumn.

He didn't have a little while.

Merv Griffin had turned a bright lime green and was wobbling all over the screen. Stella Schuman stood in front of her television adjusting the fine tuning, but with no results. She adjusted the color, the vertical and horizontal holds, but nothing helped.

"Damn," she muttered, stepping away from the television and returning to her sofa where a large bowl of caramel corn awaited her. She wore a billowy red bathrobe with black trim and black and silver slippers that Chad had bought for her several months ago.

She lowered her bulk to the sofa with a heavy sigh and put the bowl in her lap.

"*Look* at that," she said to herself, watching Merv Griffin undulate as he changed color. She swore under her breath again.

Her cat, Tubbs, hopped onto the sofa beside her and meowed loudly.

"What's matter, Tubbs?" she cooed through a mouthful of caramel corn.

The big gray cat meowed again, pacing the length of the sofa.

Stella Schuman stroked the cat's fur with a fleshy hand. Merv was interviewing a sex therapist whose explicit terminology was getting a lot of laughs from the studio audience.

She turned to the cat and frowned. Tubbs was usually a lethargic, quiet cat. She'd never seen him act so nervous. He paced over the sofa cushions a few more times, then hopped off the sofa and padded across the living room, meowing again and again.

"Are you hungry, Tubbs?" she asked placatingly, setting the bowl aside and standing. "Let's find something for Tubbs to eat, okay? Okay, kitty-kitty?"

The cat's food bowl was in the corner of the kitchen; a lump of sticky brown catfood sat in the center of it.

"You've *got* food!" she called. "And *water*. So what's your problem, cat?" She went back into the living room and found Tubbs at the window; he was standing upright with his front paws on the windowsill, meowing. *"Shush!"* she snapped, and Tubbs sprang away from the window and shot under the stereo stand.

Stella Schuman returned to the sofa and began munching caramel corn. She decided she would have to have someone look at the television tomorrow. She couldn't tolerate a bad picture, but she left the television on, mostly for the familiar sound of Merv Griffin's voice. Stella Schuman did not like silence. The radio or the television was always on. She even slept with the radio playing quietly by her bed.

Tubbs slinked back to the window and began meowing again.

He's just lonesome, Stella Schuman thought.

"Here kitty-kitty, here kitty-cat." She patted a hand on her round thigh to summon Tubbs.

He wouldn't come.

"Tubbs," she said firmly, growing impatient with the animal's yowling. "Come here, Tubbs."

Something slammed against the windowpane and Stella Schuman nearly spilled caramel corn over her lap. With a little grunt, she stood quickly and turned toward the window.

Tubbs was on all fours now, poised to attack, his ears flat against his head, his lips pulled back. He hissed at the window.

Stella Schuman's heart was fluttering in her chest. Cradling the bowl of caramel corn in one arm, she walked around the sofa to Tubbs.

"Tubbs, boy, what's matter?"

Taking a cautious step toward the window, she squinted through the glass at the night outside.

"Goddamned birds," she muttered, bending down and swooping Tubbs up in her free arm.

The cat jumped back to the floor and went to the window, putting its front paws on the sill again. A low, rumbly growl came from the animal's throat.

"Tubbs! Get away from there!"

She reached down to pull the stubborn cat from the window.

Tubbs hissed and took a swipe at the pane.

"What in the . . ." She moved closer to the window and tried to focus her eyes beyond her own reflection.

The glass exploded inward and showered over her, knocking her backward. The bowl of caramel corn fell to the floor as she stumbled, tried to keep her balance, then fell on her back as glass and cold air rushed in-

ward and as something flapped rapidly above her.
Stella could hear Tubbs growling and spitting and hissing and she tried to stand up but realized her face had
been cut; it was stinging and she could feel a warm
trickle down her cheek. She rolled over and pushed
herself up on her knees, she felt pieces of glass cutting
into her puffy flesh and cursed between gasps as she
scanned the living room to find whatever had broken
through the window. She nearly screamed when she
saw the naked man standing in a shadowy corner of
the room.

"Wh-what do you . . . wh-who are you, whattayou-
want?" she sputtered as she struggled to her feet. She
touched her cheek gingerly and winced. She felt
vaguely dizzy and nauseated. "I have a gun!" she
snapped.

The man moved slightly, but she still couldn't see his
face. She could see him only from the belly down. Stella
Schuman found her eyes lingering on the man's genitals.

He stepped forward.

"Owen!"

The studio audience on the television laughed raucously.

Stella took a step forward and nearly tripped.

"Owen, what are you doing here?"

Half his mouth turned up in a smile. "You said we
should spend more time together."

"But, but . . ." She looked him up and down. "You're
naked. And your hand . . . How did you . . ." She
pointed over her shoulder at the broken window.
"Something flew in the . . . in the . . ." She closed her
eyes and bowed her head a moment. Perhaps something had hit her in the head when the window broke
and none of this was happening.

"Stella."

She opened her eyes and looked up. He'd moved closer.

Davey Owen's lips began to twitch and they pulled back, as if in a smile. But it wasn't a smile, and as he opened his mouth wider . . .

"Oh God . . ." Stella Schuman breathed.

Davey Owen put an arm around her shoulders and pressed his mouth to her flabby throat.

Blood spattered on the smiling green face of Merv Griffin and the studio audience applauded.

Chapter Sixteen

Thursday

Benedek sat in Davey's apartment craving a cigar.

He'd arrived forty-five minutes ago to find Davey gone. After letting himself in with his lock picks, he'd pulled a ladder-back chair to the window behind the television set and seated himself quietly to stare out at the night. The only light came from the kitchen; he preferred the darkness.

He craved a cigar because the last time he'd had one was three years earlier. With Jackie. One of her patients, the wife of a sports writer at the *Times*, had had her first baby. Her husband, Francis, had come into Benedek's office with two long, fat Havanas and handed them to Benedek with a grin.

"This is the corniest thing I've ever done, but *hey*"—Francis had laughed—"it's my first kid! Give one of these to Jackie, willya?"

So he had. She'd laughed, unwrapped the cigar, cocked a brow, and said, "Gotta light, buddy?"

They'd smoked the cigars in bed, laughing like kids sneaking a smoke after school. The smell had lingered in their bedroom for the next two nights.

He wanted one now, even though he didn't particularly care for them.

Benedek took in a deep breath through his nose, telling himself he did not know what they had done with Jackie, that maybe she was alive, just being held to punish him, to bring him to them. There was no reason to panic yet.

Yet.

Benedek heard a scream. It began as a high-pitched screech from outside the building but lowered and thickened as it neared, until it was inside the apartment, the cry of a grown man.

The bedsprings squeaked under sudden weight.

The scream became sobs.

Benedek slowly went to the open bedroom door and looked inside to find Davey lying facedown, naked, trembling, on the bed. He stood there silently for several moments, waiting for Davey to calm down.

"Davey?" he said finally, his voice soft.

At first, it seemed Davey had not heard him. Then he slowly rolled onto his side and looked up at Benedek; his mouth was smeared with blood.

Benedek wondered who he had killed.

"Walter," Davey said groggily. He sat up wearily and swung his legs over the bed, stood, and went to the closet. Putting on his robe, he said, "What are you doing here?" Davey slipped his left hand into the pocket of the robe.

"Waiting for you."

Davey scrubbed his free hand over his bloody mouth,

grimacing. He pushed by Benedek and went into the bathroom.

Benedek followed him, standing just outside the door. "They took Jackie," he said as Davey washed his face over the sink.

Davey stood and turned to Benedek, his face dripping wet. "Your wife," he said flatly.

Benedek nodded.

Davey grabbed a towel, dried his face quickly, and turned off the water. They went into the living room and Davey sat on the armrest of the sofa, stuffing his left hand into the pocket again.

"They took Casey, too," he said. "I don't know when, but she's in Live Girls. She's working one of the"—he swallowed and took a breath—"one of the booths. Jesus Christ."

Benedek took his cigarettes from his coat pocket, tapped one out, and lit it. "The reason I'm here," he said, puffing smoke and walking around the sofa, "is to ask if you want to help me."

"Help you what?"

"I'm not sure yet. Stop them. Hurt them. Uncover them. I don't know where to start. But I'm going to do something. I can't just sit on my hands."

Davey shook his head slowly, looking up at Benedek. His brows were bunched together above the bridge of his nose and his eyes were filled with pain and apology.

"I'm sorry, Walter," he said. "This is all my fault."

"No, it's not, Davey. You couldn't—"

"It *is*. If I hadn't gone into that damned place, if I hadn't allowed myself to get involved with Anya . . ." He stood and went to the window, holding out his right arm and propping himself against the wall. "What is *with* me? I walk into these no-win situations like I've got a blindfold on. Patty . . . Beth . . ."

Benedek didn't know what Davey was talking about, but he let him continue, knowing he probably just needed to talk.

"It's almost as if I *want* to get hurt," he went on. "Maybe I'm trying to prove that my mother was right. And instead of *doing* anything to change it, to make things better, I just *wallow* in it." His voice was soft, but it smacked of bitter self-disgust. "Then I drag others down with me instead of pulling myself up. Like Casey. Jesus, poor Casey. And your wife . . ." He pulled his left hand from his pocket and looked at it.

The hand was gnarled, twisted, the fingers were curled under. The skin had turned a purplish-gray and the knuckles were great round knots.

Benedek almost asked him what had happened, but Davey seemed unaware of his presence; he seemed lost in thought and more than a little bit of anger.

Davey slowly lifted his eyes from his hand and looked at Benedek. "I'll help you, Walter," he whispered. "I want to hurt them, too."

"What happened to your hand?"

Davey slipped it back in the pocket and simply shook his head.

Benedek decided not to pursue it; if Davey wanted to talk about it, he would.

"Well," Benedek said, "if we're going to do something, we should do it soon." He went to the ashtray on an end table and put out his cigarette.

Davey nodded, turning to the window. As he stared through the glass, his face grew tight with concentration. After a few moments of thought, his face relaxed.

"I think I have an idea," he said to Benedek. "Can you get your hands on a syringe?"

Benedek nodded. "Yeah, I think Jackie's got a couple at home."

"Okay." Davey looked away for a moment, pursing his lips thoughtfully. "We should probably get some sleep tonight. It's after one now. In the morning, I'm going to pay a visit to a friend of mine in New Jersey who owns a gun shop. While I'm doing that, you round up a syringe, a couple Ping-Pong balls, and some liquid Drano."

Benedek frowned. "Huh?"

"Liquid Drano, you heard right. Tomorrow night, just after sunset, we'll go to Live Girls."

"I don't understand. What are we going to do with Ping-Pong balls and Drano and a syringe?"

"What do you say I explain it in the morning? You can sleep here if you want."

Benedek thought that might not be such a bad idea. He wasn't too crazy about the idea of being outside while they were after him.

"Blankets are in the hall closet by the bathroom," Davey said. "Hope you don't mind the sofa. I'm going to bed. See you in the morning."

After Davey went into his bedroom and closed the door, Benedek stood at the window and smoked another cigarette. His body ached for sleep, but he didn't bother lying down. He knew he would never be able to close his eyes long enough to drop off.

He suspected Davey wouldn't, either.

Many hours after her first feeding, Casey lay in the dark, trying to keep her mind clear of unsettling thoughts—

When will I have to do it again?

—and wishing she could sleep. Earlier, she'd felt content and relaxed, but she was becoming afraid again.

Shideh had not returned to check on her. Casey wondered when Davey would come, *if* he would come.

The door opened and someone came in, someone tall, and carrying something in its arms. The door closed again.

"Who's there?" she asked, sitting up.

"Cedric." He stepped into the yellow glow of the candle and Casey saw that he was carrying a woman. She wore a nightgown and her white hair hung down over the man's arm and swayed back and forth with each of his steps.

"Where's Shideh?" Casey asked.

"She's working at the club right now."

Club? Casey thought.

"What time is it?" she asked.

"Little after two." The man moved to the trapdoor. "Stay back," he said to her as he put the woman on the floor. He pulled the bolts on the door and lifted it. The woman at his feet stirred and sighed.

The man was wearing a tuxedo.

"Who is that?" she asked, nodding toward the woman who was now trying to sit up.

Cedric gave her a disapproving glance, as if to say she was asking too many questions. With one fluid movement, he lifted the door and shoved the woman through with his foot, letting the door fall shut.

The sound of the woman's body tumbling beneath the door was immediately followed by a chorus of grunting and smacking, and, briefly, the woman's screams.

Cedric smiled down at Casey. "They don't get to feed off live ones very often," he said happily. He used his foot to bolt the door again, then turned and left the room, chuckling.

When the sun came up, it was more visible than it had been in the past few days, shining infrequently through breaks in the clouds that darkened most of the sky.

Walking from the bus stop, he saw the Target Guns sign a few yards up the block. He kept his left hand in his coat pocket. It had gotten a bit worse during the night. Now the fingers were thin bony sticks with fat, arthritic-looking knuckles. The skin had lightened to a grayish, dead tone. Davey could not stand to look at it for more than a few seconds. It was *not* his hand; when he held it up, it seemed he was looking at something from a novelty store. He couldn't move the fingers or thumb; three of the fingers had no feeling at all. Touching the fingers was like touching beef jerky.

Davey wondered if his hand would continue to shrivel up until it just dangled by the wrist, a wrinkled, wasted piece of meat and decayed bone.

He kept it in his pocket at all times, ashamed of it, even a little afraid of it. It was a visible reminder of what he'd become and of the weakness within him that had gotten him there.

It was 10:35 when Davey walked into Target Guns.

A moose head was mounted on the far wall facing the door. Below it were several pictures of hunters with their kills.

There were guns everywhere. Guns on the walls; in glass display cases, handguns in velvet-lined oak boxes.

There were shelves of ammunition of all kinds, gun cases and sheaths, and gun-cleaning paraphernalia.

Standing behind the register was a barrel-chested man talking on the phone. Curls of his thick gray hair fell on his creased forehead. His cheeks were rosy and his jaw square and firm. His arms were big, mostly fat now, but Davey could tell that, at one time, they had been rock-hard muscle. The hand that held the telephone receiver was big and square-shaped and his forearm was hairy. The man was a bear, but there was a smiling twinkle in his gray eyes that took the edge off his size.

"Look, I gotta customer just walked in," he said into the phone. "I'll have to call you back. But don't decide until I talk to you again, okay? Later." He hung up the phone and cracked a broad smile at Davey. "Hello, there," he boomed. "What can I do ya for?"

"Morris?"

"You got him."

"Davey Owen." He held out his hand, smiling.

"Wellll." Morris laughed, pumping Davey's hand enthusiastically. "That's my boy, finally decided to pay a visit, huh?"

"Nice to meet you, finally."

"Yeah, yeah. Hey, you wanna little tour of the shop?"

"Sure. But I can't stay long, I'm afraid."

"Gotta get back to the old grind?"

Davey paused, deciding how to go about what he wanted to say. "Well, I don't work at Penn anymore, Morris."

"What? You quit?"

"Yeah. I wasn't going anywhere there. I just . . ." He shrugged.

Morris swatted him hard on the shoulder and said, "Good boy, good boy. Don't take any shit from nobody. So, what you doing now, kid?"

286

"Well, nothing at the moment."

"Yeah? Well, don't you worry about that. Jobs are tough to find these days, you know. But you'll be okay. I know, I've been there. When I was a young man, just home from the war—dubbayuh-dubbayuh two—I didn't know *what* the hell I was gonna do, you know? So I started looking into—"

Davey hesitantly interrupted him. "Morris, excuse me, but like I said, I can't stay long."

"Oh, yeah, sure. I run off at the mouth, you let me. So is there anything special you need, or you just being social?"

Davey put his hand on the countertop and said quietly, "I'm in trouble, Morris."

The old man's eyes narrowed and his lips parted as he leaned toward Davey. "Trouble? What kinda trouble, kid?"

"I need a gun."

Morris cocked a brow. "A gun, huh? Well, listen, kid. Guns are great things and I think everybody oughtta have one, but shopping for a gun when you're in some kinda trouble is a little like shopping for groceries when you got the screamin' hungries, you know what I'm sayin', kid?"

Davey nodded, closing his eyes. "I know, and if you don't want to help me, Morris, I'll understand. But I really need—"

"No, wait a sec, here, kid, I *wanna* help you. I just wanna make sure you know what you're doin'."

"That's why I came to you."

Morris squeezed Davey's arm. "Good, kid. I'm glad you did. So. What kinda trouble you in?"

"Sorry, Morris, but I can't go into it."

"Tell me this much. Your life in danger?"

A voice deep inside Davey chuckled. *Not anymore.*

Davey nodded, licking his lips. "A *lot* of lives."

Morris studied Davey's face for a long time, then pushed himself away from the counter. He reached beneath the register and pulled out two canes, took one in each hand, and, using them for support, hobbled along the counter and around the edge. When he walked, his legs made soft clicking sounds. He faced Davey and hit one of his own legs with a cane; it was wooden.

"Lost 'em in dubbayuh-dubbayuh two," he said. "So I got these stilts. Better'n nothin', huh?" He crossed the store to the entrance. After locking the door, he reached over to the window and turned the OPEN sign around so that it read CLOSED. "C'mere, kid," he said, leading Davey through a door beneath the moose head. "Step inside the inner sanctum."

It was a cramped office with a rolltop desk that was cluttered with papers and folders, a few styrofoam cups, and Hostess fruit-pie wrappers. There were pictures on the wall of Morris getting married, Morris in uniform, Morris flanked by a little boy and girl, Morris holding up a fish and smiling proudly.

"You in trouble with the cops?" he asked, leaning his canes against the wall.

"No."

"Not the cops, huh? Then it must be bad. Well, I ain't the nosy type. I won't press it." He turned to an old wooden filing cabinet and pulled out the top drawer as far as it would go. Reaching into a space behind the file folders, he removed a metal box with a handle on top. He put it on the cabinet and pushed the drawer shut, turning to Davey. "Just let me tell you one thing, kid, and this is important, okay?" When Davey didn't reply, Morris repeated, *"Okay?"*

"Yeah, okay."

Morris pointed a finger at Davey. "You never came here, you understand me? You never even met me."

Davey nodded.

"Good. Long as we understand that, we're okay." He took the metal box from the cabinet, then swept his hand over a corner of the desk, clearing a space in the mess, and set down the box. "A handgun okay?"

"Yes, that's what I need. Something easy to carry."

Morris opened a desk drawer, took out a key, and unlocked the box. Flipping up the lid, he took out a gun and hefted it in his hand. "This," he said, "is a nine-millimeter Beretta, model ninety-two. Holds fifteen shots in a magazine, easy to carry, quick to load. Powerful little bugger, too. You shoot guns much?"

"I'm afraid not."

"Here, give it a feel." He tossed the gun to Davey.

Instinctively, Davey pulled his left hand from his coat pocket and held both hands up to catch the gun. He almost dropped it, but clutched it to his chest.

Davey saw Morris's eyes linger on his twisted hand and he quickly stuffed it back in the pocket. He couldn't meet Morris's eyes and kept his head bowed.

"Hey, kid," the man said softly. "Don't look so embarrassed." He knocked his knuckles on one of his legs. "Remember? I ain't no perfect specimen either."

Slowly, Davey pulled his hand out of his pocket and held it up.

"They did this to me," he whispered.

"They? You mean the people you're in trouble with?"

Davey nodded.

"They *did* that to you?"

"Yes."

Morris looked at the hand with narrowed eyes and shook his head. "Jesus. You sure you don't wanna talk about it, Davey?"

"Yeah."

"Okay." He patted Davey's shoulder encouragingly. "Tell you what. I gotta sixty-foot range downstairs. We'll go down there and fire a few rounds, huh?"

Putting his hand in his pocket again, Davey tried to smile. "Thanks. I really appreciate all this, Morris. I don't . . . I don't want to cause you any trouble."

"Trouble?"

"Well, I don't know much about gun laws, but can't this gun be traced back to you?"

"Nope. I know *everything* about gun laws, *have* to in my business, and I always make sure I gotta few untraceable guns around. This is one of 'em. And *remember*, kid. You didn't. Get it. From *me*."

"I know. How much do I owe you?"

The man pulled in his chin and spread his arms. "Kid. We're business associates, 'member? I'm not gonna take your money for some help." He tucked in his lower lip and thought a moment. "Just promise me somethin'. I understand you're in trouble and all, pissed off at the sonsabitches done this to you. You wanna protect yourself, maybe protect somebody close to you. But take it from me, kid, don't use that thing unless you absolutely *have* to. You kill somebody, and I don't care *who* it is, you gotta live with it. And that ain't so easy to do."

Davey was touched by the man's concern.

The people I'm going to shoot, he wanted to say, *are already dead.* But he knew that Morris would think he was crazy and probably wouldn't give him the gun. Davey opted for a half- truth.

"Don't worry, Morris," he said reassuringly. "I don't plan to kill anybody."

"Good boy. Now let's go downstairs and I'll show you how to play with this toy, huh?"

Benedek entered his apartment cautiously, looking behind the door first, then quickly scanning the living room. The apartment reeked of garlic. He was glad. That meant they had probably not come in while he was gone.

Nothing had been moved. There was no sign there had been visitors. He shut the door and locked it, then went into the bathroom.

Jackie had always kept the syringes in the bottom drawer below the sink. She'd been bringing them home now and then since the first year they'd been together. He'd had a spur removed from his foot, and after he got home, Jackie gave him shots of Demerol to kill the pain. When she discovered that the syringes were handy for watering her houseplants, she'd begun bringing them home regularly.

He found a couple in the drawer, along with hypodermic needles in plastic wrappers.

Benedek still had no idea why the hell Davey wanted them or the Ping-Pong balls and Drano. Sounded pretty weird to him. But then, everything that had happened in the last few days sounded weird.

He'd dozed on Davey's sofa throughout the previous night, never falling into a deep sleep. He'd awakened once to what he'd thought was Jackie's voice. It had been a siren outside.

Benedek wasn't sure when Davey had gone—while

Benedek was nodding off, apparently. He'd found a note on the refrigerator telling him to help himself to breakfast and saying that Davey would be back by one. Benedek had eaten nothing; the burning in his stomach would not permit it.

It was 11:48 by Benedek's watch. He would have to get back to Davey's soon.

Before leaving the bathroom, Benedek glanced down at the bathtub. There was a crusty ring around the inside left behind by the bubbles he and Jackie had bathed in the night before. The brandy snifter from which Jackie had drunk was on the edge of the tub, a drop of brandy still in the bottom. He picked it up and sniffed at its stale aroma. Staring at the empty bathtub, Benedek remembered how Jackie had looked: her relaxed smile, the heaviness of her eyes, the way her nipples peeked through the clinging bubbles, the drops of moisture that mingled with the freckles on her chest.

He sat heavily on the toilet seat, wondering suddenly what he would ever do without her. He propped his elbow on the edge of the sink, put his head in his hand, and sobbed.

"Okay, Davey," Benedek said firmly when Davey came in. "I got your hypos and your Ping-Pong balls and your goddamned liquid Drano. Now are you gonna fill me in or am I supposed to *guess* what you've got in mind?"

"I'm sorry, Walter," Davey said, taking off his coat and tossing it onto the sofa. "I guess I was afraid you'd think my idea was stupid and insist we do something else."

"Hey, *you're* the expert here," Benedek replied. "Just don't keep me in the dark, okay?"

"Where's the stuff?"

"In here." Benedek led him into the kitchen. The things he'd purchased were on the table.

Davey pulled out a chair and sat down. Taking the rectangular box containing two Ping-Pong balls in his right hand, he lifted it to his mouth and tore off the cellophane wrapping with his teeth.

"When I worked at Penn," he began, "I had to read through all kinds of stories for men's action magazines, mercenary magazines, shit like that. Most of them were just guys shooting at each other, or articles about new kinds of guns, but once in a while, I came across some unusual and creative methods of blowing things up. This"—he gestured to the things before him—"is one of them."

Interested, Benedek sat across from him.

"According to this article I read," Davey continued, "if you inject one of these"—he held up a Ping-Pong ball—"with some of this"—he tapped the ball on the bottle of liquid Drano—"put a little Scotch tape over the hole, and drop it into any petroleum distillate, like gas or oil, the tape will dissolve and the reaction of the Drano mixing with the gas causes an explosion."

It sounded farfetched, but Benedek decided to go along with it for the moment.

"So how does that help us?" he asked.

"In an alley beside Live Girls, I found a window that leads beneath the building. There's a furnace down there; I'm willing to bet it's an oil furnace. I'm going to go down there tonight. If I'm right and I drop these in, it'll blow the place sky high."

"And you *with* it, if it works."

"It'll take a while for the tape to come off. I'm hoping I'll have enough time to go up and get Casey, then get out."

"I can go in while you're down in the—"

"No, Walter. You'll wait for me outside in a cab."

"Wanna be a hero, huh?"

"It's not that. I have a much better chance of getting out of there. I'm one of them. I'm not as vulnerable as you."

"Look, Davey, I can't just—"

"You don't know what they're capable of doing, Walter. If you go in there . . . they *want* you, remember?"

"They might have Jackie in there."

"It's not an option, Walter. Either you wait for me outside or don't come at all." Davey's voice cracked and he turned his eyes away from Benedek. When he spoke again, it was hardly more than a whisper. "I can't let you go in there; I'm responsible for too much already. If I find Jackie, I swear I'll do my very best to get her out."

Davey suddenly seemed to age before Benedek's eyes. He seemed to be carrying the weight of the world on his back.

"Davey, you can't blame yourself for that," Benedek said quietly. "You had nothing to do with what happened to Jackie."

"If I'd never gone into Live Girls, you never would have met me. You might've let the cops take care of your brother-in-law. You might not have gotten involved in this at all. And you might still have Jackie."

"Might, *might*. Might-haves aren't worth shit, Davey."

Davey picked up one of the hypodermic needles and tore off the plastic wrapper with his teeth. "You want to help me do this?" he asked.

"No, wait a second. If I go in there, I can look for Jackie and Casey while you're in the furnace room. It would be much safer."

"No, it wouldn't. You'd never get out alive."

"And what about you? You think they're going to sit back and let you blow the place up just because you're one of *them?*"

"I've got a gun."

"And what good is that going to do?"

"A few slugs will hold them off."

Benedek nodded. Davey was determined, he realized, to do it himself, and he was probably right. If Benedek went in there, they would never let him see the light of day again.

"Okay," Benedek said with resignation. "I'll wait in a cab outside, but I won't wait forever. If you don't come out in fifteen minutes, I'm coming in."

Davey thought about it a moment. "If you go in," he said, "and don't come out, there won't be anyone left to blow the whistle on them."

"What," Benedek snapped, "you think I'm gonna be some kinda *savior?* You think I'm just gonna walk into my editor's office and tell him there are vampires running around New York and he'll say, 'My God, Walter, we've gotta put this on the front page'?" He shook his head. "As much as I'd like to rip the lid off this, I don't know *how* I'm gonna do it. So what difference does it make?"

"I want them to burn," Davey breathed. "Anya, Shideh, the women who work those booths, I want them all to *burn*. If I have to burn with them, fine. But I'm going in there alone."

"A lot of innocent people will be killed and hurt."

"Not if I can help it. I'm going to clear the customers out of the booths."

"You're taking a lot on yourself."

"And it's about time."

"All right, Davey," Benedek said, nodding. "All right." He picked up one of the syringes and clicked a needle onto the end of it. "We'll do it your way."

Chapter Seventeen

Rain pounded on the roof of the cab and cascaded down its windows, making the city outside look like dirty melting ice cream. Everything outside seemed to be moving more slowly than usual: the cars, the pedestrians, even the wipers that swept the cab's windshield.

The cabdriver was a stocky woman with frizzy black hair who whistled softly through her teeth, keeping rhythm with the beat of the wipers.

Davey sat in the backseat with Benedek; both of them stared silently out the windows.

Davey felt a chilly sheen of perspiration on his face. He felt as if his fear had taken form and was squatting behind him on the back of the seat, its face grinning with malicious delight, breathing icy breaths down his neck.

It occurred to Davey that he'd never seen Jackie before. Turning to Benedek, he asked, "What does your wife look like?"

Without turning to him, Benedek said, "She has white hair, green eyes. She was wearing a blue nightgown when he took her." He stared out the watery window for a moment, then continued quietly: "She wasn't really my wife. I mean, we lived together eleven years but never got married. I kind of wish we had." He smiled gently. "She would have been quite a sight in a wedding gown, with her white hair . . ."

The cab came to a sudden halt and a large black man wearing tattered rags walked before it, pounding a big fist on the hood. His lips moved silently and he gestured toward them, like a witch doctor casting a spell.

"'At nut's probably gonna be president someday," the cabdriver muttered, shaking her head.

When Davey saw the flashing lights of Times Square shining through the blurry glass, he reached into his coat pocket and wrapped the fingers of his right hand around his gun. It was loaded and Morris had given him some extra magazines. Reloading would not be easy with just one hand, but Davey had practiced several times that day so he knew it was possible.

The cab stopped at the curb; Davey and Benedek turned to one another. Davey thought the man looked older than when he'd first met him just two days before.

"Davey," Benedek said, leaning toward him with determination, "are you sure you don't want me to—"

"Positive." Davey checked his coat pockets to make sure he had everything: extra magazines for the gun and the two Ping-Pong balls he and Benedek had prepared in the left pocket, the gun, a penlight, and a sturdy, newly sharpened kitchen knife in the right.

"You guys gettin' out?" the driver asked, looking at them over her shoulder.

"He's getting out," Benedek replied. "We're waiting."

"Waiting? You never said nothin' about waiting. How long . . ."

Benedek reached into his pocket and pulled out a wadded twenty and slid it under the partition.

The woman nodded, taking the bill. "So we'll wait."

As Davey opened the door to get out, Benedek put a hand on his arm and said, "I'm giving you fifteen minutes, then I'm coming in."

Davey shook his head. "Please don't, Walter."

"Like it or not, I am. So just do what you can and get your ass out of there in fifteen minutes."

Davey nodded and got out of the cab. The raindrops hit his face like cold little bullets. Up ahead, the red letters on the Live Girls sign flickered through the downpour. Live Girls looked like a blot of darkness within darkness. Davey closed the door of the cab and hurried down the sidewalk through the rain.

It was 9:12 P.M.

Casey could not calm the trembling in her arms and legs. Her stomach churned sickeningly and a burning sensation passed over her skin in waves.

Churning and burning, she thought as she hugged herself on the cushion, rocking back and forth. *Churning and burning, burning and churning . . .*

She stood clumsily and walked around the cushion, trying to overcome the weakness in her legs. As she passed the candle, the flame stirred, sending flashes of soft orange light over the walls.

Casey turned to the table lamp in the corner, felt for the switch, and turned it on. Her eyes snapped shut against the sudden light, but it cut through her eyelids like razors and her head instantly began to pound. She switched the light off again and let the darkness wash over her eyes like cool, cleansing water. She leaned on the small table for a moment, spinning around when she heard the door open behind her.

"You should be feeding," Shideh said softly as she entered the room and closed the door.

"I don't want to," Casey replied, turning away from her.

"Yes you do." There was a smile in her voice.

"I won't."

"You will."

Casey turned.

"I can see the trembling in you now," Shideh went on. "Your skin is beginning to burn, am I right? And soon, each breath you take will be like inhaling fire." Her smile widened. "Are you sure you won't feed?"

Casey remembered putting her mouth on the fleshy, disembodied penis that stuck through the hole beneath the window; she remembered using her tongue to find the pulsing vein, then briefly sliding her teeth over it, puncturing the skin and hearing the man's muffled cries of pleasure as she sucked his blood . . .

Her throat closed at the memory of the warm, sticky fluid and its coppery taste and, worst of all, how good it made her feel.

Turning again to Shideh, Casey avoided her eyes. "I won't," she said again.

"Fine. In a while, you'll beg me to let you feed. You won't last as long as you think."

"I want out."

"Hmm?"

"I said . . ." Suddenly the trembling and burning were too much and Casey found herself clenching her fists at her sides. "I want out of this goddamned room!" she shouted.

The corners of Shideh's shapely lips pulled downward slightly, and she took a step toward Casey.

When she saw Shideh's right hand slowly rising toward her, Casey moved back until she was against the wall. Shideh moved closer to her, so close their breasts were touching. She placed her hand on Casey's neck, her thumb over Casey's throat. She began to press down, slowly increasing the pressure until Casey's throat was closed and she felt as if the thumb would pop through the skin and cartilage.

"You will learn," Shideh breathed, "never to shout at me."

Suddenly the thumb was gone and her throat was open and she was able to breathe again. She put her hand on her throat and tried to take a slow, deep breath.

"I'll come back later," Shideh said as she turned to the door, "to see if you're ready to feed." She didn't look back as she closed the door.

Casey lay down on the cushion again, massaging her bruised throat and praying Davey would come soon.

When Davey rounded the corner into the alley beside Live Girls, he found three men huddled around the basement window. One of them, a thin, spindly-necked black man with stubbly white whiskers and a crooked, hand-rolled cigarette between his lips, looked up at Davey with a blank expression for a moment. The middle man wore a hat; rain pattered on its floppy brim and dribbled over the edges, veiling his face. He held a dirty, unlabeled bottle in his hand and touched it to his brim in greeting.

Davey stood behind them, looking over their shoulders at the dirty window that was only a quarter of the way open. To Davey's right, a man with bushy, matted brown hair and a beard squatted before the window, his hands dangling between his legs, his fingers flitting and squirming.

"Excuse me, fellas," Davey said. "I'd like to get through that window."

The middle man craned his head around slowly and looked at Davey over his shoulder. "You wanna get warm, son?" the man asked.

"No. I want to get in."

The twitchy one stood up and laughed; his laugh sounded like the chittering of an oversized beetle.

"Aw, you don' wan' do that," he said, shifting his weight from one foot to the other. "You, aw, no, man, you don' wan' do that."

"Why not?"

"Aw, 'cause there's, like, *things* down there, man, yeah, things, like, we can hear 'em. Sometimes they talk." He shook his head. "Aw, you, no, man, you don' wan' do that. Naw."

There'th thingth down there . . .

Davey looked down at the window. It was narrow; it would be an uncomfortably tight squeeze. There was only darkness beyond.

What could be down there? he wondered. *Probably just more of them.* Then he thought, *As if that's not enough.*

"I have to go down there," he said. "There's something down there that I need."

The men stood and stepped aside.

Davey moved forward and touched the window with his foot, seeing if he could push it open any further. With a harsh squeak it opened all the way. Davey almost lost his balance and plunged his leg into the window; he pulled his leg away from the window and stumbled against the cold brick wall.

Someone laughed; it was a repressed laugh, as if coming from behind a palm.

Davey looked at the three men; he thought, at first, it was one of them. But it had been a young girl's voice . . .

"I wouldn't stick around this building if I were you guys," Davey said nervously.

"You're, aw, jeez, man, you're gon' let 'em out, aren't you?" the twitchy one asked, backing away slowly, fearfully. "Aw, man, you can' do that, man, I hear 'em in there, talkin', they always talkin' 'bout bein' alla time *hungry*, man, so, aw, shit, no, man, you can' do that." He swept a jittery hand through his matted hair before turning and hurrying down the alley.

The other two men remained, standing a good distance from the window, watching curiously.

Davey hunkered down before the window, trying to decide upon the best way of climbing in. It would have to be feet first, of course, and probably faceup. He took the penlight from his coat and shone it into the window. The narrow beam cut through the darkness and swept over the dirty, cracked floor. When he shone the beam deeper into the room, it was swallowed by the darkness.

His palm had begun to sweat and there was the familiar fluttering of fear in his chest.

For an instant, the window resembled an open mouth.

Davey sat down on the wet ground, lifted his feet, and stuck them through the window. Scooting forward a bit at a time, he edged himself inside. When he was through the window to his waist, he looked up at the two men watching him.

They'd taken another step away from the window and were slowly inching their way backward.

The fear in their faces made him stop, made him want to pull his legs back up *now* before something down there in the dark grabbed his ankle and began to pull . . .

But he continued to squirm through the window.

His movement jerked to a halt; his coat was snagged. He heard the fabric tear with a hiss and a piece of wood creaked as Davey tried to pull the coat away from it, but it didn't come free, he would have to pull harder, probably ruin the coat, and where was he gonna get the money to buy another coat, goddammit, he couldn't afford it, but it didn't matter, did it, not in light of everything else, things like the sound Davey was hearing below him, the sound of something heavy sliding across the dirty, cracked, cement floor beneath his feet, something sliding toward him, and Davey tried to jerk the coat from its snag once again, just as something clutched the material of his pants leg and pulled hard, tearing the coat away and slamming Davey to the floor in a heap.

He began kicking his legs to push himself against the wall and to kick away whatever was in the dark before him. Pressing his back to the wall, he reached into his coat pocket and clumsily removed the gun and penlight. He flicked on the light and held it between his teeth as he gripped the gun in his right hand and prepared to use it.

At first he saw nothing. The air was dusty and smelled . . . *diseased*. It conjured up images in his head of gaping, cauterized wounds and freshly sawed bone. Something dripped steadily.

Then the blackness beyond his light began to take

shape and move. There was a whisper. Another. A stifled giggle.

Davey heard the shuffling on the floor again and swung his beam downward to what looked, at first, like no more than a big lump in the floor, until its head looked up, its eyes squinting at Davey, and reached its stub of an arm toward him, its smile revealing rotted teeth.

Davey pushed himself to his feet and moved along the wall away from the creature.

It pulled itself closer to him with its other arm, except it *wasn't* an arm, it was a stiffened twisted wing, a bat's wing with leathery folds and nail-sharp claws curling out of the top and dark veins that mapped the moist, tender-pink flesh. It had no legs. Saliva glistened on the creature's lips as they pulled back even further into a rigid, black-tongued grin.

"Another live one," it gargled, sliding closer, its fleshy stumps trailing behind.

Then the darkness behind the creature began to move with a chorus of shufflings and slitherings and a heavy, ominous *thump-sshhh . . . thump-sshhh*.

The faces oozed from the dark.

All of them were looking at *him*.

All of them were smiling.

Benedek fumbled a cigarette out of his pack and flicked his lighter.

"Hey," the driver said, scowling back at him. Her face was round and rather flat and piggish. "No smoking inna cab, I toldya once before."

Did she? he wondered, tucking the cigarette back into its pack. *Guess so.*

He wondered exactly what Davey was doing at that instant, if he'd loaded the furnace yet, or if they'd stopped him already.

Benedek rubbed his eyes, then realized the driver was staring at him with her arm stretched across the back of her seat.

"You okay?" she asked.

"Yeah, I'm, I'm fine."

"Don't look so fine." She studied him a moment, then added, "Look, if you need a smoke that bad, go ahead. It just stinks up the cab, y'know?"

Benedek almost laughed despite his anxiety, and decided to take advantage of the offer. "Yeah," he said, nodding as he took out another cigarette. "Matter of fact, I *do* need a smoke that bad." He drew the smoke in deep and let it out slowly.

"Your friend gonna be long?" the driver asked. Benedek slowly shook his head. "I hope not." It was 9:18.

A hand with only two fingers reached from the darkness.

Something waddled toward Davey making a smacking sound.

There was a flutter overhead and Davey shone his beam upward. It landed on something the size of a baby hanging upside down from a pipe, something dark and wet that licked its claw with a pink, flicking tongue.

Sweet holy God, Davey thought, backing away. The penlight beam sparkled in the eyes that watched Davey from the web of pipes and ducts overhead.

The creature on the floor was much closer. When it spoke again, its voice sounded phlegmy.

"Just gimme your foot," it said. "Just your foot . . ."

Davey lifted the gun, steadying his aim on the wrist of his dead, disfigured hand, and fired.

The creature's head jerked backward and the rear of its skull splashed over its pink bare back. Its wing began to flap, slapping wetly against the concrete floor. Its head fell forward with a *crack* and Davey took another step back when he saw the white, puffy, sluggish worms . . .

The wing continued to slap the floor.

There were murmurs in the darkness.

Davey pointed the gun at them, moving it back and forth slowly; his hand trembled.

"It bites." A woman giggled. Her voice was thick, as if she were speaking through a mouthful of pudding. When she stepped forward, Davey saw that her mouth was horribly twisted, sloping across her face at an unnatural angle; her lower jaw was crooked and lumpy. Her body was shapely and her skin pale, but she dragged something behind her, something that sounded heavy and looked, in the brief moment of light, pink and gelatinous.

Davey spun around when he felt warmth behind him and the penlight beam flashed over the rusty body of the furnace hunkering in the corner, a small bank of gauges and knobs at its base. But there was no oil tank. Two pipes went from the back of the furnace into the wall behind it.

The oil tank was beyond that wall.

There was a flurry of movement behind and above Davey and he turned around, gun raised, to see the creature that had been hanging from the pipe diving toward him, its wings flapping rapidly, its mouth gaping and its pendulous testicles bobbing beneath a huge, glistening erection.

Davey fired the gun again and the creature dropped to the floor like a wet towel, spinning around in circles like a crippled moth. It began to vomit.

Davey's knees almost gave way and he staggered to his right. His jaw was beginning to ache from clasping the penlight and spittle was dripping over his lower lip. The light wobbled between his teeth and its beam passed over a doorway to his right. He aimed the light again and held it.

The doorway was just a few feet away from him and led to the room beyond the wall, the room in which he would find the oil tank. Davey moved toward the doorway.

Something dripped on his face and he jerked back, looking up.

It was only water dripping from a pipe. He leaned against the wall and closed his eyes, allowing himself a moment to enjoy his relief. When he opened them again the woman's face was leaning close to his and she hissed:

"Give me . . . a *kisssss*."

Then she touched his face with a sticky hand. . . .

Casey gasped when the door burst open and Shideh rushed inside in a flurry of black garments and flowing white hair. Casey was curled up in the corner holding the cushion around her protectively, her limbs quaking, her teeth clenched, exhaling in puffs through her mouth. Shideh towered over her.

"What are you doing in here?" she snapped.

"N-n-nothing."

"What was that sound?"

Had there been a sound? Casey had heard two loud

cracks earlier but had thought, rather distantly, that they were the sounds of her skull breaking open because of the intolerable pounding within it.

"I d-d-don't know," Casey stammered.

Shideh bent down and pulled away the cushion, taking Casey's arm. Shideh lifted her to her feet.

"You're going to feed now," she said.

"No!" Casey began kicking and hitting until she broke away from Shideh's grasp.

Shideh tossed the cushion aside and crouched beside Casey, who was huddled, once again, in the corner.

"You will feed now," she whispered, "or I'll throw you down there." She pointed to the trapdoor. "With *them.*"

Davey made a deep-throated gasping sound as he threw himself backward, jerking his head away from the woman-creature's hand. He smacked his head against the wall and grunted at the sudden, sharp pain. In his effort to get away from her, his right hand had lowered and his left raised protectively before his face.

She froze, her arm still outstretched, staring at Davey's left hand. She leaned a bit closer, and as Davey turned his face to her, putting light on her again, he saw that her blue eyes had lost their cold, hungry look. They were soft, shimmering, almost as if they were filling with tears. She gently touched her fingertips to the side of his numbed, gray hand.

"You're like us," she whispered wetly. Her head tilted to the left, and if he ignored the rest of her disfigured face, Davey could see the sympathy in her eyes. "You believed the lie, too."

Davey pulled his hand away from hers and lifted the gun again, aiming it at her head as he inched along the wall toward the doorway. Dirt and pebbles and bits of rubble crunched beneath his feet.

The creature by the window through which Davey had entered was still slapping its wing to the floor, but more slowly now.

The thing that had dropped from the pipe was scuttling over the floor, retching.

The woman-creature watched Davey as he neared the doorway and she chuckled; it was a chuckle without humor and without malice.

"Welcome to hell," she said.

The others moved forward.

They bled out of the darkness toward him, some of them waddling on stumps, others slithering over the floor like great fat worms, and still others walked upright, cradling their deformities in their arms or dragging them heavily.

Davey turned away from them and made a move for the door but hit his foot on something heavy and soft. He looked down.

The face of a young girl peered up at him; it was attached to a squat three-foot-long body covered with matted brown fur and trailing a tapering pink tail. The girl's nostrils were flaring; she was sniffing his leg.

Davey almost dropped the penlight from his teeth; he stumbled into the doorway and looked once more over his shoulder.

They were still shuffling toward him.

Davey darted quickly through the doorway and scanned the room with the light beam.

Just inside and to the left was a steep, wooden, ladder-like staircase that led to the ceiling. It was directly beneath a trapdoor that was scarred with deep slashes like those Anya had left on Davey's windowpane.

There were some boxes and crates stacked against the far wall and eyes blinked between them, rheumy, lost-looking eyes. Things moved, shifted.

Cobwebs dangled from the pipes overhead.

Something moved above them. It cooed like a happy toddler, then laughed like a drunk.

In the corner to Davey's right was the oil tank. It was fat and rusted and stood on four short metal legs against the wall like some resting, bloated, metal beast. At the top were two gauges that sparked in the light like watchful eyes. Behind the gauges was the opening, flat and round and closed. Davey went toward it.

He put the gun in his pocket and reached for the top of the opening. It was too high; he couldn't reach it. He spun around, taking the light from his mouth and holding it before him, and eyed the crates against the opposite wall.

Something heavy slithered behind them.

Davey took a few tentative steps toward the crates. Through a space between two of them, he saw a face layered with shiny scales. He put the light in his mouth again and reached for his gun as the face slid toward him.

Its eyes blinked with vague curiosity. It didn't seem to want to hurt him.

You're like us.

Davey unwrapped his sweaty fingers from the handle of the gun in his pocket and cautiously reached for one of the boxes.

It might not like having its shelter disturbed, he thought, and the voice that murmured the warning in his mind was the voice of the same little boy who had sat in the hard rickety pew every week to listen to all those hellfire-and-damnation sermons. For an instant, that little boy was back as if he'd never been gone. *It might not just blink and stare, it might come shooting out of that narrow space with its teeth snapping, reaching just about the right height to bury those teeth between my legs and never let go . . .*

He grabbed a corner of one of the wooden boxes and pulled, expecting to be too weak from fear to be able to do more than drag it across the floor. But he lifted it easily . . .

. . . stronger than you ever thought possible . . .

. . . and pulled it away from the others.

Something long and covered with glistening open sores slid along the wall and disappeared behind another crate.

Davey backed his way to the tank, carrying the crate. He put it down, put a foot on it, testing it, then stepped up on the crate, reaching for the lid of the tank opening. Wrapping his fingers around it, he pushed and twisted until it opened upward on a hinge with a metallic screech. Reaching his right hand across his stomach to his left coat pocket, Davey pulled out the two Drano-filled Ping-Pong balls. Supporting himself against the side of the tank with his left arm, Davey held the two balls over the opening . . .

They might explode immediatey, he thought, *they might not explode at all.*

. . . and dropped them in.

The ground fell away beneath him.

Benedek was beginning to swear under his breath. He looked at his watch every thirty seconds or so.

It was 9:24, three minutes short of Davey's time limit. Benedek kneaded the seat cushion beneath him with the fingers of one hand while pressing the fingers of the other hand into the pit of his stomach where a familiar feeling was beginning to knot, the feeling that something was going very wrong.

"Excuse me," Benedek said to the driver. "Do you have the time?"

"I thought *you* had it," she mumbled, looking at her watch. "Either that or a real fascinating wrist. Um, it's about nine-thirty by my watch."

"Jesus," Benedek breathed, scooting across the seat. "Look, you just stay here, okay? I'm gonna go get my friend. Don't go anywhere, and there's another twenty for you."

"Hey, I'm in no hurry," she said with a wave of her hand.

Benedek slammed the door of the cab. Maybe the driver's watch was fast, maybe Benedek's was slow, but it didn't matter, enough time had passed for Davey to get into trouble, so Benedek broke into a jog, stumbling to a halt beneath the red-lettered sign.

Taking a deep breath, Benedek pushed through the black curtain and stepped inside Live Girls for the first time.

And the last . . .

"Please, please let me go," Casey pleaded, "just let me go, I, I need some air, th-that's all." Her whole body burned to the tips of her fingers and toes.

"It's not *air* you . . ." Shideh stopped, cocked her head. "Someone's here," she whispered. "When I come back, either you feed or you go down there." Shideh

313

stood and spun around and the black gown whispered as she hurried out of the room.

Davey fell away from the tank and into a heap among the broken wooden slats that had collapsed beneath him. The penlight dropped from his mouth and rolled away, its beam wobbling over the floor. He pulled his feet away from the broken crate and crawled on his hands and knees toward the light; it was snatched away by a gray, half-fingered hand.

Davey snapped his hand back.

The scaly creature between the boxes held the penlight up to its face, examining it with curious eyes. It worked its mouth with effort, and said in a sharp but quiet whisper, "My son used to have one of these." It slowly lifted its head to Davey. "May I keep it?" The eyes blinked as it waited for a reply.

Without looking away from the creature, Davey got to his feet and backed away. *Holy Jesus, its son!*

The penlight shone upward on the creature's face, casting shadows over parts of its flat, scaled features.

With a slack jaw, Davey nodded.

"Thank you," the creature rasped. Like a turtle pulling into its shell, it slowly retreated to its hiding place.

The room darkened as the penlight was withdrawn, but Davey could still make out his surroundings; his eyes had adjusted to the lack of light.

He turned to the steep, rickety stairs and saw that the others were coming into the room, dragging themselves through the doorway.

Somehow, they no longer seemed as threatening as before, just lost, confused. Davey resisted the urge to pull out his gun, but he kept his distance and moved very slowly toward the stairs, one long step at a time, until his foot bumped something.

There was a woman lying near the foot of the stairs; blood streaked her white hair and was splashed on the remains of her torn blue nightgown and her face.

Davey could not look at her face.

He knew it was Jackie.

Davey looked back at the creatures as he stepped over the body and put his foot on the bottom step, then the next one, never taking his eyes from the shifting audience behind him, until he could lift his right hand and push up on the trapdoor.

It would not open.

He pushed again, harder.

It remained firm.

"God . . . *dammit*," he muttered as he felt along the edges of the door, looking for some way, *any* way, to open it. He found nothing.

Something moved quickly over the floor below and Davey turned.

They were all standing aside to let something through, something that was slapping the cement floor and wheezing harshly. It was the legless creature Davey had shot earlier, pulling itself along rapidly, its head swollen and cracked, but in one piece now with worms wriggling in its hair. Heading straight for the staircase, it looked up at Davey and gurgled, "You hurt my *head!*"

Davey began to beat on the trapdoor with his fist, just as the creature reached the bottom step.

Beyond the curtain, Benedek was struck with the smell.

Like crawling inside a week-old used rubber, he thought.

315

He took a few steps into the dark, holding a hand out before him, feeling for a wall.

A door creaked open to his right.

He heard someone moving about and turned toward the sound.

Bars. A cage.

A glimpse of white hair.

Relief swept through Benedek and he wanted to scream her name.

"Jackie?" he croaked uncertainly.

He saw the white hair again, *distinctly.*

"Jackie! Oh, Christ, Jackie, honey." He pressed close to the bars, wrapping his hands around them. "Are you all right?"

Something moved toward him.

"Jackie?"

A large white hand snaked between the bars, clutched his hair, and pushed him away, then pulled his head hard into the bars.

The darkness was suddenly much, much deeper, and Benedek knew nothing.

Casey drew her knees up against her breasts and covered her ears with her wrists, trying to block out the sound of pounding beneath the floor, trying not to think of what was down there, trying with no success to ignore the raw, chitinous feeling of *need* that chewed through her body.

"*Stop it!*" she shrieked, pressing her wrists harder over her ears.

The pounding stopped.

She heard a voice, muffled at first, then louder, clearer.

"Casey?"

She pulled one wrist away and looked through her tears at the trapdoor.

"Casey, it's *me, Davey!*"

She remembered the hands that had groped for her earlier.

"Casey, are you there?"

And wondered if the voice was genuine.

"Casey, unlock this door!"

Or if they were trying to fool her again.

The pounding continued.

"Casey, *please!*"

She closed her eyes and covered both ears again, whimpering, trying to stop the pounding, the voice, and the pain of her hunger.

As Davey pounded on the trapdoor, he felt the stairs jolt beneath him. When he looked down, the creature was using its claw to heave itself painfully up the steps.

Davey took a step down and kicked the creature in the face as hard as he could without falling.

Bits of its skull shot into the darkness with the impact of Davey's foot, snickering over the floor as they landed. The creature tumbled back to the floor, but immediately rolled over and, despite the dark fluids running out of its forehead and into its eyes, began pulling itself back up the stairs again.

Davey pulled the gun from his pocket and aimed it at the creature's head once again.

"I'll hurt you some more," Davey blurted, trying to keep the gun from trembling. "I'll hurt you *bad.*"

The thing stopped on the stairs and gawked up at Davey, making a low, throaty humming sound.

The other creatures moved back a bit.

One of them laughed; it sounded more like a belch. Davey held the gun on the stubby beast.

It didn't come any closer, but it didn't back away.

There were footsteps over Davey's head; they were accompanied by the sound of something heavy being dragged over the floor.

A door opened.

A voice, its words barely distinguishable, spoke angrily: ". . . one's for you if you want it or . . . go down there and fight . . . others for it . . ."

"God, he's *alive* . . ."

Casey!

". . . him before he wakes . . ."

"No! No more, *please!*"

". . . *have* to!"

"No, no, I won't . . . him away . . ."

"All *right.*" Footsteps, more dragging. "If *that*"—fumbling clicks, and the door jarred—"is what"—more clicking—"you *want.*" The door swung open and Davey saw Shideh, soft gold-colored light flickering shadows over her tall figure, lifting a limp body by the back of its coat and dangling it over the opening.

Christ, it's Walter! Davey thought.

She dropped him in and he landed heavily on Davey, tumbling the two of them down the stairs. Davey clutched the gun tightly to keep from dropping it as they rolled over the legless creature on the stairs and sprawled onto the floor. Davey was lying face-down over Benedek and felt him move.

"Walter!" Davey hissed, getting up.

Benedek was on his back; his forehead was bleeding from two cuts.

Davey got up on his knees and began shaking the big man.

"Walter! It's Davey, Walter, for Christ's sake, get *up!*" The two balls were bobbing on the surface of the oil somewhere inside the silent, squatting tank in the corner and could blow any minute. Davey had no idea how long it would take, providing it worked. If it *did*, the whole room could be gutted by flames in a moment.

"Let go!" Casey screamed. "Please let go of me, oh *God*, don't put me down there, *please!*"

Davey looked up and saw Shideh's arms hooked beneath Casey's, lifting her, kicking frantically, over the open door.

"Walter, *get up!*" Davey shouted, giving the man one final, hard shake before starting up the stairs two at a time, keeping his eyes on Shideh's feet which stood at the very edge of the opening; he rammed her lower legs with his shoulder as he dove out of the basement.

Shideh fell back and hit the wall; Casey rolled over the floor away from her. Shideh landed on a cushion in the corner and was getting up again even before she was completely down.

"Davey!" Casey cried, and she repeated his name again, laughing and crying at once. "Davey, thank God . . ."

Davey was on his knees as Shideh lunged forward, her white hair billowing around her head. He raised the gun and fired without aiming.

Shideh's arms splayed outward and her body slammed back against the wall. A dark hole opened in the creamy skin just above the neckline of her black dress.

She tilted her head back; her face tightened and her eyes clenched shut; she pressed herself to the wall and made a deep, almost inaudible growling sound.

The bullet slowly began to ooze back out of the glistening wound in her chest until it was squeezed completely from the opening and fell to the floor with a clicking rattle.

The hole began to close.

Davey fired again and, again, she was thrown against the wall.

He fired again. And again . . . and again . . . and again . . .

Something was banging in Benedek's head and something was sticking into his back just below his right shoulder blade, something sharp and hard. He started to roll over, lifting his head painfully.

Where am I? he wondered.

There was a whispered voice to his right.

"This one's alive, too."

What had *happened?* Just an instant ago, he'd found Jackie in a cage—they were keeping her in a *cage*—he had to find her again . . .

Benedek rolled to his left, wincing at the pain in his head and back and legs as he propped himself up on an elbow and gasping when he saw her just a couple feet away from him, lying on her back, her lips slightly parted, her arms stretched out above her head.

"Jackie! Jackie!" he bellowed.

Her nightgown was torn and bloody and her hair was streaked with something dark—what *was* it?—and Benedek pulled himself toward her as the banging continued—*gunshots,* he thought vaguely—from above.

"Walter!" Davey shouted between shots. "Walter, get up here!"

Benedek felt himself smiling as he reached for

Jackie and pulled her toward him. He opened his mouth to shout to Davey that he'd found her, but the words would not come and the smile twisted into a silent scream when he saw that the left side of Jackie's face was gone, and shattered bones jutted from what used to be a smooth and kissable cheek and her mouth smiled all the way up to the empty socket of her left eye revealing jawbone and two rows of teeth and her throat was open on the left side, the skin frayed to a meaty brown around the edges and Benedek knew he was going to vomit, he felt his gorge rising fast and he pulled away from Jackie's body and emptied himself on the dirty floor. He couldn't hear the voice behind him.

"Just gimme your foot . . ."

And hardly noticed the tugging on his shoe, but only heard the gonging ring in his ears as he turned his head to look behind him just as he felt hot breath on the side of his bare foot and he sucked in a ragged gasp just as the teeth bit into his flesh.

Davey stopped shooting.

In the sudden silence, Casey's sobs seemed amplified.

Shideh was slumped against the wall, her head bent forward, her white hair cascading before her. The wall was splashed with her blood and bits of flesh. The last shot had taken out her right temple and eye.

The door slammed open and Davey spun around, pointing the gun at a tall balding man with thin, reddish-brown hair. The man made a strangled, shocked sound in his throat when he saw Shideh, then he turned on Davey, baring his fangs as he rushed forward.

Davey fired the gun and the man fell back, slapping

his left hand just below his right shoulder; blood dribbled between his fingers as he started toward Davey again.

The gun clicked.

The man lifted a hand to strike Davey.

"Roger!"

He froze, his hand in midair.

"Go!"

The bottom fell out of Davey's stomach as he looked over his shoulder and saw Shideh rising to her feet. Her head was a bloody mess. The hole that had been over her right temple was smaller.

Jesus, Davey thought, *thirteen bullets, I put thirteen bullets into her!*

Her dress glistened with trails of blood, but it was no longer flowing freely from her wounds as it had been.

She was healing.

"I'll take this one," she said, looking at Davey.

Davey stuffed the gun under his left arm and reached to his left pocket for another magazine, but Shideh was moving too quickly.

"Go!" she snapped again at the man by the open door, then turned to Davey once more. Her face, striped with blood from her gouged eye and wounded head, burned with hatred as her lips pulled back over her fangs and her snout curled into a deadly snarl.

The door slammed as the man left.

Benedek screamed downstairs: *"Jackie!"*

Casey cried Davey's name.

Davey let the gun drop from under his arm. He stuck his hand into his right coat pocket and grasped the handle of the kitchen knife; as Shideh closed in on him, Davey held the blade out before him so that she walked right into it. The knife slid inside her just above her pelvis, and she grunted as she wrapped her power-ful arms around Davey's shoulders. Putting his weight into it, Davey pulled up on the blade, slicing through the flesh and muscle of her belly all the way up to her sternum. She leaned on Davey heavily; he could feel her insides oozing against his coat, warm and wet. Her hold on him loosened, her arms slid down his sides, her face rested on his shoulder as she spit up blood with a gurgling sigh. Davey pulled out the knife, step-ping back just enough to let her guts splash to the floor, then stepped back again so Shideh had nothing to lean on, and she thumped to the floor facedown.

Davey dropped the bloody knife back into his pocket.

"Casey," he gasped, "are you okay?" He rushed around the open trapdoor to her side; she was curled against the wall across the room, trembling and crying. Davey crouched beside her and held her close. "We've got to get out of here. Can you walk by yourself?"

Her whole body quaked in his arms and she pressed herself into his embrace, hissing, "Davey, I'm so hun-gry, I'm *sooo hungry*, Davey, help me, make it stop."

He gently pulled away and moved toward the trap-door from which he could hear Benedek's struggles. He looked over the edge and saw the man trying to clamber up the stairs, his hands groping for a firm hold, his mouth open wide.

Something behind him was holding him back.

"Davey," he croaked, "they're *biting* me, Davey, they're biting my *feet!*"

Davey went two steps down the stairs and, leaning forward, braced his left elbow against the edge of the opening and reached his right hand toward Benedek.

"Grab it!" he shouted.

Benedek reached for Davey's hand, but was pulled

back down a few steps until he got his grip again and pulled himself up one step, another, one . . . more . . .

The creature behind Benedek bounded onto his back, digging the claws of its wing into Benedek's shoulder. Turning its swollen, cracked head toward Davey, the creature spat, "*We* found him *first!*" It laughed through its bloody grin as it pulled Benedek back down the stairs.

Casey tried to calm the shaking, but it only worsened until it felt as if her skin were shaking right off her bones like gelatin. She was only vaguely aware of Davey and of Benedek's cries on the stairs below and . . .

Casey turned, looked beyond the trapdoor to Shideh.

She was lying on the floor on her side, rolling onto her back. A bloody, stringy mass stretched from her belly to the floor as she turned over with a painful groan. Trying to sit up, she scooped a hand through the viscous matter beside her and clumsily lifted it onto her belly. The tendons on her neck stood out as she growled.

Shideh pressed both hands over the opening in her stomach, sucked in a deep breath, and let it out in a slow, throaty sigh. She inched her way to a sitting position and turned her head toward Davey.

Davey took the knife from his pocket and went down another two steps. Swinging the knife upward past Benedek's head, he plunged the blade into the creature's left eye, pushing it up to the hilt. A gout of blood rushed out over Davey's hand, onto Benedek's head, and the creature screamed, throwing itself backward, off of Benedek and down the stairs.

The knife remained in Davey's hand as the creature's head slid off of it.

Davey held his bloody forearm out to Benedek. "Grab my wrist!" he said.

When Benedek had a firm grip on Davey's wrist and arm with both hands, Davey stepped back, heaving Benedek up the stairs until Benedek was able to grab the edges of the opening and pull himself the rest of the way out.

Davey's heart was thundering in his chest, his lungs were on fire, and his eyes were beginning to tear, blurring his vision, but not so much that he could not, upon turning around, see Shideh sitting up against the wall. Her smile was confident. She tried to stand but stumbled, and tried again.

Davey pulled Benedek to his feet.

"Davey, they have J-Jackie down there, I f-found her, she's—"

"Walter, you've got to get out of here!" Davey snapped, turning him toward the door. "Go outside, go back to the cab, just get away from the building!"

Benedek staggered toward the door but Shideh threw herself forward and wrapped an arm around his leg, trying to use it as a crutch to lift herself to her feet. Benedek almost tripped but spun around.

She held on.

Benedek's right foot was bare and bloody, his left wore only a torn sock. Davey saw the pain in his face as he put his weight on his right foot, and the anger that flared in his eyes as he pulled his left foot back and kicked it hard into Shideh's stomach. The stockinged foot disappeared for a moment into the gash in the woman's belly, then pulled out, dripping with dark fluids.

Shideh let go of his leg and slammed against the wall, her scream strangled by the blood in her throat.

Benedek staggered away from her and fell against the door, opened it, and turned to Davey.

"Come on," he said hoarsely, nodding toward Casey. "Get her and let's go." He had to shout to be heard above Shideh's screams.

Davey hurried to Casey and lifted her up, turning toward the door as the tall balding man came back into the room, passing Benedek as if he weren't there and crouching at Shideh's side. He looked over at Davey, bared his fangs, and roared, *"What have you done to her?"* He turned to Davey and tensed, like a cat about to pounce, but Benedek moved faster, shoving the man with his foot, *hard*, throwing him over the floor just far enough to tumble him through the open trapdoor.

Davey kicked the door shut as the man began to scream.

Benedek held the door open and Davey carried Casey to it, stopping when he heard Shideh's voice, but different, thicker, deeper.

"There is nowhere you can go," she growled, "where I *can't fiiiind* you!"

Her face was dark now, covered with hair. Davey carried Casey out, through the token cage and into the front corridor. Her head was pressed to his shoulder and she was babbling senselessly.

"Here," Davey said, turning to Benedek. "Take her outside. I want to get the customers out of the booths."

"This place could go any second, goddammit!" Benedek snapped.

"I won't be long," he insisted, carefully passing Casey's trembling body to Benedek's arms. *"Get out!"*

Davey ran down the musty corridor and rounded

the corner into the room of booths. One of the men was already coming from a booth, buttoning his pants through the open front of his raincoat.

"The fuck is goin' on?" the man barked, brushing back a few greasy strings of his black hair.

"There's a fire!" Davey shouted. "Get out! Now!" He began banging on the doors with his fist, shouting, "Fire! Get out!" He grabbed the handle of one of the doors and pulled hard, jerking it open, breaking its latch.

A short old man gasped, pulling up his pants.

"*Jeez*—what the—who do you—"

Davey grabbed the collar of his coat and jerked him out of the booth. The man fell to the floor, his pants just above his knees.

"Get out of here, there's a fire!"

The man began crawling, trying to pull his pants up at the same time.

"Davey!" The voice was muffled, but Davey recognized it immediately.

He looked into the booth and saw Anya pressing her hands to the glass.

She was beautiful.

"Davey, what's happening?" she shouted. "What are you doing?"

Davey smiled coldly as he slammed the door of the booth, wishing he could stay to watch her burn.

Benedek eased Casey into the backseat of the cab, then got in beside her.

"What the hell's going on?" the driver asked. "What-samatter with *her?* Look, I don't want no *trouble*, okay?"

Ignoring her, Benedek slammed the door and said,

"Start the car and pull up there," pointing toward Live Girls.

As the cab began to move, Benedek leaned back in the seat and clenched his teeth against the throbbing pain in his foot and back. Looking through the windshield, he saw several men running out of Live Girls, their long coats slapping behind them, some with their belts unfastened and flies open.

The cab stopped and idled before Live Girls.

"God*damm*it!" Benedek hissed when he saw a tall, naked woman bound through the black curtain and run down the sidewalk, her black hair sweeping behind her as she took long, graceful strides. Another followed her. "They're getting away."

"*Who's* getting away?" the driver demanded. "Look, whatever you guys are doing, I don't want no part of it, so get your ass outta my cab!"

"Davey?" Casey whispered, huddled against the door of the cab.

Benedek put an arm around her. She was convulsing violently; her lips were pulled back in a grotesque, painful grimace as she looked up at Benedek. There were tears in her eyes as she clutched the collar of his coat.

"I'm . . . so . . . hun . . . greee . . ." she sighed. Her breath, damp with rot, made Benedek wince.

Benedek said softly, "Is there anything I can do?"

"Didn't you *hear* me?" the driver barked. "I said I want you outta—"

"I *heard* you, but I gotta sick woman back here, okay?" He leaned closer to Casey and asked again, "What can I do?"

She touched his face softly, and as she spoke, she

328

moved her hand over his ear to his neck, around his throat, fluttering it over his shoulders as she looked into his eyes.

She had beautiful eyes. Benedek had not noticed the first time he saw her just how beautiful they were, how big and soft and inviting, how embracing . . .

"I have to feed, Walter," she breathed, "I have to feed soon or, or I don't know what's going to happen to me, something bad, I, I feel like my, like my *skin* is melting off, and I'm afraid . . ."

She put her hand over his on her shoulders.

". . . that if I don't feed soon . . ."

And gently lifted it, pushing the sleeve up a bit.

". . . it *will* melt. Right. Off. My bones."

Benedek took in a deep breath as she touched her lips to the underside of his wrist, looking up at him through long lashes.

"Casey," Benedek said, but his mouth only formed the name soundlessly.

"Just a little," she whispered, her breath warming his skin. "That's all, just a little . . ."

When he felt the sting, Benedek suddenly felt weak and leaned heavily against the back of the seat.

Casey stared up at him, unblinking.

She slurped softly.

Benedek wanted to close his eyes and relax, enjoy the feeling of ease that was blanketing him, but he did not want to lose sight of her eyes . . .

"How much longer is your friend gonna be, anyway, huh?" the driver asked.

Benedek blinked, glanced at the driver in the rear-view mirror, then down at Casey. He saw a drop of blood beading at the corner of her mouth and jerked his hand away, the ease he'd felt an instant before turning to nausea as he slapped a palm over his bleeding wrist.

Casey fell away from him, leaning against the opposite door, smiling slightly and licking her bloody lips, laughing quietly deep in her throat, her whole body trembling orgasmically. She closed her eyes and folded her arms across her chest, hugging herself.

"Did you hear me?" the driver asked. "How long is your . . ."

Massaging his wrist, Benedek spotted Davey through the wet window over Casey's shoulder. He was running from Live Girls.

"He's coming now," Benedek said.

Davey stumbled to a halt on the wet sidewalk, frantically looking for the cab.

"Davey! Over here!" Benedek called.

Running toward the cab, Davey began screaming, "Drive! Drive! Drive!" as the cabdriver shouted over her shoulder, "I want you bums outta my goddamned cab or I'm gonna—" and Benedek beat a fist on the partition and roared, "Just drive the fuck outta here *now!*"

Davey threw himself inside the cab.

The door slammed.

The driver put the car in gear.

And the dark doorway of Live Girls belched fire with a bone-cracking *WHA-BOOMPH!*

The car jolted with the explosion as it pulled away from the curb.

"Faster!" Davey shouted.

"This ain't a fuckin' freeway!" the driver replied, her anger replaced by fear and confusion.

Davey and Benedek looked at one another for a

moment—Davey felt a smile pushing the corners of his lips up—then they turned their eyes to the back window.

Pedestrians were hurrying across the street away from the burning building; some fell; a woman's coat was on fire; flames licked the sidewalk and rose toward the night sky. There was another explosion and the building next to Live Girls began to burn; its windows exploded outward, showering the street with glass, and a flashing sign that promised a live sex show sprayed sparks onto the sidewalk as it fell and shattered.

A burst of flames broke away from the fire, shooting up then billowing as it swept down in a bright arc over the street, taking shape, stretching out its wings.

"Oh God," Davey whispered.

Diving downward, straight for the cab, screaming . . .

"Drive faster!" Davey shouted, hitting the partition.

It was a loud, hurt, and angry scream.

Shideh's scream.

The creature landed with a heavy jolt on the trunk, slamming its head against the window, spreading a web-like pattern of cracks over the glass.

Her face was barely distinguishable amid the flames that had already destroyed her flesh and were exposing bone beneath as she spread her burning wings over the window and screamed wordlessly as she slowly slid off the trunk and landed in a burning pile in the street, jerking violently a few times, then remaining still as the flames died away in the rain.

Davey collapsed against the door, wiping the perspiration from his face.

"Jesus," he muttered. "I didn't think . . ." He turned to Casey. She was slumped between the two men, her head back, eyes closed, a look of euphoria on her soft face. "Casey?" Davey said softly. "You all right?"

She didn't reply.

Davey saw Benedek's bloody wrist and noticed the drops of blood on Casey's chin, and he knew what had happened. "Walter, I'm sorry."

Benedek shook his head. "It's okay. I know she didn't mean to hurt me, and"—he looked down at her—"I think she needed it."

As Benedek leaned forward and gave the driver his address, Davey leaned close to Casey's ear, holding her to him.

"Casey? You okay?"

She nodded slowly.

"We're out. We're out of there now. The place is in flames."

She opened her eyes a bit, smiled for just an instant, and breathed, "Good." Then she leaned on Davey, squeezing into the crook of his arm.

"No!" the driver snapped at Benedek. "Next corner I'm lettin' you clowns out, you hear me?"

"Look, this is important. Another ten bucks if—"

"*Hey!* You already owe me twenty for *waiting.*"

"Jesus," Benedek sighed, fumbling in his pocket. "Okay, all I've got're two twenties. That okay?"

The driver thought about it, then shrugged. "Okay."

They were all silent as they rode. Davey finally felt the pounding in his chest subside, and as he calmed, he began to notice the beginnings of his own hunger.

Chapter Eighteen

Benedek stood before his medicine cabinet in his bathroom, gingerly putting two Band-Aids over the wounds on his wrist. The ringing in his ears had not stopped, and pain throbbed up his leg from his injured foot.

He looked at his reflection for a long time, noticing how trapped it looked within the chrome frame around the mirror. Trapped, as he was. Trapped with the knowledge of what was growing in the city. He knew he could not use the paper to spread the news. The editor would chuckle, and say something like, "Take it to the *Post*, Walter."

If the *Times* did anything at all with the story, it would be a small piece discreetly tucked away somewhere near the back of the paper with a headline like: POTENTIAL HEALTH CRISIS IN MANHATTAN.

Benedek rubbed his hand over the stubble on his jaw, toying with an idea.

Davey sat on the sofa with Casey lying against him. He stroked her hair gently. The relief of having her with him, alive—as alive as *he* was, at least—almost outweighed the horror of what had happened.

"You're trembling," she said.

He nodded. "I'll have to feed soon."

She pulled her head away and looked into his eyes. "What are we going to do?" she asked.

Davey sighed. "I don't know. We'll have to leave the city. The police are still after me."

"Why?"

Chad Wilkes's fearful eyes flashed in Davey's memory for a moment. Stella Schuman's strangled scream echoed in his memory. He knew the police would connect her death to him, too.

"I killed Chad," he said softly.

Casey's eyes slowly widened and she touched a knuckle to her lips, stifling a laugh.

"I'm sorry," she said. "It just, well, it just, you know, conjures up some humorous images."

Davey smiled. It was good to see that Casey had not changed too much.

"He thought he was being raped by a homosexual," he added.

She put her whole hand over her mouth and her eyes crinkled as she tried to hold the laughter in.

"And"—Davey looked away for a moment—"Miss Schuman."

She laughed out loud, but her laughter collapsed into chest-heaving sobs and she threw her arms around him, holding him tightly.

"Davey, I don't want to be like this," she cried, her voice muffled in his shoulder.

He embraced her and a large knot formed quickly in his stomach. "I'm sorry," he breathed, "I'm so sorry. It's my fault. I'm sorry."

They held one another until Benedek came into the room.

"How are you, Casey?" he asked.

She looked at Benedek with sorrowful eyes. "I'm so sorry," she whispered.

"Don't worry about it." He smiled and held up his bandaged wrist. "See? All better. I'm just glad you're okay."

"Are *you* all right, Walter?" Davey asked.

Benedek sat down in a chair facing them. "Now. Right now, I've got about a truckload of adrenaline shooting through these veins." He held his arms up for a moment. "But I suspect that in a while, I'm probably gonna be a mess."

"Sorry."

"I think there's been enough apologizing for tonight."

"What are you going to do?"

He shrugged.

"You going to write the story?"

"I'm going to write it, but not for the *Times*. They'd give me another vacation. A permanent one. But don't worry; the story will be printed. I don't know how well it will be *received*, but it will at least be printed."

Davey smiled at Benedek, standing. "Thank you," he said, shaking Benedek's hand.

The tall man stood, looking somehow weakened, wounded.

"You want something to wear?" Benedek asked, frowning as he looked at the thin robe Casey was wearing.

She shrugged as she stood. "What difference does it make?"

Benedek closed his eyes and nodded. "Yeah. Guess so."

Casey stood and the three of them walked to the window to say their good-byes.

Benedek went to the phone after they were gone. He picked up the receiver and punched Ethan Collier's number.

"Yes?" Collier cooed.

"Ethan? This is Walter."

"Walter, my friend, how are you?"

"Fair. How about you?"

"You know me, Walter. I'm always happy and gay."

Benedek chuckled.

"What can I do for you?" Collier asked. "I'm on my way out and don't have much time. The evening has just begun, you know."

"I have a favor to ask."

"Oh? So soon after the last one? How was your evening at the Midnight Club, by the way?"

"Enlightening."

"Good. I hope it loosened you up a bit. I think you could use some loosening. Did Jackie enjoy it?"

Benedek cleared his throat. "She didn't go."

"Ah. How is she?"

There was a long pause. "Jackie's dead, Ethan."

"Good God, Walter, when?"

"Late last night."

"Dear Lord, how—"

"Actually, Ethan, that's why I called. I have a story for you."

"A story? I don't understand."

"I'm going to write a story and give it to you. It's for the *Post*."

"*You* have a story for the *Post*! The paper you've spent so many years degrading? The paper you've said is far worse than a rag? What kind of story *is* this? Won't the *Times* print it?"

"No. It's kind of . . . unbelievable."

"Does it have anything to do with Jackie's death?"

"Yes, but I don't want my name on it. I'm going to write it under a pseudonym. I'd like to give it to you when it's done so you can put it on the right desk."

"The story is true?"

"I'm afraid so."

"And you think people will believe it if they read it in the *Post*?"

"At least they'll read it," Benedek replied. "And if they don't believe it, I can only hope they won't *dis*believe it." He sniffed. "Will you help me?"

There was a thoughtful silence at the other end of the line.

Collier said quietly, "Of course."

The city stretched out beneath them like a blanket of glitter.

The rain had stopped and there were breaks in the clouds that revealed twinkling stars.

The air was cold and still damp.

The sounds of the city reached them as a whisper.

Its lights fell away from them as they moved on toward someplace safe. Anyplace at all.

A place safe for them.

And safe for others.

THE LOVELIEST DEAD

RAY GARTON

To most people it's just a large house, old and a bit run-down. To the Kellar family it's a new start, but soon, it will become a living nightmare. The terrors begin before the Kellars have even finished unpacking. Who are the mysterious children playing on the rusty, vine-covered swing set in the backyard? Who is the figure sitting in the dark corner of the bedroom at night? Who—or what—waits in the basement? They are the dead and they cannot rest. Horror stalks the halls of the Kellar house. And the secrets of the past are reaching from beyond the grave to destroy the living.

JACK KETCHUM

OFF SEASON

September. A beautiful New York editor retreats to a lonely cabin on a hill in the quiet Maine beach town of Dead River—off season—awaiting her sister and friends. Nearby, a savage human family with a taste for flesh lurks in the darkening woods, watching, waiting for the moon to rise and night to fall....

And before too many hours pass, five civilized, sophisticated people and one tired old country sheriff will learn just how primitive we all are beneath the surface...and that there are no limits at all to the will to survive.

RAPTURE

THOMAS TESSIER

Jeff has always loved Georgianne, ever since they were kids—with a love so strong, so obsessive, it sometimes drives him to do crazy things. Scary things. Like stalking Georgianne and everyone she loves, including her caring husband and her innocent teenage daughter. Jeff doesn't think there's room in Georgianne's life for anyone but him, and if he has to, he's ready to kill all the others… until he's the only one left.

"Ingenious. A nerve-paralyzing story."
—*Publishers Weekly*

Dorchester Publishing Co., Inc.
P.O. Box 6640   ___5558-9
Wayne, PA 19087-8640 $6.99 US/$8.99 CAN
Please add $2.50 for shipping and handling for the first book and $.75 for each additional book. NY and PA residents, add appropriate sales tax. No cash, stamps, or CODs. Canadian orders require $2.00 for shipping and handling and must be paid in U.S. dollars. Prices and availability subject to change. **Payment must accompany all orders.**

Name: _____

Address: _____

City: _____ State:_____ Zip: _____

E-mail: _____

I have enclosed $_____ in payment for the checked book(s).

CHECK OUT OUR WEBSITE! www.dorchesterpub.com
____ Please send me a free catalog.

INTO
THE FIRE
RICHARD
LAYMON

Pretty, young Pamela was a very happy newlywed. But all that changed the night Rodney broke in. He's been obsessed with Pamela since high school, and now he intends to make her his slave for life. He thinks they'll be alone when he drives her out to the blazing desert. But someone else is out there too…someone with a gun.

Pamela hoped her nightmare was over when Rodney was shot, but something about her rescuer isn't quite right. One thing is certain: she won't be prepared for what she'll find when he drives her to a tiny, isolated town baking in the desert sun. A town with very odd customs and a unique way of welcoming strangers.